The
GQ
CANDIDATE

The
GQ
CANDIDATE

KELI GOFF

ATRIA BOOKS

New York ★ London ★ Toronto ★ Sydney

ATRIA BOOKS

A Division of Simon & Schuster, Inc.
1230 Avenue of the Americas
New York, NY 10020

First Atria Books hardcover edition July 2011

ATRIA B O O K S and colophon are trademarks of Simon & Schuster, Inc.

For information about special discounts for bulk purchases, please contact Simon & Schuster Special Sales at 1-866-506-1949 or business@simonandschuster.com.

The Simon & Schuster Speakers Bureau can bring authors to your live event. For more information or to book an event, contact the Simon & Schuster Speakers Bureau at 1-866-248-3049 or visit our website at www.simonspeakers.com.

Designed by Jaime Putorti

Manufactured in the United States of America

10   9   8   7   6   5   4   3   2   1

Library of Congress Cataloging-in-Publication Data

Goff, Keli.
  The GQ candidate : a novel / Keli Goff.
    p. cm.
1. Presidential candidates—United States—Fiction. 2. Political
campaigns—United States—Fiction. 3. Political fiction. 4. Domestic
fiction. I. Title.
  PS3607.O3443G73 2011
  813'.6—dc22
                                    2011019246

ISBN 978-1-4391-5872-2
ISBN 978-1-4391-7286-5 (ebook)

For my mother,
Opel Goff,
for not only giving me life
but giving me love and,
most of all, my voice.

"I am a success today because I had a friend who believed in me and I didn't have the heart to let him down . . ."

—PRESIDENT ABRAHAM LINCOLN

The
GQ
CANDIDATE

CHAPTER 1

Laura Cooper was having one of those days.

She was already running late that morning, having completely forgotten that her youngest son, Milo, was supposed to be at school early for a special choir practice. While she was rushing around the kitchen trying to make Milo and his brother a quick breakfast she dropped an entire carton of milk that splattered not only the kitchen floor, but the ceiling, her clothes, and even her hair. Laura rarely cursed but if there was ever a time to do so it was now. She didn't have to, though. The moment the milk dropped Laura heard a loud "Oh shit!"

It was six-year-old Milo.

"What did you say?" Laura asked.

Milo looked at her bashfully.

"Nothing."

"Where did you hear that word?" Laura demanded.

"Daddy," Milo's older brother, James, declared. "He said it when he spilt his drink in the car."

"Did he?" Laura replied. "Well that is not a nice word and it's not a word that little boys should be saying."

"But daddies can say it?" Milo asked, confused.

"Daddies shouldn't say it either."

"Is Daddy in trouble?"

"He will be when I see him," Laura said. "Which is hardly ever . . . ," she mumbled under her breath.

The last two years had been great for her husband Luke's career but terrible on their marriage. He was now Governor Luke Cooper, one of the youngest governors in the nation and among a handful who are black or Jewish—he being both. And he was widely recognized as a rising national star in the Democratic Party. His friends had taken to jokingly referring to him as "Mr. President," a nickname that Luke seemed to eat up, but which drove Laura insane. She had taken to calling him that herself, but only when she was irritated with him. As in "Mr. President. Would it be too much trouble for you to put your dishes in the dishwasher like everyone else in this family does—including your sons who are in elementary school?"

The night before Laura's spilt milk, Luke dropped a bombshell that made the moniker more than a term of endearment among his inner circle. He announced that he was considering a run for the presidency. At the behest of some of his advisors he had done some polling and it showed that he was a viable candidate for the next presidential election, less than three years away. He had decent national name recognition and his favorability rating among those who knew who he was was through the roof.

"So what do you think?" He asked her like a kid waiting to receive a gold star from a parent for good grades on a report card.

Laura stood in her nightgown staring at him for a moment.

Finally she replied, "I'm . . . I'm sorry but I'm really tired."

Luke, looking a bit like a deflated balloon said, "Oh. Well I know you've had a long day. We can talk about this tomorrow."

But that's not what Laura meant. She meant she was tired of it all. Tired of campaigning. Tired of living in a fishbowl. Tired of feeling like a single parent while he hopped from one event to another across the state seven days a week. And most of all tired of pretending that her black, Jewish husband didn't receive death threats as regularly as most people receive junk mail.

She climbed into bed.

Luke climbed in beside her an hour later. Though she was still wide-awake, the thought of a presidential campaign weighing on her, terrifying her, she pretended to be asleep. He scooted next to her and wrapped his arm around her waist, reached for her hand and whispered in her ear "Love you." She didn't say a word, but gently squeezed his hand.

★

When Laura awoke the following morning she was exhausted, having gotten only a few hours of restless sleep, and she was torn.

As much as Luke's happiness meant to her—and it meant a lot—she had to admit that while the two of them began their life with similar dreams—or so she thought—this was not the case today.

While Laura dreamed of a life out of the public eye, having been burnt by the nasty rumors and innuendo that accompanied Luke's gubernatorial race, Luke now dreamed of the White House.

She had always put their family first even when he didn't. She had loved teaching and being in the classroom but gave up her career as Luke's political star rose. And that wasn't the end of her sacrifice. There were days when he left the house at 7 a.m.—just as the boys were rising—only to return after 11 p.m. long after they had gone to sleep. More and more she began to feel not like half of a power couple, but rather like a single parent. She hadn't signed up for having her own career goals and dreams become secondary. She had wanted to become a specialist helping children with learning disabilities from disadvantaged backgrounds and once thought of pursuing her PhD in the subject. That was a distant memory now. Laura recalled once hearing a relationship "expert" say that healthy relationships are characterized by compromise on the part of both but endless sacrifice by neither. And yet after all of these years she felt as though she was the only one doing the compromising *and* sacrificing.

Luke and Laura rarely fought. Neither was really the raise-your-voice type, but they did have one legendary blowout that was still a source of teasing among Luke's friends. Both of the boys had come down with the flu and Laura had spent her day wiping noses, making soup, and cleaning up vomit. When Luke returned home around 9, the boys were sound asleep while Laura was sitting on the couch staring blankly at the TV screen, clearly exhausted. When he walked in and bellowed, "Hey, hon!" she barely looked up and simply said, "Hey."

"How are the little guys?"

"Asleep."

"Awww. Hate I missed 'em."

Then he took off his coat and threw it on a chair like he always did, and began giving a rundown of his day as he made his way to the kitchen shouting, "Hey, hon—where's the leftover meatloaf?"

"Second shelf of the fridge."

"I looked. Can't find it."

"It's on the second shelf."

"Can't find it."

"Well it's there."

"Hon, can't you just come help me find it? I'm just so tired. You know I had to work all day."

Laura sat upright. Jumped off of the couch. Walked into the kitchen. She reached for the Tupperware container, positioned smack in the middle of the second shelf, with a small label reading "meatloaf," and handed it over to him. She then pulled out a container of gravy, opened it, and proceeded to pour the cold goop over his head.

"What the!??" he screamed.

"I worked all day too!" she said. "If you'd like to trade places and stay here tomorrow cleaning up puke while I fill in for you sitting and talking with a bunch of adults, be my guest."

She then turned on her heel and walked out of the kitchen, but not before shouting back at him, "And in case you hadn't noticed, the hall closet is for hanging clothes like your coat."

Luke was stunned. In all their years together he had never seen Laura so angry.

The following morning, when Laura woke at 5 to check on the boys, Luke wasn't beside her. She looked in the spare bedroom, then on the couch.

Finally she went into Milo's bedroom and saw Luke sleeping on the floor next to his son's bed with a box of tissues on his chest and an open bottle of children's cough syrup next to him. Milo's arm was dangling down the side of the bed with his tiny fingers wrapped around Luke's thumb.

Laura walked into the kitchen to prepare herself a quiet cup of coffee and was struck by two things. The kitchen was spotless. The dishes were put away and the floor gleamed where a puddle of gravy had been the night before. There was a beautiful bouquet of yellow roses—her favorite—on the breakfast table, and a note that read "To the hardest working person in our home. I love and APPRECIATE you. Luke."

And so Laura continued with their delicate compromise, and from that day on Luke continued making an effort to let her know how much he appreciated her for it. Their compromise then took them all the way to the governor's mansion and now Luke was hoping it would take them all the way to the White House.

She needed advice. So she decided to talk to the one person she knew she could trust: her mother-in-law, Esther.

Ever since losing her own mother to cancer Laura had grown extremely close to Luke's. Esther had longed for a daughter and in Laura she had finally gotten one. They were a bit of an odd couple, and the strength of their bond perplexed some, particularly Esther's other daughters-in-law. After all, unlike them, Laura wasn't even Jewish—far from it. But this black woman who had been raised Catholic, and now attended an Episcopalian church, was the one who most reminded Esther of her younger self. Laura was tough in a quiet and unassuming sort of way. She put her kids first—ahead of her own career and ahead of her husband.

Laura and Esther often did mother–daughter things together—something they actually began to keep secret so that the other Cooper wives wouldn't grow jealous. They had a standing appointment for mani-pedis every three weeks at Bebe's Day Spa, a perfect occasion for Laura to seek Esther's help in coming to terms with Luke's new ambition. As they sat with hands and feet under dryers, Esther finally asked Laura what was wrong.

"And don't try to convince me that something's not wrong. I can always tell when something's wrong with my kids," she said.

Laura smiled. It meant so much to her that Esther thought of her as one of her children.

"It's Luke."

Esther looked worried and tense—like she thought Laura was about to drop a bomb on her, like that Luke was seriously ill or that they were getting divorced.

"Everything's fine," Laura continued not so convincingly.

"Well clearly it's not. What is it?" Esther replied.

"Luke's seriously considering this presidential thing," Laura continued. Esther's face relaxed a bit.

"I just . . . I want Luke to be happy . . . and I know that he would be a wonderful president. . . ."

"But?" Esther asked.

"I just don't know that I want this life . . . for my boys . . ."

"And for you?" Esther added.

Laura nodded. "Yes. I just want us to be a happy family and I . . . just don't know how we can stay one with all of this craziness."

It then occurred to Laura to be mindful of how loudly she discussed this in the spa.

"I know I must sound so silly. I have a wonderful husband. Beautiful family . . . a great life . . . ," Laura continued.

"And you want to protect it. There's nothing silly about that at all," Esther said. "It's what we do. Mothers have made and maintained happy homes in the craziest of circumstances—wars, famines—forever. But one thing all of those circumstances had in common is that the women made it possible for the men to go out and conquer. Now Luke doesn't want to conquer. He just wants to make the world a little better."

They sat there for a moment.

"Just think what would have happened if Coretta Scott King had said, 'I can't stand the craziness.'"

"She wouldn't have lost her husband?" Laura said.

"Perhaps," Esther replied. "But you and I wouldn't be sitting here together because we wouldn't be allowed to. And Luke wouldn't be my son."

Esther's courage and compassion had always been two qualities that Laura admired about her most. She had been a Freedom Rider during the civil rights movement and one of her childhood friends had been a high-profile murder victim at the hands of the Klan, a tragedy that seemed only to strengthen Esther's resolve. She continued supporting civil rights organizations and, to her husband's chagrin, was even arrested once during a protest march when she was well into middle age. Her bravest act to date, in Laura's eyes, was adopting a little black boy and raising him into a strong black man.

After their big talk, Laura and Esther Cooper sat in silence for a bit. Then Esther carefully reached over so as not to ruin either of their manicures and squeezed Laura's hand. Then she said, "You know what? I think we deserve a treat. What do you say we get the works today? I think I could use a facial and a massage, and you know my policy against getting spa treatments alone."

She and Laura both laughed.

"Esther?" Laura said.

"Yes, dear?"

"You won't mention our chat to anyone?"

"When you say anyone you really mean my husband and Luke."

Laura smiled and nodded.

Esther continued. "Of course not, dear. Besides, half of a successful marriage is knowing what secrets to keep from your husband."

She then winked mischievously.

They then summoned the receptionist at Bebe's so they could schedule their next round of treatments.

Over the next seventy-two hours Laura kept revisiting her conversation with Esther in her head although she didn't breathe a word of it to Luke. She assumed she had a week, max, before he would force the subject again and yet she was still undecided, despite her mother-in-law's pep talk.

Laura hated politics. She felt it brought out the worst in people, and her early brushes with being in the public eye had left her badly bruised. But she cared about policy, particularly education policy. It bothered her that there were other boys just as sweet and smart as hers who would never have the same opportunities as they just because they didn't have a father who's an elected official, a mother with a master's, and access to some of the best teachers in the state.

So on Sunday evening Laura curled into bed to watch *Education Watch*, the only political show she liked. Luke, who had appeared on the program several times, teased her that if she ever stopped watching the show, they'd lose fifty percent of their audience. U.S. Senator Laurence Sampson was one of the guests that evening. Laura couldn't stand him. She felt he was a phony who had snubbed her and Luke. They first met early in Luke's political career, when he was still a lowly state senator. Sampson had been nice to them only once Luke's political star rose. But most of all she felt that he didn't care enough about poor children and their education. She felt as though he wrote certain communities off. And the way he spoke about education policy suggested that if you weren't middle class he wasn't interested in you. To her, Sampson was both an ass and an intellectual lightweight.

Luke walked in just as the host introduced Sampson. "Your favorite," he said knowing she would roll her eyes.

Every few minutes she would say, "What a moron," prompting Luke to say, "You know, maybe you should run against him."

She rolled her eyes again.

After twenty minutes of discussing various local and federal bills and funding initiatives, the conversation finally turned to national politics. The host mentioned that political insiders were already discussing the next presidential contest and noted that some local names were being mentioned as possible contenders. He asked Sampson if he would ever consider running. Sampson, predictably, replied, "Right now I'm focused on serving the constituents of this great state and doing the job of senator." Prompting the host to reply, "So you're not ruling it out?"

"I'll listen to my constituents and wherever they want me is where I'll be."

"Another local name who's getting a lot of attention is our very own Governor Luke Cooper. What kind of president do you think he'd make?"

"Well I think he's a great governor who is certainly charming and charismatic."

"What about president?"

"Well . . ." Sampson paused. "I don't know if he's there yet. I think he's still very young in his career, relatively speaking, and I think there's a learning curve to really, really be ready. But who knows? Maybe a few years down the road. . . ." His voice dripped with condescension.

Luke chuckled but Laura didn't.

"That jackass," she snapped.

"At least he called me charming." Luke winked at her. Laura didn't crack a smile. "Aw hon," he continued. "He's harmless. A jackass, yes. But a relatively harmless one."

"I don't know about that," she replied. "If he's any indication of what the primary competition is going to look like, you could win it hands down."

Luke tilted his head, as though he hadn't heard her correctly.

She turned off the TV and began rubbing lotion on her hands. Without looking up at him she said, "You should run."

★

Luke Cooper wiped his shoes on the doormat as he had done thousands of times before.

"Who's there?" his mother's voice called out.

"Guess."

"Luke! Be right out."

Luke then slipped off his faux moccasin loafers and mentally counted down to himself, "Three, two, one . . ."

"And don't forget to take off your shoes."

He chuckled. Esther Cooper said this every single time one of her boys came home—in spite of the fact that she had been telling them to do it their entire lives. It was as impossible for them to forget as breathing.

"Let me get this out of the oven and I'll be right out," she said.

He made his way toward the kitchen.

"Hi, Mom."

"Well this is a surprise."

She removed her oven mitts and gave him a great big hug. She was so tiny her head barely reached his shoulder, yet he'd experienced the giant in her once or twice when, as a child, he made the mistake of breaking her two cardinal rules: lying and not working up to his potential. But more often than not he witnessed the giant unleashed on others—particularly those she felt were trying to hurt her children in some way. In one of the Cooper family's now legendary tales she had almost been arrested for making terrorist threats after she told the mother of a fellow student at Luke's Hebrew school that she would send her and her "little monster" home in a bodybag if the little boy ever called Luke the N-word again.

"You're so thin! Feels like I could wrap my arms around you twice. Sit down. Just finished the cake for the bake sale at the center. Plenty of food in the fridge."

The staff at the Gorman Center for children, where she had been volunteering for years, had come to rely on the leftovers she would bring throughout the week. The center was like a second home, as it was the place where, as a toddler, Luke Cooper first met the woman who would become his mother.

"We have flank steak and potatoes. I'll heat a plate up."

"I'm not hungry, Mom."

"If I let you decide when you're hungry you would have starved to death a long time ago."

It never ceased to amaze him how quickly returning to his childhood home felt like a return to childhood.

"Mom, I haven't lived at home forever and I haven't died of starvation yet."

"Where are my boys and my girl?"

Typical Esther Cooper move. If she didn't like something you just said she would ignore it and move on to something she wanted to talk about.

"Laura took the boys to a birthday party. Where's Dad?"

"Where he always is. Upstairs watching TV. It's like he's in a coma. What brings you by?"

"Just wanted to see my best girl."

As she pulled leftovers from the refrigerator Luke made his way over to the cake on the counter. As he reached for it a wooden spoon hit his hand.

"Ow!"

"Get your hands out of there."

"Well you could have said that without using your spoon."

Edmond Cooper walked in.

"Thank goodness you're here, Dad. She's trying to kill me with a spoon."

"Stop being so dramatic," his mother said. "I'm making Luke a plate. You want something?"

"Not hungry," his dad replied.

"I'm making you a plate," Esther said as though her husband hadn't spoken at all.

She turned to reach for a second plate, then a moment later Luke's father shouted, "Ow!"

"Get your hands out of there!" Esther Cooper said to her husband of more than fifty years, who like his son was trying to sneak a little bit of cake.

The three of them sat in the kitchen, Luke enjoying leftover steak and potatoes while his father nibbled on a steak sandwich. His mom watched them eat.

"Mom, aren't you going to have something?"

"No, I'm not hungry."

"Working hard or hardly working?" his father asked.

"Working pretty hard, Dad, but I think things are going pretty good."

"Umm-hmph. Well you know what they say, hard work never killed anybody and anybody it did kill . . ."

"Wasn't used to working hard enough." Luke could finish the thought because he'd heard his father say it a million times.

"Well don't work so hard that you forget to take care of yourself. You have to eat," his mother chirped.

"I know, Mom . . ." He took a few more bites then pushed his plate aside and said, "I actually wanted to talk to you both about work."

"Politics? Goodie. My favorite subject," Edmond Cooper said with a sigh and the sarcasm that was one of his trademarks. He found politics and most politicians both tedious and tiresome, but he supported Luke's interest in it the way he supported all of his sons' interests. He saw hosting a fundraiser for Luke's campaign as no different from schlepping across the country so his oldest son could try out for the Olympic wrestling team years before, even though he found watching wrestling about as fascinating as watching paint dry.

"I've been talking with my team," Luke continued.

"Your team? You make it sound like you're playing sports," his father said.

"Well, it kind of is, Dad. Like blood sport."

"Remember to wear a cup," his father mischievously replied.

"Edmond!" Esther scolded him.

"My team and I are talking about a presidential run," Luke said.

His parents sat in silence.

"You look . . . surprised," Luke said.

"Of course we're surprised. Why wouldn't we be?" Esther said defensively.

"Well?" Luke pressed.

"Well what?" his father asked.

"Well what do you think?"

"I think the bigger question is, what does the captain of your team think?" his mother said.

"The captain?" Luke replied.

"Laura," his mom pushed.

"Come on, son. Even I knew that. You didn't think *you* were the captain did you?" His father laughed.

Luke flashed a smile of commiseration. His father had spent more than half a century with his own loving but tough captain. "Laura's on board."

"Well then what are you talking to us for? That's all you need in the way of a permission slip. Now you can go on the field trip," his father said.

"I just wanted to see if you two had any reservations."

"Reservations are for restaurants," his mother countered. "If this will make you happy then you should do it."

"You know that we'll all be under a microscope. More than we've ever been."

"Well if the news media finds out any secrets about your mother, tell them I'll pay top dollar for them," his father said, displaying a grin.

"Edmond, this is serious," she snapped at him. "Go on, sweetheart."

"Well, you know our family's . . . different."

His father cut him off. "Luke, we've already talked about this. As I've told you since you were five, we can't give your brother away. We're stuck with him and his red hair. I'm sorry. You're going to have to let it go," his father deadpanned.

When his brother was in a serious car accident as an adolescent and hospitalized for a week, his father arrived at the hospital one day with his hair dyed purple. His injured brother and all of the Cooper boys found it hysterical. It was the first day his brother Matt, still in pain from the crash, had laughed since the accident. The fact that their mother was livid only made the moment funnier. Though he hadn't reached for a clown nose during this conversation, Luke could tell by his wisecracking that his dad was nervous at the prospect of this presidential adventure.

"There'll be people curious about the adoption. You might get some questions."

"What's there to ask? What's there to know? You're my son. That's the only thing anyone needs to know," his mother said.

Luke reached across the table and squeezed her hand. His mother was one of the toughest people he knew, but whenever she felt as though somehow her love for her family and capabilities as a mother were under assault it was as though she became the most vulnerable woman on the planet, particularly when she felt her bond with her youngest son challenged. When a black woman she had considered a friend casually said she thought the then seven-year-old Luke would be better off with a family he could better "relate to," Esther Cooper first instructed Luke to cover his ears, then proceeded to give the woman a tongue-lashing like no other. When they returned home that afternoon Luke heard his mother sobbing behind her closed bedroom door.

He remembered a moment at a grocery store when he saw a black family—or "brown" family, as he called them—all together and it dawned on him that his parents were a different color. He wasn't sure what age he was. Then he remembered becoming conscious of the fact that people stared at his family, particularly when he called for his mom or dad in front of strangers. Heads would swivel when he ran to them or his dad picked him up. His father told him the stares were because he was so good-looking, just like his dad. He learned to ignore them.

He tried to play with some of the other boys at the Gorman Center, where Esther volunteered—sons of the teen mothers enrolled in the training program. It was there he first understood that some people might consider him different in a way that was not good. One of the boys told him he "talked like a white boy." Luke wasn't sure what that meant. But he did notice that the boy and his friends subsequently excluded him from the game they were playing. He could never talk about the moment, not even with his family. But it stayed with him. He became conscious of wanting to be accepted by people who looked like him, and this was later one of the reasons it was so important for him to attend Morehouse College—one of the oldest and most prestigious historically black colleges for men—instead of Harvard, where each of his brothers had gone. There were other defining moments along the way, though, such as when he got into a fight with a fellow high school student who teased him by comparing him to the characters from *Diff'rent Strokes*, the TV show about a pair of black orphans adopted by a wealthy white widower.

After spending his whole life fighting for understanding and acceptance when it came to his racial identity, Luke was ready for any upcoming battles on the presidential campaign trail. But he wanted to make sure his family was up for the fight as well.

"I want to make sure that you guys are okay with all of this."

"We're okay with whatever helps you accomplish your dream."

Esther bit her lip and made a face that suggested to him that she really wasn't ready.

"You know you guys are my real parents. No matter what, but . . ."

"But what?" Esther asked, looking as though she were on the verge of tears.

"But I'm going to need to revisit the details around my adoption before someone else goes digging around in it, which they're bound to do, if they're not already. And that won't be the end of it. It's going to be a challenging year, at the very least, for all of us."

His father chimed in. "What he's saying, Esther, is that you can't threaten to send everyone who's mean to Luke home in a bodybag."

His mother stood up as though she were about to leave the kitchen in a huff, but Edmond grabbed her hand and pulled her to his lap and planted a kiss on her cheek.

"You always have to bring that up. I never *really* threatened that woman." She giggled.

"Mom. I was there, remember?" Luke said. "And yeah, you did."

CHAPTER 2

I don't give a shit what kind of computer glitch there was. It was supposed to be on my desk at 8:30 sharp and by my watch it's 8:36 and instead of reading the brief I'm talking to you. Stop apologizing and just fix it." Brock Simpson slammed the phone down.

"Mr. Simpson?" his intercom blared.

"What? I told you to hold my calls."

"I'm sorry but I think it's someone important . . ."

"Peggy, you're not paid to think. You're paid to make sure my coffee is just right and my schedule runs smoothly and so far today you've fallen short on both . . ."

"Sorry, Mr. Simpson."

Two minutes later his BlackBerry began blinking.

The message written in the subject line in all caps read: "MR. BIG SHOT TOO BUSY TO TALK TO YOUR OLD FRIENDS?"

It was from Luke Cooper, Brock's oldest and closest friend and the current governor of Michigan.

"Shit," Brock muttered to himself.

He buzzed Peggy.

"Peggy?"

"Yes, Mr. Simpson."

"Get Luke Cooper back on the phone."

"Certainly, Mr. Simpson."

"And Peggy?"

"Yes, sir?"

"Sorry about before."

Brock's wife, Tami, called Luke "the Brock antidepressant." Luke was one of the few people in the world whom Brock relaxed around. He wasn't one of the most feared divorce attorneys in the country for nothing, having famously wrangled a $250 million settlement on behalf of the wife of golfer Greg Branch, who infamously bedded dozens of porn stars. Brock even lowered his voice around Luke while everyone else got the equivalent of eardrum assault, an outdoor voice whether he was inside or not.

"Hey, Coop. How are you?"

"What are you doing calling me? I thought you were too busy to talk. Your assistant stonewalled me like I was a telemarketer or something."

"Sorry about that. I'll have to remind her that you're on my VIP list."

"Listen at you. VIP list? Do I need an appointment to get a chance to talk to my old friend? I know how valuable your time is. What are you making, like $1,000 an hour? Am I going to have to cut you a check for this call?"

"Please. You're a public servant. You can't afford me!"

They both laughed.

"How's firm life? Claim any scalps today?" Luke asked.

"No, but I plan to mount a couple of baldheaded husbands on my wall before lunchtime."

"Well if Laura runs off with the lawn guy just remember which one of us you were friends with first."

"I don't know, man. You know I like your wife better than you."

"No loyalty. No loyalty. I see how it is."

They chuckled.

"So what's up?"

"I'm heading to New York. Wanted to see if I could get the guys together for a pickup game. You around end of this week?"

"Might have to move a couple of things. What day you thinking?"

"Friday afternoon?"

"Let me see what I can do."

"Okay. You have your people get back to my people, big shot."

They laughed again.

"I'll do that."

With that they hung up.

Brock didn't really need to check his calendar. He knew he had an opening Friday afternoon because it was the day he and his wife were supposed to see a couple's counselor. He had attended only one counseling session since, a month before, he promised her he would participate. But the promise gave way to a convenient pattern. He would wait until the morning of a scheduled session and have his assistant call and cancel due to a work emergency.

He would then give Tami a gift to apologize. Unbeknownst to her, he had stocked up on various spa gift certificates and small pieces of jewelry in anticipation of his cancellations over the coming weeks—until finally, he presumed, she would get the hint and stop scheduling the sessions altogether.

But this wasn't the kind of thing that a man known publicly for negotiating people out of their marriages wanted known about his own— even to a friend like Luke.

TWENTY YEARS BEFORE

Professor Oppenheim's announcement was met with loud groans from the room of second-year law students. "Finish up chapters ten through fourteen before our next class. There may or may not be a quiz on that as well as the material we covered today."

"Damn. This man is single-handedly trying to kill my social life."

"Yeah, blame him for you not having a social life," Luke deadpanned.

"Like you're one to talk. I don't even know why you're wasting dough at law school. For as much action as you see, your ass should be going to divinity school . . . or whatever they call seminary for rabbis. . . . What do they call it?"

Garin Andrews could tease Luke about his atypical racial and religious heritage. Most people couldn't. But the two had been best friends since meeting at the exclusive Langley preparatory school, the high school for the sons and daughters of Michigan's wealthiest families. Garin was different from most of the students as he had been a scholarship student who had lived in public housing projects. He and Luke became inseparable, bonded in part by their love of basketball. After attending different colleges, they ended up at Columbia together for law school.

As they gathered up their belongings to leave, Luke asked, "Hey, you seen Baltimore lately?"

"No. Thank goodness."

"Baltimore" was the nickname they had given to another black student in their class—one who rarely spoke and never smiled and whose version of small talk, when Luke tried to make conversation with him, consisted of muttering, "From Baltimore," before walking away brusquely.

When "Baltimore" refused to loan Garin his notes after Garin missed a class and was unable to get in touch with Luke, Garin decided he didn't care for Baltimore—the city or the person.

"He's missed a couple of classes, right?"

"Do I look like his secretary? Come on. Let's grab a bite. They have this new waitress at the shop. Built like a cola bottle. I'm not sure if I'm in love but I am sure as hell in lust."

"What happened to the librarian built like a cola bottle?" Luke asked.

"I took a sip already," Garin replied with a devilish grin. "Come on."

The following week Professor Oppenheim delivered on his threat and gave a pop quiz.

After class Garin nudged Luke and whispered sarcastically, "Poor Baltimore." He glanced back at Baltimore, who had returned to class for the first time in more than a week. "No way he passed that quiz after missing more than a week. Maybe if he hadn't been such a prick someone would have loaned him their notes."

"He was out sick, Garin. Give him a break."

"Well I hope the doctor gave him some pills for his personality."

Just then the two guys looked up to see Baltimore standing behind them.

"I just wanted to say thanks. And give you this."

Baltimore passed Luke a bottle of wine.

"Thanks," Luke said.

Baltimore turned to walk away.

"Hey. It's bad to drink alone. Garin and I are having some friends at our place Friday. You should come by."

"I don't know if I can . . ."

"We understand," Garin replied a little too eagerly.

"What? Have other plans? Come by," Luke insisted.

"Okay," Baltimore replied before turning to walk away.

"What the hell just happened?" Garin asked. "You two buddies all of a sudden?"

"He was out sick, Gar. With pneumonia. So I took him notes from class."

"So that means we have to spend time with him out of class?"

"Garin, he's not a bad guy. Just takes him a little time to thaw."

A few days later, Luke spotted Baltimore on campus, but Baltimore—as always—had his nose in a book and didn't see him. As Luke was walking toward him he watched Baltimore walk headfirst, book and all, into a young woman, whose drink splattered all over her.

"Oh no!" Baltimore shouted.

"Great! Just great!" the woman screamed. "You need to watch where you're going."

"I'm sorry," Baltimore stammered, clearly mortified.

"I'm already late . . . I can't believe this is happening . . ."

Luke rushed over—in part because he was headed in Baltimore's direction anyway, but also because the woman in question was the most beautiful he had ever seen.

"Here. Let me help," he said. He pulled out some napkins. "I'm sure it may be a little big but if you want you can wear this. No one will ever know." He passed her a white, perfectly pressed Ralph Lauren Polo button-down shirt, fresh from the dry cleaners where Luke had just retrieved it.

"I couldn't," she replied.

"Of course you can. I insist."

"Well, okay. . . . How will I get it back to you?"

"Well, I'm having a party Friday. You can bring it then."

Luke wrote down the party details on one of the napkins. As the young woman turned to leave, he added, "I didn't get your name."

"That's because I didn't give it to you," she replied with a smile.

"Well how will I be able to find you?"

"I'll find you."

He stopped to give her an extra good look.

She smiled, amused as she watched his brain try to come up with what was clearly going to be a pickup line.

"Well what if you don't return the shirt and I decide to sue you?"

"Sue me?"

"Yeah. I could take you to small-claims court. Although I have to warn you, I'm a lawyer so it probably wouldn't be a fair fight." He grinned.

"Oh really. And what law firm is it that lets you wear jeans to the courtroom?" she asked, looking him up and down.

"Well, I'm almost a lawyer. . . ."

"Oh really? How almost?"

"You know. As soon as I finish law school and pass the bar exam."

"And when will that be?"

"Any day now."

"Really?" she smirked, clearly not buying it. "Well, I tell you what. If I try to abscond with your shirt, why don't you call the police? Have them put up a sketch of me. And I promise I'll turn myself in."

She then turned and rushed off.

Baltimore, clearly amused by the exchange said, "Thanks for a . . . helping out."

"No. Thank *you*."

"For what?"

"I just met the woman I'm going to marry," Luke replied.

Laura Long arrived at his and Garin's apartment for their party with Luke's shirt in tow, although all these years later it now sat in her closet, one of her favorite mementos of their relationship.

Baltimore arrived too, although Luke discovered he hated being called that so Luke began calling him by his God-given name, Brock. Though Brock Simpson and Luke Cooper could not have been more different, they developed a bond like brothers, especially after Luke invited Brock to spend Thanksgiving with his extended family in Westchester when Brock couldn't afford to travel home for the holiday.

Brock had no idea that Luke Cooper's family was white—or rich. He couldn't recall a single instance where the subjects had come up.

He sat in awe at Thanksgiving dinner. The only time he had seen a house that big was in movies. But he was also in awe of how happy they all seemed. An entire family of at least fifteen people who seemed as though they didn't have a care in the world. Money may not be able to buy happiness, Brock remembered thinking, but it sure could buy peace of mind, because this family laughed like they were floating on air.

Raised by a single mother who worked as a cleaning lady for a judge (one of the factors that inspired him to become a lawyer), he had never known that level of comfort. He had only known worry. Worry about how he was going to make life better for him and for his mother so that she wouldn't have to clean someone else's house in her golden years but would instead have someone cleaning hers.

★

Brock arrived at the West Side sports club, the most exclusive sports club in the city. Though there were three gyms closer to his Park Avenue apartment, Brock insisted that he and his wife join this one because, as he put it, "instead of working out next to just your average investment banker," they were more likely to find an A-list movie star on the treadmill to the right of them and someone socially significant, like Caroline Kennedy, to the left. Brock wasn't a very good athlete, but Luke was his best friend whom he didn't get to see very often, so he had Peggy book the court at the club. Though they were all nice enough, being around Luke and his other core group of friends—the other members of his so-called Dream Team—tended to give Brock flashbacks to his childhood days of being the last one picked for the team.

Joe and Garin had been the first to arrive, making Brock immediately feel outnumbered when he walked in. Though he was technically friends with both of them, really, they were all friends with Luke. Brock knew that he hadn't exactly been Mr. Personality in those early days at Columbia, and though Garin was always polite, at least to his face, he always had the sense that Garin remained suspicious of him, viewing him as a lifetime third wheel. Though they lived in the same city, the two rarely socialized. Their wives did, but that was something Brock wasn't thrilled with since he deemed Garin's wife, Brooke, a successful publicist, "mouthy."

Joe Nelson, on the other hand, was one of Garin and Luke's high school friends, though seeing how differently their adult lives had turned out, Luke and Garin's closeness with him puzzled some, including Brock. While Garin and Luke had been model students at their prep school, Joe had eventually been kicked out for his hard-partying, troublemaking ways. The son of an NFL Hall of Famer and a former Dallas Cowboys cheerleader and ex-Playmate, Joe resembled a Ken doll, only shorter. Joe had parlayed his lack of athletic talent but love of sports, and his father's extensive connections, into a semi-successful career as a mid-tier sports agent. What Joe lacked in athletic prowess, though, he more than made up for with ego. He did inherit two other gifts from his father: a love of cheerleaders and the ability to woo them. At last count he'd been engaged to four: one New York Knicks dancer, one New Jersey Nets dancer, a Dallas Cowboys cheerleader, and his latest love, Tiffini, a former New York Jets cheerleader turned Rockette. None of them had been over the age of twenty-four, something that prompted endless ribbing by fellow Dream Team members.

Garin was seated on a bench while Joe stood in front of him holding a ball. They were laughing about something when they looked up and spotted Brock.

"Hey Brock. What's up?" Joe asked. He extended his hand. "Good to see you, man."

Joe still looked like Joe, no doubt owing to the gazillion hours he spent in the gym every week. Apparently working for elite athletes at the agency had the same mental impact on Joe that working in the fashion industry seems to have on most women—he had become obsessed with trying to look like he belonged—so every free minute not spent working (or skirt-chasing), Joe spent in the gym. But even Joe had picked up a few flecks of gray in his blond mane since Brock had last seen him.

"Good to see you too, Joe," Brock replied. "Hey Garin."

"Hey Brock." Garin still looked like Garin, which is to say irritatingly handsome. Brock always suspected his wife, like most women, had a crush on Garin, though she would never be dumb enough to say so. The closest she came was saying, "You know it just hit me who Garin reminds me of. A younger, taller Harry Belafonte." She had clearly forgotten that she had once said that Harry Belafonte was the most beautiful man in the world when he was younger.

"How's the family?" Garin asked.

"Everyone's good. No complaints."

"And the firm?"

"No complaints there either. You know my line of work is recession-proof."

"Don't remind me," Joe said as they all chuckled, since Joe's marriage phobia was a constant source of amusement for the crew.

But Garin couldn't help thinking the line was also a slight dig from

Brock. After obtaining his law degree from Columbia, Garin never used it. Instead he joined an investment firm on Wall Street that made him independently wealthy faster than being a successful attorney had made Brock. But the recent recession had taken a toll on Garin's company, like many others. Though he still was far wealthier than the average American, he sensed Brock's recession line was intended to send a little message.

Just then Adam Leventhal, who was officially Luke's oldest friend on the planet, arrived. A successful music executive, Adam had been the first to befriend the little brown boy who stuck out like a sore thumb at their Hebrew day school. Adam looked exactly the same, still possessing both the baby face and paunch he had had since adolescence, and the glasses too—only now the glasses had the name Dior discreetly etched on the rims. There were a few other Dream Team members scattered throughout the country, but this comprised the New York crew.

"Hey Ad-Man!" Joe thundered.

Joe always seemed to turn into a quintessential fratty-jock asshole around Adam. It had been their dynamic for as long as they had known each other. Luke often ended up playing big brother to Adam, by putting Joe in his place when he needed it.

"Joe," Adam replied, feigning enthusiasm. The two men did an informal shake.

Ever the smart-ass, Joe said, "Good news, Ad-man—Garin's on *your* team."

"Really?" Adam naively replied, thinking he had hit the jackpot since Garin was without question the best athlete among all of them.

Joe then burst into laughter.

"What's so funny?" Adam asked.

"Nothing," Garin said, glaring at Joe, who after all these years was like an irritating brother he had learned to put up with. "Joe has the sense of humor of a toddler, but then again you knew that already, Adam."

Adam cracked a smile. Garin then pointed at crutches lying underneath the bench he was sitting on. Though Garin was wearing regular sneakers, the guys hadn't noticed that his ankle was wrapped.

"What happened to you?" Adam asked.

Garin proceeded to tell the same little white lie he had to anyone who asked, blaming his current state on an injury incurred while running during a game of racquetball, though the real story was slightly less macho. He had been running—out the door to work—when he tripped over his toddler daughter's toy. His wife, Brooke, the powerhouse publicist, thought he was being silly to tell the little running lie, but as a former star athlete in both high school and college, Garin's ego simply wouldn't allow him to admit to the world that he was officially middle-aged and that at forty-five things didn't bounce back as quickly as they did at twenty-five, and that these days a pink stuffed teddy bear was now enough to take him out of the game.

Brock was secretly relieved he wouldn't have to go up against Garin's wall-of-steel defense today.

After Garin's explanation Joe couldn't resist a little dig at his longtime pal. "Oh, I thought some client finally kicked you for losing all their money."

"You know, Joe, that's almost as funny as your game on the court—or should I say lack thereof?"

With that everyone burst into laughter. It had been ages since the group had been together.

Then Joe added for good measure, "Ha ha. Geez, without Garin playing it's basically me versus a bunch of old ladies."

"Shut up, Nelson," Brock barked.

"Actually, make that two old ladies and one invalid. Don't you need a doctor's note or something to play?" Joe said staring at Adam, a reference to Adam's recent heart attack scare, which turned out to be a panic attack—something that had resulted in months of ribbing by his friends.

"Fuck you, Joe," Adam replied. "Oh wait, I can't. I'm not a cheerleader."

The rest of the guys broke into assorted "oohs" and "aahs" at the dig.

"Look at that. Adam finally grew a set of balls," Joe replied. "Your mother know you talk like that, Ad-Man?"

"Let's just leave my mother out of this," Adam replied.

"Fine by me. I had more than enough of her last night," Joe chortled.

"Ignore him, Adam," a voice piped in. "We all know that unless your mom has started dancing for the Detroit Pistons lately she's safe from Nelson."

"Very funny," said Joe.

"No, very true," said Brock.

"Great to see you, Gov," Joe said, enveloping Luke in a big bear hug.

One by one each gave their old friend a hug.

"Speaking of cheerleaders, Joe, when's the big day?" Brock asked.

"What big day?" Adam asked.

"The wedding. Didn't you hear, some chick has finally managed to get Nelson locked in with a date and all," Brock continued. "So when's the big day? When do you officially become as miserable as the rest of us?"

"Speak for yourself, Brock," said Luke. "I happen to love my wife. In fact I even like her."

"Yeah, yeah, yeah, Luke. You and Laura so in love. Just like the soap opera characters."

Luke blushed. The fact that Luke and his longtime love shared the names of one of the most famous couples in soap opera history—the fictional star-crossed lovers Luke and Laura of *General Hospital* fame—was a source of much teasing by Luke's friends.

"If I did whatever my wife told me to do all the time I'd be happily married too," Brock added.

"So when is the wedding, Joe?" said Adam.

"Let's pick teams," Joe said.

"Wait a minute. Now I'm no expert in law," Adam said, "but Brock—help me out here since you're a lawyer. If a witness dodges a question, can you object?"

"You know what I object to? Those fairy glasses you're wearing. Did you get those in the ladies' section?"

"Uh-oh. Sounds like we hit a sore spot," said Brock.

"Are we here to talk or play?" Joe asked impatiently.

"Trouble in paradise?" asked Brock.

"Bite me, Brock-li."

"Uh-oh. Uh-oh," Brock replied. "Does this mean I shouldn't expect a wedding invite anytime soon?"

"Well you shouldn't expect one no matter what. So it's none of your business. We've postponed the wedding . . . just temporarily. Now let's play?"

"I knew it!" Brock shouted. "Hope you brought your checkbook, Luke—actually I hope you brought cash. I don't know that I can count on your checks clearing since you're a low-paid public servant and all."

"What are you talking about?" Joe asked.

"I told Luke your ass wouldn't make it down the aisle and put a hundred bucks on it. I should have put a thousand."

"*Fuck you*, Brock," Joe replied.

"Well, now you're free to since you're single again."

"I'm not single. For your information I'm still with Tiffini. We've just put the wedding on the back burner for a while."

With that the guys cut sideway glances at each other while trying in vain not to laugh. They all knew that this was Joe-speak for "I've lost interest." Joe was a friend, but that didn't stop them from feeling kind of bad for Tiffini. She wasn't exactly the sharpest knife in the drawer, but then none of Joe's gal pals were. She was nice enough though, and probably had no idea that she was about to be replaced, just like Brandi, Traci, and Staci before her.

"What's so funny about that?" Joe asked.

"Nothing, Joe. Nothing at all," said Luke. "Let's pick teams."

Forty-five minutes later, Brock and Joe led Adam and Luke 12–10. Due to his injury Garin was serving as referee and so far had racked up courtside Knicks tickets from Joe and a free dinner at Le Cirque from Brock to make calls go their way. Luke called them both "shameless" in their efforts to rig the game. A minute later Garin called Luke for traveling with the ball. "I did not," said Luke. "Did too," Brock chimed in. "Ref—with all due respect, I think you need to get your eyes checked," Luke said. Garin, with a wicked grin replied, "Adam—you might want to talk to your teammate. He's flirting with a technical." They all began to laugh. As play resumed, Joe shouted to Luke, "Maybe next time you should try shamelessly offering up something. Too bad the Pistons are playing so shitty this year. Probably couldn't give those tickets away. Any good restaurants in Michigan?" Everyone laughed.

Just then Luke, ever the cheerleader for his home state said, "Screw you, Nelson. I'll have you know we have some very fine dining establishments in our great state . . . and they also have some great ones in D.C."

"What does D.C. have to do with anything?" Joe replied.

"I might be spending more time there."

"Why on earth would anyone want to spend time in Washington unless they absolutely have to? It's almost as bad as the Midwest."

"You are such a snob, Nelson," Garin shouted. "You're from Michigan, for crying out loud. . . ."

"I may have grown up there but I was always a New Yorker at heart."

"Whatever you say, Joe," said Garin.

"Are you up for an appointment or something, Coop?" Adam asked.

"No," Luke said. "I'm going to run for president."

"Of what?" Adam asked.

"The PTA," Luke replied sarcastically. "What do you think?"

With that pronouncement they all froze.

All of them except Luke, that is. He stole the ball from Joe and began dribbling down the court. As his friends stood there with their mouths hanging open, Luke shot a beautiful three-pointer.

"Well, if I knew it was that easy to throw off your defense I would have mentioned it to you guys much, much earlier."

"Are you serious, Luke?" asked Joe.

"As a heart attack," Luke replied. "Oh—sorry, Adam."

They all burst into laughter.

*

"Why now?" Brock asked.

"Well, we've looked at the numbers . . ."

"Numbers?" Adam asked.

"The polling. My team thinks our numbers are never going to be better than they are right now. It's not exactly now or never, but basically tomorrow's not going to be any better than today. It seems I've got a bank of goodwill stored up with the public, and what's to say it's going to be there forever."

The Dream Team knew what goodwill Luke was referring to. He had gone from lowly state elected official to nationally known hero virtually overnight thanks to an unlikely encounter with a white supremacist that sounded straight out of a Hollywood script.

Luke had initially been drafted to run as lieutenant governor on a ticket with Attorney General Jamie Griffin, the heir to a local political dynasty. The Democratic candidate's frontrunner status had been hobbled by allegations of racial insensitivity after video surfaced depicting him laughing heartily at racially charged jokes, including one using the N-word, at a friend's bachelor party. After only a year and a half in office, Governor Griffin was forced out, his fondness for prostitutes having been made public by one of them. Just five short years after entering politics, Luke Cooper had gone from lowly state senator to the most powerful elected official in Michigan and one of the youngest sitting governors in the nation.

Though he faced a tough re-election fight because of his youth, perceived inexperience, and the corruption of his predecessor, in the end he managed to hold on to his seat. His family and friends all pitched in to help, raising money from their own friends, relatives, and acquaintances throughout the nation. They even knocked on doors on Election Day. Luke nicknamed them the Dream Team. Fate struck again when Luke's rival was incapacitated by a stroke in the days before the election, and Luke went on to win his first major race, and earn his first round of national attention—although it wouldn't be the last.

Just a few months into his first official term as governor of Michigan, while en route to an economic development conference in Florida, the SUV carrying the governor and a local elected official came across a group of protesters. Luke was informed that a group of self-described "white nationalists" had gathered to protest a rise in crime they blamed on growing communities of Haitian and Mexican immigrants. Luke asked the driver to stop the car and listened as protesters on both sides of the issue—the white nationalists and those shouting them down—tried to make their case for the surrounding crowd and the news cameras. Then something extraordinary happened. A racial slur was hurled and in an instant fists were flying. As police intervened to break up the melee, the SUV driver turned to encourage the governor to return to the vehicle, but Luke was nowhere to be found.

As the driver would later recount the story, minutes later he spotted Luke in the crowd but then lost him again. Panicked, he grabbed a police officer and said, "The governor of Michigan is in this crowd. If something happens to him we're all in trouble."

A moment later Luke was spotted again before his head disappeared back into the crowd. With a police officer in tow, the driver made a beeline for the spot where he had last seen what looked like the back of Luke's head. Together they found him on the ground. He was bleeding with a small cut to his forehead but insisted that he was fine. He then apologized to the police officer for being a distraction, the officer would later recall in interviews. Luke refused to go to a hospital, noting that he had already made them late enough for the conference, and opted instead for a simple Band-Aid. He gave a brief statement to police, noting that his scrape was merely a result of falling when the chaos erupted, and told the police officers to feel free to contact him should they need any additional information. It was not until that evening that his driver found out exactly how the governor earned his minor injury. Footage aired on the local news that night showed the crowd as they erupted into a blur of shoving and swinging fists. Only seconds later the camera captured an extraordinary sight: as a white nationalist lay on the ground bleeding, another man removed his tie and used it as a tourniquet to help the man with his injury. Just then a protester hauled his leg back as if ready to kick the white nationalist, but the man helping him blocked his leg.

The man helping the white nationalist was Luke.

Over the next seventy-two hours the clip would be played endlessly on television. The story of Luke—the black-Jewish governor who protected a racist—became a national sensation and Luke became one of the most recognizable elected officials in the nation. People who didn't even know the name of the governor in their own state now knew the name of the governor of Michigan. While talk swirled of film offers, Luke agreed to a total of five interviews on the subject. He did an interview with the Southern Poverty Law Center, a research institution that studies the role and impact of hate groups. He did one interview with a high school newspaper in his home state of Michigan. He did one interview with the Museum of Tolerance, inspired by Holocaust survivor Simon Wiesenthal's Center. He did one interview with a local news anchor in Michigan. The lone national interview he did was with *Good Morning America*—but only because he had been previously booked for a segment regarding several controversial death penalty cases in Michigan. Luke's press secretary stipulated that the *Good Morning America* anchor could ask only one question about the "incident" or the interview would be canceled. Luke agreed to one more national appearance, but it wasn't for an interview. He appeared as a guest on *Sesame Street*, for an episode on tolerance. He pointedly declined all further requests from political reporters because, according to his press secretary, he "didn't want to politicize something that had nothing to do with politics but was about simply being a human being." When later pressed about the small number of interviews, Luke added that he believed that if given a choice the citizens of Michigan would probably prefer to see their tax dollars pay for a "governor who works, not just gives interviews."

But that didn't stop the media from talking—or from dubbing him a rising political star. In fact, Luke's decidedly nonpolitical response to the media siege only added to the mystery and hype surrounding him. *TIME* magazine named him to its annual list of the world's most influential people, "for reminding all of us that there is just one race: the human race." *GQ* magazine named him to its list of "Political Power Players," noting that "the handsome governor is known so much for his debonair suits that some in the Michigan statehouse have been known to refer to him as 'Mr. GQ.'"

That was a total fabrication perpetuated by the media (in fact Luke's real nickname among those who knew him best was Coop). But the moniker stuck nonetheless, and with it the GQ candidate was born.

So here Luke was barely a year into his first official term as governor, and he was already planning a White House run.

As understated as ever, Joe shouted an enthusiastic "Hell yeah, Coop! I've always wanted to play ball in the White House!"

"Well, I don't know that they have an indoor court there, Joe," Luke replied with a smile.

"Yeah but if you're president you can get one if you want."

"Well I got to get there first."

"You'll get there, Coop. There's not a single thing you've set your mind to that you haven't accomplished. In fact the more I think about it, you got some kind of magic voodoo or something you're working with? Maybe we ought to rub your head for good luck." With that Garin stood and steadied himself on his one good ankle and proceeded to get the possible future president in a headlock and rub his head."

"Alright, alright, Garin. That's enough!" Luke said, laughing.

"Just making sure that president or not you never forget you're the same old Coop to us. And if you do ever forget it I'll leak all your secrets to the media."

"Garin, I don't want to start my presidential campaign off by being accused of assaulting an old man with a bum leg so let me go before I have to hurt you."

"Old man, huh?" Garin proceeded to rub Luke's head even harder, as though it were a genie lamp, before letting go.

"Please, like Mr. Squeaky Clean here has any secrets worth selling," Joe piped up. "You know, now that I think about it, it all makes sense. That's why you've always been so . . . so . . . so . . . what's another word for 'boring'?"

"Joe, you think Hugh Hefner's life is boring," Garin teased.

"Well, the man did sleep with the same three chicks for, what, a year? Two?"

They all began to laugh, and the fact that Joe was dead serious in his comment only made them laugh harder.

Then Brock and Adam got quiet.

"Adam? What do you think? Do I have your vote?" Luke asked.

"Of course, Coop."

"Well try not to get too excited," Luke said.

Adam stood there silently for a moment and then did something completely unexpected.

He leaned in and gave Luke a big hug. When he let him go he said, "I can't believe I just hugged the next president. Anything you need. Anything at all." He looked as though he was tearing up and for once Joe didn't tease him.

"Thanks, Adam," Luke said, squeezing Adam's shoulder.

Adam wasn't known for big displays of affection, so his gesture made the moment more real for all of them.

They stood there awkwardly in the way men often do when things get too intimate, too emotional.

"Brock? Any thoughts?" Luke said.

"I'm just taking it all in," he said noncommittally.

"Say what's on your mind. We're all brothers here," Luke said.

"Well, Coop . . . isn't it a bit early? I mean, your governor's race was close. Don't you want to stay in there, show everyone what you can really do, and then make your move?"

"We talked about that, but five years is an eternity. Who knows where things will be by then? I mean, I could be the answer to a trivia question," Luke said.

"Your people are right. You gotta strike when the iron's hot. It's hot for you now," Garin added.

"I agree, Coop. It's like when I talk to a family who's torn between sending Junior to college or the league. You can't control when you're going to be at the top of your game. You have to move when you're there. Not wait a few years and hope you stay there," Joe added.

"Well, I want everyone in my family to be on board because you know this is going to be a crazy ride whether they want to be on it or not. I mean, there's going to be press digging around in my past, talking to every person I ever said hi to on the street. And this goes without saying, but I can't do this alone. I'm going to need my Dream Team to get me to the championships again. So what do you all say?" Luke asked.

"I'm in. All the way, Coop." Garin then put his hand out, the way he and Luke did in high school in their basketball huddle.

"Me too," Joe said, putting his hand in.

"Me three," Adam said, putting his hand on top of Joe's.

They all looked at Brock.

"Come on, Brock. Don't hate just because Luke is going to make it to the White House before you. Just think, he can appoint you to the Supreme Court."

All of the guys laughed. Brock feigned a chuckle, but inwardly he was pissed at Garin.

"I only have one question," Brock said. "When can me and my missus host a fundraiser for your presidential campaign?" Brock put his hand on top of Adam's. Then Luke put his on top of Brock's.

★

The Political Post-Express

TWO MORE DEMS MULL PRESIDENTIAL BIDS

Congressman Jay Billings of Ohio took his first official steps toward becoming a presidential candidate today by launching an exploratory committee. Though Billings, who announced his intentions on "Meet the Press" days ago, is considered a long shot by many members of the Democratic establishment, some insiders say he could potentially draw support from "ABB" voters, those looking to vote for "Anyone But Abigail Beaman," the senator and daughter of the late President Michael Carter Beaman. But according to sources, "ABB" voters may soon have another surprising choice. Luke Cooper, the charismatic governor of Michigan, is said to be seriously considering throwing his hat in the ring. The governor, who gained national acclaim when he intervened on behalf of a white supremacist who was being attacked, could potentially draw from two key Democratic constituencies, African-American and Jewish voters. The governor, who is African-American, was adopted and raised in the Jewish faith, and has in previous interviews identified himself as "Black and Jewish."

But before a single vote is cast, candidates have to win the pre-primary primary, known colloquially as "the money primary." Sen. Beaman, who it has been said has been preparing for (and been prepared for) this race her entire life, has approximately $8 million on hand for her presidential run. Though spokespeople for Billings and Cooper both declined to give specific figures, they both acknowledged that their current money totals are nowhere near the $8 million figure. Both candidates also acknowledged that that has to change soon for their campaigns to be taken seriously.

CHAPTER 3

Tami took her babies out and, as had become her ritual, immediately hid the evidence—the boxes and the shopping bags.

She had already gone over her monthly shopping allowance, and if Brock knew that she had purchased two more pairs of shoes, he would flip, especially if he learned they came from Giuseppe Zanotti and Jimmy Choo. It was amazing to her that a man who primarily wore Gap khakis and Brooks Brothers suits off the rack could know that Jimmy Choo wasn't a Chinese takeout chain, and also knew how much a pair cost. But that was Brock for you. He made it his business to know the names—and prices—of the labels that Tami wore.

Forty-eight hours earlier Brock had informed her that they would be hosting a fundraiser for his friend Luke Cooper, the governor of some Midwestern state, and they had ten days to pull it together, and by they, he really meant her. In typical Brock fashion he had told, not asked, her.

She shopped when she was stressed. Shopped or ate. And while Brock disapproved of overindulging in either habit, his reaction to her putting on 60 pounds while pregnant with the twins made it clear that he disapproved of her overeating more. From his perspective, he married a model, and he wanted to stay married to one, or at least someone who still looked like one. She once asked him point blank if her being overweight made him love her any less and he coolly replied, "Not any less than you would love me if I quit the law firm and hopped on the back of a sanitation truck."

That exchange pretty much summed up their relationship.

Tami had never really run an event this big on her own. She was on the boards of a couple of small nonprofits and worked on committees, but those were different. The one upside was that Luke's cousin Jessica was an event planner and had agreed to help. She was even trying to get a couple of celebrities on board. Brooke, the wife of Garin, an old friend of Brock and Luke, had also agreed to pitch in. Brooke always struck Tami as both tough and no-nonsense—someone who didn't take any crap from anyone, least of all her husband. It was a trait Tami had always admired, and even envied.

After the shoes were safely hidden away Tami headed down the stairs to the kitchen of their Park Avenue duplex and opened the fridge. She opened the produce drawer and saw a smorgasbord of apples to choose from. She then closed the drawer and spotted a bushel of fresh grapes and next to them some strawberries, and above them two cartons of blueberries. "What is this, a freaking farmer's market?" she thought to herself.

Her nutritionist—that highly enthusiastic and annoying man Brock had gotten for her as a "gift" for her thirty-fifth birthday—had cheerily told her to "think of brown rice as your friend." Just staring at the bowl of rice made her want to punch him . . . and Brock. She reached for it and removed the Saran wrap. She then proceeded to pour it down the garbage disposal. She returned to the refrigerator, opened the freezer portion, pulled out the Tupperware bowl labeled "homemade chicken noodle soup," and opened it. She then grabbed a spoon from the drawer and began digging into the pint of Häagen-Dazs butter pecan hidden inside.

Two minutes later her phone began to ring. It was Peggy, Brock's assistant, calling. For a moment Tami wondered if he had secretly implanted some chip in her while she was sleeping so that he could tell whenever she was going over her suggested daily caloric intake. It was like he had ESP or something—either that or cameras in the house. Tami swallowed one last scoop of ice cream then flipped open the phone. "Hi, Peggy. How are you?"

"I'm well, Mrs. Simpson. Thank you for asking. Mr. Simpson asked me to remind you about a couple of things."

"Of course he did," she thought to herself. "Because he thinks I wouldn't remember to wake up in the morning if he didn't leave me a Post-it note." She considered expressing these thoughts aloud, but instead she simply said, "Sure, Peggy. Just let me grab a pen."

★

The moment Jessica saw the light on her phone flashing she knew, in the same way that a twin knows that the other is in danger, or that a woman knows to hack into her boyfriend's cell phone for evidence of cheating. Your gut instinct just tells you something. Her assistant paged her on the intercom:

"Jessica?"

"Yeah, Sam?"

"It's Ashley again."

"Are you kidding me?"

"No. Sorry . . . do you want me to put her into voice mail?"

"No, you can put her through—but buzz me in *exactly* two minutes to get me off the call."

"Will do."

Samantha followed Jessica's instructions.

"Hi, Jess. Sorry to bug you again." "For the fourth time in an hour," Jessica thought.

"Not a problem. What's up, Ashley?"

"Diamond feels like we should rethink the caterers. Maybe try something French instead?"

"Well, Ashley, we already have a deposit down with Spoonbread."

"Yes, she knows, but French cuisine might be a better way to go. She's had me prepare a list of suggestions . . ."

"Well does Diamond plan on paying the fees for being in breach of contract with Spoonbread?"

There was a long pause.

"Jess, you know I'm just the messenger."

"Well then please take the message back to her that the answer is no. It's too late in the game. Particularly when we already changed it once—at her suggestion." Right on cue Samantha buzzed her.

"Ashley, can you hold on a sec?"

"Sure."

She put Ashley on hold for a reasonable length of time—the usual 45 seconds—then picked up and said, "Ash—sorry, but I got to take this."

"No problem. Can we check in later?"

"Of course," but she was really thinking "Of course not."

Jessica thought she had seen it all through her career as an event planner, but this one, more specifically the hosts of the event, was driving her up a wall. Actually, one of them in particular made her want to drive headfirst into the wall.

She had agreed to work on this event only as a favor to her cousin Luke. She probably would have said no to almost any other family member, but Luke was one of her favorite cousins. He was the reason this Westchester girl, destined to marry a successful doctor someday, got backstage to meet Tupac Shakur, thanks to his friend Adam's music industry connections. Her classmates were so jealous they could hardly stand it and Mark Smith, the most gorgeous specimen walking the campus—who had barely acknowledged her most of the school year—actually came up to her during lunch and sat down next to her to find out what "Pac" was really like in person. She still had the pictures with "Pac" to prove it hanging in her bedroom. Luke rarely called and asked her for anything, so when he asked for help with this event she said yes. But as they say, "No good deed goes unpunished."

Diamond Moon was a former defense attorney turned talk show host, but her biggest claim to fame was being the cohost of a TV show called *Love Him or Leave Him*. On it, she and two other attorneys would help counsel women on the pros and cons of staying with or ditching a troublesome spouse. Surprisingly, the syndicated show became one of the highest-rated in daytime television. All was going swimmingly for Diamond (or "Lady Di," as she became affectionately known), until a now notorious on-air altercation. Di, a longtime bachelorette, was "swept off her feet," as she would later tell *People* magazine, by a young lawyer nearly twenty years her junior. Six weeks after meeting him the two eloped to Barbados. As the wedding took place during a *Love Him or Leave Him* hiatus, the blessed union would not be celebrated on the show until more than a month after it took place, allowing plenty of time for the newlyweds to honeymoon together.

When the show returned for its premiere in the fall, viewers (not to mention the show's crew) were shocked, to say the least. Gone was the Lady Di they knew and loved. In her place was a Barbie caricature, with a smaller nose and larger breasts, and in place of her signature pixie cut was a long, flowing wig. It was as though during her honeymoon she had gone into a plastic surgeon's office and asked to be given "the Lil' Kim"— a makeover from top to bottom.

At first, at Di's request (or, rather, demands), her cohosts made no mention of the new Lady Di. But as viewers began to weigh in the media, discretion eventually went out the window. When they did a show about a husband pressuring his wife to get skinny and get plastic surgery, Griffin Donnelly, the male cohost, advised "Never do something for someone else or you'll always resent him. You have to be happy with you."

Diamond piped in, "Honey, if you start changing for him today, you're going to be too busy being who he wants you to be and you're not going to have any time left to be who *you* want to be."

Some of the audience applauded but others simply sat there, as did the hosts, in an uncomfortable silence. The guest then said, "You bought a whole new body just to get a husband. What's wrong with me wanting to get one just to keep mine?"

Diamond jumped out of her chair like a linebacker. It took both Griffin and the other attorney, along with the stage manager—all 280 pounds of him—to restrain her. The audience went berserk, while the guest hid behind a seat.

Love Him or Leave Him got more press coverage than ever before But the saying "there's no such thing as bad publicity" did not prove true for Diamond. She was given a sizable buyout to walk away from *Love Him or Leave Him*. Since then she had not been able to find a steady TV job. Relegated to lobbying unsuccessfully for guest spots here and there on programs like *Dancing with the Stars*, Diamond wasn't an A-list celebrity, which meant she had the free time to go over invitations with a fine-tooth comb and rewrite the catering menu fifteen times for Jessica. But Jessica was so fed up with her that she was tempted to ask one of her TV friends to offer Diamond a job just to get her out of her hair.

Jessica hadn't even wanted to include Diamond, but with Brock being Luke's best friend there was little she could do about it. Diamond and Brock had been colleagues in the early days of their legal careers and they remained good friends. Brock and his wife Tami regularly socialized with Diamond and her new husband, Cory. They had just traveled to St. Bart's together, something Jessica knew only because photos of Diamond from the trip had been featured prominently in *Star* magazine's "Worst Beach Bodies of the Stars" issue. Since her makeover, Diamond had begun dressing like the hot high school cheerleader she never was—even for red carpet events. "If I had spent thousands of dollars on plastic surgery and *any* of my body parts made a 'worst' anything list I would sue my plastic surgeon for malpractice," Jessica thought to herself. "Although considering the state of her career, Diamond should kind of be flattered they would include her in anything featuring the word 'star' in it." She then dissolved into laughter.

Besides, as much of a pain in the ass as Diamond was, Jessica recognized that they weren't in much of a position to be choosy on the celebrity front. Luke was recognizable enough to political junkies and had had a brief brush with fame thanks to the high-profile incident in which he saved the white supremacist. But that didn't make him an A-list celebrity in a city that was full of them. Not to mention that in New York the competition for dollars and celebrity face time is particularly fierce. Senator Abigail Sanchez Beaman, Luke's principal competition for the Democratic nomination, was the daughter of a beloved former president. Furthermore, she was also the first Latina woman elected to the Senate. Her mother was of Mexican descent. But perhaps most important, since President Beaman's death her mother's longtime companion had been Senator Sid Burstein.

Sidney Burstein was the senior U.S. senator from New York, widely recognized as one of the most brilliant political tacticians in the nation. He won his senate seat in a race that more than a decade later still ranks as one of the nastiest and most expensive in U.S. history. A popular joke among Washington media and political insiders was: "Where's the most dangerous place to be?" The punch line: "Between Sid Burstein and a news camera." Hence his reputation for being ruthless and media-obsessed. A former congressional colleague once described Burstein as someone who knew "how to run a winning campaign better than anyone I know. He also knows how to hold a grudge better than anyone I know."

So while Brock had no trouble lining up friends in the legal world for fundraisers during Luke's run for governor (in fact Sid Burstein even served as guest of honor for one), with word out that Luke was planning to make a bid for the White House—against Burstein's chosen candidate, no less—Brock and company were finding it tougher to get their calls returned by certain donors.

If Luke's campaign was going to have any serious chance of competing on Beaman/Burstein turf they were going to have to think (and raise money) out of the box. This was one of the reasons that Jessica had been brought in. She knew a lot of people, particularly rich, young people in New York, and if she could get some of them to show up at this event and bring their checkbooks they would be in good shape. She had no interest in politics but wanted this event to be a success for Luke. But Lady Di had been one of the biggest "names" they had gotten to commit. Since desperate times called for desperate measures, Jessica called the person, she least wanted to, her ex . . . something, T.J. Greeley.

She picked up the phone and dialed.

A star player for the New York Giants, T.J. had been a longtime friend before one night of tequila shots turned them into more than that. They spent one amazing weekend together—no commitments—and then the following week she learned from the gossip column Page Six that he was back with his on-again, off-again girlfriend, a *Sports Illustrated* swimsuit model. "Aren't they all?" she thought to herself.

After the Page Six piece ran, their relationship dwindled to occasional e-mail exchanges usually consisting of no more than a sentence or two, the last one, sent by him three months earlier, wishing her a happy birthday. It was nice that he still remembered all these months later. But she didn't write back. What was there really left to say?

The phone rang twice before she hung up. She then remembered that while her cell phone number was blocked, her office number wasn't, so she called back.

"Hello."

"Hey! It's me."

Silence.

"It's me, Jessica."

"Oh. Sorry. Hey, Jess. What's up? Did you just call?"

"No. I asked my assistant to get you on the line and she somehow dropped the call and . . . so . . . I . . . figured I should do it myself. . . ."

"Oh. Okay. So what's up?" T.J. asked.

"Nothing much."

"How was your trip?"

She had mentioned in passing during their fling that she was cel-ebrating her birthday with a girls' getaway to Cabo San Lucas. She couldn't believe he remembered.

"Good. Good. Good. Real good"—"Say something other than 'good,' for crying out loud," she thought to herself. "Thanks for asking. . . . How are things with you?"

"Good, good," he said with a wry giggle. He was obviously teasing her. "You know. Same old same old."

There was an awkward silence for a bit.

"Jess. Are you okay?" he asked.

"I'm fine. Why do you ask?"

"Well, I just haven't heard from you in a while and you sound kind of . . . like you're someplace else."

"Actually, I kind of need a favor. . . . You know I hate to ask but . . ."

"Sure. Name it. What is it?"

"I'm helping to put together an event for my cousin, a fundraiser, and I was hoping you could make it."

"Sure. What kind of charity is it?"

"It's not a charity, exactly. It's a political fundraiser. He's a governor."

"Your cousin's the governor of New York!? Damn. You never men-tioned that. That's hot."

"No. Not of New York. Of Michigan."

"Oh. So you want me to come to an event in Michigan?"

"No. He's governor of Michigan but we're having the event here."

"Oh. Okay . . . why?"

"Well, a lot of politicians raise money in New York and I'm just trying to help him out."

"If he's already been elected governor then what does he need help with?"

"He's running for president."

"Your cousin's running for president? Get out. Wow. That's some seri-ous shit. What's his name?"

"Luke Cooper."

"Wait a minute. Luke Cooper . . . the black guy?"

". . . Yeah."

"He's your cousin?"

She simply said, "Yeah, he's my cousin."

"Get the hell out of here. Well, I can't wait to see what the rest of your family looks like," he said with a laugh. "What day is the party?"

"Not this Thursday, but next Thursday."

"Yeah, that should be fine. How much you trying to raise?"

"Well, the more the merrier."

"I hear that."

"Tickets start at two hundred and fifty."

"Thousand?"

"No. Just two hundred and fifty bucks. Two hundred fifty to a thousand bucks."

"No problem. Okay. I'll be there and I'll see about rounding up a few friends."

Jessica had to restrain herself from squealing. "Thanks, T.J. Thanks a lot. I really appreciate it."

"Anytime, Jess. E-mail me deets and I'll see you there."

★

Now that they lived in different states, pulled by the demands of work and family, Garin and Luke almost never got a chance to hang, just the two of them. Usually when Luke was back in New York, his schedule was so tight that it ended up being a gathering of the entire Dream Team crew, like their recent basketball game. But Luke had his scheduler carve out an extra hour for him to meet up with Garin for an early drink before his fundraiser at Brock's.

The two tucked into a booth at Tillman's, one of Garin's favorite places to grab a drink and some ribs.

They immediately began reminiscing.

"You're never going to believe who I ran into," Garin began.

"Who?"

"Denise Solomon."

"You're kidding!"

"Swear to God."

"I thought she'd gotten married and left New York."

"She did. But she's divorced and back . . . with five kids."

"No!"

"Yes. Even showed me pictures."

Denise Solomon was a City University of New York student Garin had dated briefly while he and Luke were in law school, before she showed some *Fatal Attraction*–like tendencies.

"How'd she look?"

"Like she'd had five kids."

"Denise Solomon. That's a blast from the past. How old's the oldest? You sure there's not a little Garin junior in the bunch?"

Luke giggled mischievously. After Denise broke into their apartment and poured bleach on Garin's clothes—and, by accident, a few of Luke's—Garin's playboy ways finally ended for good. He became a one-woman man, eventually settling down with his wife Brooke.

"I tell you this much, that girl single-handedly got me back into church. I was so thankful God helped me get rid of her I started going every Sunday."

"How was she when you talked? Did she act like nothing had happened?"

"I was completely caught off guard. Was grabbing coffee in a Starbucks and heard a voice say *Garin*? Hardly recognized her. I think it's safe to say it's been a rough twenty years for her."

"Who'd she marry?"

"Don't know. Didn't ask. I wanted to get out of there as quickly as possible. When the last conversation you have with someone involves discussing a restraining order, that's not exactly grounds for a Hallmark reunion."

Luke laughed. "Whatever happened to Sheila . . . Sheila . . . ?"

"Gitroy?"

"Yeah. Yeah."

"Married, with kids. Out in California somewhere."

"Still practicing law?"

"Last I heard she was taking a couple of years off to be with her kids. It's not like she needs the money. Her husband's some bigwig at Google or one of the other major tech companies."

"She was something else."

"She was and from what I hear still is. Total package: beauty and brains."

"And so nice."

"Until she was in the courtroom. She's supposed to be a hell of a litigator."

"Yeah, I could see that."

"Oh, you know who else is supposed to be back in town?"

"Who?"

"Ranya." Garin let the name roll off of his tongue.

"Really?" Luke tried to sound nonchalant but he was no longer look-ing Garin in the eye. "When did she get back?"

"I don't know. I didn't see her. Joe did."

"Joe?" Luke said distractedly.

"Yep. Joe."

Luke was now nervously tapping his foot.

Luke didn't say anything, so Garin added, "You know, Joe? He's about five-feet-ten, blond hair, blue eyes, you've known him most of your life."

"Funny," Luke said. "So where'd he see her?"

"Some celeb party, of course. Apparently she was there with some French actor or director or something."

"Of course she was," Luke mumbled under his breath.

Luke and Ranya had a tempestuous affair while she was studying film as an undergrad at NYU and he was in law school. She was high-strung, temperamental, and demanding, but one of the most beautiful women he had ever seen, and the sex had been incredible. Her father was Egyp-tian and her mother Ethiopian, and she spoke with this accent that drove Luke wild. They had met at a downtown party and were serious for what seemed like an eternity but was really for only a year. She cheated on Luke with a famous film director she had been interning for. She was the only woman who had ever broken Luke's heart. They continued to rendezvous occasionally even after the official breakup. When he and Laura became official, he and Ranya severed all contact, although he heard through the grapevine that she relocated to Europe and worked in the film industry there.

"Joe said she came up to him and said hi. He couldn't believe she remembered him."

Luke just nodded without saying a word.

"Don't you want to know how she looked? Aren't you even the least bit curious?"

"Another glass?" the waiter then asked.

"Not for me, or I won't make it through my speech tonight," Luke replied.

"You always were a lightweight," Garin teased. "I'll have another."

"Brooke going to be able to make the event tonight?" Luke asked, changing the subject.

"Wouldn't miss it."

"She's great."

"She is but I hate to break this to you. She's not coming just to support you. She's also coming to support Tami, but she's mainly coming because she knows how much her presence irritates Brock. Apparently he's deemed her some kind of bad influence on Tami."

"No comment," Luke said.

"You callin' my wife a bad influence?"

"I wouldn't dream of it. But I tell you this much, if I were in combat and had to choose someone to cover me, it wouldn't even be a contest."

"My best friend better not be saying he'd choose my 130-pound wife to back him up over his oldest, toughest, most athletic friend."

"One of those adjectives was right. I believe it was 'oldest.' Besides, don't act so surprised. Even you're afraid of your wife, and you're not afraid of anybody."

"For the record, I am not afraid of my wife."

The waiter filled Garin's glass and walked away.

"Really now?" Luke said, raising an eyebrow that clearly denoted "I don't believe you."

"No. I am not. I just find that things tend to go more smoothly when I agree with her."

Luke let out a loud laugh then said through his laughter, "Words to live by, my brother. Words to live by. You know what they say . . . 'Happy wife . . .'"

"Happy life," Garin said, as he and Luke clinked glasses.

"Okay," Luke began. "All bullshit aside. Just the two of us here. You think I can pull this off?"

"This?"

"You think I have a shot at winning?"

"Well," Garin paused. "I think that if I were a gambling man I would say the odds are a lot more likely that you will be elected president next year than they are that Tiffini will get Joe down the aisle."

The two then had a hearty laugh.

"Seriously, Garin. You think I can pull this off?"

"I once watched you convince a police officer that if he didn't let me out of a ticket, he could be tried as an accessory in my murder when my father killed me."

Luke laughed.

"I've been watching you pull off the impossible, for more than half my life."

"I know Matt doesn't want me to run. He won't say it, but he's thinking it."

"He's your brother. He's probably worried about you and your family."

"Yeah, but you're like my brother. The thing is, I sometimes think my real brothers are so worried about protecting me . . . I don't know if it's because I'm the youngest, or the race thing or what, but it's like sometimes they're treating me with kid gloves, and I know you've never done that. You always tell me what I need to hear. Not what I want to hear. Promise me that will never change no matter what happens. You'll always shoot straight."

"Have I ever shot crooked with you?"

Luke cracked a wan smile. "You know what I mean. So I'm not crazy . . . to do this . . . right now?"

Garin took a deep breath and chose his words very deliberately. "Yes. You are crazy. To do this. Right now. But you'd be even crazier to pass up the opportunity to do this right now."

Luke cracked a smile of relief. "I want to ask you something. Important. Will you be the treasurer of my campaign? There're all these bigwigs my team wants me to ask."

"Thanks for letting me know I'm not a bigwig," Garin said.

"No, you know what I mean . . . I want someone in there I can trust. Who won't bail if things start heading downhill."

"You need me, I'm there."

"You need to talk to Brooke, or will she be okay with it?"

"Please. You know Brooke likes you more than I do. She'd probably threaten to divorce me if I don't say yes."

"Thanks, man," Luke said.

"Well, I'm not doing it for free. Low-paid public servant or not, this round of drinks is on you."

"Thanks, Garin. Seriously, means a lot."

"You're my brother."

★

Despite getting off to a somewhat bumpy start, by the day of the fund-raiser things had finally come together. Adding T.J.'s name to the official invite moved more tickets in one day than Lady Di's name had in a week. They now had more than seventy attendees confirmed, which was safely over the "disaster threshold." In Brock's words, fifty was the magic number they needed to hit to "avoid embarrassment."

But Jessica still wasn't able to breathe a complete sigh of relief. Lady Di was making sure of that. Thirty-six hours before the event, she had her assistant call Jessica to inform her that Diamond would be arriving at the event with a camera crew in tow, to shoot footage for her upcoming reality show. When Jessica told her that per instructions from Luke's campaign staff, no press was allowed, she received a tersely worded e-mail from Lady Di herself—written in the third person—that said in so many words, "Screw you and I don't care what you say, I'm bringing them anyway."

Jessica called Tami for backup, but she told Jessica to speak directly with Brock, who didn't get back to her. For the next twenty-four hours Jessica didn't hear from Diamond or her assistant. In some ways this was the answer to her prayers, but as they say, be careful what you wish and pray for. Jessica knew that in this case silence was not golden and probably meant Diamond was up to trouble.

Jessica tried to focus on the positive. Brooke had gotten both Sandra Stevens and Monique Montgomery to agree to attend. Sandra handled investments for a few of the athletes Brooke represented as a publicist. She was an investment wiz at Morgan Stanley, one of the few African American women being openly groomed for senior management. She was featured in a number of national publications, from the *Wall Street Journal* to *Essence* magazine. Her support could ultimately open up the wallets of many others, so securing her attendance was a huge coup.

Monique was one of Brooke's former clients, a former Miss USA first runner-up who was known for the famous men she had been linked to. She met her first husband, Sam Smith, during her reign as Miss New Jersey USA, when he was a celebrated player for the New Jersey Nets. They divorced after less than a year. A week after the divorce became final she met the actor Mason Broderick at a birthday party for his friend Wesley

Snipes. Two months later she and Broderick were engaged. The engagement lasted three years, during which time she solidified her status as the kind of aspiring actress who would always be "aspiring" by posing in a selection of men's magazines, including *Playboy, King,* and *Smooth.* The engagement was called off, but not before the two had a son. Rumors linked her to a number of other famous and powerful men over the years, including former boxing great Greg Duffy. It was believed that one of these men gave her the startup money for the upscale boutique she now operated in Harlem, the eponymous Monique's.

Monique reminded Tami of that girl from high school who pretended to be your friend while plotting to steal your boyfriend. But Monique knew lots of people. She was a staple of the black blogosphere, popping up at this or that celebrity event. She drew coverage, and that was good for Luke. That was all that mattered, really, but Tami certainly wouldn't leave her alone with her husband, that's for sure.

The morning of the fundraiser Tami woke up with a splitting headache and still had a to-do list to check. Her household staff had been busy for days with the preparations. Brock wanted to make sure that if there were another star of the evening besides Luke, it would be their sprawling 3,600-square-foot duplex.

Brock had grown up a fat, nerdy kid with dark chocolate skin and thick Coke-bottle glasses. His childhood was so painful he rarely spoke of it. He subscribed to the notion that living well was the best revenge. So he believed that everyone he associated with in his new life should be picture-perfect. That's why he was so tough—or as Tami's friends described him, "dictatorial"—about her weight. That was also why after spending nearly thirty years—her entire life—as Tamika Smith, she gained not one but two new names on their wedding day. Brock rechristened her the abbreviated "Tami," a name he deemed more befitting the wife of an Upper East Side attorney. Goodbye, Tamika Smith, the working-class kid turned C-list model. Hello, Tami Simpson, Park Avenue trophy wife.

Tami wasn't naive. She was nice, but not an idiot. She knew that part of why Brock wanted to marry her was he wanted a black trophy wife. She was not too tall, but not too short, not too thick, but not too thin. She was curvy in all the right places, and her head was full of big, bouncy curls—no weave necessary (Brock hated those). After a day at the beach her skin was still the color of Halle Berry's. Brock would never admit to being so shallow, but he did want babies with "good hair," so he set out to marry a woman whom he believed could deliver—literally.

When they first began dating they seemed to walk everywhere. At first she thought maybe Brock was lying about his profession and simply couldn't afford taxis. After a few weeks she realized that he liked walking around with her, as though he were showing her off. She began to notice the way he would clasp her hand or nuzzle her head whenever a good-looking man began to eye her. He wanted the whole world to know she was his.

It was a short courtship. He proposed after five months and they were married within a year. She wanted to prove to his skeptical family, and to herself, that she didn't marry him for his money. She reminded herself that she was employed, and comfortable, as a working model when they met. A catalog model approaching thirty. She did think of Brock as her Prince Charming. He rescued her from a life of working at some job that she hated once she was discarded by the modeling industry for committing the cardinal sin of aging. And she did love him—most of the time—although he sometimes made it a challenge.

A couple of weeks before the wedding, at a dinner party, Brock got into a debate about a former professional basketball player, Jay Jefferson, who was considering a run for Congress. While the other lawyers were enthusiastic about him, noting he was a great speaker with a graduate degree in government, Brock dubbed him "an unqualified joke." Tami sat silently through much of the back-and-forth until one of the other lawyers asked, "What do you think?"

"I don't follow politics that closely, or basketball," she replied.

"Tami follows clothes, that's about it," Brock said, winking at the other lawyers.

Tami didn't laugh, and then added, "But I have met Jay before and he's a bright guy."

Brock looked surprised and annoyed.

"I knew you were marrying a smart woman, Brock," said one of the other lawyers.

To which Brock replied, "Yes, so smart she almost finished community college." The fact that Brock had a law degree from Columbia, while Tami only had a few years of community college under her belt, was something he never let her forget—particularly when they disagreed over something.

Brock had to fight for every opportunity he had ever gotten, creating a chip on his shoulder that at times threatened to weigh him—and those who loved him—down. He was particularly resentful of those from more privileged backgrounds, who, he felt, would never have to work as hard as he. Years later he still stewed over some of the perceived slights visited on him by wealthy blacks, including a fellow law student who made a point of inviting only those from equally pedigreed backgrounds to a Labor Day party at his home in the Hamptons. Years later, when the same classmate made partner at a rival firm before he did, Brock purchased an apartment that the man wanted. The man allegedly offered to buy it from Brock—at a twenty percent profit—but he refused. Then, after the man and his fiancée settled into another apartment with what Brock gleefully deemed a "less desirable view," Brock turned around and sold the original apartment his rival had wanted to someone else, at a loss.

While Brock's competitive streak had doomed a string of personal relationships over the years, Luke was one of the few people around with whom Brock seemed to keep his competitiveness in check. Despite his privileged upbringing, not only did Luke not flaunt his wealth, he was one of the most generous people Brock had ever known. As a testament to their close bond, Brock named one of his sons after his best friend. It was particularly touching to Luke because it was a long-held Jewish tradition that no child be named after a living relative, meaning Luke would never have a Little Luke of his own.

So because this evening was important to Luke, it was important to Brock, and that made its success extremely important to Tami.

Cocktails were scheduled to start precisely at 6:30 p.m., but Tami was realistic. Brooke was one of the few exceptions to "CP time" in their circle. She arrived at 6:30 on the dot with a few of her girlfriends in tow.

"Tami!" Brooke squealed, leaning in to give her a hug.

"Hey Brooke! How are you?"

"I'm good. Hanging in there. How are you?"

"Same old same old. And how is Ms. Allie doing?"

"Becoming more and more of a little diva every day. How about the twins?"

"About to drive Mommy up a wall."

At that they both laughed.

"Well, as usual you look fabulous, Ms. Tami."

"Thanks, Brooke!"

"Are those the new Jimmy Choo slingbacks?"

"They are. But shhh! Don't tell," she said with a laugh.

"Well, whatever they cost, they were worth every penny because you look mighty fierce."

Just then Tami began to feel a little woozy. She excused herself from the girls to get a glass of water. As she made her way over to the bar area she stopped to steady herself against a table. She had been so determined to look great that night that she hadn't had anything to eat all day—well, actually all week. In the seven days before the event she had begun the master cleanse, surviving on little more than a liquid concoction of maple syrup, lemon juice, and cayenne pepper. In a few more hours the event would be over and Tami could reward herself with a full meal. But for now, she would have another glass of water and she would be fine.

Jessica had arrived at 5:30. Barely more than five feet tall, she barked orders and got people to follow them with the gusto of a seven-feet-tall drill sergeant. Jessica was frazzled, though, and Tami could tell. She knew that Diamond was at least partly to blame. Though Tami considered Diamond a friend—she could be a lot of fun—you had to remember that she would always put her own needs ahead of everyone else's. She actually asked Brock if he and Tami would be willing to reschedule the twins' christening because it conflicted with the Daytime Emmys and Diamond's show was nominated that year.

After Jessica put the kibosh on the film crew for Diamond, there had been an eerie silence from her camp. Jessica e-mailed Brock explaining the situation. He finally wrote back the morning of the fundraiser with a cryptic: "All taken care of." She breathed a sigh of relief, but Jessica still hadn't been able to get Ashley or Diamond on the phone the day of the event, which made her nervous.

Peggy called to say that Brock's conference call was running behind schedule so he would be a little late. Adam had to head out of town at the last minute on a business trip, but he sent his regards and more important, he sent a check, along with his wife Terry, a fellow music executive who arrived with two friends—with three additional checks in tow. Joe was also supposed to attend and Tami was looking forward to seeing which bimbo he would have on his arm this time. Joe had a tendency to date women who were all slight variations of one another: petite, blonde, aspiring model/actress/dancer types whose names inevitably seemed to end with an "i," as in Brandi or Tiffini.

Joe eventually arrived accompanied by three fratty-looking guys who looked like younger versions of him. They were junior agents at his firm. Tami could tell they were trying to impress Joe, and Joe ate it up. Joe always struck Tami as one of those men who had been going through a mid-life crisis since puberty. Without an expensive sports car in his driveway and a thin—and young—woman on his arm, life, for him, was not worth living. Tami never quite got what Luke saw in him. She made her way over to say hello. Joe gave her a polite peck on the cheek and then stared at her breasts. While she knew she should be offended, it actually flattered her. She was glad someone still noticed her, since her husband rarely seemed to anymore.

The crowd—a nice assortment of the fundraising circuit's usual suspects: doctors, lawyers, investment bankers, and some media types—finally started to stream in a little after seven. T.J.—someone Tami was not at all familiar with because she didn't follow sports—was very dapper looking in a custom-cut Brioni suit. He brought a few of his teammates. (Two of them had the biggest necks she had ever seen on a human being in her entire life, she thought to herself.) Many of the men began to circle them. Usually in New York, particularly at events like this, there was an unspoken rule that people would go out of their way to act cool and unimpressed with the setting and the guests, but Tami watched as Lloyd Friedlander, Brock's onetime boss, who was now a partner at another firm, pulled out his camera phone to take a photo with T.J. And of course some of the women did the same, although Tami had a feeling that for a few of them it had nothing to do with their interest in football. Tami noticed that Jessica and T.J. seemed quite cozy. He enveloped her in a big bear hug—the kind that seemed to indicate that there was more to their relationship than business, and possibly more than friendship too.

And of course one of these women was Monique Montgomery, who by the look of things was already well acquainted with T.J. and his buddies. As if that was a surprise.

Monique looked exactly like her pictures—like Pamela Anderson with brown skin and a much bigger butt. For someone who ran a fashion boutique, she didn't seem to know very much about how to dress appropriately. There was Monique in a skintight red Herve Leger dress that was more appropriate for clubbing than mingling. She was joined by her friend Leila Dawson who, like Monique, was less known for her professional accomplishments than the men she was linked to. Though she described herself as a "writer," her sole writing credit was an as-yet-unpublished memoir about her brief marriage to Donovan "Donnie" Tyson, the NBA All-Star most famous for his acquittal on charges of rape in a high-profile trial years earlier. But her most notable accomplishment was securing a $20 million settlement out of divorce proceedings that lasted longer than their one-year marriage, and the manner in which she was rumored to have gone about negotiating her settlement. During a raucous birthday threesome that she surprised him with shortly before filing divorce papers, she allegedly got Donnie to sign a new and improved prenuptial agreement that was much more favorable to her in the settlement.

Tami's cell phone rang. It was Brock. "How's the turnout looking?"

"Great, sweetheart. It's a really, really good crowd. Some bankers. Some ball players. I think Luke's people will be very pleased."

"That's wonderful news! I'm really proud of you for pulling this off."

Tami beamed. It was one of the most romantic things he had said to her in months.

"I'm on my way now and will see you soon, dear," he said, then hung up.

"Love you!" Tami said. But the line was already dead.

When her phone rang a second later from a blocked number, Tami thought it might be Brock calling from his BlackBerry, which he often did when his cell phone died.

"Calling back to tell me you love me too?" she chirped.

"Not originally, but you know you are one of my favorite people on the planet."

"Luke!" Tami exclaimed.

"How are you?"

"I'm well."

"That's great to hear. I hope this event hasn't been driving you too nuts."

"Oh, it's been a breeze," Tami said.

"Well then, I should hire you to work for me. You and my little cousin are quite the tag team, I've heard. Maybe you should open your own consulting business. You're doing a better job than half the jokers out there we've paid in the past."

Tami savored the compliment. When she once expressed interest in starting her own cosmetics line to Brock he said, "Tami, you can barely balance a checkbook, which means you couldn't manage a McDonald's let alone start and run your own business." Luke was so nice to her that whenever they spoke she wondered why she could not have met him *before* meeting Brock.

"Anyway, I just want to say how grateful I am to you and Brock for all of your generosity and friendship. Couldn't be making this journey without you. You're a part of my family."

"It's our pleasure Luke, really."

"See you soon," he said then hung up.

Tami let Jessica know that both Brock and the guest of honor would be there shortly.

That was the good news. The bad news was that Lady Di was nowhere to be found and she was supposed to introduce Luke.

Garin and Luke arrived just before 7:30, with Shereka Dobson, a member of Luke's campaign staff out of Detroit. Luke still looked like he always did, handsome in a harmless kind of way. They were heading over toward Brooke when Brock walked in two minutes behind them and intercepted. "Luke already knows Brooke, has her vote and has her check. He needs to meet people he doesn't yet know."

Jessica spotted Cory, Diamond's husband, and made a beeline for him.

Skipping the usual hi's and hellos, she simply said, "Is Diamond with you?"

"I'm really sorry, Jessica, but unfortunately Diamond isn't feeling well so she asked me to come in person to send her regrets."

Jessica could feel her entire body—all four feet eleven-and-a-half inches of her—turning bright red.

"Are you fucking kidding me?" she said.

"Look, Jessica, first of all I don't think that type of language is necessary . . ."

"Oh really? Well then you probably shouldn't hang around to hear what I'm going to say next."

She then turned on her heel and walked over to Brock, who was chatting with a colleague while Luke laughed with guests nearby, and said, "Excuse me, Brock. I need to have a word with you, please."

The two stepped away, but Garin could tell that they were involved in a heated conversation. A few minutes later Brock stepped into a corner and whipped out his cell phone.

Luke spotted Jessica, smiled broadly and motioned for her to come over. She smiled back and shook her head no, waving her hands in a manner to indicate that she didn't want to interrupt his conversation.

Moments later Brock came back over to Jessica and said, "Okay. She says she's sick. She sounds sick. Let's figure out a plan B."

"You know damn well there is nothing wrong with her except her attitude. The only place that woman is sick is in the head."

"Watch it, Jessica. You're talking about a friend of mine."

"Oh sorry, I couldn't tell. See, my friends don't usually leave me hanging the way that your alleged friend just did to you."

"Look, let's not be overdramatic here. This isn't a crisis . . . I can introduce Luke."

Just then T.J. walked by, heading to the bar, and smiled and winked at her.

"Fine." Jessica said. "You'll welcome everyone and then apologize for Diamond not being able to make it. Recognize T.J. and his teammates, then introduce Luke."

"Believe it or not, I have given a speech before, Jessica."

Just then Luke walked up and yelled, "Cuz!" He leaned in and gave her a big hug. "Have you grown since the last time I saw you?"

"Ha ha," she said.

"I just wanted to thank you guys for putting this together," he continued. "The turnout is terrific. My staff better watch out. It looks like you're gunning for their jobs," he said with a chuckle.

"Anytime, Luke. Anytime," Brock said.

Jessica shot Brock a dirty look before saying, "We actually have some unfortunate news."

Brock jumped in. "Diamond's a bit under the weather so she can't make it."

"Oh, that's too bad," Luke said.

"But don't worry," Brock said. "T.J. Greeley is here."

"Yep, he is," Jessica said, then pointedly added, "he owed me a favor."

"What would I do without you, Jess?"

Jessica smiled and could feel herself starting to relax.

"Come on. Let me introduce you to T.J.," she said.

"And you're alright too," Luke said to Brock, slapping him on the back. "No, seriously. You guys are amazing."

As Jessica led Luke through the crowd, she spotted T.J. across the room. She saw that he was chatting with a woman in a tight red dress. Once she and Luke were closer, Jessica realized that woman was Monique Montgomery, whom she saw pass a card to T.J. Jessica knew she shouldn't care, but she did.

She tried to muster up the coolest voice possible and said, "I hope I'm not interrupting."

"Not at all, Jess," T.J. said in his typically charming voice.

"Hi. I'm Monique," the woman said, extending a hand while flashing an annoyingly perfect smile.

"Good to meet you. Jessica." Jessica spit out her own name, barely acknowledging Monique. "I'm sorry, Mary, will you excuse us, please?"

"It's Monique."

"Oh, right. Sorry. Will you excuse us?"

"Sure," Monique replied. "T.J., great catching up. I'll see you soon." She then leaned in—or, as Jessica noticed, her breasts leaned in—and gave T.J. a kiss on the cheek.

She then turned to Luke and said, "We haven't met. I'm Monique Montgomery."

"Hi. I'm Luke Cooper."

"Oh, Governor! I'm sorry I didn't recognize you. It's a real pleasure."

What an idiot, Jessica thought.

"Pleasure's all mine," Luke said.

"Governor, would you mind terribly if I get a photo?"

"Not at all," Luke said.

"Jenny, would you mind taking a photo of the three of us? Come on, T.J., you have to be in it too."

Monique extended her camera to Jessica.

Jessica made a point to smile and then cheerfully said, "It's Jessica. And I'm sorry but I don't know that I'm actually tall enough to get all of you in a photo."

T.J. and Luke both began to laugh.

"But maybe later someone else can. I just have to borrow these two for a minute. Hope you don't mind," Jessica added.

"Of course not," Monique said, although her eyes conveyed that she did.

"Well, I will expect a rain check from you two gentlemen later." Monique winked at both of them before sauntering off.

"Of course," T.J. and Luke practically sang in unison.

What was it about beautiful women that rendered even the most accomplished men utterly stupid? Jessica wanted to vomit. Instead she introduced T.J. and Luke to one another and then briefed both of them on the evening's program, including the update that Diamond would not be attending. Brock would begin introductions shortly and would mention T.J. and his teammates for a moment of recognition, then introduce Luke to begin his remarks.

Brock came over to discuss a few talking points before he tapped his wine glass with a fork to call everyone to attention. Jessica and her assistant then began floating through the crowd in an effort to shush everyone.

Brock began by thanking everyone for coming out to show support. He apologized for Lady Di's absence but noted that her husband Cory was there in her stead since she was ill. "Cory—would you raise your hand?"

Everyone looked around the room but no one's hand was raised. After about a minute of perusing the crowd, Brock continued with "Okay. Looks like Cory must have headed home to take care of his wife. In any case, we are so grateful for both of their support. Let's give them a round of applause in absentia."

To Jessica's amusement there was only a smattering of applause.

"Speaking of wives, I'd like to thank mine. Many of you probably corresponded with my lovely wife Tami over the last several days regarding this event. Didn't she do a wonderful job?"

As the audience began to applaud, Tami raised her hand and waved. Just then she started feeling woozy again. She still hadn't eaten anything.

At the fundraiser all she allowed herself was a glass of seltzer water. She began to feel lightheaded and started seeing double. Then amid the applause she collapsed.

The next minute was chaos: Brooke shouted for someone to call 911, then knelt down and grabbed Tami's hand. Luke asked if any doctors present would please step forward to help. Brooke asked Tami if she could hear her. Tami opened her eyes. She was alert but said that her head hurt. Brock made his way to her and asked what happened. Tyler Sinett, a pediatrician in the crowd, came rushing over and asked Tami to describe her symptoms before her collapse. He asked her what she had had to eat and drink throughout the day. As they helped lift Tami into a chair she told Dr. Sinett that she had been "too busy with the event to eat today."

Dr. Sinett told her that she was probably just dehydrated, but that it would be a good idea to head to the hospital for some tests just to be safe. "There's a reason that we tell our little patients that an apple a day keeps the doctor away. The same rule applies to big patients as well. You should never be too busy to eat, young lady," he said with a fatherly smile.

As he knelt beside her, playing the role of dutiful husband, Brock said within earshot of Brooke, Tami, and Dr. Sinett, "So basically you're saying that she's not really sick, just hungry?" Brock asked, with irritation dripping in his voice, "What else is new?"

"Shut up, Brock," Brooke said.

"It's okay, Brooke," Tami said. "I'm so sorry for scaring everyone. Please don't let me ruin this wonderful event."

"Too late," Brock mumbled under his breath.

Luke made his way through the cluster, knelt by Tami's side and asked, "Are you okay?"

"I'm fine. Just embarrassed. I'm so sorry for disrupting your event."

"Don't be ridiculous. First of all there wouldn't have been an event if it weren't for you," Luke said. "I just want to make sure you're alright."

"Really, I'm fine."

Just then Jessica announced that the ambulance had arrived.

"I should come with you," Brock said, helping Tami out of her chair.

"Yes, you should," Brooke snapped at him.

"No," Tami said. "Luke needs you here, Brock."

"Tami—really, I don't need him as much as you do right now. Don't be silly," Luke said.

"Well we can't both leave. It's *our* house. Really, I wouldn't forgive myself if I tore him away. Brooke—would you mind coming with me?"

"Of course not, sweetheart."

Brooke accompanied Tami to the ambulance.

Brock then turned to the crowd and said, "Okay. First of all I want to let everyone know that my beautiful wife Tami is okay."

At that everyone applauded.

"And she has me under strict instructions to go on with the event, so if it's okay with you all, let's keep things moving along. It might be tough to top the excitement we've had so far this evening but my good friend Luke, also known as the governor, is going to try."

At that Luke and Brock hugged.

Luke then stepped before the audience and began his remarks. "First off, I want to start by thanking my wonderful family for their help and support putting together this event. My little cousin Jessica really stepped up to the plate to help me out and helped to get so many of you here."

At that Jessica began to smile while her assistant pointed her out to the audience, who applauded.

"She told me she would only do it if I promised to stop telling embarrassing stories about her from childhood."

At that the crowd broke into laughter. "I said I wanted to thank my family and I have to say that Brock and Tami really are like family to me. So I know everyone's having a good time mixing and mingling, and I certainly don't want to distract from the fun, so I promise to keep my remarks fairly brief. In politician-speak that means I'll try not to go over an hour. . . ."

"I'm kidding."

A chorus of laughter again.

"But I would like to share some thoughts with you on how I see the future of our great country. . . ."

★

The next morning Jessica awoke to the screeching of her cell. Bleary-eyed, she rolled over and looked at the time. It was only 6 a.m. She had a text from her assistant. It read, in all caps, "URGENT. READ PAGE SIX."

Jessica reached for her glasses, grabbed her laptop, and went to NYpost.com.

★

PUTTING THE 'FUN' IN FUNDRAISER

Lady Di may not have made it to her scheduled appearance last night at a fundraiser for rumored presidential candidate Luke Cooper, the governor of Michigan, but her husband Cory certainly did. According to sources, Cory, the recent law school graduate young enough to be the legal eagle's son came, saw and conquered. Members of the catering staff report that after downing a few cocktails Cory became extremely friendly, particularly with one member of their team—a strapping blonde who is an aspiring dancer. But perhaps the former daytime diva shouldn't be too alarmed, as the dancer whom Cory pirouetted off into the night with was of the male persuasion.

Other friendly matches were made as well. Maneater Monique Montgomery was on the prowl. After flirting up a storm with the handsome governor she then exchanged digits with Giants star T.J. Greeley. The excitement appeared to be too much for some. One guest fainted and had to be carried out by ambulance. One source joked, "If this is how the governor and his posse rolls, I can't wait to see how they party at the White House."

Jessica stared at the computer screen. "Holy shit."

CHAPTER 4

After the Page Six story ran, Lady Di went ballistic. She accused Jessica of planting the story to get back at her for missing the event, and then did what any high-profile lawyer would: she threatened to sue everybody.

Page Six (for defamation), and Jessica and her company. Brock nipped that in the bud out of his loyalty to Luke, but Brock believed Jessica had *something* to do with the story and he was not amused. Luke was cooler than anyone about the situation. "At least they called me handsome," he said about the publicity. But the rest of his core team didn't find it funny at all. Including his wife.

Michigan wasn't exactly teeming with superstars. Besides players for the Pistons, local news anchors were pretty much the only celebrities the state had—along with high-ranking politicians. In Luke's first year as governor, Laura became a popular fixture on the local society pages, owing to her penchant for exotic fashions and her beauty, which was most defined by cheekbones that one gossip columnist declared "could cut glass," and pin-straight jet black hair. Laura didn't strive to be a magnet for the media, but like it or not, now she was one.

And the more time she spent in the public eye, the more she knew she didn't like it. Her reticence was due in large part to the media fallout from one particular appearance she made. The steroids doctors used to treat hives—a condition that had plagued her since childhood—left her with an unfortunate, albeit temporary, side effect. Her face was swollen just in time for a ribbon-cutting ceremony for a new pediatric AIDS wing at a local community hospital. The rumor mill grinded away with stories that she was suffering from a secret illness or, worse, had a substance-abuse problem. One local gossip columnist ran a headline that read "Lovely Laura Looking Lumpy." After days of issuing a simple "no comment," the campaign issued a statement explaining that "the First Lady had an allergic reaction but is doing just fine."

The rumors persisted, though. No matter how bad she may have thought the media in Michigan were, she knew that the scrutiny of the national press would be much, much worse. So when she read the Page Six item, she winced but she was not shocked.

Though Laura didn't need another reason to mull over the Page Six story, she got one. She answered the phone to hear:

"Who on earth is running Luke's campaign? The three stooges?"

"I didn't realize Page Six was required reading where you are, Veronica."

"Oh, please. Page Six is required reading for anyone who matters, period."

"Well I don't read it."

"Why am I not surprised to hear that, dear?"

A typical Veronica comment, Laura thought.

"Laura, you know I love Luke to death but running a JV campaign is certainly not the way to become a varsity starting quarterback." Her Southern drawl was melodic, like a nice, soothing song, until you actually listened to the words.

"Veronica, you know that I know absolutely nothing about sports so you're going to have to speak English."

"Well, in plain English, if Luke doesn't shake up his operation and get some professionals in there instead of these hacks he's been relying on, he will become best known for running one of the shortest presidential campaigns in history instead of for actually being elected president."

Laura knew that one of the reasons Veronica dismissed Luke's team as "hacks" was because she detested the man who ran it, Luke's senior political advisor, Johnny Highlands. In Veronica's eyes he didn't measure up. He was raised in public housing, earned a degree from the school of hard knocks, and had the gall to be proud of it. The pièce de résistance came when, the day before Veronica was scheduled to host a sold-out fundraiser for Luke, she read an e-mail where Johnny derisively labeled her "the princess."

"Veronica, why are you telling me this? You know I have nothing to do with Luke's campaign or personnel decisions."

"Well maybe you should. You certainly couldn't do any worse than these jokers," she snapped.

Laura proceeded to change the subject. "So are you heading to Fashion Week?"

Though related, Laura and her cousin Veronica Devereaux were polar opposites. Both were the daughters of successful lawyers who had married teachers who were sisters from an old, prosperous family. As such, both were bona fide members of the black elite. While Laura had always been ambivalent about her status, Veronica had reveled in hers, participating in debutante balls and becoming a prominent black socialite in her native Louisiana and her adopted home of San Francisco, where she had settled with a high-profile surgeon from a wealthy California family. Veronica could be a handful—Brooke's nickname for her was "the Diva"—but she was loyal and smart and had raised a ton of money for Luke's gubernatorial campaign. As such, her input had to be taken seriously, but her attitude and flamboyance had to be taken with a grain of salt.

While Laura was innately stylish and felt just as comfortable in a great pair of Levi's as a high-end designer label, Veronica was allergic to any label that didn't cost as much as a small car. Laura's mother once told her that "there are three types of people in this world. Those who brag about how much they spend, those who brag about how little they spend, and those who don't brag at all."

Veronica was the first.

"Oh darling, I don't know. Si's parents might be using the plane during Fashion Week, and you know I simply can't fly commercial."

Laura let her ramble on for the next ten minutes, interjecting an occasional "uh-huh" every thirty seconds or so before telling her that she had to get to the boys' elementary school for an event.

"Oh Laura, I don't know how you can do it. Cooking, cleaning, and wiping noses all day. I would go insane, but you are so good at all that. Always have been."

When they were still in their teens Laura's mother told her that Veronica used material things to compensate for all of the nonmaterial things missing in her life, just like her mother had before her. In Veronica's case she had all of the money she could want, but she was miserable in her marriage. Her husband already had grown children from his first marriage when he married Veronica, and had made it clear he didn't want any more. So while she got to live out her dream of being a rich, high-society queen bee, she was denied motherhood. Laura knew this, so she cut Veronica slack.

So far Laura had managed to stay out of the spat between Veronica and Johnny.

Johnny Highlands was Luke's longtime political advisor, but he was much more than that. Some referred to him as Luke's "consigliere," a nod to one of Luke's all-time favorite films, *The Godfather*. Only Luke wasn't Don Corleone. He was Michael—*before* Michael decided to join the family business.

Johnny had been the first one to encourage Luke to run for office and had in many ways become a second father to him—the surrogate black dad he never had. He was the first to inspire Luke's political gifts. Like Luke, Johnny was the youngest of four boys. But unlike Luke, Johnny was the only one in his family not to end up in prison. A local policeman became his de facto mentor, playing basketball with him on a regular basis. For that reason Johnny started a local basketball league to help other kids in need of positive role models, and he later founded a nonprofit, called Second Chance, to help men like his brothers rebuild their lives after leaving prison. Johnny was known for being a tough, relentless player and coach, but his on-court personality was tame compared to his political game. His nickname was "Sharp," an ode to the way he played on and off of the basketball court: with sharp elbows. After his basketball program was denied government funding thanks to a local councilman, he quickly found an opponent to run against the official. Though Johnny had known nothing about politics, he displayed a knack for political strategy, outmaneuvering the incumbent and guiding his candidate to victory. Two years later he steered that same candidate to Congress. In the nearly two decades since, Johnny "Sharp" Highlands had become one of the most important political players in Detroit, but even as his political star rose, Johnny still found time to make the basketball and prison programs priorities.

Though it was family tradition that the Cooper boys spent summers helping out at the Cooper families' multimillion dollar real estate business, Luke decided to spend his summers at Second Chance, helping men who never had the opportunities that he did. It was while working there that his political star first began to rise. After some of the men in the Second Chance program, all nonviolent drug offenders who had recently obtained their GEDs, were told that the newly opened Value-Mart in town was no longer hiring, Luke submitted an application and was asked to come in for an interview that afternoon. He was offered a job on the spot. Johnny was vacationing in Africa so Luke made two calls, one to the *Michigan Tribune*, the state's leading paper, and the other to the office of Congressman Bayard Searcy—the congressman Johnny first helped elect all those years ago.

The front-page article in the *Michigan Tribune*, "Investigation Shows Bias in Value-Mart Hiring," was accompanied by an op-ed written by Luke. In it he introduced readers to two men: one a child of privilege who was raised by two loving and powerful parents, and who attended the best schools and had every opportunity handed to him, and another who was born to a drug-addicted single mother and then raised by a series of flawed government programs and various foster parents before turning to drugs himself. "But eventually," Luke wrote, "this young man did something amazing: he turned his life around." And then Luke posed this question: "So both of these men started out with very different odds, one with a greater advantage than the other, and after various twists and turns they have ended up at the same place, applying for the same job. Which man do you think deserves the advantage now? The one who has had them handed to him all of his life or the one who has had to earn them?" He then wrote, "Speaking as the guy who has had every single advantage life could possibly offer handed to me on a silver platter, I think I know the answer, and it's not me."

Within days of the *Tribune* piece, Congressman Searcy had organized a group of local officials to denounce Value-Mart's hiring practices. The store immediately issued an apology and created a task force to improve community relations. Its owners also agreed to create a special "Value Transitions" program for qualified candidates who had prison records. When Johnny returned from vacation, he was stunned that

Luke had triggered all of this. He knew he had a winner on his hands. It took Johnny a few years to convince Luke to throw his hat in the political ring, but eventually he did. Luke proved to be a natural, and Johnny was by his side every step of the way.

Laura liked Johnny—he was hard not to like—but he interacted with Luke like a stage parent; the-show-must-go-on-so-the-cash-can-keep-coming-in kind of parent. She had been particularly peeved when he arrived at the hospital the day she gave birth to their second son and impressed upon Luke how important it was for him to make his appearance at the Super Bowl being held in Detroit that year. "It is simply too important to miss," he said.

As if their son's very first day on earth wasn't.

Over the years she clashed with Johnny a few times, like when he tried to pressure Luke to miss a wedding because it conflicted with one day of the Democratic National Convention that year. Johnny had, more seriously, been the subject of some articles claiming that he had used his relationship with the governor as leverage for business opportunities. A number of businessmen claimed on the record that he used lines like "The Gov and I are like family. After all, he wouldn't be governor without me, so you have nothing to worry about."

Shortly before Luke left for New York, Laura encouraged him to clear the air with Johnny and have a serious heart-to-heart. It ended with the men having only their second argument. The first was when Luke accepted the offer to become lieutenant governor—a move that Johnny opposed. He argued that Luke's soon-to-be running mate could not be trusted and warned that the lieutenant governor's slot was where those with "no real political talent went to idle." Laura told Luke that she believed he put his own interests ahead of Luke's. Laura believed that the real reason Johnny didn't want Luke to take the job was because his potential running mate had declined to hire Johnny years earlier. Ultimately Luke made what turned out to be the best decision of his career. While Luke didn't reveal to Laura exactly what words were exchanged during their second argument, the incident ended with Johnny—who was originally scheduled to join Luke in New York—canceling the morning of their scheduled departure. He announced that Lorraine Busby, one of Johnny's lieutenants, would also be unavailable.

Though Luke tried to laugh off the fundraiser fallout, Laura, along with Dan Gregory, his chief of staff, were not laughing. Veronica's assessment of Luke's campaign was right. You don't get a second chance to make a first impression. And the impression now in the press was that Luke was not ready for prime time.

"What do you want me to do, Laura?" Luke asked her. "The man's like family. You know that."

"I know. And he can stay in the family, but I don't think it's a good idea for him to stay in your campaign. Didn't you tell me that your dad once fired your brother?"

"When he was nineteen."

"But he did it. He wasn't going to risk everything your family's worked so hard to build, for one person. And you shouldn't be risking everything that you've asked all of us to sacrifice to help you build, for one person."

"What's that supposed to mean?"

"Can Johnny run a presidential campaign? Let me rephrase that. Can he run a winning presidential campaign?"

She waited a minute.

"Okay," she continued, "I think your silence answers that, so let me ask you another question. Can Johnny be anyone's number two? Can he take orders from anyone?"

Luke continued to sit in silence.

"So let me get this straight. You expect us, your family, to sacrifice our lives, our privacy, our time with you, so that you can go on some kamikaze mission to spend a year having someone run a losing presidential campaign for you? Is that where we're at, Luke? Because if that's where we're at then you are the most selfish person alive and I will not have any part in this."

"What does that mean?"

"I didn't stutter, did I? If we're going to do this, then we're doing it all the way. Not half-assed. I will be the best presidential campaign spouse I can possibly be, but you have to be the best candidate you can possibly be. That means the best team. If not, then why bother? Huh?"

They stood in silence for a moment before she threw down the gauntlet.

"It's your call. You let me know when you make your decision."

She then left the room.

Luke sat by himself in the study for the next hour.

The next day Luke asked Johnny to join him and Laura at their home for dinner.

After about an hour of chit-chat about their families and of "Uncle Johnny" doing his famous magic tricks for the boys, Laura said James and Milo's least favorite words: "Bedtime. Uncle Johnny and Daddy have to talk big-guy stuff."

Each of the boys grabbed hold of one of Uncle Johnny's long, gangly legs on his six-feet five-inch frame.

"You boys listen to your mother. I'll show you my other trick some other time. You know I'll be back," Johnny said.

He then dramatically swung first his left leg, then his right, causing the boys—who had been hanging off of him like he was a tree—to fall off and land on the floor in a pool of giggles.

"Good night, boys."

"Good night, Uncle Johnny!" They turned to run up the stairs.

"Hey! What about me?"

The boys turned around, ran over to their dad, and enveloped him in hugs.

"Love you guys."

"Love you, Daddy," they said in unison.

Then they followed their mom upstairs.

"They're such good boys," Johnny said.

"Yeah. I'm a lucky man," Luke said.

"They are too. To get a dad like you. I think almost every prison in America would be empty if every person spent their first few years with just one parent who looks at them the way you look at your boys."

"Thanks, Johnny. How are things at Second Chance?"

"You asking me as the governor or as my friend?"

Luke just smiled.

"Good. Contributions are down, as to be expected with the economy."

"I'll check in with my folks. You know they're always happy to help."

"Thanks. I appreciate it."

"So I wanted to talk to you, Johnny. About the presidential race."

"Great. I have a few ideas I wanted to run by you. I think we should focus just on southern states early on. Build up our numbers so . . ."

"Johnny. I've thought a lot about this and I think I can't afford to have you distracted."

"Distracted?"

"I need you minding the shop for me here in Michigan. I don't want to become one of those candidates who gets criticized for sleeping on their day job while trying to run for office. You're too valuable."

"Luke. How long have we known each other?"

"Forever, seems like."

"So why don't you talk to me like that? I think I've earned that. You're pulling me off of the presidential campaign?"

"Don't look at it that way."

"How the hell am I supposed to look at it? So I was good enough to get you to the governor's mansion but not good enough to get you to the White House, is that it?"

"You know that's not true, Johnny."

"No, actually, I don't. Who are you replacing me with, some Washington, D.C. Ivy Leaguer? Well, don't come running back to me when you fail!"

"Johnny . . ." Luke looked like a puppy that had been kicked.

"How long have you been planning this? Ever since your little heroics made you famous?" Johnny began packing up his papers and belongings. "I didn't think it would happen with you. Forgetting where you come from and who your real friends are. Bet you've been planning this since you became governor. Bet you just couldn't wait."

"That's not true and you know it," said Laura from the stairwell.

"I should have known. Should have known that you were in on this. You never liked me. You and your snobby fucking family."

"Johnny!" Luke snapped.

"It's true. You started to change when you married her. It's funny. I always admired the fact that a black guy raised by rich, white parents never forgot that he was black, and then you marry into a black family with all of their Jack and Jill bullshit and forget who you are."

At that Luke stood up. "It is a testament to the fact that I love you and our twenty-five years of history together that I'm going to say this. Get the hell out of my house."

"That's supposed to show me how much you love me, huh?"

"Yes, it is. Because if I didn't, I would have physically thrown you out already."

"You need me," he said, his lip quivering.

"I need my wife, Johnny."

With that Luke got Johnny's coat and held the door open for his father figure to leave.

CHAPTER 5

Luke knew that he wanted to work with Nate Crosby within minutes of meeting him.

Nate arrived at their meeting wearing shorts—despite the fact that it was 40 degrees outside. And a sweatshirt that looked like it was three sizes too big.

"Apologies for the Halloween costume," he said with a bright smile. "Airline lost my luggage."

Thirty-six hours before, Nate had arrived from Africa, where he had been volunteering at a clinic for pediatric AIDS patients. Luke's team faced a big challenge just to get in touch with him, let alone to get him to agree to a meeting. Strangely, Luke soon felt like he was there to be interviewed, not the other way around.

Nate Crosby was a bit of an enigma in Washington. Unlike just about everyone else who lived there, he didn't seem to get off on the two p's: power and press coverage. Despite his impressive resume he was notoriously press shy, bordering on reclusive. He was famous for turning down invitations to fancy affairs like White House state dinners for decidedly less fancy ones like camping with friends. He once showed up at the White House Correspondents' Association Dinner wearing jeans—with a tuxedo jacket and bow tie. The president actually made an impromptu joke about Nate's attire during his remarks: "Nice to see that Nate Crosby felt compelled to put on his Sunday best for all of us tonight." By the time the president finished speaking Nate was gone, having quietly slipped out a side entrance—not because he was too thin-skinned to appreciate the president's ribbing, but because George Clinton and Parliament

Funkadelic were playing a rare reunion concert in the nation's capital that evening and he had no intention of missing it. As far as he was concerned he could eat rubber chicken and listen to a bunch of political types pretend to be funny anytime, but seeing the original Parliament live was a once-in-a-lifetime experience.

In addition to his aversion to publicity, Crosby was known for two things: piercing blue eyes and a small, well-kept afro, both the product of his diverse heritage, which included a black mother and white father. He was now spending some time with his dad, an African studies professor at a local college in Boston. Between his afro and current outfit, Nate looked like one of thousands of Boston college students.

Until he opened his mouth.

"So, you don't have a lot of time, do you?"

"No. I've cleared most of the afternoon so we can talk," Luke replied.

"That's not what I mean, Gov."

"Call me Luke."

"Great. Call me Nate," Nate replied with a wry smile. "What I mean is you're already behind the curve in terms of the calendar. Anyone who's serious about running started staffing up months ago, which gives them a gigantic head start over you in every state that matters. Months are an eternity in an election, as I'm sure you know. So it's not going to be enough for you to hit the ground running. You're going to have to fly."

The waitress came over to see what they needed, giving them both a breather. Once she left, Luke asked:

"You've already made a decision, haven't you?"

"What makes you say that?" Nate replied, while glancing at the menu.

"Am I wrong?"

"Not entirely."

"What made you decide, without really knowing me?"

Nate put down the menu and looked Luke in the eye. "There are two kinds of people who run for office. People whose egos make them do it, and people whose egos let them do it. People whose egos make them do it are so narcissistic, self-obsessed, and power hungry that they actually consider life meaningless without the power that goes with elected office. Which makes them dangerous . . . to themselves and to others. People whose egos let them do it are people who could and would just as soon do something else and could actually be happy, but they are cursed with being the kind of person that other people really think can make a difference. So even though politics may not be the thing that drives them when they wake up every morning, they've got a thick enough skin and healthy enough ego that even if someone runs ads calling them an asshole every day for three hundred and sixty-five days straight, they tough it out, for all of the people they don't want to let down."

"I've worked for the former. I think you're the latter."

The waitress came back.

Nate looked up at her. "I'll have the veggie omelet with fries, please, and green tea, if you have it. You having anything, Luke?"

"No. Already ate." As the waitress walked away he asked, "So what's next?"

"What's next is we have a lot of work to do. Your field operation is practically nonexistent and your fundraising operation is a shit show. I have a friend. Her name is Mimi Van der Wohl. I'll put you in touch. Time is of the essence so you need to connect with her by COB today to get the ball rolling. She's expensive but she's a friend of mine so we'll work something out, and frankly at this point you can't afford not to hire her."

Luke jotted down Mimi's name then said, "Anything else?"

"Your biggest liabilities are pretty obvious. You're black and you're Jewish, and I haven't seen a lot of black Jews in the White House. Your biggest assets? You're black and you're Jewish. That gives you two prime Democratic constituencies who are there for the taking if you can convince them. So far you haven't. You have a sort of identity crisis thing going on. Like you don't really know who you are so you can't tell voters who you are."

"Nate. With all due respect, I know who I am. I've had my entire life to get comfortable with my identity even when people around me weren't."

"And that's great. But people you meet in college or at the gym are different from voters. Most of them will never meet you—except for through a few TV commercials, some interviews, and maybe ten minutes of a debate, if that. And with so little to go on most voters are inclined to vote for who they know and in the absence of that what they know. A voter is standing in the voting booth. They don't know anything about two of the candidates on the ballot except that one's named

Murphy and one's named Smith. The voter's dad is Irish Catholic. Who does the voter go with? Honestly, Luke? You and I know they go with Murphy. Why? Because they feel some kinship with him, that's why. Even though they've never met him. Will probably never meet him. He's connected to them in some way, at least enough to make the voter feel comfortable. Your problem is black Jews are not a big enough constituency to get you into the White House."

"Well, there are a few thousand of us scattered around the world, but I take your point." Luke smiled.

"Jews don't look at you and see a Jew and blacks don't look at you and your family portrait and see one of their own. You haven't won them over yet—either group—but you can."

"You sound pretty confident about that."

"I am. The easy way to look at you and your prospects would be to say this is who isn't supporting you. I just happen to look at things a little differently than most. I look at you and think, these are all the people who aren't supporting him . . . *yet*, but will when given the right reasons to."

"Such as?"

"Well for instance, you're a black kid raised by white Jews who went to a historically black college. A guy who doesn't feel a connection to the black community doesn't do that. He also doesn't marry a black wife. But most blacks don't know that about you. They just know your parents are white and you saved a skinhead. Not exactly compelling reasons for them to vote for you. And then a lot of Jews don't know that you passed up on really big job opportunities in D.C. and New York just to stay close to your fam because you really are a loving Jewish son. And as un-PC as this may be to say, the fact of the matter is that you are a loving Jewish son who happens to have a last name that is conveniently ethnically ambiguous—meaning there are some voters who may hear Cooper and think 'Jewish candidate' and others who won't. The numbers, specifically your name recognition and favorability ratings compared to unfavorables, show that people are open to hearing your story, but you've got to tell it to them. And when you do, a lot of people are going to vote for you. That's why you're the candidate the others are most afraid of."

Luke tilted his head slightly, in an expression that conveyed disbelief.

"The media's framing this as a race between frontrunner Abigail Beaman and the guy most likely to shore up the ABB—Anybody but

Beaman—vote," Nate continued. "They expected that to be some good-old Southern boy, which meant basically two white guys from Southern or Midwestern states would come along and have a Civil War over the Southern vote—which always has a sizable African American population. No one counted on a black candidate—a serious one, not some activist type, but a real, solid candidate—popping up this election and throwing things off. That would be you. You're the wild card and at the moment that's the most valuable card in the deck."

The waitress brought over Nate's plate. He began sprinkling pepper on his omelet and asked, "What else do you want to know?"

"When can you start?" Luke asked.

Nate chewed his first bite, wiped his mouth with a napkin and said, "Well, I'm billing you for this breakfast so consider this Day One."

★

DemocraticInsider.com

STAFF CHANGES SHOW COOPER CAMPAIGN MEANS BUSINESS

Until now, Michigan Governor Luke Cooper's presidential run has been viewed like many first-time presidential runs before his: as an audition for a more serious run down the road. But in recent weeks Cooper's campaign has been hiring staff that signals he's ready to take center stage.

After years of being guided by longtime political advisor Johnny Highlands, a legendary local political figure in Michigan, Cooper has hired DC legend-in-the-making Nate Crosby to run his presidential campaign. Crosby is best known as the longtime right-hand man of Sen. Sid Burstein, and is credited with helping Burstein lead the Democratic Senatorial Campaign Committee to record gains last election cycle. Crosby was viewed as a surprising yet inspired choice by many of the political insiders we spoke to. He's considered that rare political operative who possesses the total package: grassroots tactical experience with a wealth of internet and technological savvy.

★

Twenty-four hours after his meeting with Nate, Luke did something he hated and swore he'd never do: he asked someone he detested for money.

Jack Saunderson was a retired real estate magnate who, Luke recalled, made an off-color joke about Hispanics at a cocktail party the two men had both attended in New York years earlier. The party was cohosted by a friend of Luke's, so in an effort to avoid making a scene, Luke didn't say anything, something he later regretted. Instead he simply walked away, hoping that showing his displeasure with his feet counted for something. He also avoided Jack Saunderson, not even offering so much as a hello when the two found themselves in the same room on two other occasions. So he was stunned to discover that Saunderson not only agreed to give money to his campaign, but actually gave the maximum amount. Apparently he was an "old friend" of Luke's new fundraising guru.

After saying the magic words, "Thanks so much for your support. Yes, looking forward to connecting sometime soon," after Saunderson said "the check's in the mail," Luke felt instinctually dirty, but Mimi Van der Wohl, his new director of fundraising, told him, "You'll learn to take a bath and get over it if you're serious about becoming president."

That remark was quintessential Mimi.

Mimi Van der Wohl, an Amazonian, forty-something blonde (who never revealed her exact age but who, thanks to her Beverly Hills upkeep, could easily pass for thirty-something) was the fourth and final wife of Carl Van der Wohl, a Hollywood mogul who was forty years her senior at the time of their marriage. When he died, a messy battle ensued over his estate during which Mimi was infamously quoted by a gossip columnist as saying, "I just find it kind of funny how the children of wealthy men always denounce younger wives as golddiggers, when the only reason they hate stepmommy dearest is because they're afraid she might vault to the front of the inheritance line ahead of them. I mean, they didn't earn the money either." It wasn't exactly the kind of quote that wins friends, no matter how true, so it wasn't a surprise among Hollywood's old guard that the only Van der Wohl family friends who spoke up on Mimi's behalf in the press were Jack Nicholson and Hugh Hefner, both of whom she'd been "friendly" with prior to marrying Carl. It also wasn't a surprise that Mimi ultimately lost the battle for a bigger share of the Van der Wohl pie.

Between his three previous wives and his six children (three of whom were older than Mimi), she was left with less than one percent of his fortune—a mere two million dollars, more than enough for the average American but not nearly enough for the lifestyle Mimi had grown accustomed to during their relationship. As a result, she was forced to find some form of gainful employment, so she turned to doing what she knew best: partying.

She had spent most of her marriage aggressively honing her craft as a social climber, a craft that was paying off in spades now. With friends in high places from Hollywood to Aspen, and even glamorous expats, she had cultivated a global rolodex that even a sitting president would envy—which made her a sought-after fundraiser and party planner for nonprofits as well as political candidates. Unlike most in the political consulting world, Mimi was not party loyal. She was people loyal. If she liked someone, she'd raise money for them. If she didn't, she wouldn't. She liked Nate Crosby. A lot. And when Nate called and asked for a favor—which he rarely did—Mimi said yes.

Mimi Van der Wohl's smile had been likened, by one gossip columnist, to the kind seen in toothpaste commercials. Her pearly whites belied a steely nature that made her a force. The same calculating aggression she used to land her wealthy husband (and a string of wealthy boyfriends before him), she now used to land donors for her various causes.

Nate called just before returning from Africa and asked Mimi if she could help Luke. Within days she was on the phone training Luke in the art of the subtly aggressive ask. For Luke, an hour with Mimi was like a cross between fundraising and seduction boot camp. She had a way of asking for money that made it sound like she was asking someone out on a date . . . a date they would actually want to go on. It was a remarkable skill. Luke listened intently, trying to follow Mimi's lead.

Though Luke's parents were wealthy and supported all of their children's hopes, dreams, and goals, they had made it clear that they would not act as a lifetime ATM for any of their children's endeavors, hobbies, or businesses. The Cooper boys could request an occasional loan, for a restaurant, to finance a film, or a run for political office, with a contract signed by all parties involved. But they could not expect a blank check from the bank of Mom and Dad.

When Luke saw the lengthy list of potential donors she expected him to call, he said, "You know, I actually have a day job, right Mimi?"

"Yes. And if you plan to have another one next year you need to call these guys, pronto."

"Isn't that what we hired you for?"

"Luke, I'm not going to ask you if you've ever used an escort service."

"Gee. Thanks, I really appreciate that!" he replied incredulously.

"But I'm sure you're familiar with how one works. I mean, you've seen them in movies and on TV, and while I'm sure you're too square to do so yourself, I'm sure a friend or two has probably used one and told you all about it."

Luke immediately thought of Joe, who'd rendezvoused with his first prostitute while they were in high school, and, Luke surmised, probably still rendezvoused with them occasionally now, although Joe would never admit it.

"Here's what I mean," Mimi continued. "A guy who calls an escort service is not interested in the guy who answers the phone and handles all the details, sets things up. In his eyes that's just an administrator who's only there for the sole purpose of facilitating helping him get laid."

"You mean the pimp?"

"Okay. If that's the term you prefer. But the point's the same. He's a lot of things: the administrator, the muscle, the enforcer, the protector, the aggressor, the accountant. But the star attraction, the one who really matters in the whole operation, is the woman with big tits and a smile. There is no business without her. In this case, that would be you."

"Mimi, did you just call me a ho?"

"No. It's only whoring if you sell yourself short." Her tone indicated that she thought she had just said the most obvious thing in the world, like "the sky is blue." She then drove her point home: "I can make the calls, Luke. But you're the one who has to close the deal."

Upon Googling her, Luke had discovered that Mimi had been working as a Las Vegas showgirl when Carl Van der Wohl "discovered her" and made her his wife. Though her makeover from showgirl to Beverly Hills trophy wife had been completed years before, she still occasionally spoke like someone who had been around the block.

Mimi thought of herself as similar to a personal trainer, only with a much better wardrobe. Some clients were completely out of shape and needed someone who would whip them into shape with a combination of a restrictive diet and take-no-prisoners workout routine. Others simply needed someone to show them how to use the gym equipment properly. Luke needed discipline. She could give it to him. She would get him to eat his greens, so to speak, and keep his ambitions strong.

She continued. "So we're doing two events in Los Angeles for next month. Nate says we can make it happen with your schedule. Also, I've been in touch with Veronica and she's going to do an event for us too."

"Veronica?"

"Yes. She's your cousin, right?"

"Oh, Veronica!" Laura's high-maintenance cousin, the one who hated Johnny and Luke needed a Valium to deal with.

"I've actually known Veronica for years. Actually, I've known her husband's family for years. My husband and I used to socialize with them."

"Of course," Luke thought to himself.

CHAPTER 6

"Hey, hey, hey. I'm wondering if you can help me out. I'm trying to track down the guy who stole my Run-D.M.C. tickets and my girl all in the same night," Luke said.

"Coop! How you been?"

TWENTY-FIVE YEARS BEFORE

"How do I look?" Luke asked Theo, his first and only roommate at Morehouse College.

"Doesn't matter. She's going to be too distracted by how you smell to notice."

"You don't like it? It's supposed to be the most expensive cologne there is."

"Yeah, but doesn't it come with directions about how much to use? I don't think you're supposed to pour the whole bottle on, are you?"

"Oh Theo, my naive young friend. If I took advice on the opposite sex from you, then I would be spending the night here with you, curled up with a book too, instead of curled up with Miss Patrice Johnson."

"You're awfully sure of yourself, aren't you?"

"No. I'm awfully sure of Patrice. She's supposed to be a sure thing. That's why I'm going out with her."

"Luke . . ." Theo said disapprovingly. The son of Reverend Theodore Edwards Jr. of the historic Mount Sage Baptist Church, Theo defied the stereotype of preacher's kids being the worst in the church. Theo was one of the nicest, kindest, most well-mannered people on the planet.

"Don't give me that look," Luke said.

Though he'd never admitted it to Theo, Luke was in fact a virgin, something that had become a source of teasing among his closest friends from home—Joe and Garin, who had both lost their virginity in high school.

"But Luke, why are you going to do that nice girl from Spelman like that? She likes you."

"Yeah, she likes me so much I haven't gotten so much as a kiss in three dates."

"She's a good girl. Didn't you say her daddy's a pastor?"

"Yeah, well her daddy's not here. Besides, you know what they say: 'Some girls you marry, some girls you date.' Saundra is great marriage material, but I'm not looking for that right now." Luke had finally given up on Saundra Walters when on their third date, to see a movie, he tried the old yawn, stretch routine and reached for her breast. She responded by moving his hand back up to her shoulder. That night, Luke scheduled a date with Patrice.

Theo gave a disapproving look. "Well, what am I supposed to tell Saundra when she calls?"

"I don't know. Tell her I'm sick."

"So now you want me to lie for you?"

"Then don't. Tell her whatever you want." Luke grabbed his Members Only jacket and said, "Have a good night. I know I will!"

Only Luke's evening didn't turn out as planned. When he arrived to meet Patrice, her ex-boyfriend, who had recently been released from prison, was there and didn't take too kindly to Luke's presence. Luke ended up running a good mile to get away from him. Since getting lucky was now clearly out of the question, Luke decided he would have to see Run-D.M.C. by himself. Only when he checked the pockets of his Members Only jacket his tickets weren't there. Then it hit him. He left them lying on his dresser, right next to his bottle of cologne.

The concert began at 7:30 and, thanks to the boyfriend drama, it was already 8. There was no way Luke would ever make it back to the dorm in time. "What a waste," he thought to himself. The tickets had been third-row center, thanks to his childhood friend Adam, who interned for the record label the band was on.

Luke got back to the dorm to discover that Theo and the tickets were gone.

Theo answered when Saundra, the preacher's daughter, called for Luke. At first he tried to lie about his whereabouts, but when she began to cry, Theo was undone. He told her, "You're a good girl, and one day you'll find a real man who can appreciate that." Theo then said, "I know this sounds strange, but I happen to have an extra ticket to the Run-D.M.C. concert. You wouldn't be interested in joining me, would you?"

They were married after graduation and were still going strong more than twenty years later.

★

"I've been hanging in there," Theo said. "I'm doing alright, Mister President. Doing alright."

"Don't call me that . . . at least not yet," Luke said with a mischievous giggle. "How's the Mrs.?"

"She's great, Luke. She's great. How's yours?"

"Laura's fabulous. Kids are driving her a little nuts and so am I, but she's a good sport about it all."

"How's she with this whole presidential thing?"

"You know, I'll be honest. She's taking it so much better than I thought she would. She actually called me with an idea for how to respond to something one of the other campaigns said about me. You know, she never used to pay attention to campaign stuff, but she's turning into a real pro."

"Well, we're all pulling for you and we're all so proud of you. My dad especially. You should have heard him when I told him. 'Little Luke's going to be commander-in-chief. I'll be.' He just kept saying it over and over."

"How's the good reverend doing?"

"Moving a little slower these days, but you know him, not letting anything slow him down too much."

For forty years, Reverend Theodore Edwards, Jr. had served as senior pastor of the historic Mount Sage Baptist Church, where his father had served as pastor before him. Reverend Edwards was a contemporary of

Dr. Martin Luther King, Jr., whom he had marched alongside and even shared a jail cell with on occasion. Theodore Edwards III (or Theo, as everyone called him) had been groomed since childhood to assume the reins of Mount Sage.

Luke and the preacher's kid formed a tight bond and the Edwards family would become his surrogate family away from home. Luke teasingly blamed Theo's mother for the freshman fifteen he put on his first year because she always made sure "her boys," as she called them, had home-cooked meals. He thought he was having a heart attack after his first Sunday dinner with the Edwards—his first experience with soul food—that started with the spiciest gumbo ever and finished off with collard greens, catfish, cornbread, and a peach cobbler so good that Luke still had daydreams about it.

"What's your name?" was the first question Theo asked when they met. The second: "Have you selected a bed yet?" The third: "Have you found a church home here in Atlanta?" When Luke replied, "Not exactly," Theo immediately invited him to worship with him at Mount Sage Baptist. Countless Morehouse students, faculty, and alumni had worshipped, married, and been baptized there. As Luke later learned, Morehouse was so much a part of the Mount Sage family that it was the only college Theo considered attending, like his father and grandfather before him.

It was only after Luke agreed to join Theo at Mount Sage that the subject of his own religious beliefs came up. Theo asked Luke where he had been baptized and Luke calmly said, "I haven't been baptized. I've been bar-mitzvah-ed. I'm Jewish." Theo laughed so hard his eyes started to water, then slowly the laughter subsided and the smile faded. "You're serious?" Theo asked.

"I am."

They stood in silence for a moment before Theo said, "Well I have to say, I've never seen any Jews that look like you."

"Well, you haven't met my parents yet, but you will when my dad comes through for business next month . . . I'm adopted. My family's Jewish and so am I."

"Oh," Theo said.

After an awkward minute or so Theo said, "So will I still see you for service this weekend?"

Without skipping a beat, Luke replied, "Well, that depends. Will I be seeing you at temple next weekend?"

Theo blanched, then smiled nervously while Luke let out a hearty laugh.

The closest Luke had ever come to a black church was what he had seen on television, but he agreed to join Theo that Sunday and found the experience stirring. The choir was amazing and Theo's father was a truly magnificent orator. "Transcendent" was the word Luke used to describe his first time in the church.

It was the beginning of an unusual friendship and the beginning of a unique journey of faith for Luke, who would visit Mount Sage regularly just to hear Theo's father preach. He remained, however, a practicing Jew. It would have killed his mother—literally—for him to do otherwise.

★

"So I know you're always busy with goings on at Mount Sage, but I'm wondering if you have any openings in your schedule the beginning of next month, on the seventh."

"The next couple of weeks are crazy busy, Coop. We're gearing up for our hundredth anniversary celebration in two months, which is also Dad's birthday."

"That's right! One hundred years. That means the big guy will be, what, eighty?"

"That's right. Though he claims he's going to tell everyone he's seventy-nine the rest of his life."

They both laughed.

"I hope I still have his spirit when I'm his age."

"Me too—but maybe not his hips," Theo said. "He had to have a replacement a few months back."

"What? You never told me that."

"You know him. He hates people making a fuss. He told me that if he didn't wake up from the surgery then I had his permission to tell people."

That sounded like Theo's dad, Luke thought to himself.

"Anyway, he's been in and out of the hospital with a few complications since then, but he's as upbeat as ever and his mind is as healthy as it's ever been. So no complaints. We're blessed."

"Well, you let me know if there's anything I can do."

"Will do, Coop. Will do. So what's going on?"

"Well, we're doing the official campaign kickoff down in Florida. And I was wondering if maybe you could make it."

"Florida, huh? Why there?"

"Well, you know they still haven't recovered from the effects of that environmental disaster. They're still really struggling, and since one of the things I'm campaigning on is the failure of the current administration to address it adequately, or to address the needs of any of the middle class adequately, we're going to do our official kickoff there."

There was silence. "Theo, you there?" Luke asked.

"I'm here. It's just . . . you already sound presidential. I'm just taking it all in . . ."

"Oh stop."

"Well, Luke, you know I love you and support everything you do, but I gotta be careful now that I'm senior pastor. You know we get in trouble if we're seen as endorsing or anything. And to be honest I've already gotten a talking to from older members who supported President Beaman who told me to make sure I keep my politics out of the pulpit when it comes to his daughter." The reference was to Luke's main primary challenger, Senator Abigail "Abby" Sanchez Beaman.

"I understand."

"You know I love you, man."

"Of course. Don't even worry about it."

"But I tell you what. Would it be alright if I called you the morning of your kickoff and prayed with you over the phone?"

Luke was touched.

"I'd love that."

"Okay, man. You let me know what time works for you. Love you, man."

"Love you too. Hey, and Theo?"

"Yeah?"

"Tell the woman who would have been my wife if you hadn't stolen her from me that I said hello."

Theo laughed, loudly.

CHAPTER 7

AddictedToPolitics.com

COOPER CAMPAIGN COMES OUT SWINGING AT FLORIDA LAUNCH

Michigan Governor Says Administration Failing Florida and America

The official rollout of a presidential campaign is often a ceremonial affair, intended to confirm for voters, donors and the media, what we already know: that another candidate is running for the nation's highest office. But in rare instances, they can actually set the tone for a race, and this month's competing kickoffs between Sen. Abigail Sanchez Beaman (D-PA) and Gov. Luke Cooper (D-MI) appear to have done just that. While Beaman launched her campaign amidst the comfort of her hometown, in front of the community center her father, the former president, founded before entering politics, Cooper launched his hundreds of miles away from his home, amidst the lingering disaster and disrepair of the Gulf. Aside from being a bold choice from a policy standpoint, Florida is also the state that helped put Cooper on the map after his role in saving the life of a white separatist there.

While Beaman's inaugural campaign speech took a largely optimistic tone, highlighting her family's commitment to public service "to a country that allowed the son of immigrants, a skinny kid with no money, no connections but the kind of heart and dreams that money can't buy, to grow up and have not one but two dream jobs, including one that allowed him to help others live the American Dream," the Cooper campaign struck a surprisingly confrontational tone, citing "the failures of Washington to make the American Dream accessible to all those who deserve it—all Americans, not just those who can afford to buy it: the firefighters, the teachers, the farmers, the truck drivers. I'm running for president because I want to change that. I want to make the American Dream as accessible for my grandchildren as it was for my grandparents, and our current leaders are simply not doing enough to make that a reality."

The move is certainly an interesting strategic choice, no doubt guided by the governor's senior advisor, Nate Crosby, a former aide to New York senator Sid Burstein (who's famous for turning political confrontation into an art form). Though the governor ran a tough statewide campaign, he is widely described by most political observers with two adjectives: "young" and "likable," attributes that, while useful in a presidential campaign, are perhaps not as useful as ones like "experienced" and "tough." But if the governor's remarks today are any indication, he might just add "tough" to his description soon enough.

★

"Daddy! Can we look for shells while we're on the beach?"

"Well, the beach we're going to had an accident last year so I don't know if it's really a good idea for us to pick up shells there and take them home."

Milo looked disappointed.

"But I guess there's no harm in looking," Luke added, causing Milo to break into a wide smile.

Luke, his closest family, and a couple of friends and staff were in a holding suite in a hotel near the beach where he would officially begin his presidential adventure.

Luke squatted to look Milo eye to eye and grabbed his hand. "You excited about today?"

"Yeah! We're going to the beach!"

Luke paused, taking in the moment. In Milo's eyes this wasn't the biggest day of his dad's life, it was the day he and his dad might go look for shells on the beach.

"Okay, we've got to let Daddy focus. He's got to study."

"Study?" Milo asked. "Does he have a test today?"

"You could say that, sweetheart," Luke's mom said, winking.

"Uh-oh. Are you ready for your test, Daddy?"

"I think so," he said, smiling.

"You were born ready, son," Esther Cooper said while squeezing Luke's chin, the only part of his face she could really reach even though she was standing on her tiptoes.

"Mom." Luke sighed.

"What? I can't touch my own son? You're never too old, too big, or too important for me to show you some love, and don't you ever forget it."

Luke squeezed her hand then kissed it. "I won't. I love you, Mom."

Esther's eyes began to well. The two just stood there for a moment before they were interrupted . . . by a loud belch.

"'Scuse me," Milo said.

"Milo!" Esther replied.

"I said 'scuse me, Grandma."

"He did, Mom. I heard him," Luke said giggling. He enveloped Milo in a big hug.

"I'm hungry," Milo said.

"Okay, well let's find you something to eat, then, not that you sound like you need it," Esther Cooper replied.

"Please don't go too far, Mrs. Cooper. We'll be departing shortly." It was one of Luke's new campaign aides, who had walked in undetected.

"What do you think I'm going to do? Run off to Vegas?" She then grabbed Milo's hand and began walking away.

Luke was amazed at how quickly his campaign staff ballooned in the last few weeks from virtually zero to more aides than he could count. The presence of all those handlers required an adjustment, not just for him but his entire family. Some were handling it better than others. When an aide had made suggestions to his parents regarding what they should wear to the campaign kickoff, she came scarily close to receiving one of Esther Cooper's dressing downs.

"Listen, young lady, I've been dressing myself for quite a long time and I don't think I need your help—or anyone else's—to continue doing so."

At which point Luke's dad distracted Luke's mother by asking her a question about one of his heart medications, a tactic he'd been employing for years. But the exchange set the tone for Esther Cooper's relationship with Luke's advisors and aides. She decided she didn't care for most of them, finding them patronizing know-it-alls. Except for Nate, who shortly after the mishap of the suggested clothing makeover sent her flowers for her birthday.

In addition to his parents, one of his brothers was also there for the big launch, along with Laura's cousin Veronica, who never missed an opportunity to possibly be on television. Garin and Brooke were also there for moral support.

After arriving by private plane, Veronica made her entrance with two Louis Vuitton trunks for her 48-hour stay.

"Hello, my dear!" she said upon seeing Laura for the first time in months. After air kisses on both cheeks, she said, "What an exciting day!"

"Yes it is," Laura said, and she meant it. Though she had initially been cool to the idea of Luke's candidacy, she had to admit that this was all exciting and extraordinary and she couldn't be prouder of her husband.

"You look lovely," Veronica said, not sounding like her usual, critical self.

"Thanks, Cuz," she said.

"Now, when are they doing your makeup?"

And just like that, the old Veronica was back.

"Actually, I already did my own makeup, Veronica."

A look of horror spread across Veronica's face.

"Laura, dear. I know you pride yourself on being a natural beauty, but the camera requires all of us to employ a little extra help—no matter how good our genetic stock. And I know we both come from *fabulous* stock. Now, I can call Phillipe and see who he knows in this neighborhood who can swoop in for last-minute emergencies. Although based on the quality of this hotel, my hopes aren't high for the caliber of whom he might recommend."

Phillipe was Veronica's personal makeup artist. In addition to her and a handful of other socialites, he had a host of B- and C-list celebrity clients and had once appeared on an episode of *The Oprah Winfrey Show*, something Veronica never let anyone forget.

"Veronica, that's very kind, but we really don't have time for that now, so I'm afraid my plain old face will have to do."

Thankfully for Laura, Brooke had a way of putting her at ease. In addition to being a great friend, Brooke was also a great publicist, a quality about her Laura was coming to value more and more as the campaign picked up steam. Though as First Lady of Michigan Laura had a staff, it was nothing like the team of handlers who had emerged in the recent weeks of the presidential campaign to tell her what to say and when to say it. With Brooke around, Laura felt like she had an ally, someone whose professional expertise was just as valid as that of all of the experts, but whose motives Laura never had to question. After all, unlike the so-called experts, Brooke would still be there right by Laura's side whether Luke was elected president or not.

Brooke's loyalty and toughness were on full display the morning of the kickoff.

"Mrs. Cooper, you look lovely," a consultant said.

"Thank you. You're very sweet to say so." The aides suggested that Laura wear a dress, preferably one in a bright color, to accentuate her femininity, something that screamed young, attractive wife and mom. So Laura wore her "lucky" teal Diane von Furstenberg wrap dress. It was lucky because she had purchased it on sale for half off, and days later Luke won his race for governor.

"But we're not sure the color will work. It's just there's blue in our signs and we don't want there to be a clash."

"Oh . . . ," Laura said, puzzled. "Well, I have one more dress in my—"

"Not to worry," he quickly replied. "We actually happen to have a couple for you to choose from."

"You do?" Laura asked, surprised.

"Yes." He then called for another young female aide who appeared seemingly out of nowhere. The aide opened a garment bag and proceeded to pull out three dresses. One was Pepto Bismol pink—a color Laura never wore. The other was a sleeveless floral print, something Laura also never wore. The last one was a yellow church lady number that Laura would never wear. If the choice had been between those monstrosities and a trash bag, Laura thought to herself, she would accessorize the hell out of the trash bag and hope for the best.

"Umm . . . those are . . ." Laura paused for what felt like an eternity as she searched for the right word. "Those are . . . very . . . pretty, but they're not really me."

She, the consultant, and the aide stood in an awkward silence.

Laura forced a smile. "As I said, I have another dress that I'm happy to . . ."

The consultant interrupted her. "The thing is, Mrs. Cooper, you're so beautiful and definitely convey an air of sophistication which is . . . great," although he said it in a way that let Laura know he didn't mean it. He continued, "It's just that not all Americans relate to that. The dress you're wearing screams classy and, forgive me for saying so if I'm speaking out of turn, sexy . . . but not necessarily the all-American mom . . . at least not the way a mom in Nebraska might define it."

"That's funny. Because I was born and bred in Nebraska and I happen to love her dress," Brooke interjected.

The consultant smiled in a way that said, "Who the hell are you and why are you butting in?" Instead he said, "I was using Nebraska just as a hypothetical example."

"Well I certainly hope so, because last I checked Nebraska wasn't even a swing state, so if you're basing my friend's election strategy on winning over voters there, then this campaign's in trouble before it's even begun. And unlike you I don't even get paid to know such things."

Brooke smiled the smile she used on reporters who had crossed one of her clients. It was a smile that said, "If you ever do that again, I will kill you—not metaphorically, but literally."

The consultant pointedly turned away from Brooke and faced Laura directly. "Mrs. Cooper, if you'd like to think about it, we'll just leave the dresses here for you."

"That's okay," Laura replied with a smile.

"Well, we'll leave them here, just in case."

To which Brooke replied, "I haven't had my coffee yet and according to my husband I can pass as Satan's demonic twin sister before my first cup, so you'll have to bear with me as I try to ask this in the least bitchy way possible. Are you deaf?"

The consultant stood there in silence.

"That wasn't a rhetorical question," Brooke continued. "I just heard her tell you that it's not necessary for you to leave those dresses there and it would seem to me that if you're a consultant to the campaign to get her husband elected president and her First Lady then that would mean that you work for her, not the other way around, and she just told you that she doesn't want you to leave the dresses. So that leaves me to presume that either, one, you don't respect your client or, two, you didn't hear her clearly, which, considering you are standing only a few feet from one another, would seem to indicate that you're hearing impaired. Are you?"

The consultant looked as though he wanted to punch her. Brooke picked up the garment bag and handed it to him and said, "It was nice meeting you."

The consultant and the aide stormed out.

★

Luke barely slept the night before the launch. Though his remarks had theoretically been completed the day before, he was not satisfied with the closing.

At 5 a.m. he checked his BlackBerry and saw that he had a message from Garin. "Just made it to FL. Longest trip ever because of the weather but I wouldn't miss it for the world. So proud of you. Catching a quick nap but will see you later.—G"

Luke was in the sitting area of their suite so as not to disturb Laura. He didn't want his voice to carry so he pulled out his phone to text.

"Up?"

Ever the smart-ass, Garin replied, "No. Sound asleep. You?"

"Me too, wiseass," Luke typed. "Snoring as I type this. Where r u now?"

"Just checked in."

"Meet in the lobby in 5?"

"Sure."

Fifteen minutes later Luke stepped off of the lobby elevator. He had been trying to take one last crack at a sentence in his speech. His delay prompted Garin to text, "Lost?"

"Hey," Luke said.

"Hey yourself," Garin replied. He looked like he was in the middle of a nap.

"You look like shit," Luke said.

"So do you," Garin replied. "Only you have to try to convince a bunch of people to vote for you in a few hours. I don't."

"Gee thanks," Luke said.

He sat down next to Garin.

They sat in silence for a moment.

"What's up?" Garin finally asked.

"What do you mean?" Luke asked.

"What do you mean what do I mean? Today's the most important day of your life, so what the hell are we both doing down here?"

Luke didn't respond.

"Luke, you're ready."

Luke remained silent.

"Besides," Garin continued, "it's too late to call the whole thing off. It's like a wedding. The preacher and church are booked. Might as well go through with it and just deal with an annulment later if you have to."

"Thanks a lot," Luke replied.

"I'm just messing with you."

Luke was silent for another minute before saying, "It's this damn speech. I just can't . . . I don't know. Something doesn't feel right about the ending. I can't put my finger on it but something's off. . . ."

Garin yawned.

"You look exhausted," Luke said. "You should get some sleep. I'll see you for the launch."

"I'm not tired," Garin said. Then he yawned again.

"Yeah, I can see that," Luke said smiling.

"No, really," Garin said. "Not tired at all." He stretched like a cat waking from a comfy rest. "I have an idea."

Garin jumped off of the couch, walked over to the front desk and had a conversation with the manager on duty.

Luke couldn't hear them but could tell Garin was flirting. Luke could tell it worked because Garin turned around and winked at him.

The manager passed him something. Then Garin motioned for Luke to follow him.

"Where are we going?"

"Just trust me," Garin replied.

They went down a flight of stairs into what appeared to be the hotel's basement. Garin unlocked a door. There was a Ping-Pong table in the center of the room.

Luke was puzzled.

"Ping-Pong?" he asked Garin.

"No," Garin replied. "Hockey."

Luke was confused. He didn't see any hockey rink, though like just about every kid from a well-to-do white Michigan family, he did play. Then he looked in the corner. There was an air hockey machine.

"I saw it on the list of amenities when I checked in." Garin flashed a wide smile, the kind of smile only Garin could.

Luke and Garin played all the time during law school, particularly when they needed a break from studying.

"You have got to be kidding!" Luke said.

"Afraid I'll kick your ass like I used to?"

Garin took off his jacket and began rolling up his sleeves.

"Hardly," Luke said. "Are you forgetting who beat who?"

"You cheated that night."

They had played with their kids, here and there, since then but had not played each other in almost twenty years, not since shortly before their law school graduation.

Garin plugged in the machine. "Need some warm-up time?"

"Naw, I'm good," Luke said. "But then I'm not as old as you."

"You know, Coop, I hope you maintain that sense of humor when I beat you."

For twenty minutes it was as though neither man had another care in the world—except for getting that little puck into the other man's goal. They trash talked as though they were playing ball in an NBA championship, not playing a game usually found at Chuck E. Cheese's, in a hotel basement.

When they finished, they were actually out of breath, in part from laughing so hard.

"Oh shit, I gotta run," Luke said, looking at his watch.

"What? You gotta go run for president or something?" Garin said with a smile. "If I had a nickel for every time someone's used that excuse to get out of playing me . . ."

Luke laughed.

"I understand," Garin continued. "You're intimidated that I'm finally hitting my stride. I get it."

"Hardly," Luke said laughing.

Garin unplugged the machine and they headed for the door.

Both men had forgotten how tired they had been before.

As they walked up the stairs Garin said, "Today's going to be great. You'll see."

"Thanks, man." The two men embraced.

"I wonder if there's an air hockey machine at the White House?" Garin asked.

Luke laughed. "That was a very Joe thing to say."

"I know," Garin said, grinning. "That's what happens when I spend too much time with him, but you know he always has good tickets to games."

Luke returned to his suite with a clear head and spirit and within twenty minutes had put the finishing touches on his speech.

★

After his mother and son left him the morning of his launch, Luke took advantage of some alone time. He knew he should read over his remarks one more time. But instead he just enjoyed the silence and took the moment in. Was this the day his entire life would change? After only a few minutes there was a knock at the door.

"Have time to talk to a voter?" a female voice said.

It was Laura.

"Sure do."

Luke smiled—and relaxed a bit more. They had barely spent any time alone together the last thirty-six hours. She walked in and shut the door and locked it.

"Good. Because I'm undecided at the moment," she said with a grin.

"Is that right?" Luke asked, his own smile growing wider.

"Yes. I need someone to help me decide who to vote for."

"You do?" he replied. He moved his prepared remarks from his lap to the lampstand next to him.

"I do," Laura said. She slipped off her shoes and despite her long legs, managed to curl up on his lap. She placed her head on his shoulder.

He loved the way her hair smelled. Whenever they were apart it was the physical trait of hers that he could remember most vividly, and doing so would always help him drift off to sleep when she wasn't in bed beside him.

"Hey, you," he said and kissed the top of her head.

"Hey yourself," she replied.

They sat for a moment, enjoying the silence and the fact that it was just the two of them, a reality that they knew would become increasingly rare in the coming months.

"You look beautiful," Luke finally said. "You know, I think I may just win this thing for having the hottest wife."

Laura giggled. "Although I don't have that much competition. I mean, Senator Beaman's married to a man."

"Yeah, but have you seen him?" Luke asked. "I'd still win hottest spouse, hands down."

Laura laughed.

"I'm being serious," Luke continued. "Too bad I have to give this damn speech. I can think of a lot of other things I'd much rather do." He gave her rear a firm squeeze.

"You bad boy. You're supposed to be concentrating," she giggled.

"Well then stop coming in here distracting me with all of your womanly charms."

Just then there was a knock at the door.

"Saved by the bell!" Laura said.

"Give us a minute," Luke shouted. "Actually, give us ten!" He then whispered to Laura, "That should be enough time, right honey?"

"Since when has ten minutes ever *not* been enough time?" Laura said with a wicked, teasing grin.

"Oooh! That's harsh! That's harsh," Luke said, grabbing his heart dramatically like he was struck, but he was laughing. Laura always had the ability to make him laugh when he really needed to.

She stood up and slipped her shoes on. Luke grabbed her hand.

"I love you."

Laura leaned down and gave him a deep, lingering kiss, so long, in fact, that the knock at the door became louder and more persistent.

When she finished, Luke looked as though he had been swimming underwater and was coming back up for air. She used her thumb to wipe a little lipstick off of him, then walked to the door. Luke watched her walk. Her smell was not the only feature of hers that he loved.

She stopped, turned back to him and said, "Go get 'em, Governor," then opened the door.

On the other side of it was his frantic-looking aide. "Governor, I'm sorry but we're already running behind schedule."

She then said, "Oh my god, are you bleeding?" The aide pulled a tissue out of her purse and walked over to Luke.

"No. I'm fine," Luke said.

"But you have a little—right there," she said, reaching for the lipstick Laura had left.

"No, it's nothing really," Luke said.

"Oh," the aide said uncomfortably, a look of realization falling over her face. She cleared her throat and said, "Here's a mirror."

"I told him to lay off of the makeup," Laura said with a smile.

Luke laughed. Laura blew him a kiss.

Luke's private cell phone rang.

He asked his aide to answer it so he could review his speech one last time.

"Governor Cooper's phone . . . I'm sorry he's unavailable at the moment. May I take a message? Can you spell that? I'm sorry, how's that spelled? T-H-E-O?"

Luke looked up. "Who's that on the phone?"

"Someone named Theo."

"I gotta take that."

"Governor, we're already behind schedule," the aide pleaded.

"So a few more minutes won't kill us." He took the phone from her hand.

"Did I catch you at a bad time, Coop?"

"Nah, man. You're right on time. Right on time."

"Well, I'm so sorry I couldn't be there for your big day."

"Don't worry about it, man. If all goes well there will be a bunch more of my campaign invitations in the next couple of months for you to turn down."

"Ah, don't do me like that, Luke. You know I'd be there if I could."

"I know. I know. I'm just messing with you. How's my favorite preacher doing?"

"I'm hanging in there."

"I wasn't talking about you. I was talking about your dad."

"Gee. Thanks a lot," Theo said. He and Luke always teased each other. "He's actually back in the hospital."

"Aw, I'm sorry to hear that, Theo. Is there anything I can do?"

"Well, you know him, he's still in fighting form. In fact, that's part of why I called. I know we talked about praying together on your big day, but I thought about it and don't think I can."

"Oh . . . well . . . okay." Luke was confused. He assumed that was why Theo called.

"But can you hold on a sec?"

"I actually have to run soon, Theo."

"Just one sec, Coop."

Just then another voice picked up. "Hello? Hello? Hello? I can't hear anyone on this darn thing."

It was Reverend Edwards, Theo's father.

"I thought you'd rather have your favorite preacher pray with you," Theo's voice piped up. He had managed to get the three of them on the line together.

"Reverend!" Luke said.

"Can you hear me, Luke?"

"I can, sir! How are you?"

"Don't call me sir! I'm not that old. Well, I am but I'm in denial about it."

Luke laughed.

"No, sir, you're not old at all."

"Son, if you managed to say that with a straight face then you already have one of the most important qualities necessary to be a successful politician." Luke laughed harder. For someone in the hospital he still sounded like the same old Reverend, Luke thought to himself. "Speaking of, how are things?" Reverend Edwards continued.

"I'm doing okay. Doing okay. No complaints. I'm actually about to head out to my official launch now so they're probably going to snatch this phone out of my hand any second."

"Okay. Praying under pressure. Not to worry. I've done it before, usually when faced with bodily harm, but we'll make this quick. You boys bow your heads." And with that instruction they all did. "Dear heavenly father," he began, "please watch over Luke as he embarks on this journey. Please bless him with the wisdom and humility to be the leader that you want him to be. Please protect him and his family . . ." The reverend continued praying with them for what seemed like no time at all. But when Luke opened his eyes his aide was standing beside him.

After the reverend said "Amen," he then said, "Give 'em hell, Luke."

Luke and Theo both laughed loudly.

"Will do, Rev, and you take care of yourself." He hung up the phone.

"You ready?" his aide asked.

"I'm ready," Luke replied.

As he prepared to exit the suite amidst the aides, family members, and friends of the campaign swirling about, Luke spotted Garin and patted him on the back. He then leaned in and whispered in Garin's ear, "I got something important to tell you."

Garin froze, ready for Luke to speak his last words to him before he officially became a presidential candidate—the words that Garin would repeat in Luke's A&E *Biography* special—if there ever was one—years from now.

"Yeah, Luke, what is it?" Garin asked. Did Luke need one last pep talk? Garin wondered.

"Let me tell you something," Luke said. Garin braced himself. "I know you let me win this morning. And I don't need or appreciate your pity. So you better be ready for a rematch," he flashed a smile.

Garin let out a laugh so loud that it actually startled the aide standing near them. Luke then added for good measure, "By the way, what on earth did your wife say to my staff? They're terrified of her." As he whispered this to Garin, Luke waved at Brooke who was standing across the room, out of earshot.

Brooke beamed and waved back, oblivious to what he'd just said.

"You know Brooke. Instilling terror is one of her hobbies," Garin said while also smiling at the woman he loved—and also feared—more than any other on the planet, now that his mother was deceased. The two men then laughed conspiratorially as they had a thousand times before.

Then, with his wife Laura beside him and his closest friend behind him, Luke Cooper walked out the door and into the biggest adventure of his life.

CHAPTER 8

"N amaste," Laura's instructor said, signaling the end of her class. Laura felt lighter and more alive, the way she always did when she finished practicing yoga.

Yoga was one of Laura's few sanctuaries. Her closest Michigan friend, Robin, had turned her on to it long before it officially replaced aerobics and Pilates as the "in" form of exercise. Robin was the first, and in some ways only, real friend Laura had in Michigan. There were, of course, the other Michigan political wives and the mothers of Milo and James's playmates, all of whom she socialized with, but they weren't confidantes who would unconditionally stand by her.

Moving to Michigan was a tough adjustment for an East Coast city girl. Her in-laws made it easier, but she missed New York and an identity beyond the Cooper family. So she put her education degree to use and began teaching at a local elementary school. She loved the kids but most of the teachers left something to be desired. Many of them seemed to resent Laura on sight. She was too young, too idealistic, too Ivy League and fancy, and too pretty. But one teacher, Robin, extended not only a hand, but a hug, welcoming Laura into the fold.

They were a study in contrasts. Robin was as short and plump as Laura was tall and thin. Where Laura often wore her jet-black, straight hair elegantly pulled back, Robin wore reddish brown gray dreadlocks. While Laura was meticulous, Robin spilled food on her clothing so often that it was like an accessory.

They became inseparable friends. Even after Laura left teaching to become a full-time mom, and full-time political wife, they spoke on the phone daily, and Auntie Robin would often stop by to see "her boys."

They went to yoga together. Sometimes Robin would simply "lead" a one-on-one class with Laura at home.

Robin also served as one of her few sounding boards about Luke. Robin liked him but didn't make excuses for him. When he chose to attend a political event on Laura's birthday, at his former advisor Johnny's urging, Robin sent him an e-mail titled "Ten Reasons You're a Jackass." In the body of the e-mail, reasons one through ten all said the same thing: "Because you're missing your wife's birthday for an event you won't even remember in another year." After that, Luke got his mother to babysit and took Laura away for a belated romantic birthday getaway at a four-star hotel where she was pampered with spa treatments. And he presented her with an antique necklace she'd had her eye on for months.

Luke didn't mention the e-mail or its salutation—"Dear Mr. President . . ."—until years later, when Laura was grieving the loss of her beloved friend. Hearing the story of Robin's "You're a Jackass" e-mail prompted the first laugh Laura had in the weeks following Robin's death, eighteen months before Luke was asked to become Lieutenant Governor. Laura was so devastated she couldn't set foot in a yoga class for more than a year. But she finally began to ease back in. First going a few times a year. Then working her way up to once a month, with occasional sessions at home, before she was going weekly again, just as she had with Robin.

She was friendly to everyone in her class, though not really friends with any of them. Laura had never really made friends easily, her shyness often being mistaken for aloofness, and since Robin's death she had been afraid to become so close to anyone again.

But she was always polite and cordial, exchanging pleasantries with the other ladies in her class.

She knew that there were those who knew that she was married to the governor, but she always appreciated that no one treated her differently, at least as far as she could tell.

That would soon change.

Laura rolled up her mat, tucked it under her arm, and proceeded to head for the cubby that was holding her shoes.

There two young women she had seen off and on at the studio for the last year stood chatting. Laura leaned in to grab her shoes, when one of them said, "I'm sorry to bother you, but I just wanted to say that I think it's great that your husband is running for president. He has my vote."

Laura was caught off guard, but she smiled and said, "Thank you."

"You must be so excited."

Laura smiled and shrugged, not quite sure how to respond, particularly as she was aware that a group of people had gathered, all under the pretext of grabbing their belongings from the cubby at precisely the right moment to eavesdrop on their conversation.

"Well, there's only one downside, of course. I'm sure you guys will miss Michigan. I've been to D.C., and excuse me for saying so, but it sucks." Her friend laughed.

"Well, that's not the only downside," Laura said with a friendly smile.

The woman's friend piped up, "I can't imagine how tough it must be. The loss of privacy must feel insane."

Her friend nudged her and said, "You commenting on her loss of privacy while we bother her at yoga is the very definition of irony."

Laura laughed.

"Are you ready for all of this life-changing craziness?"

"You're never really ready for something like this. It's not like there's a how-to guide or something, but we're having fun."

At that point the yoga instructor appeared.

"Well, sorry to bother you again. Just wanted to say hello."

"Nice meeting you," Laura replied.

As the women turned to leave, the instructor touched Laura's arm and said, "We consider this a sacred place for all of us, so if you ever feel bothered or uncomfortable please do let me know."

"That's very kind of you, but they were really sweet."

"Okay," he said. "See you next week."

★

"Hello."

"Laura?"

"Who's calling, please?" Laura asked, thinking the unrecognizable voice was most likely a telemarketer, or someone else she was uninterested in speaking to.

"Hi! It's Marnie."

Laura didn't respond.

"Marnie from the campaign."

"Hi," Laura replied.

"I can tell by your voice that you must not have received the e-mail introducing me."

"I'm afraid I didn't."

"Oh. That's strange, they copied me on it. We might want to get your e-mail account looked at since that will be our primary form of communication."

Laura realized there was nothing wrong with her e-mail or with the BlackBerry she had been given by the campaign—other than the fact that she usually forgot to turn it on or carry it with her.

"I'm hungry!" Laura heard Milo shout.

"I'm sorry, but this isn't really a great time for me," Laura told her.

"I'll only be a minute. I really just wanted to formally introduce myself since we'll be working together, and also just go over—quickly—how I think we'd like to address Yoga-gate."

"Yoga what?"

"That's what the blogs are calling it. You know, the comments that are getting some attention."

"I don't mean to be rude but I really don't know what you're talking about, and I . . ."

"Mom—Milo took the last cookie!" James shouted.

"Neither one of you are supposed to be eating cookies this close to dinner!" Laura shouted in response. She then continued, "I'm sorry, where were we?"

"I was just about to explain my suggestion for how we deal with these comments that are obviously being misconstrued."

"What comments are you talking about?"

"Oh boy," Marnie replied. "Okay . . . I didn't realize you didn't know any of this."

"Know any of what?"

"Well, a local political blog in Michigan reported that you told some students in your yoga class that you don't think the governor is ready to be president."

Laura paused, taking the words in.

"Laura? Are you there?"

"Yes. I'm here."

"I'm not going to ask you if you said it, and I'm going to assume that if for some reason it sounded like you did that's because what you were really trying to say was taken completely out of context, obviously."

"I didn't say it."

"Well that certainly makes things easier."

"Great. As long as it makes things easier," Laura said tersely.

There was a pause.

"Look," Marnie said, "I know this is difficult having all of these intruders storm into your life, but I want you to know that I am one hundred percent on your side. I work for your husband's campaign but I'm on your team. My job is to make sure that your voice is heard as authentically as possible, and to make sure that the public has a chance to get to know the wonderful woman behind our wonderful candidate."

"Beside," Laura corrected her.

"Excuse me?"

"Luke's mom has always said to me that *beside* every great man is a great woman, not behind."

"Of course," Marnie continued. "So, with your permission I'd like to get a statement out as soon as possible debunking this obviously fabricated story. What do you think of this: 'It appears that these anonymous students may have still been coming down off of their yoga high when they imagined this story. Laura not only considers her husband ready to be president, but also knows he is by far the most qualified candidate for the job.'

"What do you think?" Marnie asked.

"Mom! James took the remote control!"

"I'm sorry, Marnie, but I have to go."

"Understood. Can you just sign off on this statement for me?"

"Sure. Fine."

"Great. I'll be in touch in the next day or two. We should plan to be in regular contact, so I'll have the tech guys figure out what's going on with your e-mail."

"I think I can figure it out, Marnie."

"Are you sure?"

"Yes."

"Okay. Looking forward to working with you."

Laura simply offered a low-key "Thanks" before adding quickly, "Marnie, one question."

"Sure. Ask me anything."

"What exactly is it that you do?"

"Well, I'm what you'd call a consultant. I'll be helping you out with communications and a few other things for the time being. But considering we're still in the early stages of the campaign think of me as your jack of all trades, so anything you need that's campaign related don't hesitate to pick up the phone or shoot me an e-mail. In fact that's actually preferred—e-mail, that is. And I should say for the record that I know you were probably hoping to become more visible later on in the race but we're probably going to need to get you out there sooner. You know, to drive the point home that you believe in Luke, and his candidacy."

Laura was quiet for a moment before asking, "Anything else?"

"It's probably best if you not return to that yoga studio, and if you do insist on going to a studio, as opposed to practicing at home, please be careful what you say and who you say it to. I know this is all a big adjustment. Trust me, I know. But these little things can make a big difference in the long run. Anyhoo, I've talked your ear off enough. I'll check in with your scheduler at the governor's office on carving out time to connect you with our media trainer. She's great. You'll like her a lot. Again, so excited to be working with you. Have a good night."

"You too," Laura muttered.

After she hung up the phone, she stood there staring blankly until her children snapped her back to reality.

Later that evening, after getting out of the shower, Laura had a voice mail from her husband, who was on a campaign trip out of state. "Babe, you gotta do me a favor. If my mother calls and asks you for the names of any of your yoga classmates, don't give them out. She's threatening to put them in bodybags." He then let out a mischievous laugh. "Anyway, sorry I missed you, hon. I love you lots and can't wait to see you soon. And for the record—I can't wait to see *all* of you. . . ."

Laura blushed and smiled.

She was tempted to e-mail Marnie a revision to her statement on "Yoga-gate." "Not only do I consider my husband to be the most qualified candidate, but the cutest too."

★

"Okay, I've scheduled you for two sessions with Sheila Brandt next week. She's the best media trainer in the biz. You'll be able to handle an hour on the hot seat with everyone from Sam Donaldson to Judge Judy when she's done with you. We'll brush up with her periodically throughout the campaign as needed."

"Nate, I told you, I've done a ton of interviews the last couple of years."

"But none like the ones you're going to be doing the next couple of months, and if all goes well the next couple of years . . . which actually brings me to something I've put off bringing up as long as possible, but I can't avoid it anymore."

"What? Are you going to ask me for a raise?" Luke joked. He often used humor to deflect tension.

"That would actually be easier to bring up with you than what I'm about to. We just finished a focus group. You're doing well, better than we expected this early."

"That's bad news?" Luke asked, puzzled.

"But Laura's not, Luke. She's not testing well with women. She's not testing well with men. She's not testing well with anybody."

"Well who the hell are you testing? A bunch of people with substandard IQs?"

"I know this is . . . tough to hear . . ."

"What could they possibly not like about her? She's beautiful. She's smart. She's kind."

In moments like this Nate had learned that honesty wasn't always the best policy, sort of like when your girlfriend asks, "Do these pants make my butt look big?"

"Well, that's probably it, Luke. She's so glamorous and good-looking and smart that she may intimidate a lot of people."

He could sense Luke's blood pressure going down. It would not have had he told Luke the whole truth, which was that the focus groups simply didn't like his wife. She came across as the quintessential angry black woman. She had actually worn a jacket with an African print to a photo op. Most of the members in the focus group literally recoiled at the picture—including two elderly black women in the group. In addition to the yoga class misstep there were other quotes that continued to haunt her, such as when Luke told a reporter, "It's not a secret that while I may run the state, my wife runs the house." There was also the time she was asked by a reporter, shortly after Luke's election, whether or not she could ever picture herself being First Lady of the United States, and Laura replied, "No. I can't picture it and wouldn't want to. It seems like a thankless job." Of course her full quote never actually made it into print in its entirety, and the sentiments expressed were the difference between night and day. "Well, it would obviously be such a once-in-a-lifetime adventure and honor to serve our country in such a wonderful way, on the one hand, but on the other hand, the level of scrutiny on everything from your clothes to what you say, kind of makes it seem like a thankless job at times, at least I would imagine, and it seems like all of that would make it a tough environment to raise kids in. And that's my focus. So to answer your question, I guess the answer is no, I can't picture it, at least not right now, but I'm sure if you asked every First Lady who's served, they'd probably say it was all worth it, and I'm sure they would be right."

She also once said in jest, at a fundraiser for a Jewish charity where Luke's father was being honored, that "growing up in a Catholic household, I never dreamed of ending up with a Jewish family, particularly since I had never planned to date a Jewish guy or I guess any white guys, for that matter. But I somehow ended up with more Jewish relatives than I can count, and they now far outnumber my Catholic relatives." The remark was greeted with uproarious laughter at the time. She then added, "And I couldn't imagine my life and family without each and every one of them." But that sentence was largely forgotten in media reports of the comments. Context and nuance are often tough to convey on the written page and since there was no video of the event, and the humorous, light-hearted tone of that evening didn't translate well into print, the comment left a bad taste in the mouths of some members of the focus group, most notably the white males.

"So we have a little work to do to get voters to love Laura as much as you and everybody else who knows her does. You know as well as anybody that candidates are judged by the company they keep."

"She's not company I'm keeping, she's my wife and she's a great one and those numbskulls would be lucky to have her as First Lady. Bunch of dumbasses."

Nate actually had to bite his lip to keep from laughing. There was something endearing and chivalrous about Luke's defense of the woman he loved. The cynical political operative in him actually fantasized about capitalizing on the moment, realizing that if voters heard this they would actually love Luke even more.

"Look, Luke, we've discussed this. How many times have I said that running for president isn't like running for school board or even Congress? Then, people are voting for the person they think is the best candidate. When it comes to president, they're voting for the candidate they think is the best person. And part of deciding that is judging their families and religion and hobbies and friends in a way they don't with the other offices. I'm not saying it's right or makes any sense. But it's the way it is. You're not the only one running for president. Everyone you love and whoever loved you is in a sense running too. They will be put under a microscope, dissected, and it's not always going to be pretty, but if you believe and they believe that you are here to serve a cause greater than yourself and you think the downsides are worth it, then we've got to learn not to focus on the negatives but instead focus on how to address them."

There was a long silence.

"What are you suggesting?"

"Well, Lucy Simonds is one of Sheila's business partners. She's an image consultant and she can work with Laura on everything from her hair to her wardrobe."

"I love her hair!" Luke exclaimed. "No one's touching a single hair on her head."

"She has lovely hair," Nate offered. "But Lucy will be great at assessing whether or not she is wearing it in a way that brings out her personality, in a way that's accessible to voters. We want them to see in Laura what you see in her."

Luke paused.

"Who's going to tell her?"

"Well, I can have Marnie gently suggest it, or if you'd like to let her know—"

"No *thanks*," Luke said. He'd made the mistake of asking Laura if she was planning to "wear that"—a dress he deemed too revealing—to a fundraiser one night years before and she responded by taking the dress off—to his initial relief. She then replaced it with her bathrobe and house slippers and told him to go to the dinner by himself.

"Okay. I'll have Marnie talk to her, then."

"Fine. But Nate, please don't have anyone call my mother about *her* hair. I can protect you guys from Laura but not from her."

Nate broke into a laugh. Luke said, "I'm not kidding."

★

"Some people may think I fell in love with my husband because of his fashion sense. Others think that I fell in love with him because he's Mr. Serious."

"Cut! Laura, we'd like to try that again. Give us a sec while we tinker with that line."

Laura was sitting in the home of her in-laws, a place she'd been to a million times and usually felt incredibly happy and relaxed in, but not today. Now accompanying the couch, loveseat, and scores of family photos that filled the Cooper family room were various pieces of film and lighting equipment. In what Luke's consultants called "an effort to humanize the candidate" and to "strengthen his identity" with black voters, Laura Cooper was shooting her first advertisement for the campaign.

"Okay, Laura," the director called out. "Let's start again. This time let's try, 'Some people think I fell in love with my husband because he's such a dapper dresser.' Got it?"

"Got it," she replied, unenthusiastically. "How could I not get it?" Laura thought to herself. The director spoke to her in the belittling tone that colleagues used to speak to learning-disabled kids at the elementary school where Laura once taught.

"Everything okay, Laura?"

"Yep," she said without giving eye contact.

Laura had been sitting in the exact same spot for more than thirty minutes, for a campaign ad that would last no more than thirty seconds. She was in an outfit she would never wear in real life—a pink cardigan sweater set that Lucy Simonds had picked out for her, finished off with a chunky strand of pearls. Simonds called herself a "lifestyle enhancer." Simonds explained that she often worked with people like Laura, who were not public figures in their own right but had the good luck, or misfortune, depending on how you looked at it, to fall in love with and share a life with one.

Lucy showed Laura "before" and "after" photographs of some of her previous clients. One of them was a recent First Lady (or its equivalent) in England and another was an American model turned princess of a small European nation. The photos displayed extraordinary transformations. The English First Lady had gone from a gray-pantsuit-wearing barrister with short, no-nonsense hair to a dress-wearing, bangs-having embodiment of the perfect "mum" who looked ready to throw the perfect tea party at a moment's notice. The American model had gone from a jean-cutoffs-wearing surfer chick to a regal looking version of Princess Diana Barbie. Laura then realized why she had been asked to meet with Simonds. The campaign wanted her to undergo an *Extreme Makeover: Campaign Edition*. Laura had sworn that she would do whatever she could to help her husband fulfill his dream, but she wasn't expecting this.

"Wait a minute. She has a stray hair. Let's fix please," the director barked as they continued the shoot.

A stylist moved in to polish Laura's updo.

"Okay!" The director shouted. "And three, two, one . . ."

"Some people think I fell in love with my husband because he's such a dapper dresser. Others think that I fell in love with him because he's Mr. Serious. But the truth is, I fell in love with him because I always found his passion for giving back to our community endearing and downright irresistible, which is why when he told me he wanted to run for office, so that he could serve as many people as possible, well, I fell in love with him all over again."

"Nice, Laura! Nice," the director said, yet still managed to make it sound condescending. "Now let's do it one more time, a bit more upbeat, okay?"

Laura shot him a look that screamed, "If I had a gun right now my eyes would not be the only thing shooting at you."

Just then Luke's mother entered.

"I made cookies for everyone," she said.

Esther Cooper loved having guests. It reminded her of when her boys were kids and the Cooper house was the second home of much of the neighborhood.

Esther beamed as the room filled with one of her favorite sounds: "Mmmm." The only thing she loved more than baking and cooking for people was watching people enjoy what she baked or cooked for them.

"You didn't take a cookie," she said to the director.

"Oh, I'm fine. Thanks."

"You have an allergy or something?" she pressed.

"No. Just not really a chocolate chip fan."

"Well, it's not chocolate chip," Esther replied. "It's triple chocolate chip."

"And they're delicious," an intern said. The director glared at him.

"Thank you, sweetheart. Have another," Esther replied, passing the intern the serving tray. She then turned to the director and said, "Well, I'll leave one here for you in case you change your mind."

"That's really not necessary," he said.

"It's no problem at all."

"Thanks, but I'm all set."

"Well here you go, just in case." She pressed a cookie into his hand.

Laura tried to suppress the first laugh she'd had all day.

With the cookie in hand the director said, "Look, Mrs. Cooper, we have a lot of shooting to do." Esther looked like a balloon that had been deflated.

"Well, I'm sorry I interrupted," she said.

"I'm not. I could use a cookie, and no one makes them like you do," Laura said, then reached for the tray and gave her mother-in-law an affectionate squeeze on her arm. Esther smiled.

The director finally said, "Okay, fine. Let's take five. Let's call this one a wrap and let's move on to the next script with Laura again, and then we'll shoot with Mr. and Mrs. Cooper." In addition to filming ads featuring Laura that day, they were supposed to shoot as a family, but Luke's schedule changed at the last minute so today's session had been scaled back to include just Laura and Luke's parents, who, the consultants hoped, would help "humanize" him with different audiences—namely white ones.

"Can we get some makeup on Mrs. Cooper?" the director yelled. He then finally took a bite of the cookie. "This is pretty good," he said.

Esther Cooper, who barely reached the director's chest, looked up at him and said, "I'm already wearing makeup. Just what are you implying, young man?"

The room fell silent.

The director then began to stammer, "I . . . I . . . I'm not implying anything . . . ma'am."

Esther Cooper then reached for his hand, grabbed the half-eaten cookie and said, "You don't deserve this," before storming out of the room.

Just then Marnie, Laura's new aide, entered the room and said, "What's happening?"

Laura followed Esther Cooper into the kitchen.

"That man is a rude jackass!" she shouted when Laura walked in.

"Shhh, Esther, he might hear you," the always calm Mr. Cooper replied.

"Good! I hope he does. How dare he come barging into our home being so discourteous."

"Yes. Yes he is," Laura replied. "He is a rude, discourteous jackass. But he's here to help Luke. So why don't we try to bear it?"

"Are you taking his side?"

"Esther," Laura said. "Now you know I'm not taking his side, and certainly not over you, but it's not about him. It's about Luke. Remember?"

Just then Marnie poked her head in. "I'm sorry to bother you, but it's the governor on the line."

"Hey, hon," Laura said, taking the phone.

"What happened?" Luke asked. "What's the bodybag count over there? Is the poor director still alive?"

Laura wanted to laugh but she pretended Luke had said something else.

"Yeah, everything's okay. This commercial thing is a little tougher than I think we all thought. But your mom made cookies, so that made the day worthwhile for me." She winked at Esther, who smiled.

"Nice answer," Luke replied. His wife really had become a Cooper over the years, knowing just what to say and how to say it when it came to his mom. "Okay, let me talk to her and see what I can do."

Laura turned to Esther and said, "He says he wants to talk to his favorite girl." Laura passed Esther the phone as she grinned from ear to ear.

"Hi, son," she chirped.

For the next five minutes Esther Cooper told her side of the story, which consisted primarily of "that director is a rude, discourteous jackass," before finally going silent, then eventually erupting into laughter. It was the kind of laughter that only the men in her life, her husband or her boys, could bring. She then uttered the words, "Okay. I love you, son."

She passed the phone back to Laura.

"We should be all set now," Luke said to Laura. "But call me if there are any more problems. And for God's sake, tell that man to just eat the fucking cookie next time."

CHAPTER 9

Each member of Luke's "Dream Team" remembered distinctly when it dawned on him that one of his closest friends might become the most powerful person in the land—when the idea moved from abstract concept to crystal clear reality.

For Joe, the moment came when he heard from his father, Joe, Sr., out of the blue for the first time in months.

"Hey, kiddo!"

"Dad!" Joe squealed. Hearing from his father always brought out the little kid in Joe, specifically the ten-year-old boy he was when his father walked out on him and his mom for a ballerina, his third wife. His father was now on his fifth.

"How ya doin'?"

"I'm good, Dad. I'm good."

"What's your distance?"

"Six, sir."

"And what's your time?"

"Forty-six minutes, sir."

Over the years Joe had learned that he could rely on his father for very little except for two things: occasional money and over-the-top gifts to assuage his guilt over being such a neglectful father, and the fact that he would open every one of their conversations with a question about Joe's exercise regimen. He would usually ask him how many miles he was running each day and how many minutes his mile took him. Exercise, sports, and women were the only subjects he and Joe could bond over.

He could go months without hearing from his father, who had missed more of Joe's birthdays than he cared to count, but Joe also knew that he owed his career to his father and his name.

Having been suspended from college after an indecency incident involving a professor's wife (Joe told Luke he and the woman had been having an affair, and when the professor found out, the wife claimed Joe stalked her), Joe was adrift. His father's longtime sports agent then gave him an entry-level job at his firm. Joe never returned to college, something his father, who was drafted after graduating with honors from Oklahoma University and its legendary football program, never let him forget.

"I'm going to be up your way in a few weeks. Let's catch up, son."

"That'd be great!" Joe said. He couldn't remember the last time he had actually seen his father, although he knew it had been more than a year.

"We'll grab dinner at the Brig."

"The Brig?"

"Yeah. Perry's an old friend of mine."

The Brig was a restaurant that had opened only the week before but already had a three-month waiting list for reservations. And unbeknownst to Joe, his father was friends with the owner. "Of course he is," Joe thought to himself.

As a football legend, Joe's dad had a lot of friends, or at least a lot of people who claimed to be his friends. He had squandered much of his fortune over the years on countless women, kids, and bad investments, but thanks to his name, fame, and famous friends he still enjoyed the high life, or at least the illusion of it.

"That sounds great, Dad."

"How's your friend Luke doing?"

"Luke?" Now Joe was really impressed. His dad hardly ever remembered the names of people in Joe's life who mattered to him and was usually too self-absorbed to ask about those he did remember. He did take Joe, Luke, and a couple of other friends to a game in high school, so Joe presumed perhaps that's why he remembered Luke.

"He's good, Dad. He's actually governor now."

"He might even become president, I hear."

"Yeah! Can you believe it?"

"Well, listen, Bobby just told me that his dream job is to work in the White House someday."

"Bobby?"

"Pilar's son."

"Pilar?"

"My girlfriend."

Joe was confused. "What happened to Brenda?"

"Joe, we've been separated for months."

"Of course you have," Joe thought to himself.

"You'd love Pilar. She was a swimsuit model—was even in *Sports Illustrated* once. Now she teaches yoga. That's how we met. Her class changed my life. In more ways than one." His father laughed. "And you wouldn't believe how flexible she is."

Most adult children would feel uncomfortable hearing their parent talk like that but Joe was used to it. His father had given him an issue of *Playboy* for his twelfth birthday.

"Anyway," his dad continued, "her son Bobby's in college and would really love to work for your friend. Can you set something up?"

"Sure, Dad. Sure."

"That's my boy! So I'll have Bobby e-mail you his resume, okay?"

"Okay, Dad," Joe said solemnly.

"Terrific, son."

"Actually, you could just bring his res when we meet up for dinner when you're in town."

"Joe, you know better than anyone how unpredictable my schedule is, so better for him to e-mail you and I'll be sure to let you know when I can make it to town. Okay?"

"Yeah, Dad."

"Okay, kiddo. I gotta run."

★

Garin's moments of realization came in stages. The first was when he and Brooke were dining at one of their favorite restaurants. They could tell that a celebrity was there based on the limo waiting outside and how much the staff seemed to be buzzing back and forth to the private back room, so they decided to ask Tim, a young waiter who had served them before.

"It's not anyone *that* famous," Tim said, just after rattling off that night's dinner specials. "Just that tech guy. Bud Gates?"

"Buff Gates?"

"Yeah, that's him."

Garin looked at Brooke. Buff Gates wasn't just a tech guy, he was one of the richest men in the world.

"On a hot date?" Brooke asked, teasingly.

"No. He's here with some politician."

"Really? Mind if I ask which one?"

"A senator. In fact she's running for president."

"Beaman?" Garin asked.

"That's her."

Brooke and Garin shared a sideways glance.

"Think you'll vote for her?" Brooke asked.

"I don't know," Tim said. "I'm a Democrat but I don't really follow that closely."

"What do you think about that guy running against her?"

"The congressman?"

"No, the governor."

"I don't know too much about him. My mom likes him, though."

"Really?" Garin said. He and Brooke smiled.

"I don't know that she has a good reason. She just kind of likes him."

"Well we do too," Brooke said. She winked at Garin.

"If I were a betting man I'd put my money on him," Garin said. "Governor Cooper has a great record on education. The *Washington Post* said he's done more than any governor in the nation to lead the fight to make college more affordable in his state, and crime rates have gone down since he took office. And he's one of the most honest people on the planet."

"Geez. You really know your stuff. Do you work for him or something?"

Brooke laughed. "Kind of," she said.

Garin smiled. "Not exactly. But he is an old friend."

"Well, you're a good friend. You sold me," Tim said. "He's got my vote."

"Are you just saying that for a good tip, Tim? Because you know I always take care of you."

Tim laughed. "No, really. You're a good guy, Mr. Andrews. You should see the way some of the folks who come in here treat me, so if this Cooper guy is a friend of yours, he must be a good guy too."

"Thanks, Tim," Garin was touched.

It may have been a small victory for Luke's campaign, but every vote counted.

The moment he and Brooke returned home he did what any friend would do. He notified Luke's fundraiser, Mimi, that one of the richest men in the world was meeting with Luke's rival.

Garin's other moment of realization that his life would change—possibly forever—because of his friend, was not quite as pleasant.

He had been notified that he was to receive an award from The Guild, a networking group for black financial professionals. Days later he received a call from the group's executive director.

"Hi, Garin. It's Kathy from The Guild."

"Hey Kathy! I was just about to e-mail you about the event. I'm sure my company will buy a table but I was going to ask if—"

"Garin," she interrupted, "this is really difficult for me to say, but as much as we were looking forward to including you in this year's program we are unable to. I hope you will forgive me. I'm mortified that we are having to backtrack like this."

Garin was speechless.

"Garin, I'm so sorry," she continued.

"Okay," he said. "Are you eliminating the award?"

"Not exactly."

"Oh."

They sat in an awkward silence for a moment.

"So may I ask who I was bumped for?"

"Mara Burstein."

"Senator Burstein's daughter-in-law?"

Kathy sighed loudly into the receiver. "Garin. This is so uncomfortable for me. You know that Senator Burstein's brother is on the board of our organization and . . . well, between you and me, there's already been some tension because two of the younger board members are supporting your friend Luke for president, and I guess there was just some sensitivity from Mr. Burstein regarding sending a message with you receiving an award from our group and you being so publicly identified with the governor. I'm so sorry. I wish there was something more I could have done but my hands were kind of tied."

Garin was silent before saying, "I understand."

"And I realize this may be a hollow consolation, but we'd love to offer you and Brooke complimentary tickets to the gala, although frankly I'll understand if you don't wish to attend at all."

Garin was tempted to tell her and the organization where they could take their tickets and shove them. Instead he said, "No, we'll be there. We've been at every one for the last ten years. We're not going to ruin our streak."

"That's so great, Garin. Thanks for being such a good sport."

"I just have one request," Garin continued.

"Name it."

"I want to sit with Senator Burstein."

Kathy laughed. "You're great to have such a sense of humor about this."

"I'm not joking, Kathy. You guys might have been intimidated by him, but I'm not. So I look forward to seeing you and him at the gala and to seeing our names on the place settings at his table."

"Okay, Garin."

"Great. Have a nice day, Kathy."

★

Though Brock had become a wealthy man, there were moments when he was forced to come to grips with the fact that there were still some things that money could not buy. He was reminded of this when he received the letter from the Gershwin School—the city's most competitive kindergarten—notifying him that his twins had been wait-listed. Their only hope of enrolling in the school was if other students decided not to go, and since the Gershwin School was the first choice of every other family who applied, Brock knew that being wait-listed was the equivalent of being rejected. He was livid. Not just because his children were not admitted, but because the children of another attorney at his firm, Smith Gray, were. And to add insult to injury Smith wasn't even a partner. But his wife was the world famous supermodel Tatiana, and the children of A-list celebrities always had a leg up at Gershwin.

From Brock's vantage point the success of the supermodel spawn reinforced the idea that it wasn't his fault that the twins were wait-listed but further proof of Tami's shortcomings as a mother. After all, Brock and the other attorney were essentially equals. The other child had a leg up because her mother was a real model—the kind who had appeared in *Vogue*, not the kind who appeared in advertisements for Macy's and catalogs for monogrammed pajamas, like Tami had.

Though Brock's first instinct was to send a letter threatening legal action against the school's admissions director, he had been warned that parents dubbed "difficult" by an admissions officer at one school would find themselves essentially blacklisted by most others. The world of elite private schools was a small one, and he still had to get the twins into a quality junior high and high school. So instead he waited and seethed.

But just one month before he was to submit the retainer check to the twins' safety school, Briarley Academy, Brock ran into Smith at the firm. Brock had done his best to avoid him since learning his daughter had been admitted, while his boys had not. Though at the time Brock lied and said, "We're still waiting to hear."

When Brock spotted Smith in the hallway he actually tried to pretend he had not and then attempted to turn in another direction as though he had forgotten something, but Smith saw him and shouted, "Brock! Wait up. I was hoping I'd run into you."

"Smith . . . I didn't see you," Brock lied. "How have you been?"

"Great. Thanks for asking."

"Of course you're great," Brock thought to himself. "You're sleeping with one of the world's most beautiful women and your kids are going to the world's best school, you smug son of a bitch."

Instead he said, "I'm sorry, I'm just late for a thing but we should catch up soon."

"Well, I'll walk with you," Smith said and began following Brock . . . like a gnat, Brock thought.

"So listen. I hope I'm not talking out of turn, but Tatiana and I were at the school the other evening."

Brock stared at him blankly.

"You know, Gershwin?" Smith actually whispered the words, as though he was disclosing that Brock had leprosy, although in certain New York circles being rejected from the right kindergarten was the equivalent, Brock thought to himself.

"Yes, I'm familiar," Brock said, his irritation brimming just below the surface.

"Well, they had a welcome reception and tour for new parents, and the headmaster let it slip that they have three slots that just opened up on the wait-list."

At this Brock perked up. "Really?"

"Anyway, he asked Tatiana and I if we had any suggestions and of course we mentioned your boys." Brock couldn't believe it. He knew if given the chance he never would have done the same thing for Smith.

"That's very kind of you, Smith."

"Don't mention it. You'd do the same thing for me."

Brock blanched.

"Anyway, from what I've gathered it's between you and three other families. One of them is some distant relative of one of the European royals, but Tatiana tells me the mother has a problem, if you know what I mean." Smith tapped his nose to signal cocaine. "Schools like the Gershwin don't want to deal with that. The other family is a hedge funder. *Lots* of dough. Like, could buy the school ten times over kind of dough, and I think his oldest daughter, who's in college, went to Gershwin, so there's that. Daddy's on his third marriage. They got the application in late so I think the wait-listing is just a formality to try to show that the school enforces the rules equally no matter how rich you are, which we all know is just for show. I don't know much about the last family except that they're rich and Asian and well . . . I think they've already accepted a number of those. Then there's you."

Brock stood there calculating the odds in his head. Because he had twins, he had more work cut out for him. They essentially had to knock two families out of the running. One was doable, he thought. Two was tougher.

Smith could see the concern on his face.

"Tatiana and I talked you and your family up, of course, Brock, but I think it wouldn't hurt to look for an extra edge."

"No kidding?" Brock said.

Smith smiled and said, "Well, something interesting did come up last night."

"What's that?" Brock asked.

"It turns out that Kent, the chair of the board of trustees, has an older daughter who's a student at Dartmouth and she's looking to get into politics. She wants a job on a presidential campaign. I hope you don't mind, but I mentioned you're friends with the governor. Maybe he could write a letter of recommendation for your boys? Maybe even meet with Kent's daughter about working on his campaign?"

Brock was speechless. Now all of his nightmares were coming true—simultaneously. An attorney whom he considered intellectually inferior to him was lecturing him on how to solve a problem and the solution to said problem involved asking a friend for a favor—the kind of favor that would essentially be the equivalent of admitting that his friend was more accomplished, more successful and more powerful than he.

"Oh, I didn't realize how late it is. I got to hop," Smith said.

"Let me know how it goes with your friend. Tatiana and I need to have some allies at Gershwin." Smith winked and patted Brock on the arm.

Though Smith's cheeriness was genuine, Brock could barely suppress the urge to punch him. Why did some people's lives seem to go so perfectly? It just wasn't fair.

He never shared his dilemma with Tami, but forty-eight hours after his conversation with Smith, Brock e-mailed Luke asking for a letter of recommendation . . . for his 4-year-olds.

In typical Luke form, he responded with the sense of humor and grace that was a Luke hallmark.

"Letter of recommendation for a kindergarten? You're pulling my leg! Can I just write, 'They are officially two of the cutest kids on the planet and they have the best names too.'" This was a reference to the fact that one of the boys was named for his "Uncle Luke."

Brock sent the letter in days later. By the end of the month he was notified that his twins were the newest students at the Gershwin School.

CHAPTER 9

Thanks to Burstein and his cohorts' efforts to paint Luke's Jewish identity as a fraud, polling showed that a worrisome portion of Jewish voters in key states like Florida and New York were moving from the undecided category to the decidedly negative category when it came to Luke. This had Nate and the rest of Luke's advisors especially nervous.

"We have a small problem that's quickly turning into a bigger problem. It's the religion thing."

In typical Luke fashion, he cracked a calm smile. "Well, Nate, I thought you knew I was Jewish when you agreed to take this job."

Nate smiled. Luke had a way of bringing the temperature down in just about any situation. Luke then continued, "So lay it on me."

"Well, in a nutshell, we're not moving the needle as quickly as we need to. A lot of older Jewish voters in Florida simply don't look at you and see one of their own."

Nate paused to give Luke a moment to take this in. The least fun part of being a political consultant was breaking bad and potentially hurtful news to a candidate. Telling someone that the religion you practice and hold dear, and the fact that you happened to be adopted, are potentially rendering you unelectable certainly fit the bill.

"What, exactly, is it about me that doesn't scream Jewish?" Luke asked with a frown. "I couldn't look more Jewish if I tried."

Nate was speechless. Truly speechless. He had broken a lot of bad news to candidates over the years but this—the fact that as a big black guy you don't look like the people you consider *your* people—would be a first.

Luke then burst into a boisterous laugh.

"You should have seen your face," he said to Nate. "You clearly thought I was on a train to Crazy-ville."

Nate cracked a smile. He had to hand it to him. The man had a sense of humor. If ever there was a time for one, this was it.

"The upside is you're polling great with Jews under thirty. The downside is they don't really matter in a Florida primary. The ads with your mom are helping, but we're going to really need all hands on deck. We need to get your whole family—brothers, in-laws—on board. . . ."

Two of Luke's brothers valued their privacy and shared their father's disdain for politics. Luke had promised them that while the presidential campaign would certainly impact their lives, it would not turn them completely upside down—no stump speeches or kissing babies for them. Now here he was, essentially having to go back on his word. He knew his brothers would give him a kidney if he needed one, but somehow this felt like a tougher ask.

"And moving forward we might want to reconsider pulling a Kennedy."

"Pulling a Kennedy" was code for giving a speech on his religion.

It was something Nate had originally deemed unnecessary, and Luke agreed, but with the poll numbers in Florida dropping, other advisors on the campaign were lobbying for Luke to confront the issue head on.

Because President Beaman had won the New Hampshire primary convincingly years before and the Beaman family maintained a summer home there, it was considered Beaman turf. And since the governor of Iowa was a longtime Beaman family ally as well, Nate made the strategic choice to focus on states more demographically favorable to Luke: South Carolina, with a sizable black population, and then Florida, with a sizable Jewish one.

But the Beaman campaign was now hitting them with a coordinated assault on two fronts. In addition to questions and wild conspiracy theories permeating the blogosphere regarding Luke's family and his Jewish identity (including a rumor that he was paying the Cooper family to pretend to be his family for the sake of the primary), the Beaman campaign had lined up a number of high-profile black activists and clergy, old friends of President Beaman, to subtly undermine Luke's credibility in the black community. Reverend Otis James, a well known civil rights activist and contemporary of Martin Luther King, Jr., was chairing "Followers of Faith for Beaman." He had begun appearing in ads for the Beaman campaign in South Carolina, but more problematic, he had been making comments during personal appearances that were construed as direct digs at Luke's faith. "As the saying goes, not everyone who's our skinfolk is our kinfolk," James would quip, and "it's more important to have a brother or sister in Christ than a brother or sister in skin. Can I get an amen?"

The rumors were affecting the campaign's fundraising, and at the rate things were going, Nate was beginning to secretly worry that they might not make it to South Carolina.

"There's one more thing," Nate continued. "I think we need to consider getting Laura's father more involved."

Luke took a deep breath.

"I know how you feel about that," Nate said. "But I wouldn't be asking if this wasn't really important. We're in trouble, Luke, and having an older black man who knows you and can vouch for you the way a father can could make a difference."

Luke had a cordial but complicated relationship with his father-in-law. The two men had exactly three things in common: they were both black, they both had law degrees, and they both loved Laura.

Griswold "Wally" Long had always been perfectly polite to Luke, but he was polite in a way that made it perfectly clear he would be no nicer than absolutely necessary. While Laura's parents were a million times more welcoming than other members of her family, particularly the Veronica branch, they still had certain expectations for their daughter and those expectations did not include her marrying a man like Luke. Her father assumed Laura would marry a doctor or lawyer from a traditional black family like their own. Not one from a family like Luke's. Her father had loved Laura's high school boyfriend like a son, and she had often joked that her father had been more heartbroken than she was when they broke up. He also wasn't a huge fan of Luke's politics. Despite having actually worked on some civil rights cases as a young attorney, Laura's father was a lifelong registered Republican, describing his own politics as being from "The Party of Personal Responsibility."

"Let me think about it, okay? I mean we'll have to run this by Laura of course."

"Okay," Nate replied. "And I know you know this already, but I'm going to say it anyway. We don't have a lot of time."

"I know. I know," Luke replied.

★

The first major debate of the primary season, held at the University of New Hampshire, was a key opportunity for Luke to address the questions over his identity.

When the moderator began, "One of the questions submitted in advance by the audience is about religious faith," Luke could see Senator Beaman practically gloating with her eyes. She knew this was going to be a potential "gotcha" moment for Luke and, unfortunately, within minutes he proved her right.

"It's actually a two-part question. What role, if any, does your religious faith play in how you lead? And is worship service of any kind a regular part of your routine? Senator Beaman, we'll start with you."

"Well, religious faith plays a huge role in my life and always has for my family. Many of you will recall that I was baptized at the historic Abyssinian Baptist Church in Harlem because of my father's close friendship with Reverend Adam Clayton Powell, who was a great leader there. In addition to Reverend Powell, my father developed many close friendships with a host of religious leaders during his work on poverty issues throughout his career, including Bishop Leary and Rabbi Saperstein, who was at our home so much that I called him Uncle Saperstein. We have always been regular churchgoers. And my children are as well."

It was like a one-two punch. She solidified her family's closeness with the black community and also reminded anyone who was watching of her closeness with one of the country's most respected rabbis, in one fell swoop.

"Governor, same question."

"Well, first of all," Luke began, "one of the things I love about our country is its diversity and religious freedom. Those are some of America's greatest . . . greatest . . . ," he stumbled along, ". . . greatest . . . values." He knew he sounded nervous, and he was. "My faith colors everything that I do, and more than anything I believe in the power of prayer, and that certainly plays a key role in guiding me in any leadership role, and I pray regularly."

Luke had not attended synagogue regularly for years except on special occasions, and while Laura visited a small Episcopalian church off and on, he tended to spend most Sundays enjoying some rare alone time jogging, reading, or watching *Meet the Press*—that is, if he wasn't working.

He needed a home run in the debate and he knew that his answer had fallen flat. It might not have blatantly cost him voters, but it certainly hadn't won him any.

It was all downhill from there. He flubbed a question on the environment and confused the names of two different terrorists. He knew it had gone badly, but he wasn't quite sure just how badly until he checked his voice mail.

He had three messages: one each from two of his closest friends, Adam and Garin, and one from his mom. It wasn't what they said in the messages, but rather what they didn't.

"Hi, honey. It's Mom. I just called to say I love you and we're always proud of you and everything you're doing."

"Hey, it's me. Just calling . . . well. No reason really. Just miss my best friend." It was Adam. "I think what you're doing is awesome and, well, that's pretty much it. Can't wait to catch up."

The fact that his mother and Adam didn't dare mention the debate at all was bad enough and spoke volumes, but what Garin said was almost worse.

"Hey, man. It's me," Garin's typically enthusiastic baritone began. "Just calling to check in . . . let you know that we're raising lots of dough here in the Big Apple, which is good news. By the way, that tie you were rocking tonight was something serious. You're going to have to let me borrow that sometime."

Luke couldn't help but laugh. It was the equivalent of when someone sounded terrible on *American Idol*, and after Simon Cowell eviscerated the person, Paula Abdul use to chime in with a pity-induced "But you look great!"

Luke picked up the phone and dialed.

"Hello?" Garin answered.

"My tie? That's all you have to say? You liked my tie?"

Garin was quiet, until Luke began to laugh.

Garin relaxed before saying, "Well, I thought that was better than saying, 'You'll get 'em next time.'"

Luke laughed even harder.

They then proceeded to talk about everything under the sun besides politics for the next twenty minutes, mainly sports, and the jerks at Garin's office.

"Not only is he an ass, Coop, but that guy has the worst breath ever. It smells like . . ."

"Stop it, Garin, you're killing me!" Luke laughed.

". . . like cottage cheese mixed with . . ."

"Stop it!"

". . . mixed with socks or something, and yet his girlfriend looks like a cross between Tyra Banks circa 1999 and Christie Brinkley circa 1989. I want to be that rich where I can have breath like that and a woman like that."

"You are *terrible!*" Luke replied.

"And yet you're laughing, so you're just as bad as I am."

"Don't let the media find that out."

They continued laughing before Luke added, "It feels good to laugh about something today."

"Okay," Garin said. "I have a confession."

"Yeah? What's that?" Luke asked.

"I didn't really like your tie."

Luke laughed even louder.

"But I love you, man," Garin said. "But next time, *please* call me and I will loan you one of my ties if I have to." Garin was the sharpest dresser Luke knew. That was one of the reasons he ribbed Luke so much about his "GQ candidate" label. The two of them, and their circle, knew that if anyone was Mr. GQ in the group, it was Garin.

"I'll keep that in mind," Luke said.

"Okay, now can I bring up one quick thing about work?"

"Sure, as long as it's not about the debate," Luke said. "I'd like to forget it."

"Please—I don't want to mention anything that depressing ever again. No, seriously, Coop, a couple of friends of mine and Brooke's are hosting fundraisers for you in the city next week and just wanted to give you a little backstory on a few of them."

"Sure. Shoot."

★

After he and Garin wrapped up a few minutes later Luke checked his messages. Laura had called while he'd been on with Garin. Luke didn't bother listening to the message, which he presumed was just as depressing as all of the others.

Laura had missed the debate in person and on television because the boys' school had their annual science fair. Luke mentioned the debate to her in their last two conversations, but he got the sense she didn't fully grasp how important it really was. Although he had begun to wonder if perhaps she simply wanted to appear as though she didn't grasp how important it was because she wanted him to have some sense of tranquillity and normalcy when they spoke. When he would say, "Nate says this is really important," her standard reply would be, "Well, running for president is really important, but so is Halloween. Don't forget you have to help the boys pick out their costumes," or something else to help remind him of what was really important in their lives, and would be long after the campaign ended.

He picked up and dialed her cell, so as not to wake up the boys. He expected to get voice mail, but to his surprise she answered.

"Hello."

"Hey, stranger," he said.

"Guess who I'm talking to?" she asked.

Luke was confused but played along. "Who?"

"The father of the winner of the Fairfield Science Fair!"

"You're kidding!"

"No! Can you believe it?"

James had done an experiment designed to determine which food was most nutritionally healthy for pet gerbils. Luke worked with him on it while he was home, and would call regularly to check in on it on the nights that he wasn't.

"That is *awesome. Awesome.* That's so terrific."

"You should have seen him. He was like our very own little Einstein up there."

Sensing Luke's disappointment at not being there, Laura said, "You should have heard him. He told everyone, 'My daddy's at work running for president.' He's so proud of you."

"I can't believe I missed it," Luke said. "Did you get pictures?"

"You didn't miss it, Governor, because I got something better than pictures. I got one of the parents to help me figure out how to use that newfangled recorder we have, so we have video. It will be just like you were there . . . you know, as soon as someone shows me how to get the video off of the camera and into a format where I can actually send it to you."

Luke laughed. Technology was not one of Laura's strong suits, but she had many others.

"He's looking so much like a little version of you these days," she continued.

Luke smiled.

"So did he have to give a speech or something when he won?" he asked.

"Don't you want to wait for the video?"

"It's okay. You can give me a little teaser."

"Well. He was very grown-up and said, 'Thank you very much. I want to thank Mrs. Geltsin for being a very good teacher. I want to thank my mom and my brother too. And I want to thank my dad for helping me come up with the idea.'"

"Aww. That's great." Luke felt like his heart was about to explode.

"Then he ended with: 'He's not here because he's running for president, but I know he's going to be happy.'"

Luke began to tear up.

"Hon—are you there?"

"Yeah, I'm here."

"Oh, I'm sorry I've been yammering on. How was your day?"

"It was good," Luke said calmly, confidently. For the first time tonight he could say that and mean it.

"Anything exciting happen?"

Luke paused and said, "You know, not really."

"I find that hard to believe," Laura said giggling.

"Well, nothing as exciting as winning a science fair."

"Okay, well you and I both have got to get some sleep. I love you."

"I love you too, baby."

For the first time all day Luke was one hundred percent relaxed. He got ready for bed.

After settling in he skimmed the e-mails on his BlackBerry. He checked his new Gmail account—the one he had specifically established for those closest to him after launching his presidential bid. His other accounts had become so bombarded with requests from the media, and press releases from special-interest groups and from voters, that he wondered if the addresses were plastered on a bathroom wall somewhere. So he checked his Gmail when he needed a pick-me-up or just a lifeline to the world outside the bubble of the campaign.

His brother had forwarded him a funny cartoon, something the two of them shared a fondness for. They had been swapping cartoons for years, although since the launch of the campaign Luke had very much fallen behind in his cartoon sharing duties.

He then noticed a note from Theo that he had glossed over the previous day when he was in debate prep mode, and now he took a moment to take a look.

The subject line read "Celebration." The e-mail read, "hey Luke, I know you have absolutely nothing better to do with your time right now than party :) but just in case you missed it before I wanted to send you the invite to our joint celebration honoring pop on his 80th birthday and the 100th anniversary of the church. Official invite is attached. I know you probably can't make it with how busy your schedule is now but thought I'd send it along just in case. Keeping you in my prayers, Theo"

Luke opened the attachment on his berry. There was a photo of Reverend Edwards as a young man with his toddler son on his lap. The toddler was Theo.

Luke smiled.

He then tapped out a quick note on his BlackBerry to his scheduler.

> Subject: Detour next week
> Hey there—I have a personal engagement I need to attend to next Sunday down in Atlanta. Please cancel anything else on the schedule that conflicts. This is non-negotiable.

CHAPTER 11

As Luke's driver pulled up in front of the church, a host of memories came flooding back.

One in particular made him laugh every time he thought of it.

★

TWENTY-FIVE YEARS EARLIER

"Sister Mabeline, have you met my other son?" Aurelia Edwards, Theo's mother, also known as the First Lady of Mount Sage, began after Luke attended Sunday service one day.

"Other son? No, I don't think I have," Mabeline replied with a puzzled look on her face.

"This is Luke."

"How do you do?" Mabeline said, tentatively extending her hand the way Southern belles do. "I wasn't aware you and the reverend had any more boys," she said arching her brow.

"Oh, *we* don't," Mrs. Edwards replied. "Luke's daddy is Jewish."

Sister Mabeline's facial expression registered what could only be described as sheer horror. She stood there momentarily speechless before saying, dramatically, "Oh, dear. I think I need my fan. And my smelling salts." She began fanning herself with a monogrammed handkerchief. Luke thought she sounded like a character out of *Gone with the Wind*.

"Is everything alright, Sister?" Mrs. Edwards asked with a wide smile.

"I . . . I . . . I . . . you will excuse me. I have to . . . go. . . ." Sister Mabeline then turned and sauntered off.

Mrs. Edwards squeezed his hand and said, "Well, that should do it."

"Do what?" Luke asked.

"Get rid of her for a while. I wouldn't be surprised if she stopped speaking to me altogether now. She can't dare to be associated with a whiff of scandal with her old snobby behind."

"I don't understand," Luke continued.

"Well, since I told her you're my son, she now perceives me to be a woman of ill repute, so that means she and her horrible little friends just like her will finally stop trying to rope me into all of their gossip and mess."

"She really thinks I'm your son?"

"Well, you are," she said, squeezing his cheek lovingly.

A few minutes later, Reverend Edwards walked up. "Aurelia my dear. What on earth did you say to Sister Mabeline? She's told half the church we have an illegitimate son."

"Did she?" Mrs. Edwards asked innocently. She then winked at Luke.

★

The last time Luke had set foot in the church had been for Mrs. Edwards' funeral, five years before. He slipped into the main reception hall, with a single traveling campaign aide in tow, and introduced himself to a couple of unsuspecting parishioners. But within minutes a murmur began to ripple around the room, and soon the entire room burst into applause. The man once known as Theo's little buddy might become president of the United States, and he was here in their banquet hall. Reverend Edwards, whom Luke had hoped to surprise, turned around in his seat and broke into a wide smile. Luke stopped to shake a few hands and pose for photographs before a member of the church's staff came over to help guide him through the crowd. When Luke arrived at the Edwards family table, he was enveloped in a sea of hugs, the biggest of which came from the reverend himself.

"Mr. President," he said as he put both hands on Luke's face.

"Not yet, sir. Not yet, but maybe you can put in a word with the man upstairs?"

The reverend laughed.

"I'm already talking to him about you. Have been for years. Every day, son. Every day."

"Much appreciated, sir. Much appreciated. Where's Theo?"

"He's running around here somewhere. You know how busy the pastor always is at church events."

Just then Sister Bryson, who had been a member of Mount Sage since before Reverend Edwards became senior pastor, looked at the reverend and squealed, "Don't forget! You owe me a birthday dance." At ninety-three, she still did a mean electric slide. Luke remembered her from his days back in college. She always wore the biggest, boldest, most colorful hats he, or anyone else, had ever seen.

"I don't want to keep you from your dance partner," Luke said to the reverend.

"Don't mind her. You know she'll still be out there scooting around in another hour. Help me up. Let's go where we can talk."

Luke helped him to his feet and gave the reverend his arm. The reverend then leaned over to one of the church staffers and told him to let Theo know that he and Luke would be in the sanctuary for a bit. Two staffers then accompanied Luke and his aide in guiding them through the reverend's office, which was a shortcut to the sanctuary.

Luke always remembered Mount Sage sanctuary as one of the most gorgeous buildings he had ever seen, and all these years later it still was. Its stained-glass windows had been listed as among some of the most beautiful in the world. One of them featured an elaborate depiction of the crucifixion, only in this rendering Jesus was not white. He wasn't quite black either. But when this rendering was done, in the late 1800s, the fact that Jesus didn't have blue eyes and porcelain skin was enough to stir controversy. Since the death of the artist who had constructed the image, his works had become collector's items, making the Mount Sage, officially, a work of art.

Luke and Reverend Edwards settled into one of the middle pews.

"You know, sometimes I come and sit when no one else is here, and when I close my eyes I can still hear my father's voice saying, 'This is the day that the Lord had made. And it is a good day. A blessed day, a day to do His work, for we are all God's children. Now please join me in turning to Colossians 3:9: Lie not one to another, seeing that ye have put off the old man with his deeds; And have put on the new man, which is renewed in knowledge after the image of him that created him: Where there is neither Greek nor Jew, circumcision nor uncircumcision, Barbarian, Scythian, bond nor free: but Christ is all, and in all. . . .'

"I'm officially an old man now and I still miss my daddy."

"You're not an old man," Luke said reassuringly.

"You shouldn't lie in a church, boy."

Luke smiled.

They sat in silence for a moment before the reverend asked, "How are things?"

"Good. Laura and the boys are well. They're getting big. You'd hardly recognize them."

"I mean with the campaign."

"Fine. . . ." Luke said not so convincingly.

The reverend shot him a look, as if to remind him again about lying in a church.

"Could be better," Luke said.

The reverend began to nod in agreement. He then turned his head and gazed back toward the pulpit. "You know, a parishioner asked me if I could vote for someone who wasn't a true believer. I asked her what she meant by true believer. And she said, 'You know . . . someone who shares our faith and commitment to our God, reverend.' I said, 'Well, if that's the criteria we're using, I should say that I only see your husband at service about every other month, but I still head over to his shop every time I need my car fixed. You know why? Because he makes my engine purr like a kitten and that's all I'm looking for in a mechanic. Someone who can get the job done. I figure I can do enough praying for the both of us. . . . You get my meaning?'"

Luke smiled. "What'd she have to say about that?"

"Not much. She stormed out, but on her way I heard her call me some not-so-Christian names."

They both laughed.

"You know, Luke, I know we never talked much about the differences between our faith over the years. That's because at the end of the day I don't think the differences are profound enough to spend a lot of time carrying on about."

"Yes, sir," Luke replied.

"Plenty of Jewish brothers and sisters marched side by side with me and Reverend King—got locked up side by side with us, even prayed side by side with us during the struggle. Our prayers just tended to end a little different, that's all."

Luke smiled and nodded.

"I think," the reverend continued, "that you've got to find a way to convey that to people."

As a candidate Luke was used to receiving unsolicited advice from . . . everyone. It was part of the package. Even his barber once told him—unprompted—that he thought one of his campaign ads looked like it had "been shot by a film student at a community college," but Reverend Edwards was one of the few people whose advice he valued, on any subject.

"You can't run away from the issue. You've got to walk right up to it and stare it dead in the eye. 'Cause at the end of the day most people feel same as I do. If you're going in for surgery you'll take the guy that can cut in a straight line over the guy who cuts crooked but goes to the same church as you, any day of the week. You've got to find a way to convey that to people, plain and simple, in ways they understand. You're the guy that can cut straight. The others can't. You understand what I'm saying?"

"I do, sir."

"Good."

"And as far as the good Reverend James goes,"—referring to Otis James, one of Luke's most vocal clergy critics—the reverend paused as he searched for the words. "He is what we Christians refer to in official terms as . . . a horse's behind."

Luke let out a loud, boisterous laugh.

The reverend continued, "He wasn't always that way, but in his later years he . . . seems to have lost his way. But don't let him make you lose yours. Okay?"

"Yes, sir."

Comfortable that business was out of the way, the reverend steered the conversation in a different direction.

"How are your parents?"

"They're good. Planning a vacation to Europe soon, just the two of them."

"That's nice. I still regret that my Aurelia and I didn't do more traveling. I still miss her a great deal."

Luke put his hand on the reverend's back and the two men sat in silence for a few minutes.

Just then a voice said, "I was getting ready to have the choir sing 'Hail to the Chief,' but then we couldn't find the future president anywhere. Anybody seen him?"

It was Theo.

Luke got up and the two men embraced.

"How ya been, Coop?"

"Hangin' in there. Hangin' in there. But just barely," he said with a smile.

"Pop, Sister Bryson told me to tell you she's still waiting on her dance."

"I'll bet she is. I'll just bet she is," the reverend replied as Luke and Theo chuckled.

"Well, we could send Luke out there to dance with her. She'd call it a night in no time."

Luke was a terrible dancer, a fact that earned him endless ribbing from his friends, particularly those from his days at a historically black college.

Theo gave a mischievous grin as Luke said, "Now wait a minute. I've picked up a few moves in the last couple of years."

"Luke, you could go to a *Soul Train* boot camp for an entire summer and when you came back you still wouldn't be able to dance. They can't teach rhythm."

The three of them laughed—with Luke laughing the hardest. They chatted for a few more minutes before returning to the party.

CHAPTER 12

Early on Nate warned Luke about one of his former boss's favorite, and arguably most lethal, chess moves when it came to dealing with Democrats who had crossed him. Senator Sid Burstein would try to shut down the New York political money pipeline to prevent it from flowing into Luke's campaign. A substantial portion of the money that funded all Democratic campaigns nationwide came out of New York (something Luke had benefited from during his gubernatorial campaign) and it was virtually impossible to mount a presidential campaign without New York money. For this reason Nate instructed Mimi to be as aggressive as possible, as early as possible, in securing commitments from New York donors.

They also both agreed that it would be important to create a core group of new donors—ones who had not been particularly interested in politics per se, but may be interested in Luke. At the top of this group were wealthy black donors, particularly younger ones who may not yet be on Burstein or the rest of the Democratic National Committee's radar and younger celebrities. Nate knew from firsthand experience that most donors—even for the party that was supposed to be a bastion of diversity—were still overwhelmingly white. Yet he also knew that there were more potential donors out there like Luke's friends—black professionals who had too few opportunities to elect people like them: fellow educated, talented black professionals who were not their parents' age.

Upon joining the campaign, Mimi arranged a string of fundraisers in New York. In addition to securing commitments from a couple of her celebrity friends, she also secured commitments from some of her socialite contacts, among them Karen Hendricks, one of the most prominent African American art dealers in the nation. Karen was also an incredibly popular fixture on the New York social scene and sat on the boards of a number of charitable institutions, including the Soho Museum of Contemporary Art, where she served as chairman, and the Grio Dance Company whose board elected her president of its Young Leaders Committee. She and Mimi had been seated next to one another at a fundraising event for another museum and stayed in touch. The axis of the world of fundraising turned on one word: reciprocity. Mimi made contributions to both the Grio Dance Company and the Soho Museum shortly after she and Karen met the previous year, and Mimi had never asked her for anything in return until now. This is why Mimi was so good at what she did. She always waited for just the right moment and just the right cause to make the perfect ask. As a policy, she never, ever asked people for money to fund causes or events she didn't think they would genuinely be interested in or feel some sort of connection to.

Karen Hendrick's husband, Rob, was white and Jewish. She didn't know much about Luke before Mimi got in touch, but read the material Mimi sent over and googled to learn more. She found his personal story so compelling that she immediately e-mailed Mimi: "Rob and I don't have kids yet, but it is inspiring to see someone out there who comes from the kind of mixed cultural upbringing our children will someday, spreading such a positive message. How can I help?"

Karen and Rob hosted the fundraiser in their sprawling Tribeca loft. Karen, who had recently been called "one of the most stylish women in Manhattan" by New York Social Diary, dazzled in a vintage Halston gown. The crowd was the kind you were more likely to see at a gallery opening than at a political fundraiser. It was diverse, downtown, hip, and artistic. Most of the people there had never written a check for any sort of political cause. In fact Mimi presumed that more than a few had never even voted, but here they were supporting Luke Cooper for president, or at least giving him money, and all because the right person, Karen Hendricks, had asked them to.

On the way to the event Luke asked Mimi for the traditional pre-fundraiser briefing, which consisted of pertinent background information on the host and guests. Luke was by far more disciplined than most candidates at reading the briefing books his staff dutifully supplied to him daily, but it was always important to dig deeper when it came to donors. And he had learned over the years that there were always one or two helpful details that never made it into the briefing book that could make the difference between someone being a one-time donor/supporter or a lifetime donor/supporter.

"So, what do I need to know?" Luke said in the car on the way there.

"Well first off, lose the tie," Mimi replied without looking up from her BlackBerry.

Luke chuckled. Mimi didn't crack a smile.

"I wasn't kidding. I'll hold it for you until the event is over," she said, holding her hand out to him. "If you walk in there dressed like an accountant, we'll be lucky if the crowd lasts through the second round of drinks."

Luke began removing his tie.

"Also," she continued, "I didn't get a copy of your remarks but make sure they are remarks and not a speech."

"What's the difference?"

"Remarks mean no more than ten minutes."

"Mimi, all due respect—I think if people pay a couple of hundred dollars they are expecting a little more than a few soundbites and a round of drinks."

"You're right. They're hoping to network their asses off with the people in the room who are more powerful or socially connected than they are, and the less you do to impede their ability to do that, the more positive the response to you will be."

Mimi said this all without so much as glancing up from her BlackBerry.

"Tie," Mimi said. Luke placed it in her hand.

"Don't lose it," Luke warned.

"Please, I'd be doing you a favor," Mimi replied. "Where did you get this from anyway?" She held it up as if she were examining a urine sample.

"It was a gift from my kids."

"Oh," Mimi said, expressionless. She stuffed the tie into her $20,000 Hermès Birkin bag, one of three she owned, then said, "Okay. So you know to thank Karen and Rob, the hosts. You should also make a point to mention what a fan of Rothko you are."

"Rothko?"

"The painter."

"I'm aware of who Rothko is, Mimi."

"Okay. So what's the question?"

"Why am I saying I'm a fan of his, when I'm not?"

"Because Karen is. And the *New York Times* Style section just did a glowing piece about her efforts to secure a landmark exhibition of his work for the Soho Museum. So it's important for you to congratulate her and mention how you can't wait to see the exhibit yourself. I took the liberty of printing a summary of the exhibit for you to review." Mimi then passed Luke the summary. He barely looked at it before passing it back to her.

When they entered the event Luke immediately noticed two things. Number one, that Mimi had been one hundred percent right about the tie. The room looked like it had been staged by a casting agent working for Calvin Klein. There was not a single traditional business suit in the room—save for the one being worn by an androgynous female model-type.

Number two, Mimi was right about Rothko. Not two minutes after arriving, Mimi recognized a redheaded woman by the door and said, "Eleanor!"

"Mimi! How lovely to see you."

The two women greeted each other with air kisses.

"I want you to meet Governor Luke Cooper, the guest of honor," Mimi said.

"It's a pleasure," Eleanor said, extending her hand to Luke.

"Pleasure's all mine," Luke replied.

"So glad you could make our little soiree," Mimi added.

"I wouldn't miss it. My mom is one of the founders of the Soho Museum," Eleanor continued.

"Oh, wonderful," Luke said.

"Are you an art aficionado, Governor?" Eleanor continued.

"Well, I'm no expert but I certainly appreciate art."

"Who are some of your favorites?"

"Well, I'm a big fan of Archibald Motley."

"Yes, some wonderful artists came out of the Harlem Renaissance, although I'm more of an expressionist and contemporary fan myself."

"Yes, some very innovative talent came out of those periods," Luke said. It sounded like a safe, meaningless thing to say to keep the conversation going.

"Indeed," Eleanor replied. "Who do you think is the most significant?"

"Significant . . . ?" Luke replied.

"Talent to come out of those periods?" Eleanor asked Luke.

"Well," Luke began, trying to stall. He then felt Mimi pinch his arm.

"Well, I think Rothko is fascinating," he said.

"Oh," Eleanor said, a big smile spreading across her face. "You know we have a new Rothko exhibit at the museum."

"Really?" Luke and Mimi said in unison, feigning surprise.

"How long will it be there?" Mimi added.

"It just opened so you have plenty of time to see it. You know, we should arrange a private tour for the governor and his family next time they're in town," Eleanor said excitedly.

"That would be delightful," Luke replied.

"Thanks so much, Eleanor. I'll be sure to follow up and put you all in touch. It was great seeing you, as always. By the way, you look beautiful," Mimi said. She then hooked her arm through Luke's and turned to guide him across the room.

As they walked away she leaned in and whispered in his ear, "Nicely done. You may have raised more money in that conversation than you will the rest of the night. Rumor has it her dad is a billionaire."

★

Garin was discovering that being the friend of a presidential candidate was different from being the friend of a Midwestern governor. In a city like New York, where seeing an A-list celebrity at a restaurant is not out of the norm, and befriending a B- or C-list celebrity, if you are wealthy, is practically a given, being friends with the most powerful person in a so-called fly-over state was considered about as impressive as being friends with the most successful actress in one. In other words, it wasn't that impressive. But being friends with someone in the running to become the most powerful person in the country—even if it was a long shot—was considered impressive, as Garin was learning based on the more enthusiastic reactions his fundraising efforts were receiving this time around compared to Luke's gubernatorial run.

The other difference, Garin learned, was that being friends with a governor was considerably less expensive than being friends with a presidential candidate. As Garin combed through his rolodex to call yet another so-called "friend" from law school he hadn't spoken to in years, to casually ask him for $1,000 on behalf of "their old friend Luke," it dawned on him that one of the biggest differences between being a politician and, say, an accountant or a lawyer, is that accountants and lawyers may call their friends and ask them to refer business, but they don't ask them for money outright to help them get a job in the first place, which is essentially what a campaign contribution is: money to subsidize one very long job interview.

The first time Garin called someone he wasn't really friends with and made a "friendly" request for $1,000 on behalf of their "old friend," it was uncomfortable. But by his fifth call it was old hat. He'd even gotten it down to a formula for efficiency that ensured that he could wrap the call up in under eight minutes flat.

The conversation usually went like this:

"Tom? Hey, man. It's Garin, Garin Andrews."

"Garin?! Long time. Talk about a blast from the past. How ya been?"

"Good. Good. You?"

"Can't complain. Can't complain."

(After an embarrassing exchange in which Garin asked one potential donor, "How's the missus?"—since he couldn't remember her name—and he was met with the reply, "I'm assuming she's great, since she and my ex-best friend are now spending half of my money on a yacht somewhere, thanks to our divorce," Garin learned to modify his small talk to the more generic, "How's the family?")

"How's the family?"

"Good! Good. Jake is graduating this year. Can you believe it?"

"No! You're kidding. We're getting old," Garin said, even though he didn't remember that Tom had a son or that his name was Jake.

"How about you?"

"My little Allie is getting so big. I cannot believe how fast she's growing."

"It goes by so fast, Garin. Take it all in, because before you know it she'll be the one graduating."

"Never!" Garin replied dramatically. "I plan on putting her in a tower like that fairy tale with the princess—what's the one with the hair?"

"Rapunzel?"

"Yeah! I'm going to keep her a little princess forever, locked up away from boys."

"Good luck with that! So what's up?"

"Well, you remember Luke?"

"Coooop!! How could I forget? You were like two peas in a pod back in law school."

"That's right." Garin laughed. "Well, you may have heard he's running for office."

"I saw he'd run for—what was it?—Congress back in Minnesota or something?"

"Governor of Michigan."

"Right, right."

"Well, my wife and I are actually having a party for him next time he's in town, for his presidential run."

There was usually a little hesitation at this point, when it becomes clear to the other person on the line that this is a call for money, not for catching up on old times.

"Gar—you know I love you guys, but I'm not that into politics."

"I hear you, man. I'm not either, but you know Coop's a good guy, and I think we could do a lot worse than having someone like him at the helm. Just think, he could make history as the first ever honest guy in the White House."

Tom (or whoever) would then usually laugh before asking, "How much you looking for?"

"Tickets are between five hundred and a thousand dollars." There was usually another pause, at which point Garin would close the deal by saying, "But listen, I'd really love for you to meet my wife and daughter and just to catch up with Coop and the gang, so why don't you just plan to come as my guest, and if you like what you hear from Coop, write a check. No pressure. How's that sound?"

"What the hell. It'd be great to see you guys, so count me in."

As Garin had learned from previous events, no self-respecting, socially conscious New Yorker wanted to be seen as taking a handout, so it was practically a given that once at the event, the "guest" in question would in fact write a check for Luke's campaign, but without feeling as though Garin had twisted his arm to do so.

And this became the way Garin spent every free moment he had in the weeks and months after his friend decided to run for president.

Garin certainly did his fair share to help Luke in his previous campaigns, but there was a sense of urgency with this one that did not exist in the others. For starters, this campaign required significantly more money. When Luke's advisors told him how much money they needed to raise, and how quickly, just to keep Luke in the race—not even to win it—Garin practically fell out of his chair. He felt as though he had gone from funding a friend's student film the year before to being asked to help fund a blockbuster action film this year—only in less time and with no guarantee the film would ever make it to theaters. But Luke was his best friend. Garin also considered him a great human being, and knew that he would be a great leader, so Garin was committed to doing his best not to let him down.

One month, Garin enlisted his dentist, his personal attorney, his accountant, a co-worker, and Brooke's gynecologist, Dr. Colvin, to all host fundraisers for Luke. Brooke was mortified when she found out he'd asked her doctor.

"You asked my doctor for money? That's so tacky!"

"What's tacky about it?"

"Well, it's just embarrassing."

"Let me get this straight," Garin said to her. "You're embarrassed that I asked the man to host a fundraiser for our friend, but you're not embarrassed to let him see you naked once a year?"

"That's different!" Brooke protested.

Although Garin sensed she was actually just irritated that he beat her to the punch by thinking to ask Dr. Colvin first, after running into him at a reception without Brooke.

In addition to feeling pressured, out of loyalty to his old friend, to raise as much money as humanly possible, Garin felt pressured by Luke's rottweiler-esque fundraising director, Mimi.

While some found Mimi's temperament taxing, Garin actually liked her, though he could see why others didn't. She had a way of asking for things that made it clear she wasn't really asking, but was actually demanding in a way that bordered on threatening. She once copied Garin on an e-mail to another member of the campaign's finance committee that read, "I would really appreciate it if we could get this taken care of by close of business today because I would hate to have to inform Luke that I can't continue doing my job to help him get elected because someone on our team let us down."

But she was good at her job and Garin told Luke so, which rankled Brock, who, Garin wasn't surprised to hear, couldn't stand her. Brock began referring to her as "that blond bimbo" following a falling out over a fundraising event the two were supposed to be working on together but which went awry.

Brock had been determined to redeem himself after his first fundraising debacle, so he eagerly volunteered to host another event for Luke. But this time the campaign insisted on forming a host committee to ensure that sole responsibility for securing donors was not left to him. They decided to put together an event comprised of prominent New York attorneys, informally known as Lawyers for Luke.

Jonathan Saxby, general counsel for Harlem Alliance Media Group, publisher of a variety of popular black magazines, agreed to sign on, as did Sheila Inglewood, partner at Mather and Inglewood, a boutique law firm specializing in securities litigation. Mimi also contacted Sasha Ellis, a social acquaintance of hers whose husband was a partner at a major law firm.

Mimi was delighted to discover that Sasha already knew Luke. She had been an attorney before becoming a stay-at-home mom and Luke and her husband, Roderick, had attended law school together. At Mimi's suggestion Luke called Roderick directly and asked him for his support. Roderick and his wife had actually contributed to both Democrats and Republicans over the years—including Senator Sid Burstein—but this campaign Luke had gotten to him first, and the personal connection and personal touch of a phone call made a difference. Roderick agreed to cohost the event.

There was just one problem, Mimi soon discovered. Brock hated Roderick. In fact, Roderick had been the lawyer in question who inspired such ire in Brock that he infamously purchased an apartment just so Roderick wouldn't get it, an act of pettiness Brock often dismissed, to friends who were aware of it, as "a mere coincidence." Mimi learned of the tension after her assistant sent over a draft copy of the invitation to Brock for review.

Though he never fully admitted the real reason to anyone, Brock hated Roderick simply for being Roderick. Roderick was from an upper-class black family that had been that way for generations. His grandparents were all college graduates and his father had been a judge. Roderick's family—all of whom were extremely light-skinned—had ties to Sag Harbor, which had long been the summering enclave of choice for well-to-do black New Yorkers, going back half a century. In essence, he was the polar opposite of Brock.

But to anyone who asked, Brock claimed he simply didn't trust him. Brock swore that Roderick once cheated off of him in law school, but Luke had always suspected that Brock's animosity really stemmed from the time Roderick invited a group of classmates to his family's home in the Hamptons. A group of classmates that did not include Brock.

Luke presumed that was all water under the bridge, however, so he didn't think twice about asking for Roderick's involvement in his fundraiser, particularly considering how helpful Roddy could be. Luke presumed wrong.

Moments after e-mailing a copy of the draft invite over to Brock, Mimi received a call from Brock's assistant, Peggy. "Ms. Van der Wohl, I have Mr. Simpson on the line."

"Sure, Peggy, put him through."

"What is Roderick Ellis doing on this invitation?" Brock demanded.

Mimi was caught off guard. "Hi, Brock . . . ummm, Mr. Ellis has agreed to serve as a cohost."

"Like hell he is."

"I'm sorry . . . I don't understand. What exactly is the problem?"

"No one cleared this with me."

"Well, we all agreed that there would be multiple cohosts for this event so that we can maximize . . ."

"No one cleared this with me."

"Well, Brock . . ." She searched for the right words.

"No one cleared this with me," he repeated.

"Brock . . ." She struggled to get a word in as he kept repeating "No one cleared this with me."

"I mean this as diplomatically as possible, but I don't work for you. No one here does, so I don't need to clear anything with you . . ."

"This is *my* event!"

Mimi made a point not to raise her voice. "Actually, Brock, it's Luke's event. Not yours and not mine, Luke's."

"It is *my* event. In *my* home and—"

"So we'll move it to a different home if there's a problem, which clearly you seem to have, although I'm still not clear on what it is. Do you have some sort of problem with the Ellises that I should know about?"

"My problem is that you made a decision about an event I'm supposed to be hosting and I was not consulted!" Brock snapped.

"Well, I wasn't aware that you needed to be consulted on every decision. If you'd like I'm happy to send over a list of the different types of napkins and nametags that we're considering using at the event. That way you won't feel left out of any decision. How's that sound?"

Mimi's deceased husband used to refer to her as Princess Smart-ass. Occasionally she lived up to her nickname at inopportune times, and this conversation was one of them. But she caught herself—remembering Luke was an important client and that Brock, pain in the ass or not, was a longtime friend of his, so she needed to try to find a resolution.

"Look, Brock," she continued, "this is not something that can't be resolved. We are all working towards the same goal, which is to help Luke as much as possible."

"I'm aware of what the goal is! I was raising money for Luke long before you showed up," he yelled.

"Great, so let's all agree to do what we can to help him keep doing that. Why don't we just plan for a separate event down the road so you and Roderick won't have to do this one together."

There was silence before Brock said, "Fine."

Crisis averted, Mimi thought.

"Okay, great. I'll be back in touch about dates that work for you and your wife later."

"Dates?"

"Yes. Dates for you and Tami to host another event down the road."

"Wait a minute—wait just a goddamn minute," he screeched. "I'm not rescheduling anything. He can cohost another event down the road!"

"You cannot seriously expect me to disinvite the man all because you don't like him. That's absurd."

"This is my event!"

"As I said before, it's not *your* event. It's Luke's. And if you're really Luke's friend then you should be willing to do what's best for him. I'm sure you may find this hard to believe, but not everything is about you."

Brock erupted. "Do you know who you're talking to?"

Mimi calmly replied, "In a nanosecond I'll be talking to no one," and hung up.

Mimi usually enjoyed her job. It was essentially party planning, only instead of BYOB (bring your own beer) the policy was BYOC (bring your own checks), but every now and then run-ins with rich "eccentrics" like Brock reminded her how much she missed the days of being a trophy wife of leisure. One of her favorite sayings was "A difficult person with no money is just plain crazy, while the same person with money is just eccentric." You take a temperamental person and give him or her seven figures or more and it was often a recipe for crazy, as Mimi knew all too well from her stepchildren. The Brocks of the world were par for the course in the fundraising game. You either learned to deal with them or you found a new profession.

Mimi removed Brock's name from the invite and called Roderick Ellis's assistant to see if it would be possible to move the event to the Ellis home instead

The day after the Brock blowup she received a call from Nate.

"Hey, Mimi."

"Heeeeeyyy, Nate," she said flirtatiously.

"How are things?"

"Better than expected. The next couple of events we have set up are really moving."

"Not surprised. You're always my lucky charm when it comes to making the money rain."

"Awww. Flattery will get you everywhere, as you well know."

"Listen, I'm calling about some wacky e-mail Luke forwarded my way from someone named Brock Simpson, a donor . . ."

"Ugh . . . are you kidding me?"

"No, I'm afraid not," Nate said laughing. He had dealt with his share of demanding, difficult and downright crazy donors over the years.

"He's not a real donor. He's one of Luke's friends and he's crazy with a capital C."

"A donor who's crazy? No!" Nate said sarcastically.

Mimi laughed. "He started screaming at me because I refused to bump another donor from the event just because he didn't like him."

"Oh boy."

"What did his e-mail say, anyway?"

"I'll spare you the gory details, but let's just say that he felt that perhaps your services were no longer needed."

"He tried to get me fired?!"

"Don't worry about it. . . . don't worry about it. . . . Luke gets it. He knew that there were two sides to this story, which is why I'm the one calling you instead of him. I'll handle it. You just keep doing what you're doing."

"But I told Brock we'd do another event with him down the road . . ."

"Ummm . . . why don't we jump off that road when we get there, sound good?"

"Sounds good."

"You're doing a great job, Mimi."

"Thanks, hon."

Nate ran interference, something any experienced political operative becomes accustomed to doing, and placed a brief call to Brock "on behalf of the campaign" to say that they "very much valued Brock as a key supporter" and that "Mimi had been spoken with about treating supporters of his caliber with the necessary respect."

In the course of a five-minute phone call, Nate, who was known for being able to recognize at least one redeeming quality in every person he interacted with, decided that Brock Simpson was by far one of the most obnoxious human beings he had ever encountered. After Brock finished ranting about Mimi, and Nate was confident that the situation had been sufficiently resolved, Nate ordered a bottle of champagne and had it delivered to Mimi with a note reading "Keep up the great work."

The Lawyers for Luke event, sans Brock Simpson, ended up raising a healthy $100,000 for the Cooper campaign.

And the event later hosted by Brock Simpson, which he insisted Mimi not be involved in, raised $25,000, a disappointing outcome that Brock, ironically, then blamed her for.

★

Because Mimi actually liked Garin and, more important, because he had actually raised a sizable amount of money for her boss, she made the kind of exception she rarely did, agreeing, at Garin's request, to be personally involved in a low-dollar fundraiser hosted by two young friends of his. Garin told Mimi that these friends were actually like family to him, so her involvement in ensuring the event's success meant a lot.

Brooke and Garin had both been rising stars at their respective companies when they made a decision that would change the course of their lives. They each decided to become mentors. It was while volunteering for the Manhattan chapter of Big Brothers and Big Sisters years before that the two of them first crossed paths. It turned out they were mentoring a brother and sister, Sheryl and Jason Matthews, who lived in the Stansbury projects in Harlem. They met one Saturday afternoon when they arrived simultaneously to see the two siblings. The chemistry between them was so apparent that Sheryl, Jason, and their mother set about playing matchmaker, and within two months after meeting Brooke and Garin were dating. The funniest part was they were oblivious to the fact that they had been set up, and tried to keep their coupling a secret from the Matthews family until they had been dating for a full year. Mrs. Matthews finally let the cat out of the bag that the family had known all along they were a couple and had maneuvered to make them one.

Now, thirteen years later, Sheryl and Jason were both young, successful professionals in their own right—Jason was an associate at a major law firm while Sheryl worked in marketing for Ralph Lauren. They both lived in Harlem and offered to host a Young Professionals for Cooper fundraiser there. Mimi was somewhat skeptical when Garin first got in touch with the offer. She was under a tight deadline to raise big money fast, and her experience was that often the amount raised at so-called low-dollar events was not worth the time and effort involved in mounting them. But Garin was a close friend of the candidate's and he was nice, so she wanted to be accommodating.

Mimi spoke with Sheryl, the primary contact for the event, who said she was confident they could get at least one hundred people there. Mimi thought this sounded like a stretch but figured she would indulge her. They set the minimum ticket price at $150 and decided they would set a VIP level at $250, which would include a private cocktail reception with Luke beforehand, which Mimi was convinced no twentysomething, particularly in Harlem, would be willing to pay. Within forty-eight hours all one hundred tickets for $150 were gone. They decided to move the event to a larger venue that could accommodate twice as many people and, to Mimi's amazement, within twenty-four hours they had sold another eighty tickets.

Mimi was stunned. Unbeknownst to her, in addition to the adoring coverage Luke received in mainstream outlets he had become somewhat of a phenomenon in the black blogosphere, something she (along with most white people and those over thirty-five) knew absolutely nothing about. His Morehouse pedigree and election as one of only a handful of black governors in the nation's history, not to mention his good looks, had made him a popular fixture on black blogs such as Bossip and Ybf which, long before he announced his campaign for president, ran items featuring Luke and his photogenic family under headlines like "Could this be our next president?" It was safe to say that Luke Cooper was one of the only candidates for president who had enjoyed coverage in both *Hip Hop Weekly* and the *Wall Street Journal* in the same month. Mimi also underestimated the importance of Luke's Morehouse ties. Jason had himself attended Morehouse, and though he had met Luke only once, Luke had written him a letter of recommendation. The Morehouse connection ran deep and strong. Mimi later discovered that more than fifty of the twentysomething donors who had RSVP'd so far were alums of Morehouse or its sister college, Spelman.

Based on the response, Mimi worked with Sheryl to create a fully fleshed out host committee comprised of others she believed could move as many tickets as she and her brother already had. Mimi liked to think of herself as both younger and hipper than the average fortysomething, but in the course of planning the Young Professionals event she came to realize that in some ways she was a bit out of date in her thinking.

When Mimi agreed to meet with Sheryl and the other host committee members, and discovered that the meeting would be taking place at Sheryl's apartment in Harlem, at first she tried to diplomatically suggest that the evening meeting be turned into a conference call instead. Mimi considered the fact that she had interracially dated a few times a mark of her significant open-mindedness, although it was worth noting that the black men she dated really hadn't been all that different from the white guys she dated.

All of them were also rich.

But Mimi had never ventured above 93rd Street. It wasn't a conscious choice. It just wasn't something women like her did. Whether she admitted it or not, she harbored just as many stereotypes about Harlem as the average close-minded tourist.

So when she arrived at Sheryl's address she was stunned to see a luxury high-rise before her, and even more stunned to be greeted by a doorman in full uniform (which immediately put her at ease). She entered Sheryl's apartment, which featured gleaming hardwood floors and all brand-new amenities. One by one, the other host committee members arrived, all young, all stylish, all attractive, all black. And all but one was a Harlemite. She noticed that each of the young women there had something in common that caught her eye. Though all dressed differently to reflect their various professions, which ranged from banking to fashion, they each sported a fabulous handbag. This was not the image of Harlem Mimi had pictured all of these years, and if these young people were indicative of the crowd for the fundraiser—and the host committee always was—then this one was going to be a success, a fashionable, buzz-building success.

The night of the event, Mimi watched the way Luke interacted with the people in the room. She could see how he had gone from "long shot" to having a real shot so quickly. She had seen so many candidates treat donors—particularly ones who were not at the top of the food chain—as nuisances. Often they were barely able to hide their contempt for the fact that someone who was "only giving a couple of hundred dollars" could have the temerity to expect their time, attention, and respect. But Luke was different.

Not only did he make a point to say hello to every person in the VIP reception, he actually insisted on shaking as many hands as possible at the general reception. But it was what he did after the reception that showed Mimi the kind of person he really was.

The afternoon of the reception, Sheryl and Jason's mother was rushed to the hospital with chest pains. She remained under observation, and while she insisted that at least one of them attend the event they had worked so hard on, one of them, Sheryl, stayed by her bedside.

Luke was supposed to meet another donor—a high-dollar one—for a drink at 9, and they were already going to be late for the meeting, but Luke insisted, that he, with Garin, Brooke, and Jason Matthews in tow, head to the hospital first.

It was after visiting hours when they arrived, but Luke sweet-talked a nurse—who, lucky for him, was originally from Michigan and was somewhat star struck by meeting the state's governor.

She checked first to make sure that Mrs. Matthews was still awake and up for seeing another guest.

Mrs. Matthews and Sheryl assumed she meant Jason.

Instead, Luke popped his head in. "Hi there."

Mrs. Matthews didn't have her glasses on, and sat there squinting before her daughter said, "Oh my gosh. Mom—it's the governor."

To which Mrs. Matthews replied, "I'm not dressed to meet a governor."

"You look beautiful," Luke replied.

"You must need glasses as badly as I do," she cracked.

Luke giggled before replying, "Now, I would have brought you some cake from our party, but I was told I wasn't allowed to. Doctor's orders."

Mrs. Matthews laughed, then added, "I wish you had. The food here sucks."

"Mom!" Sheryl replied.

"Well, when you're well, you'll have to let me take you and your lovely family out to dinner."

"That's a deal," Mrs. Matthews said beaming.

"Your kids certainly did a lot to help me try to get where I'm going. I can't thank you and your brother enough, Sheryl—really. Tonight was outstanding."

Now Sheryl was beaming too, as was her brother, who had joined them in the room.

"Mrs. Matthews, you've raised such wonderful kids. You must be so proud."

"I am," she said, smiling from ear to ear, before adding, "maybe they can work for you in the White House."

"Mom!" Sheryl and Jason said in unison.

Jason then whispered "sorry" in Luke's ear.

"What are you two embarrassed for?" Luke replied. "You're both smart and accomplished. I'd be lucky to have you. Maybe I should put your mom in charge of hiring for my campaign. She's clearly got great instincts." Luke grinned, patted Jason on the shoulder, then looked at Mrs. Matthews and said, "Okay, you need your rest so I'm going to go."

"Thanks so much again, guys. And you get well and take care of yourself."

They were late for the meeting with the donor—something that normally would have made Mimi irate, but not this time.

And the event that Mimi initially presumed might be a little waste of time ended up being a big success, raising almost $50,000. But just as important as the money raised that evening was the idea it spawned. Mimi asked Sheryl about the possibility of putting together a string of similar "Young Professional Fundraisers" throughout the nation.

CHAPTER 13

Luke Cooper's friends weren't the only ones adjusting to a new life of permanently passing the collection plate for him.

Next to giving campaign speeches, campaign fundraising was one of Laura Cooper's least favorite activities, and yet it wasn't the only adjustment for her. Adjusting to a life of being perpetually "handled" by a host of consultants, experts, and aides there to make sure that whenever a camera was rolling on her (and even when one was not), she said the right thing at the right time, smiled at the right time, even appeared sad or empathetic at the right time, was a challenge.

As First Lady of Michigan, Laura was known for being friendly and protective of her staff, which consisted of an executive assistant, an event scheduler, and a revolving host of interns, all of whom adored her. But as candidate for First Lady of the United States she now had a new host of aides and advisors, many of whom seemed to be under the impression that she worked for them, not the other way around. But Laura wanted Luke to win, and these so-called experts were supposed to be the ones who could help him accomplish his goal, so she indulged them.

Most of the time. But there were moments when she did subtly, and sometimes not so subtly, remind them who worked for whom.

The campaign staff considered fundraisers a safe and easy way to begin easing Laura and her mother-in-law onto the campaign trail as the faces of "Women for Cooper." Fundraisers were controlled environments that were off the record and where she would be surrounded by supporters, a safe starting point for her as she dipped her toes deeper into the presidential campaign waters. As the campaign progressed, there would be "Women for Cooper" events throughout the nation, mounted by the campaign's various female supporters in local communities. But the early incarnations of "Women for Cooper" consisted primarily of fundraisers helmed by Laura. This meant that she began working more closely with the campaign staff's self-appointed First Lady, Mimi Van der Wohl.

In canine terms, Mimi combined the looks of an award-winning standard show poodle with the aggressiveness of a pit bull. She constantly pushed Luke to squeeze in just one more call to yet another potential donor, even when his other staff explained that he was already running late for another engagement. As the one who made the money tree shake, Mimi was in theory the most important person on the Cooper campaign, and she could be quick to remind others of that. But she soon was reminded that she was not the most important, nor most powerful, person in Cooperworld.

Mimi called excitedly from the West Coast to announce that she had just landed Luke a private dinner with a high-profile Hollywood director. After trying the governor's cell phone and getting no answer, she dialed his home. It was midnight in Michigan, a fact she had either temporarily forgotten or remembered but didn't think mattered.

But after about two minutes on the line, the governor asked Mimi to hold for a moment. He soon returned to the phone and spoke very slowly and very deliberately as if reading from a script. "Mimi, while I appreciate the significance of this particular meeting and all of the other work you are doing for the campaign, I have to ask that you not call my home after 10:00 p.m. unless it is an absolute emergency, since I have little ones." In the background Mimi heard a voice say loud enough for her to hear, "And a wife." The governor continued, "Also, we have a centralized process for scheduling requests to ensure that there are no unforeseen conflicts with my family obligations."

His core Michigan staff referred to this as "RFT"—Reserved Family Time. When "RFT" was written on a particular date or time, nothing work-related was scheduled, *ever*, owing to a blowout that was now referred to by the staff as "The Chuck E. Cheese Massacre," so called after Luke missed most of his son's birthday party and he and his team faced the wrath of his wife.

Luke appreciated that there would be a learning curve with some of the presidential campaign staff, so he continued with Mimi, "Again, I appreciate your hard work and everything you're doing, but this meeting should be submitted to my scheduler so that she can make sure it fits in with my other commitments."

"Luke, I don't think you're grasping just how important this donor is," Mimi replied.

"No, I certainly do, Mimi, and again I appreciate you making this happen, but I also need to try my best to make my sons' games and activities, which are also important."

To which Mimi, who had no children of her own, calmly replied, "Please tell me you're kidding. Right?"

At which point a female voice came on the line and said, "No, he's not. And neither am I. Any other questions?"

The First Lady had joined the conversation from another phone.

After a brief silence Mimi, who was rarely speechless, mumbled, "Ugh . . . No . . . I . . . don't think so."

"Glad to hear it. And just in case you didn't get the message the first time it was delivered, don't you call my house after 10 p.m. again, waking my kids up, unless it's a matter of life or death, or I assure you it *will* be a matter of life and death by the next time we talk. Are we clear?"

"Crystal," Mimi muttered.

"Great. You have yourself a good night." With that Laura hung up.

The exchange was never discussed again, but from that moment on Mimi limited her semi-diva behavior to everyone on the campaign except Mrs. Cooper, whom she bent over backwards to avoid. And when that wasn't possible, she bent over backwards to accommodate.

★

One of Laura's first Women for Cooper fundraisers was to be hosted by her cousin Veronica, who dressed in a brand new St. John suit for the event. Looking like a walking ad for a society lady who lunches, she lightly tapped her glass with a salad fork.

"Ladies, it's such an honor to welcome you all to my home, in support of my wonderful cousin's wonderful husband, the next president of the United States, Governor Luke Cooper."

The women in the room, most of whom, like Veronica, were ladies who earned their fortune the old-fashioned way, by marrying it, burst into applause.

"Obviously I am somewhat biased because I know the governor personally, but more importantly I know our family, and as you ladies know, the women in our family only marry quality men."

The women in the room laughed knowingly. After his first wife died, Dr. Si Anderson had been one of San Francisco's most eligible bachelors before Veronica snagged him. Despite its liberal reputation, much of San Francisco society had still been surprised, to say the least, when the scion of such an old-money family married a black woman. Though the Andersons were not quite as old and monied as the Getty oil clan, they certainly held their own. Veronica's late mother-in-law, Betsy Anderson, had her name stamped on a fair share of school libraries, auditoriums, and even a museum wing. Veronica attempted to pick up right where her mother-in-law left off, joining the boards of the right San Francisco philanthropic institutions and befriending the right socialites. Though neither she nor they would ever admit it, there were still some in the circle who would never fully accept her as one of them, but they'd be more than happy to accept her and her family's money. Since she was now part of the package, as far as Veronica was concerned that level of acceptance was enough. The caliber of women gathered that afternoon to toast her cousin—out of respect, or rather deference, to Veronica— was a testament to that.

The room was essentially filled with three types of women.

The first were Veronica's true friends. Out of the fifty women in attendance, there were just three of those, and one of them was Veronica's housekeeper.

The second set was comprised of strivers—as in those social climbers who were trying to buy their way into Veronica's social circle and were willing to scrape together $500 or more to do it.

The third set was women Veronica—though she'd never admit it— was still striving to impress, despite her wealth and influence.

Among them was Gigi Lang, who had married into one of San Francisco's most prominent families fifty years before. She was one of the few women on the planet who had the distinction of being a close friend of both Nancy Reagan and Ethel Kennedy. She was also one of the few people on the planet whose approval clearly mattered to Veronica.

Laura had never seen her cousin be so accommodating with anyone—besides her husband, whom she catered to. After all, she owed the life she enjoyed to him.

Gigi walked on water, to hear Veronica speak of her.

"And Gigi told me she just loved the dress, and you know Gigi does not give compliments lightly," she said, as though she were a little girl who received a pat on the head from a difficult-to-please parent.

Veronica was referring to her very first magazine profile in *San Francisco Social*, a glossy magazine dedicated to the kind of women who were at the fundraising luncheon: attractive, well-dressed, rich women who didn't have a lot of real-world problems and, frankly, weren't particularly interested in reading about any. Instead, they wanted to look at pretty pictures of women like themselves, dressed in pretty clothes. Veronica was photographed in a strapless gray silk number by the one and only B. Michael, the go-to designer for any black socialite "who mattered," Veronica was fond of saying. Though Veronica was a fashion plate who wore everyone from Donna Karan to Vivienne Tam (and was such a loyal customer that she had sat front row at their shows, and others, several times), for the big events it was always B. Michael, who was not only her favorite designer but her friend. Laura hadn't been sure whether Veronica really believed in Luke's quest for the White House until she said, "Now remember, Laura dear, you'll have to schedule your fitting with B. Michael well in advance of the inauguration because he's always booked months ahead."

It was in some ways such a classic, shallow Veronica thing to say, considering the million other things Laura had to worry about related to her husband running for president, among them her husband's health and safety, not to mention her family's privacy. But in Veronica's own small way it was one of the nicest things she could say. It meant she really believed in Luke—and believed in Laura too.

"Gigi, you look resplendent as always," Veronica said, leaning in to give Gigi an air kiss on the cheek.

"Why thank you, Veronica. And you're looking lovely."

"Well, I took your advice and visited Idella's. You were right. Her tailoring is perfection."

"As I've always said, I can't cook, I can't clean, and I can't sew, but I'm a wiz at hiring the best people to do all of the above."

Veronica and a woman seated next to Gigi laughed. Laura didn't. She smiled, uncomfortably. Laura had met Gigi once before and found her to be the snobbiest, most condescending person she'd ever met . . . next to Veronica. She also got the sense that Gigi didn't exactly care for her kind. She never said or did anything overt. There was just something about her that screamed, "I really wish I didn't have to talk to you, but I'm stuck, so I'll try to be cordial."

"Gigi, you remember my cousin Laura."

"Why of course. How do you do?"

"Very well, thank you. On behalf of my husband, I'd like to thank you very much for your support."

"Well, Veronica was kind enough to invite me as a guest, and she can be very convincing."

Veronica made an uncomfortable face at Laura. "Guest" was code for "didn't pay to attend the event."

Veronica had pointedly told Laura there was no room at the event to accommodate two local high-school students from underprivileged backgrounds who had been volunteering for the campaign because "this is a fundraiser not a soup kitchen," and yet Gigi and her sidekick, who had all of the money in the world, were there despite not having given a cent to attend.

"As Veronica knows, I can be very eclectic in my politics. After all, I think I'm one of the only people who's spent Thanksgiving with the Reagans and the Kennedys."

Veronica laughed. "Isn't she a hoot?" she said to Laura.

Laura faked a laugh.

"But, Laura, I will say this: your husband is certainly charming and so well-spoken and articulate," Gigi said, as though genuinely surprised.

Laura nodded and managed to squeak out a "thank you," though she really wanted to say something else, specifically a two-word phrase that also ended with the word "you" but that had a four-letter word beginning with the letter "F" just before it.

Laura didn't consider herself one of those people who dwelled on race or searched for signs of discrimination at every turn, but she did find it patronizing when someone, particularly an older white person, seemed to diminish an accomplished, educated black person's intellect by appearing surprised or impressed that the person could speak proper English.

The Chris Rock joke about this immediately sprang into her head: "What the f*!k do you expect Colin Powell to sound like? 'I's be's the president?'"

She wanted to say to Gigi, "Well, my husband was born in this country and earned a law degree from Columbia, and you have to speak pretty decently to be an attorney, but thanks so much for noticing."

Instead she said, "My apologies. I completely forgot to introduce my assistant to the woman over there whose son wants to intern for the campaign, and I see that she's leaving. Will you please excuse me?"

"But of course. Lovely to see you, dear," Gigi said.

"You as well."

Laura made her getaway and continued circling the room.

Veronica stayed by Gigi's side much of the rest of the afternoon, and to Laura's irritation was there forty minutes later when it was time for Laura to go. Laura couldn't tell if she was the guest of honor or if Gigi was, based on the number of aspiring social climbers who had lined up to pay homage to her throughout the afternoon while Veronica beamed, reveling in her moment as social arbiter. Laura had had enough of Gigi—and, frankly, Veronica—to last her a lifetime, but she couldn't sneak out without saying good-bye to her hostess, so she approached Veronica gingerly.

As she got closer, she could tell that there was some sort of commotion going on.

She then heard Gigi announce, or rather spit out the words, "Janice, get my purse. We are leaving!"

Laura then watched as Gigi and her sidekick stormed toward the door (as quickly as a seventy-five-year-old woman in kitten heels could storm).

"Everything alright?" Laura asked.

"Now it is," Veronica replied coolly.

None of the women standing nearby looked her in the eye. One of them then said, "It's been such a nice afternoon but I have to . . . to . . . leave. . . ."

And one by one, the remaining guests filed out.

"What happened?" Laura asked.

"Nothing worth revisiting," Veronica replied. But Laura could tell something happened, and it must have been bad because Veronica's café au lait skin had turned a distinct shade of red.

"Well, my cleaning crew certainly has their work cut out for them. They should get started on cleaning up this mess," Veronica continued.

"I've got to go. I cannot thank you enough, Veronica. It was such a lovely event."

"Oh please. You know I'd do anything for you. You're family."

Laura was caught off guard. That was a very un-Veronica-like thing to say.

"Cuz, are you sure you're alright?"

"Of course I am. I'm just frazzled. We have a lot of work to do to get Luke to the White House. This is just the beginning." She smiled at Laura, then did something she almost never did: initiated a hug.

Now Laura was really worried.

It was not until safely ensconced in her car with her aide that Laura finally discovered what drove Gigi Lang out in a huff.

"And then apparently Gigi said to one of the other guests that a Jew had about as much chance being elected president as she did, and a black jew even less," Laura's aide said excitedly—like she was back in high school telling a juicy piece of gossip about the homecoming queen.

"She said *what*?" Laura asked, although she realized she wasn't really that surprised. Her instincts had simply been proven correct.

"But Veronica heard her, and you will *never* believe what she said."

"What?"

"Apparently, she said—I'm paraphrasing, of course—'Gigi, just because your husband left you for the mayor doesn't make you a political expert. And I would add that the fact that Luke has done more with his life than simply drop out of high school and marry well probably does make him infinitely more electable than you.'"

Laura sat in shock for a moment.

"Can you believe she said that?"

"No, I can't." And Laura really couldn't.

"Your cousin might have just cost us a few thousand dollars in future donations," her aide continued, "but she's kind of a badass."

"Yeah. She kind of is," Laura said with a smile.

★

Even though they were in good hands with their grandparents, Laura hated being away from the boys, so the campaign tried to schedule a series of events over a few days each month so she could spend as much time home as possible the rest of the month.

Though she was now surrounded by more people than ever on a regular basis, Laura Cooper was also lonelier than she had ever been in her life. She missed her best friend Robin, who had passed away just as Luke's political career was really taking off. Occasionally while she was waiting to speak at an event, her mind would drift to her friend—to what Robin would have thought of this grand adventure. She had seen a therapist off and on following Robin's passing, but after Johnny, Luke's former consultant, made an offhand comment about voters not trusting candidates who "saw shrinks" or were "married to people who saw shrinks," she stopped.

Laura had plenty of social friends, but none of them so close that she really felt that she could truly confide in them and know without question it wouldn't end up on a blog somewhere. She didn't have siblings and she wasn't close with her father, not in that way. He was a kind, smart, regal man, and Laura felt fortunate to have been raised by him, but he was so regal that emotional intimacy was something he simply did not do. And while she was close with Luke's mother, she didn't like to worry her when she knew Esther Cooper was wrestling with her own fears about her son's candidacy.

But she did have Brooke. Though the two women had been friends for years, theirs was a peripheral friendship typical of spouses of best friends. They would talk by phone occasionally and meet up for lunch whenever Laura found herself in New York. But as the campaign progressed, Brooke's e-mails and phone calls became more frequent. Sometimes they would consist of only a few words: "Saw a pic of you online today. You looked GORGEOUS. Can't wait for us to have a First Lady who actually has a sense of style. Xoxo —Brooke." Her notes often came at the moments Laura most needed them to, after a day when some reporter had written something unflattering about her or Luke or her children that had really hit a nerve. Or she would call and just check in and ask Laura if she needed anything. Laura realized that the notes and calls from Brooke had become a sort of lifeline, and she began to view her not just as the wife of Luke's friend, but as her friend.

Of course, Laura also had Luke. No matter where his campaign travels took him, he made it a point to call and check in once a day, or at least to leave her a message saying, "I love you." Usually if he missed her, he would actually sing into her voice mail a few bars of Stevie Wonder's "I Just Called to Say I Love You," one of Laura's favorite songs. He was a terrible singer so it always made her laugh, which was the main reason he did it. His voice kept her going when the last thing she wanted to do was shake another hand or smile in the face of another obnoxious snob whom she was counting on to give her husband money.

In an effort to capitalize on Luke's Morehouse connections, the campaign booked Laura to attend a series of fundraisers in Atlanta one weekend, a city where a young, booming black professional class was particularly enthusiastic about Luke's candidacy.

Though Mount Sage was in Atlanta, Theo was unable to personally host an event for his old friend. To protect its nonprofit status the church had to officially stay out of politics as much as possible. So unofficially, Theo did the next best thing. His wife Saundra, known as "the First Lady of Mount Sage," whom Luke had briefly dated all those years before, was hosting a Women for Cooper event at their home. The guest list consisted of Saundra's sisters from one of the oldest black sororities in the nation.

Brock's wife Tami had been one of the charter members of Women for Cooper, having given the maximum contribution to his campaign when they hosted a fundraiser for him at their home and offering to do whatever she could to help the campaign down the road. She was visiting family in Atlanta that week, and since she had met Theo's wife before, thought it would be nice to attend her event.

Tami was also looking forward to another opportunity to chat with Laura. Though Tami considered Laura and Brooke to be real friends, she considered her relationship with Laura just friendly. Laura had always been lovely to Tami, but Tami felt hopelessly intimidated by Laura's social pedigree, Ivy League degree, and seemingly effortless looks. She was the kind of woman Tami aspired to be, but knew she never would be.

Tami arrived at Theo and Saundra's sprawling home in the Cascade Heights section of Atlanta. Living in Manhattan, Tami sometimes forgot what real houses with real square footage looked like. Brock would have been horrified to see that a pastor's lawn was almost larger than their apartment, she thought to herself.

The beautiful foyer had two spiral staircases that descended into a marble entranceway. The first floor was decorated in all white, almost angelic. How fitting, Tami thought, for a minister.

Tami proceeded through check-in, her nametag affixed to her navy blue, belted Armani pantsuit. She had seen Angelina Jolie wearing the black version of her suit in an interview and knew she had to have it. She finished the look off with Jimmy Choo slingbacks. She joined the other ladies who were already mingling in the living area.

Upon entering, Tami immediately felt slightly out of place. First off, every woman there was wearing some version of the Southern Sunday suit, a prim dress with matching jacket. And all of them were wearing bright, bold colors. Her fashion sense was one of the few things Tami usually felt one hundred percent confident about, but now she felt like a banker—albeit a well-dressed one—who had mistakenly wandered into an Easter service on her way to a cocktail reception.

She proceeded toward the bar for a glass of wine, knowing that would relax her. Unfortunately for her, while Theo wasn't actually there, his presence was still very much felt. There was no alcohol on the premises.

She settled for a ginger ale and then willed herself to say hello to someone.

She saw a group of three women chatting not too far from where she was standing and decided to introduce herself. A compliment was always a safe way to start a conversation with any woman, so Tami walked over and said, "That's a lovely suit."

"Thank you," the woman nearest to her replied.

It was actually a hideous looking lemon yellow Chanel knockoff with a floral print, but Tami was trying.

"I'm Tami," she said, extending her hand.

"I'm Adele," said the one in the yellow. "That's Martha, and that's Elaine."

"I don't think we've met at Saundra's other luncheons. Are you new to the area?" said Adele.

"Kind of. I'm visiting from New York," Tami said.

"Oh," Adele said, not that enthusiastically.

"So you're with the chapter up there?"

"No, I . . ."

"Don't tell me we have a spy from another house in our midst. Saundra just loves to let ladies from other houses crash our events."

Martha and Elaine began to laugh.

"Not to worry," Tami said with a calm smile.

"Well which one are you with?"

"I'm actually not with one . . . I never joined a sorority," Tami continued.

"Let me guess, mom and dad worried you'd start partying and wouldn't focus on the books, huh?" Adele continued as her two buddies chuckled.

Tami smiled uncomfortably. "Not exactly," she replied.

"Where'd you attend school?" Elaine asked.

"I actually attended Hostos briefly . . ."

"Hostos? I don't think I'm familiar with that. Is it an arts school?" Martha asked.

"It's small. It's actually an associate's college," Tami replied.

"Oh," Adele, Martha, and Elaine said in unison.

"I was working as a model, so I didn't really have a chance to attend college full time," Tami added.

"Oh . . . ," they repeated, but their eyes were saying a lot more.

"Modeling? That sounds fun," Martha said in an incredibly patronizing way. Tami wasn't surprised. Martha put the H-O-M-E in homely and Tami was used to being dissed by homely girls. She had been since childhood. Even at fifteen pounds heavier than her modeling days, she was still thinner and younger looking than a lot of women and was used to being treated accordingly.

"So we have our very own Naomi Campbell here?" Adele chimed in.

Tami was pretty sure this was some sort of backhanded compliment but simply replied, "Well . . . not exactly. I was much more of a working model than a partying model."

"Ever work with her, though?" Elaine asked.

"I did more commercial work," Tami replied.

"Oh, you were in commercials?" Elaine asked.

"No, I mean mainly commercial work . . . catalogs and such."

"Oh," the group said again in unison.

Just then another woman came and tapped Adele on the shoulder and they both squealed in delight before hugging.

"Hey Sharon!" Adele said. "It's so good to see you."

Martha and Elaine both hugged her too.

"Juanita is here too," Sharon said, pointing at a woman across the room.

"Oh great!" Adele said.

Tami stood there silently in the awkward way that someone waiting to be introduced does, before Martha said, "Oh—I'm sorry. This is Teri."

"Tami," Tami said.

"Nice to meet you," Sharon said, not particularly interested.

"How is everything?" Adele asked Sharon.

"Ugh . . . where to start? Well my little brother is engaged."

"Congratulations!" the women chirped.

"It's not something to celebrate," Sharon snapped.

"I thought he got rid of what's her name?" Martha replied.

"Tabitha? Yes, he got rid of Tabitha 'the dancer,'" she said, making the hand gesture for quotation marks. "And replaced her with Tamika, the so-called 'model.' I thought Mother was going to die when he told her. I mean it's bad enough she has no real job and no education to speak of, but you know my mother. I mean, when I was pregnant she told me if I named any of her grandchildren Shanequa or Tamika or anything like it, I would have to find myself a new mother."

Tami, the former model, formerly known as Tamika before she became Mrs. Brock Simpson, felt herself blushing. It was just like being back in high school, only this time Tami was the odd girl out.

"I'm sorry. I'm just chattering on," Sharon said. "So Tami, I don't think we've met before. New to Atlanta?"

"Not exactly," Tami said.

"Tami is not a fellow sister," Adele chimed in.

"Oh," Sharon replied.

"She's visiting from New York . . . ," Elaine added.

"Where she used to be a model." Martha concluded, with a mischievous glimmer in her eye.

"Oh . . . well . . . how . . . nice," Sharon said condescendingly.

They stood in a brief silence before Sharon said, "Well, I know Juanita would just love to catch up with you ladies." She made it clear she was speaking to every lady in the group except Tami.

Adele turned to Tami and said, "Well, it was very nice meeting you."

She was clearly the queen bee of this little bunch, and on cue the others said "bye" practically in unison, turned on their heels, and followed her across the room.

Tami stood there feeling lonelier than she had in a while, even though she was in a room full of women. Adele, in spite of her ugly suit, was clearly the room's reigning diva, because for the next twenty minutes virtually no one talked to Tami. Saundra waved at Tami from across the room briefly, but then disappeared and was now nowhere to be found. Tami didn't know Saundra well and had only met her a handful of times, Luke's swearing in being one such occasion. She had always seemed friendly enough, but Tami was beginning to wonder how any truly nice human being could call these witches sisters.

"Why couldn't there be alcohol on the premises," Tami thought to herself.

Forty minutes after the scheduled start time, Laura arrived with her campaign aide. She rushed in with Saundra—who had gone outside to meet her at the door and brief her on those who were in attendance—by her side.

Laura said some brief hellos to a few of the ladies, including Tami, whose hand she gave a gentle but firm squeeze.

Saundra officially introduced her, then Laura began her brief remarks—first apologizing profusely for being late. She then offered the obligatory thank yous that are a hallmark of all political speeches by elected officials, candidates and their spouses.

"First of all, I'd like to thank Saundra Edwards for being such a gracious hostess to all of us today," she began. "Saundra, I cannot thank you enough for welcoming us all into your lovely home. It is one of the most beautiful I have ever seen and I am so grateful for the kindness and friendship that you and Theo have shown Luke and me over the years. Thank you so much for introducing me to your friends—your 'sisters'— and I thank all of you for welcoming me into your sisterhood today."

At that, the women in the room burst into applause.

Laura continued, "I'd also like to thank a few more people who helped make this event possible and so special. First, as always, the wonderful campaign staff, especially Jenna, who helped work on this event, as well as our volunteers—please raise your hands so we can see you—and also the rest of our dedicated team here in Georgia. Let's give them all a round of applause." The room followed Laura's lead in applauding.

"There would truly be no campaign without these dedicated people. I'd also like to thank my dear friend Tami Simpson for traveling here all the way from New York to show her support." She turned toward Tami and gestured in her direction. "Tami is one of the national cochairs of Women for Cooper. Tami, you and your husband Brock have been there from the very beginning, and Luke and I are so appreciative for your unwavering support. Thank you for all that you do."

Tami blew a kiss in Laura's direction. She tried not to let the gloating show on her face, but inside she was beaming.

Laura then began, "Now, I know I kept you ladies waiting, so I am going to make it up to you by only making my speech an hour."

No one laughed.

Laura hurriedly added, "I'm kidding. That was a joke."

The rest of the women then broke into feigned laughter.

"Seriously, I would just like to share with you some of the issues that I as a mother and wife and woman care about most, and why I believe my husband is the best candidate for president to address those issues."

For the next twenty minutes Laura spoke about education, affordable child-care, and after-school tutoring—staying away from any controversial topics. One of the toughest questions she received from the crowd was, "Which sorority are you a member of?" (She wasn't a member of one, so she deflected the question by joking that "my parents thought I would get distracted from school if I joined one. Little did they know you didn't have to actually join a sorority to party with one." The room erupted in giggles.)

Laura closed by saying, "I hope that I will get a chance to chat with each and every one of you before you go, at least to say hello. Thank you so much again!"

After Laura finished speaking, Saundra escorted her around the room, introducing her to the women.

Tami noticed that during Laura's speech she'd missed two calls—one from Brock's assistant and one from Millie her housekeeper, who was helping with the kids while she was away. She stepped out of the room to return the first call. Brock had to leave that evening for a business trip and wanted Tami to return home immediately.

Tami made her way back inside. She needed to call a car and wanted to say good-bye to Laura and to Saundra, whom she hadn't yet had a chance to really chat with. The two of them were talking with a small group of women not too far from the refreshment area, so Tami made her way over for yet another nonalcoholic beverage before easing her way into Laura and Saundra's line of sight and then saying her good-byes. As she reached for some punch, she turned to find Sharon, a member of the mean girls' posse that had surrounded her before, standing there.

"Tami—hi," Sharon said with a wide smile. "I wanted to introduce you to my friend Juanita. Juanita—this is Tami."

"Hello," Tami said coolly.

"Hi!" Juanita said eagerly.

"Listen, Juanita is national president of Ebony Moms United. It's a nationwide membership organization for mothers of color. We do everything from fundraising for disadvantaged children to scheduling play dates, attending children's theater outings, arranging etiquette classes. It's really great."

Tami proceeded to give Sharon the same aloof response she had given Tami an hour earlier, an unenthusiastic "Oh . . . how nice."

"Well, we'd love to get someone like you involved," Sharon continued.

"Really?" Tami asked.

"Absolutely," Juanita continued.

"Are you sure models named Tamika are allowed?"

Sharon's smile began to fade—but just a tad. She then feigned confusion, "I'm sorry. I don't understand."

Juanita—who was genuinely confused—then said, "Did I miss something?"

Tami replied, "Oh, just an inside joke between Sharon and I."

Just then Laura turned around and said, "Tami! So good to see you. Are you on your way out?"

"I am," Tami said.

"Okay. Need a ride?"

"That would be great," Tami replied.

Saundra then leaned in and gave Tami a kiss on the cheek. "Thank you for coming!"

"My pleasure!" Tami said. "You have a lovely home."

"So do you. I couldn't believe those pictures from Luke's fundraiser. I need your decorator's number."

Just then Laura's campaign aide motioned her toward the door.

"Okay. That's our cue, Ms. Tami. We have to roll."

Laura gave Saundra a big hug. "Thank you. Thank you. Thank you, Saundra."

"Any time. I mean it. Our home is always open to family, and you and Luke are family."

"Thank you," Laura mouthed to her while squeezing her hand.

"Thank you, everyone!" Laura turned and said to the remaining attendees as she and Tami headed toward the door.

As she glanced back, Tami saw Sharon and Juanita, now joined by Martha, Adele, and Elaine all standing together.

Apparently Adele drew the short straw, because she walked up to Tami and said, "Tami—do you have a card? I'd love to stay in touch."

Tami smiled and said, "I'm sorry but I don't carry cards. Why don't you give me one of yours?"

"Great. Thanks," Tami said, accepting the card before turning to join Laura. As the two of them walked out the door, Tami promptly tossed the card in the bushes of Saundra's perfectly manicured lawn.

Once they were comfortably settled in Laura's campaign car, Laura thanked Tami again for making the trip down. They chit-chatted briefly about the beautiful homes in Saundra's neighborhood. Then finally Laura looked at Tami and asked, "Okay. Is it just me, or were those women kind of scary?"

CHAPTER 14

As Luke's schedule became more chaotic the amount of "RFT" on his schedule noticeably decreased. But that wasn't the biggest change in the couple's lives. The biggest, most noticeable change was that Laura actually didn't seem to mind. Luke knew that she did, but she tried hard to act as though she didn't. She would remind him with her oft-repeated admonishment that "we're not going to half-ass this. We're going to do it all the way, and if you missing this soccer game is what it takes, you'll have to miss this one."

But Luke knew deep down inside it bothered her, because deep down inside it bothered him too. For the first time in his son's young life he was missing more of his soccer games than he made. He was heartbroken that he had missed seeing Milo score the winning goal at a game the week before. So he made a point to get home for one of the last games of the season.

No matter where his travels took him, he tried to speak with his boys at least once a day by phone, even if it was just to ask them how school was and to say, "I love you." But he decided to surprise them before the game, arriving at the house around 11:30 a.m., just before they headed out to the field. The boys were ecstatic. Milo actually ran and jumped into his arms, shouting "Daddy!" Laura maintained her usual poker face, saying calmly, "Welcome home, stranger." She instructed the boys to double-check their rooms to make sure that they had everything before leaving, then as soon as they were out of sight, she planted a deep, lingering "you're getting lucky tonight" kiss on Luke.

They all headed to the soccer field, where Milo's team lost by an impressive 6–1, a league record. Luke decided lunch at Milo's favorite, T.G.I. Friday's, was in order to lift his spirits, and so they could have yet another talk about the importance of good sportsmanship over hot fudge sundaes and french fries. On the way there, Milo was silent.

"I know you're disappointed, but you played a good game, son," Luke said.

"You were terrific," Laura added.

"It's just today . . ." Luke continued.

"The other team beat you bad!" his older brother, James, said.

"Shut up!" Milo replied.

"Don't tell me to shut up," James replied.

"Well, I will," Laura said. "Be quiet and leave your brother alone."

The rode in silence for a few minutes.

"You can't win 'em all, son. Even the greatest players lose every now and then. Even Michael Jordan lost sometimes. And he's one of the greatest ever."

They rode in silence for a while longer before Milo said, "Dad?"

"Yes, son?"

"What's an anti-Semite?"

Luke and Laura looked at each other.

"Where did you hear that word, son?" Luke asked.

"Eric said his dad says you won't win because too many people are anti-Semites."

"Eric's father is an idiot," Laura hissed, "who should worry more about his wife's drinking problem than about—"

"Laura!" Luke said.

"Well . . ." Luke sputtered. He could barely focus on driving. "An anti-Semite is someone who doesn't like certain people . . . um . . . Jewish people . . ."

"Why not?" Milo asked.

"Because they're crazy," Laura interjected.

Luke shot her a pleading look.

"Well, son . . . you remember how at school there was a boy that some kids were being mean to even though he hadn't done anything to them? And remember your teacher had a talk about how it's not good to be a bully?"

"Yeah."

"Well . . . you could say anti-Semites are like that. They don't have a good reason for not liking Jewish people. They just don't. Some of them were taught the wrong thing by their parents . . . and some of them were taught the right thing but grew up and decided to believe the wrong thing . . . maybe because they're unhappy. . . . All we can do is pray for them and be good people and hope that one day they realize how wrong they are."

"Are they going to make you lose?" Milo asked.

Luke clenched the steering wheel.

"I don't think you have to worry about that," Luke tried to say as calmly as he could. "You know, I'm a little better at running for president than I am at air hockey, son," trying to elicit a laugh from Milo.

He didn't respond.

"I tell you what," Luke continued. "I'll bet you that not only are we going to win, but I'll bet you something even bigger . . ."

"What?" Milo asked without looking up.

"I'll bet you I can finish off not only a T.G.I. Friday's burger platter but three whole hot fudge sundaes."

"Bet you can't!" Milo shouted.

"Bet I can," Luke shouted back.

"You're going to make yourself sick," Laura whispered to Luke.

"I'm no coward," Luke said, winking at her.

That evening Luke lay in bed with a horrendous stomachache, thanks to the nearly one gallon of ice cream he'd ingested, much to his sons' delight and his wife's horror. He was so uncomfortable, he had to do something he rarely did—turn down his wife's offer of sex. He then took two Alka-Seltzers and prayed they'd work their magic by the morning.

But as he lay in bed next to his wife, he couldn't get the conversation with his son out of his head. How do you get a child to understand that there are people who will hate you for the rest of their lives for absolutely no reason at all?

He began to think that perhaps Nate and the rest of the team were right. He may have to pull a Kennedy and address the issue of his religious identity more fully.

Laura was reading Toni Morrison's *Song of Solomon* for the third time. It was one of her favorite books. She was wearing her reading glasses, which gave her a sort of naughty secretary look that he loved.

"Hon. I need to ask you a favor."

"I tried to offer you a favor earlier and you said your stomach hurt," she said with a sly smile.

He laughed. "Well, the campaign wants me to ask you for a favor."

"Uh-oh. Is this going to involve me wearing more ridiculous clothes? Because I think I've bent over as far backwards on that one as I possibly can."

"The campaign thinks we need your dad. How do you feel about that?"

"Well, that depends. Do you mean how do I feel about him helping you out, or how do I feel about asking him to?" She made a face.

"I know. I know." Luke appreciated the magnitude of what he was asking. But he had to ask nonetheless. "The campaign says I'm struggling with older black men, and he could really help by speaking up on my behalf."

"Honey, I mean this in the least mean way possible, but are you sure you want to take the chance of the public hearing what my dad has to say about you? I mean, to say this could backfire in a big way is probably an understatement."

"Whew. That's harsh," Luke said trying to smile.

Laura then leaned over and kissed his forehead.

"Let me think about it, okay? You know Daddy. You have to catch him in the right moment. We'll figure something out. Now, how you feeling? Want me to rub your tummy?"

★

Two weeks later Laura's father was in her living room. She called and told him that she had to travel on behalf of the campaign for a couple of days and that Luke's parents weren't available to watch the boys, so he volunteered to watch his "favorite" and only grandsons.

Griswold "Wally" Long had served with the Tuskegee Airmen in World War II and was later a successful attorney when there were very few blacks who were. He was always unfailingly polite, but tough and no-nonsense with everyone, especially his only child. Yet the man who had been so incredibly strict with Laura growing up had been transformed into a grandfather who told her to "lighten up" with his grandsons and let each of them stay up past their bedtime and have a second slice of cake.

He had already been there for three hours and hadn't so much as asked about the presidential campaign or Luke.

Once the boys were in bed, Laura said, "So I'm leaving in the morning. Back in two days."

"I'll try not to burn the house down," her father quipped without looking up from the newspaper he was now reading.

Laura smiled. Her father was a good man but he was just from a different generation, she tried to remind herself, a generation when black men weren't allowed to show how they really felt. He rarely said the words "I love you," and hugs were a foreign concept. The only time she saw him cry was the day her mother died. Though he was much more affectionate with the boys than he had ever been with her, he still usually said something like "Who's my favorite grandson?" in place of "I love you."

"Listen, Daddy, I wanted to ask you something."

"You don't have to announce a question, Laura. Just ask it." He turned the page of the newspaper without looking up.

"We're planning some activities for the campaign that will include every member of the family. And you're my family and I'd like you there."

"You're not running for president," her father replied without skipping a beat or glancing up at her.

"That's true, but I am running for First Lady, and I want people to see and know the kind of people I come from. Meet the man who raised me."

Her father folded the paper and placed it in his lap.

"Did Luke put you up to this?"

Laura took a deep breath, crossed her fingers behind her back and prayed that God would forgive her for the lie she was about to tell. "No. As you know, there have been some commercials running with Luke's mom in them, and the boys asked why Grandpa Wally wasn't in any commercials, and I didn't really know how to explain it to them. I didn't want to tell them you didn't want to do it."

"Well you never even asked me!" he said, sounding genuinely concerned.

"I know, Dad. It's just you're so busy."

"Well I'm never too busy for the little guys. When are you all doing these get-togethers you're talking about?"

"Well, if you're actually interested in participating, I'll check with the campaign on when the next time is."

The next morning, when Laura Cooper crept into her boys' room to wake them up for school before she left on her trip, she said, "Hey guys, I have a surprise for you. I packed some extra cookies in your lunch and some homemade Rice Krispies Treats."

"Yay!" they said in unison. She then whispered, "Shhh. Mommy just needs you to do something."

"Okay."

"When you see Grandpa Wally, can you thank him for taking pictures for Daddy's campaign?"

Laura Cooper felt a twinge of guilt, like she was possibly being a bad mother. But she knew she was being a very good wife.

CHAPTER 15

Two weeks after Laura's little white lie to her father, the campaign had an advertisement featuring him in heavy rotation in South Carolina. The ad included photos of him in his Tuskegee Airmen's uniform decades earlier and, finally, a photo of him with Luke and Laura at their wedding. Though he refused to call Luke "son," despite the director's urging, he did agree to look into the camera and say, "He's a great husband, and a great father, and I know he will make a great president."

Twenty takes later they got one that was believable enough to use.

Though the campaign anticipated the ad would help significantly with older black voters, they didn't know if it would be enough, so Luke had secretly begun working on his own "Kennedy speech" to address the public's uncertainty about his religious identity. He was sitting in a hotel room in South Carolina, tackling another draft, when his Black-Berry began vibrating. But his cell phone alerted him to a message at the same time. He picked up his phone first. There was a text from Nate. "URGENT," it read. "Check berry." He then picked up his Berry and saw that the subject line read, "URGENT Fw: Hate Group Planned Attacks on Churches for MLK holiday." Luke began reading. He wrote back to Nate and copied his communications director, "What more do we know?"

"Still gathering details . . . May want to release some sort of statement . . . Will get back once I know more," his communications director wrote back.

Nate replied and said, "Call me ASAP." His first words to Luke were, "Are you sitting down?"

"No," Luke replied.

"Well, you might want to."

"Just tell me."

"The hate group story . . ."

"Yes?"

"I've gotten two calls from outlets who say that the informer who tipped off the government to the attacks is Jack Means . . ."

"Luke, did you hear me?" Nate pressed. "Luke?"

"Yeah . . . I'm here."

★

The revelation that Jack Means, the white supremacist Luke saved years before, had potentially helped prevent a domestic terror attack became the leading news story in America.

The campaign was cautious, initially refusing to comment until more news had been confirmed. The FBI held its official press conference about the thwarted attack but never mentioned the name Jack Means and did not take questions from reporters. The campaign released a brief statement: "Gov. Cooper is extremely pleased to hear that religious institutions were successfully protected by the fine work of law enforcement officials. He has always said America has the best law enforcement in the world and this is yet another example that proves it."

But over the next thirty-six hours word of Jack Means's connection to the investigation grew from rumor to accepted fact, even though it was still unconfirmed. And two days after Nate's initial heads-up e-mail to Luke, the mother of Jack Means granted her first and only interview, to *Today Show* host Matt Lauer, of whom she was a longtime fan. The interview wound up providing the Cooper campaign with the kind of free media money couldn't buy. She not only credited Luke with saving her son's physical life, but his spiritual one as well.

She recounted how, after his encounter with Governor Cooper, her son began a journey that eventually led him from work with hate groups to work with underprivileged kids. The so-called money quote from the interview—the exchange that was played endlessly on other networks and online—was when Matt looked at her and asked Mrs. Means, "So do you credit Governor Cooper with turning your son's life around?" and she replied, "Yes, sir . . . I'd have to. He showed my son kindness and now my son is trying to follow his example with his life today, and that's why he tried to help save all of these lives."

She added that though she was a registered Republican, she considered Governor Cooper a "nice man with cute kids and a nice family who clearly can help change other people's lives for the better."

Within hours of the ensuing press coverage, the campaign was inundated with interview requests and speaking invitations. Some local Democratic activists in primary states who they had trouble getting on the phone before were now calling the campaign requesting Luke's presence at their clambake or barbecue or parade. Luke even received his second invitation to appear on *The Tonight Show*. He'd turned down the first shortly following the Means incident years before.

Nate wanted to use the new scrutiny as an opportunity to prove that Luke was focused not on being a celebrity but on being an effective leader. In the days following the Means revelation the campaign released position papers on Luke's plans for targeting both domestic and international terror as president.

They also announced some prominent endorsements, among them one from retired General Ben Rosenthal, who was best known for four things: being a highly decorated war veteran, becoming the first Jewish chairman of the Joint Chiefs of Staff, having a volcanic temper, and for his long-running feud with Senator Sid Burstein. After Burstein criticized him on a television show, Rosenthal was later asked in an interview what he thought of Burstein's remarks, and Rosenthal famously replied, "I'd like just three minutes alone with him to show him what I think of them."

To his campaign advisors' growing chagrin, Luke had steadfastly refused to capitalize on, or even discuss in detail, the events from the day he saved Jack Means. Now he didn't have to. Mrs. Means had done it for him. She had painted Luke Cooper as a hero who had the power to change and transform lives and make America better, exactly what Americans want in a president, and that was now the story defining the presidential race, instead of Luke's ethnicity or his faith.

The campaign quietly scrapped plans for Luke's landmark speech on his religious faith. In her simple way, Mrs. Means had conveyed the benefits of Luke Cooper's unique racial and religious identity in a way that was accessible to voters, far better than the candidate could have.

Within seventy-two hours of the Means interview, Luke Cooper's poll numbers shot up in every state among every demographic in America. He was still not the front-runner, but he was no longer a long shot either.

★

Luke had finished up a full day of events and was eating a slice of pizza in a hotel room when his phone rang.

"Well, I always said you were the luckiest motherfucker alive and now I know it's official because if I didn't actually know you I would be convinced that you're into some voodoo shit with this Means guy popping up like that," Garin said.

"If I was into voodoo my plan wouldn't have been this elaborate. I'd just have the other guys drop out of the race or maybe at the very least have Fogerty get caught in a sex scandal, just for kicks." Garin laughed.

Larry Fogerty was one of the no-name, no-chance-in-hell candidates in the presidential race. He, and the other no-names alongside him, were running not because they thought they actually had a chance of winning but simply to raise their profiles and, along with that, their fees on the speaking circuit once their campaigns flamed out. Fogerty was most famous for being self-righteous about "family values" and also for attacking Luke, whom he made clear he didn't like in the first debate—and had been making it clearer ever since.

"I don't think you need to count on a voodoo doll for that," Garin continued. "I told you that Fogerty character's shady. I never trust guys who go on and on about how happily married they are like that. It's sort of like how Brooke says she always knows when one of her sorority sisters is about to get a divorce, because they start bragging about their sex lives like they're Pam and Tommy Lee or something. Just like people who actually have their finances straight don't run around buying fifty Hummers and tons of bling, I think people who have their family situations straight don't run around bragging about how *Leave It to Beaver* their lives are all the damn time. I'm telling you he's shady, and you remember I said so when he gets caught with his hand in the cookie jar, and by cookie jar I mean..."

"I know what you mean," Luke said with a laugh. "No need to elaborate. How have you been?"

"Busy. Even more so than usual, thanks to you and our old friend Mr.

Means. People I couldn't get to return my calls last week are all of a sudden not just offering to write you checks but to cohost events."

"Yeah, Mimi said it's going to be a good month."

"Damn good month, and Mimi's loving every minute of it. You know, she actually said she never thought she'd see the day where she'd want to even kiss a skinhead, but thanks to all the money this Means thing has brought in she'd be willing to sleep with a few as a thank you. Can you believe she actually said that?"

"Yes. Yes I can," Luke replied, shaking his head.

"Well, Sheila's fundraiser is now at capacity."

"Really?" Luke was genuinely surprised.

Sheila was their old law school classmate who was now a stay-at-home mom, but her husband was CFO of one of Silicon Valley's hottest properties. Though Abby Beaman had seemed to have a lock on much of the Democratic donor landscape in California early in the race, between the Means story and Mimi's own connections there, the campaign had begun making serious inroads for Luke.

"Don't you know, you're no longer just a lowly bureaucrat anymore? You're like a real life famous person. Hell, Marcus may even try to get you to do a walk-on on his show."

"Gee. Just what I've always dreamed of," Luke said.

"Speaking of, I'm guessing now that you're back in the news again he's called?"

"How'd you guess?"

Marcus Templeton was Luke's friend from Morehouse, although with Marcus "friend" was more of a relative concept, depending on how useful you could be to him at any given moment. The son and grandson of a doctor, he had broken family tradition by becoming an actor and now starred on the sci-fi crime drama *Shooting Stars*, which one TV critic summed up as "*CSI* meets *Star Trek* with writing that makes the WWE look like Shakespeare." Luke could go years without hearing from Marcus, but whenever Luke's career was on an upswing, Marcus always seemed to conveniently reappear.

"He actually offered to host a fundraiser with some of his actor friends," Luke said.

"There's a shock," Garin said sarcastically. "Well money's money and you can't run this campaign without it, as Mimi keeps reminding me, so take him up on his offer. Only maybe you should get him to sign a contract that says he can't cancel on a whim if your poll numbers start dropping."

Garin wasn't a fan of Marcus, finding him to be a pretentious pretty boy.

"Oh come on, Gar. Marcus always liked you."

"Oh I'm sure he does. I'm sure he likes me a whole hell of a lot."

"That's not what I meant and you know it."

Garin and his wife Brooke and other friends on the periphery of the celebrity world had heard for years from reliable sources that Marcus was gay. The fact that Marcus bragged incessantly about his various conquests with young models and video vixens only heightened Garin's suspicions.

"Remember what I said about people who brag about their situations being shady?"

"Oh come on, Garin, if you regularly slept with models you mean to tell me you wouldn't brag to your friends? After you slept with Bambi or Baby or whatever that porn star's name was—you called me before you'd even gotten dressed and made it out of her apartment."

"For the record her name was B.J., and bragging to you when I was twenty-five is different from bragging to Howard Stern when you're forty-five."

Luke sighed.

"So speaking of your real friends who would give you a kidney if you needed one, are you sitting down?" Garin asked.

"Nope."

"Joe's getting married."

"Who's he engaged to now?"

"No, Coop. He's really getting married. To Tiffini. They set a date and it's soon. Next month."

"What? Is she pregnant or something?"

"I thought the same thing!" Garin said laughing.

Luke felt bad for the remark. His first words should have been ex-pressions of happiness for his friend, but he just knew Joe too well. Luke loved Joe like a brother. Joe had been the first person he'd ever smoked pot with and the first person he called when he lost his virginity, but over the years he had come to accept the fact that Joe's relationships with women were not exactly what you'd call healthy. His parents' divorce and his father's endless string of infidelities during his multiple marriages had really taken a toll, but it was not until they had reached full-fledged adulthood and Luke watched him ruin one relationship after another that he realized just how damaged Joe really was. He eventually assumed that Joe was destined to end up as the guy at the nursing home that the nurses called funny, the male residents called fun, and the female residents called a creep. That was just Joe. So Luke was genuinely surprised to hear that a woman had finally reeled him in.

"Joe swears she's not. He said he's just ready to do it. Like the Nike ad, he said. He can't even discuss his wedding without a sports reference." Garin laughed again. "Look, I tried to convince him to wait until after the campaign's over so you can make it, but he's determined."

"Don't be silly!" Luke said. "I don't expect the entire world to stop because I'm running for office."

"No. I know, but still he's waited almost half a century to get married. A few more months won't kill him. I really don't see the rush. You know, if he's telling the truth about her not carrying a little Joe. Can you imagine Joe as a dad?"

They both chuckled to themselves.

"If God has a sense of humor he's going to have a little girl someday."

Joe's sexual exploits were legendary among the crew, as was his reputation for breaking young hearts—including those of his previous fiancées.

"Well, I'm happy for him," Luke said. "I really hope it works out for him. He deserves to be happy."

"Yeah, me too, Coop."

There was a strange pause.

"Should I call him and congratulate him? Or should I wait until he tells me himself? I haven't heard from him in a bit," Luke asked.

Actually, it had been more than a bit. Joe e-mailed Luke a note about some son of his father's latest girlfriend who wanted to work on the campaign and Luke promised to have someone get in touch with the kid. He hadn't heard from Joe since. It had been more than a month.

"Well, I think it's been a rough patch for him. Joe Senior reappeared for a bit then pulled one of his disappearing acts."

Joe's dad was notorious for popping into Joe's life, showering him with gifts and affection—usually when he was in between wives or girl-friends and usually to irritate Joe's mother—and then disappearing from Joe's life just as quickly as he appeared.

"He borrowed some dough from Joe, then stood him up for dinner, and he hasn't heard from him since. Happened last month."

It all made sense to Luke now. Joe's dad asked him for help getting his girlfriend's son a job. His dutiful son sends the e-mail to Luke. Then his dad disappears again. Typical. No wonder Luke hadn't heard from him. Joe always had a hard time right after his dad pulled one of his in-and-out routines.

"Besides, I think he probably knows that you may not be able to make the wedding because of your schedule, and for all these years if he ever needed a best man, the plan was for it to be you."

"I wouldn't miss his big day for the world."

"I'm sure hearing that would mean a lot to him. But for the record, I've actually put dibs on being best man. I owe him one."

Luke laughed. "Come on, Garin. You've got to let it go. We're in our forties now. We're too old for that kind of fratty shit."

"Speak for yourself. I almost didn't get laid on my honeymoon thanks to him."

Brooke had warned all of Garin's friends that if he didn't show up at their wedding in one piece and sober she would hunt each one of his bachelor party buddies down and make them pay.

Garin made it to the ceremony looking his usual handsome, perfect self. It was only when he and Brooke kneeled at the altar to receive a blessing from the minister that Joe's bachelor party prank became obvious. Written in bright silver ink on the soles of Garin's shoes were two words: SAVE on his left sole, and ME on his right. He and Brooke couldn't understand why the congregation began snickering at that moment and continued to do so throughout the remainder of the ceremony.

Brooke was so mad when she found out the source of the laughter that she hit Joe hard enough with her bouquet to scatter most of the petals—which only made her madder. It took a year for her to forgive him—and only after Joe gave them an extraordinary one-year anniversary present, an all-expenses-paid trip to the Maldives Islands where one of Joe's retired basketball clients owned a five-star resort.

"Well, you can write on his shoes if you want, but leave me out of it," Luke said.

"Coward," Garin teased.

"Call me what you want to. All I know is I'm too old to get attacked by an angry cheerleader brandishing a bouquet."

The two of them laughed.

★

After hanging up with Garin, Luke scrolled through his 200 unread e-mails. His staff marked the time-sensitive ones URGENT and anything important but less time-sensitive PRIORITY, so Luke looked for those first and then skimmed to see if there were any from friends and family. He saw that he had one from Terry, Adam's wife. The subject read, "Know you're busy but please call when you can . . ."

"Hey Luke," it began. "So I know you're crazy busy but was hoping you could call me—preferably at the office in the next day or so. I sent you a couple of e-mails before but know you're a little busy at the moment :) but if you can call soon would be great. – T"

Adam's birthday was in a few weeks so Luke assumed Terry wanted to talk about a surprise party or something, though Luke knew whatever it was he probably wouldn't be able to make it. His schedule was officially too chaotic. He had just learned that he would have to miss his nephew's bar mitzvah because of a fundraiser, and had not yet worked up the nerve to tell his family.

It was too late to reach Terry at the office so he shot her a note.

"Hey Terry! Sorry to be a MIA. Things have been a little nuts the past few days. What time can I get you in the office?"

She wrote right back.

"What time can you talk and I'll make sure I'm free."

"Can you do 7 est? Sorry, but earlier's better for me . . ."

"Talk then, Coop . . ."

As usual Luke was behind schedule before his day even really began. His communications director called him at 6:45 and he looked up and realized that half an hour later he had already kept Terry waiting fifteen minutes. She was a vice president at a record label, and he knew that her time was not just as valuable as his but probably *more* valuable, and Terry was what Adam called "a psycho about punctuality."

"Terry! So sorry I'm late. My other call ran long."

"Don't worry about it, Luke. I know you're a little busy right now."

That was a very un-Terry-like thing to say. He once arrived late to meet her and Adam for dinner and she greeted him with "Listen, you may be the most important person in your state but not in mine. So for keeping us waiting for our dinner, you're buying."

"What's going on?" Luke asked.

"We're both busy, so I'm not going to waste our time bullshitting. I'm worried about Adam."

"Is he all right?" Luke's heart began to race. Having known him since they were five, Adam was literally like another brother.

"He's not sick or anything, Luke, but I think he's . . . well, I think he's depressed . . . actually I know he's depressed."

"What makes you say that?"

"Ever since he lost his job he just hasn't been himself."

"He lost his job?"

"He didn't tell you?"

"I don't remember him saying anything about that. What happened?"

"Layoffs. You know, those of us in the music industry are feeling a lot of solidarity with the guys who are watching their factories get shut down as they're replaced by machines."

"When did it happen?"

"Six weeks ago."

Luke had definitely spoken with Adam since then, but his old friend hadn't said a word.

"I thought he would bounce back after a couple of weeks," she said, "but he's barely getting out of bed. I'm sorry to call you now at, like, the worst possible time for you, but I didn't know what else to do. Obviously I can't call his family."

"Of course not."

Adam's father was perpetually disappointed in his only son. Nothing Adam ever did pleased him. His mother was overbearing and his sister was the princess who could do no wrong, mainly because she grew up and married someone incredibly wealthy.

Luke and Adam bonded forty years before after Adam stuck up for

Luke—the only other kid in their school with a mini-fro like his—when other kids teased him about his hair.

"How can I help?" Luke asked Terry.

"Could you call him? You can get through to him in a way I can't."

"Terry, you know I want to help, but what should I say?"

"I don't know, but you always manage to say the right thing. That's why you're such a good politician."

★

During his next moment of downtime Luke called Laura. "Hi hon. I need a small favor."

That afternoon Laura called Adam.

"Hey Adam. I'm sorry to bother you. I know how busy you are but this is important. It's about Luke."

"What's going on?"

"Well the thing is . . . I'm just going to say it. I'm really worried about Luke."

"What do you mean? I thought the campaign was going well."

"Well, it's going better but he's been down lately."

"I just saw him on TV. He seemed pretty upbeat."

"Well you know Luke. He tries to please everybody, protect us from any pain he's going through."

"That's true," Adam agreed. "What can I do?"

A week later, Adam began traveling with the Cooper campaign as a part-time volunteer/full-time friend of the candidate.

CHAPTER 16

Most days Mimi Van der Wohl loved her job.
This was not one of those days.

Brian Colby, a star player for the Lakers, had agreed to serve as celebrity cohost along with famed director Buddy Jacobs at an L.A. fundraiser for Luke. He did so at the request of his close friend, Gray Matthews, one of the most influential agents in the history of sports who now served as a partner at the agency that repped Brian. Matthews also happened to be Joe's boss.

Though she knew Hollywood inside and out, Mimi never followed sports and could hardly distinguish between a professional basketball player and a professional baseball player. So it never ceased to amaze her when men—particularly successful ones—fell all over themselves to meet some athlete. Thanks to Colby joining the event, there were now a host of wealthy men, from bankers to entertainment lawyers, who were attending and planning to bring their wives, girlfriends, and wealthy friends with them.

Colby was infamous for alienating teammates and coaches alike, but in the eyes of many fans his gifts on the court made up for his shortcomings elsewhere. His wife, Sunny, meanwhile, had a reputation for alienating everyone. An aspiring "model" when she and Colby met on the set of a rap video, she accidentally-on-purpose became pregnant on their third date. She was seventeen. He was nineteen and didn't want to see his multimillion-dollar future go down the tubes because of an ill-advised tryst with someone who "technically" was a minor. So instead he married her and had been paying for the tryst, among other things, ever since. Sunny gave birth to their daughter six months after their marriage. (In an effort to maintain Colby's golden-boy reputation, it was rumored the birth certificate was fudged to make it appear as if the baby was born prematurely, and not as if she was conceived at an age that was legally questionable for the mother.) Nine months later Colby's first son was born—to another woman. Ever since then Sunny had gone out of her way to make Colby's life, and the lives of everyone else, it seemed, as miserable as possible. (It was rumored that Sunny, an Asian beauty, was particularly incensed that he had had the nerve to cheat on her with a black woman, even though Colby was black himself.) If she was going to be bitter and unhappy, so was everyone else. In the course of one year the couple had cycled through three nannies and four housekeepers—one of whom threatened to sue Sunny for abuse before a settlement made the problem quietly go away.

Mimi had heard the stories and wasn't thrilled about the prospect of having to deal with Mrs. Colby, or Mr. Colby, for that matter, but in the world of fundraising—even among celebrities—Colby wasn't just a big fish. He was the equivalent of reeling in a shark. Once Colby signed on, others soon followed, eager to get a chance to spend an evening with the man who had been named Most Valuable Player of the NBA Finals two years in a row. Colby had a reputation for being "difficult," but his wife had a reputation for being worse. And in the weeks leading up to the fundraiser she lived up to her reputation, and then some.

Buddy Jacobs and Gray Matthews had been absolute delights to deal with. They pretty much let Mimi and her team handle everything, which made them a fundraiser's dream. They lent their names to the event, then stayed out of the way. The Colbys, or rather Mrs. Colby, was another matter.

And Mimi was finally at her breaking point. "It's her again," Mimi's assistant said.

"Tell *her*," Mimi said with dramatic emphasis, "I'm in a meeting."

"She says it's urgent."

"She always says it's urgent. It was urgent when she wanted a high school friend added to the guest list. It was urgent when she wanted the same friend removed because they had a fight. It was urgent that she didn't like the caterer. Ask her if she actually knows the meaning of the word urgent. If she does, I'll take the call, but considering she dropped out of high school to become a full-time groupie it appears that she doesn't, so you can put her into my voice mail." Mimi's assistant didn't know how to respond. She wasn't exactly caught between a rock and a hard place—more like between one bitch and another.

Five minutes later her assistant buzzed again.

"It's her again. She says it's about the guest list." It was Mrs. Colby's twelfth call of the day.

"You have got to be fucking kidding me!" Mimi screamed.

"What do you want me to do?"

"Tell her I died or joined the witness protection program. I am *not* talking to that woman again today. I didn't spend as much time coddling my husband as I have this psycho, and being his wife paid a hell of a lot better than this gig."

Two minutes later Mimi received the following e-mail message:

Mimi I need to speek with you. Its ergint. If you are to busy to talk then maybe it is best we don't partisipate in your event.

Mimi was torn between wanting to laugh out loud and wanting to throw her laptop across the room. The woman lived in a $20 million mansion, carried a $10,000 handbag, and yet clearly had not invested any of her wealth in developing her spelling and grammatical skills beyond kindergarten.

She closed her eyes and began breathing slowly and deeply. She had once taken several meditation classes with a few other Beverly Hills trophy wives but nowadays limited herself to the breathing exercises, only when she really felt on the verge of killing someone, like right now.

After three minutes she felt lighter and calmer.

Mimi didn't know much about athletes, but she knew a lot about men and what made them tick. She turned to her computer and began typing.

No prob. Please just let me know as soon as possible because we were planning to include some other players from the team

> **in the event but based on Mr. Colby's history with some of them
> we didn't want things to be uncomfortable. I'd love to call them
> all before close of business to let them know we would like their
> participation so please let me know if you are dropping out ASAP.
> Cheers, Mimi**

Mimi knew that Brian's management team, including Gray, was doing damage control to try to improve his image. He was perceived as an arrogant loner who was not liked by the rest of the team, and if he dropped out of this fundraiser, and then other players miraculously replaced him at the event, it would simply reinforce that. And subsequently further impact his reputation, which would impact his endorsements and, ultimately, Sunny's collection of Hermès bags, which clearly Sunny did not want.

Ten minutes later she received the following e-mail message from Sunny:

> **I think you misunderstood me. We're definitely hapy to par-
> tisipate . . . If you could just send me the names of some of the
> gests . . . or just the girl gests, that would be great . . .**

Just then it all clicked. Sunny wanted to scan the guest list to see if there would be anyone there she needed to worry about—any models or young actresses she perceived as a threat or were rumored to have had liaisons with Brian. The woman was a complete and utter bitch, but in that moment Mimi actually felt sorry for her. Here was a young, beautiful nineteen-year-old woman who was wealthier than 99.9 percent of the population, yet was so desperately unhappy and insecure.

She wrote her back,

> **Will check with my team and try. Mimi**

★

Luke's schedule changed so often that he had trouble keeping up with it himself. His mother surprised him by actually knowing the date of one of his debates before he did because she saw it mentioned in the newspaper.

He made a point to call her at least once a week, although he was debating skipping this week because he knew his next conversation with her was likely to be an unpleasant one.

With the multitude of drafts his schedule went through, it had become harder and harder to carve out meaningful chunks of RFT—Reserved Family Time—though he and Laura fought their hardest to try.

In addition to the science fair and soccer games and the multitude of family dinners, there had also been James's debut in the school play. But they were coping.

But when Luke looked on his schedule and saw the date for his L.A. fundraiser with Brian Colby, he knew the date looked familiar but couldn't place why. Then it hit him. It was his nephew Brian's bar mitzvah. He knew moving or missing the fundraiser was simply not an option, although he was torn. He wasn't sure who was scarier, Mimi or his mother.

He picked up the phone and dialed.

"Hey!" he said.

"Hey yourself. I would have thought you had been kidnapped by aliens or something if I wasn't seeing you on TV all the time," his brother Josh said.

"I know. I know. I'm sorry things have been so busy. I hardly have a chance to take a piss anymore."

"Geez, if you're this busy just running for president then I guess I better get ready to never hear from you when you're actually running the country."

"Now you're making me feel as guilty as Mom."

"Please. I wouldn't even make the Olympics for guilt with Mom competing. She's like the Mark Spitz of guilt."

Luke laughed, hard.

"So how are things going, squirt?" his brother asked.

"I thought I told you not to call me that anymore."

"No. You told me not to call you that in public anymore, and we're not in public."

"Some things never change," Luke mumbled.

"Damn right. Just remember, no matter how big you get you'll still be squirt to me, even in a big, white house."

As his oldest brother, Josh had served as Luke's ultimate protector growing up. He'd also been his ultimate tormentor, teasing him endlessly in the way big brothers do. He had been calling Luke squirt for as long as anyone could remember, not, as many thought, because of Luke's small size as a boy, but because of an incident involving Luke, a tube of toothpaste, and their father's briefcase that Luke's brothers would never let him live it down.

"How's the campaign going?" Josh asked.

"It's going."

"That Fogerty guy's a real asshole, but that Beaman's got some great legs. If they have a swimsuit competition in this thing, you're toast."

"Gee, glad I can count on your vote, Josh," Luke said.

"I never said that," Josh said, laughing.

"How are Kate and the boys?"

"Kate's good except for the avocadoes."

"Avocadoes?"

"She's on some crazy new avocado diet."

"Avocadoes?"

"Yeah. Speaking of, when you become president can you take care of that?"

"And how do you expect me to do that?"

"I don't know. Can't you pass a law outlawing stupid diet books? Or the people who write them?"

"Yes, Josh, that's exactly what presidents do."

"Or maybe you could just outlaw avocadoes. Because honestly, if I have to eat another meal with them in it I might just commit a homicide at this point."

"Well, I have to become president first, and I can't even get my own brother to commit to voting for me."

"Consider it to be my way of getting back at you for being Mom's favorite."

"Oh here we go . . ."

They both laughed.

"How are the boys?" Luke asked.

"Ethan's good."

"And how's the big guy?"

"Bri's doing better. Had a rough patch, but he's getting back on track."

"What happened?"

"Well, he got into a little trouble at school."

"Brian?" Luke asked, surprised. "Brian doesn't get into trouble."

"Well, welcome to the world of living with an almost-teenager."

"What happened?"

"Some kids were being assholes and he got into a fight."

"Brian was fighting? Brian?"

"It's not that unbelievable. After all, he is my kid."

"I know, but he seemed to have lucked out and gotten his mom's good looks and good sense."

"Very funny. The other kid started it, and let's just say Brian finished it. How are your guys?"

"They're good. I miss 'em. It's hard being away so much. They're getting so big, you know?"

"Yeah, I know. It's like you blink and they're grown up. Can you believe Brian's bar mitzvah's in a couple of weeks?"

Luke saw his opening. This was the moment he should confess that he wasn't going to be able to make it. That he was going to have to miss one of the most important moments in his nephew's life because he would be on the campaign trail.

"We're getting old," his brother sighed.

Luke willed himself to say it, to say that he couldn't make it. But instead he said, "Speak for yourself, older brother. My *much* older brother."

"But much better looking," Josh replied.

"You keep telling yourself that."

They bantered about life, sports, and their parents for another ten minutes as Luke tried to work up the nerve to bring up the bar mitzvah again, when finally his brother said, "Shit. I didn't realize the time. I gotta hop. I'm already late."

"Go. Go. Sorry I kept you."

"No, it was good to catch up. Seriously you're so busy all the damn time. I worry about bugging you."

"You never bug me, Josh. Hearing from you guys is what keeps me sane out here. So let's make sure we catch up more often. Okay?"

"Okay, squirt. You got it."

"Do you have to call me that?"

"Yep."

"How did I know you were going to say that?"

"Because you know me so well."

"Tell Kate and the boys I said hi, and tell Brian I said to stay out of trouble. Nothing's worth throwing a punch for."

"I don't know about that."

"I forgot who I'm talking to."

"Look, some people you can reason with, Luke. But some people are assholes. This kid and his parents are assholes. I told Bri I was proud of him."

"What did the kid do?"

"You really want to know?"

"Yeah."

"He was talking shit about you. It went on for a while and Brian had finally had enough and one day said if he said another word about his uncle he'd deck him. The kid mouthed off and Brian clocked him. I know it may not be right to say, but I've honestly never been prouder of him in my life."

Luke was speechless. Finally he said, "Josh, I don't want to cause him trouble."

"You didn't cause it. The kid caused it. Actually, it was the kid's parents. I always knew they were jerks and this just confirmed it. Anyway, Bri owes you a thank you. He got a new iPod out of it. Kate was a little miffed, but I thought he deserved a present. You know, Mom always taught us to stand up for family, and that's what he did."

Luke was touched but also felt guilty for the way his life was taking over the lives of those he loved.

"Hey, wanna know the best part?" Josh asked.

"What?"

"The kid was bigger than Bri. Had a few inches and about twenty pounds on him. It was like Rocky taking down the Russian. Oh, and this cute girl that Bri's had a crush on forever is talking to him now. So don't be surprised if he thanks you at the bar mitzvah for landing him his first kiss."

"Glad I could do some good."

After hanging up Luke shot Mimi an e-mail about the Colby fund-raiser. He informed her that he had a scheduling conflict.

CHAPTER 17

Since the Means revelation, the media had been treating the Cooper campaign as if Luke really could become the next commander in chief. Now Luke, Laura, and the whole family were under more scrutiny than they had ever been.

In a conversation with an entertainment reporter with the show *Celebrity Beat*, Laura was asked about her favorite music. She mentioned Kool & the Gang, Fleetwood Mac, and the Gap Band (all answers she had cleared with the campaign). When they asked for her thoughts on younger artists, Laura drew a blank. The reporter then asked her thoughts on hip-hop's reigning queen, TaMara, known as much for her scantily clad costumes as her music. Laura replied, "That's not really my kind of music." The reporter pressed and asked if Luke or the boys enjoyed TaMara's music. Laura replied, "I don't know that that type of entertainment is appropriate for children, at least not mine."

The quote was picked up, with some drawing comparisons to Tipper Gore and other mothers of the eighties who had campaigned against racy lyrics by artists such as Prince, thus engendering the permanent enmity of some in the entertainment biz.

Unbeknownst to Laura, however, TaMara and her rapper husband had recently given the maximum contribution to Luke's campaign and, at least until the quote appeared, were in discussions about possibly hosting a fundraiser for him.

The incident left Laura rattled. She was exhausted all of the time, constantly worried about saying the wrong thing, worried about wearing the wrong thing, and worried about the impact Luke being away from their children, and her, was having on their family. One of her aunts (a three-time divorcée) used to always say "Absence makes the heart grow yonder, not fonder" and "The average man is as faithful as his options," and though Luke had never given her any reason to worry, he was yonder a lot more and he had a lot more options. When Laura heard that the actress Tracy Gilmore, on whom Luke once had a huge crush, had agreed to cohost an event for Luke with Luke's college buddy Marcus, it gave her pause.

But she didn't dare voice her fears to anyone. This was a once-in-a-lifetime experience. She just had to hang tough. But sometimes she felt like she was hanging by a thread.

Days after the TaMara interview, Laura spoke with Brooke by phone.

"How's the next First Lady?"

"You sound a lot more sure of that happening than I am right now."

"Rough week?"

"Yeah." Laura was really down.

"Laura, you can't let it all get to you."

"I wish it were that easy. You know TaMara and her husband canceled a fundraiser because of me?"

"Well, I'm sorry to hear she has such a thin skin. I mean, everyone knows that her dance routines look like they came straight from a strip club and aren't appropriate for kids. You just had the balls to say it out loud."

Laura smiled for the first time in days.

"Anyway," Brooke continued, "we've wasted enough brain power and conversation on her. I was calling to talk about something much more important."

"Sure. What's up?"

"I heard you're going to be back in town soon."

"Oh right. I have some Women for Cooper fundraisers, I think. Hopefully you and Tami can make it?"

"Laura, if you need me there I'm happy to attend, but I actually wanted to know if you wanted to do a spa date."

Laura hadn't really thought about it, but in the last two months the most relaxing and self-indulgent thing she had done was sleep.

"I don't know, Brooke."

"What's not to know? Look, you can't let this completely consume your life. You gotta keep living or you're going to go insane."

Brooke was reading her mind.

"I'll invite Tami and we'll make a girls' day of it. Sound good?"

"Sounds great," Laura said.

"Okay, well I'm heading to L.A. in a couple of days, but I'll try to connect with your scheduling person about setting something up."

"You're going to L.A.?" Laura asked.

"Yeah. I finally got Nico on a magazine cover and the shoot is at the end of the week, so I have to go out to hold her hand."

"My condolences to the photographer. I'll say a prayer for him."

Brooke laughed. "How about a prayer for me? He'll be rid of her after one afternoon. I'm the one who will be stuck with her indefinitely." Nico Stiles was a Hollywood starlet famous for being famous. Her parents were longtime celebrity hangers-on and had groomed their daughter accordingly, so though Nico had no discernible talent, she was often seen in the company of those who did. After she grew sick of being a tabloid co-star she decided to set out to become a tabloid star herself, and did so by co-starring in a film with two of her B-list celebrity pals, a sex tape that in days made Nico a household name. Brooke wasn't exactly proud of representing her, but three of her professional athlete clients had recently retired. Nico was single-handedly keeping Brooke's business afloat, so she had to put up with Nico's antics, embarrassing and irritating as they may be.

"You know, Luke's doing some events out there."

"Yeah, I heard. One with Brian Colby and one with Marcus. Garin told me."

"Apparently Tracy Gilmore will be at one."

"Oh really?"

"Yeah, and some of her actress friends, Ramona Jeffries and Genie Booth." Ramona and Genie were two of Hollywood's hottest up-and-coming black actresses. Ramona had proclaimed in a recent interview that she had a "crush" on the governor.

"Really?" Brooke replied.

"Yep."

"Funny that Garin didn't mention *that*."

Laura trusted her husband completely, but her trips on the campaign trail reminded her that she couldn't always trust other women. She had seen more than a couple—black, white, and every color in between—pass their business cards to her handsome, charming, powerful husband. Though she had always seen him pass those cards along to an aide, at least a part of her subscribed to the words her aunt had imparted upon her years before: "The average man is as faithful as his options." And now her husband was heading off to L.A. to mingle with a bevy of beautiful young models and actresses, without his wife.

"Well, I'm sure you have absolutely nothing to worry about," Brooke continued, "because when it comes to men, Luke is in the ninetieth percentile of great ones. But why don't I swing by just to say hello and get a few autographs from these ladies just the same? Besides, I'm sure my husband will be just thrilled to have me tagging along." She laughed.

Brooke reminded Laura yet again why she liked her so much.

★

"What is this I hear about you missing some important fundraiser?" Esther Cooper said when her son called for his weekly check-in.

"What are you talking about?"

"That baseball player. The one who was nice enough to offer to help you raise money to become president, and I heard you're not attending."

"How did you know about that?"

"How I know isn't important."

"First of all, he's a basketball player, Mom."

"Whatever. I knew that he played some kind of ball. That's not the issue. When someone offers to do something nice for you it's not nice to stand them up. It's rude."

"Mom, it's the same day as Brian's bar mitzvah."

"I know that. I also know that he's unable to do it any other day and it was extremely generous of him to offer to help you and you can use the help, so you should take it."

Luke couldn't believe what he was hearing. His mother had always insisted "family first."

"What about family comes first?"

"Well, we are your family and we are putting you first. This is a once-in-a-lifetime opportunity and we don't want you to say woulda, shoulda, coulda. Besides, I don't know who this ballplayer fellow is, but I'm sure

Brian does and I'm sure that he would enjoy receiving a bar mitzvah call from this gentleman, maybe even an autograph or something."

Luke was speechless. Finally all he could say was, "Who tattled?"

"That's for me to know. So just so we're clear, you can officially consider this an order. I expect you to attend that fundraiser, young man, no ifs ands or buts."

Luke knew better than to argue with her. It was a lost cause, so he just said what he always did, "Yes, ma'am."

The following day Nate sent Mrs. Cooper a thank-you bouquet.

CHAPTER 18

L uke was in California for only forty-eight hours, but each minute was jam-packed.

He really appreciated having Adam on the trail with him at moments like these, when he felt so exhausted that he wasn't sure if he could go on. They hadn't spent this much time together since they were kids. Adam returned home to Michigan here and there, but in the weeks since Laura contacted him he had been a constant presence by Luke's side, making himself useful doing everything from holding campaign signs at events to running errands for the candidate.

Even though Luke essentially had Laura trick Adam into joining him on the trail as a way to help his old friend, Luke had really come to rely on him. Adam's most important job was to serve as Luke's sounding board, the one person he could talk to on the campaign trail who wasn't being paid to give him a certain answer.

Their morning jogs became one of the highlights of Luke's day. But he knew how much he truly valued having Adam there after returning to his car shortly after a disastrous meeting with a union, which Luke knew had just cost him their endorsement. He was mad at the union rep who antagonized him during the meeting, mad at his policy staff for not prepping him strongly enough, and mad that things were not going well.

Yet when he slid into his black SUV, there was Adam, laughing.

Luke was silent.

"Hey," Adam said.

"Hey," Luke mumbled.

Adam's giggling had turned into full-throated laughter again.

Luke barked, "What's so funny?"

"Nothing," Adam said, sensing Luke was upset. He wiped the smile off of his face and fell silent, biting his lip trying to stop the laughter.

Finally Luke said, "Well, clearly it's something."

"No. It's nothing . . . it's just . . ."

"What?" Luke asked.

"It's just . . . I was watching this old 'Three Stooges' episode on my laptop. It's the one where they're cavemen. I always crack up when they start throwing the eggs."

". . . and rocks. I remember that one," Luke said.

"I wasn't sure if you'd remember."

"Of course I do. We tried imitating them and you ended up with a black eye and I ended up grounded."

Adam pulled open his laptop and began playing the episode. Luke laughed so loud that his driver turned and asked, "What's so funny back there?"

Luke repeated Adam's earlier reply, "Nothing," as tears of laughter began streaming down his face.

★

It was only noon and Luke had already squeezed in a full day's work. He started at a fundraising breakfast for local Democratic activists at 7:30 a.m., followed by a visit to an elementary school at 9:15 a.m., followed by a rally at a local college at 11:30 a.m.

The crowd was impressive, considering it was raining lightly. There were more than 400 students with "Cooper for President" and "College Students for Cooper" signs.

Though Joe had flown in specifically for the Colby fundraiser, Luke convinced him to attend the rally so they'd have a chance to catch up over lunch.

At first Adam was annoyed when Luke mentioned Joe would be stopping by. His memories of Joe bullying him in school had not faded. Luke was surprised. He knew Joe was not Adam's favorite person but he didn't realize Joe had tormented him so when they were teens.

"You know, it's just because he was having a tough time."

"Yeah, I'm sure the blond-haired blue-eyed jock god had a real tough time in high school compared to me, who was short, fat, and wore glasses."

"Yeah, but you had your parents to go home to. Joe never had that. Deep down he envied you. Do you know how many of his football games his dad made? One. And that was only because Joe's mom threatened to castrate him if he didn't. How many of your band performances did your folks miss?"

Adam paused before quietly saying, "None."

"There you go."

★

The rally officially began when the campus chair of Students for Cooper came out and welcomed the crowd. She then introduced the guest of honor, Luke.

Luke came out to boisterous applause and said in his best announcer voice, "Hellloooo California College!!"

The crowd went wild and took minutes to settle down.

"Thank you!" Luke shouted. "Thank you!"

Finally the applause began to subside.

Luke began his stump speech, slightly modified to address issues of concern to college students, such as student loan debt.

A few minutes into his speech three students began chanting, "Cooper is a homophobe! Cooper is a homophobe!" They unfurled a banner that read "Gay Soldiers Deserve Dignity Too."

A week before, at a candidate's forum, Luke had been challenged on his stance on openly gay and lesbian service members serving in the military. His noncommittal response—that while he "honored the service of military members of all sexual orientations," he would "ultimately look to military leaders for guidance on the issue and defer to them"—had displeased gay and lesbian advocacy groups, who were publicly praising Senator Beaman, who believed that gay and lesbian service members should be permitted to serve openly, no questions asked.

Joe turned to the students and shouted, "Why don't you shut the fuck up and let him speak?"

The students continued chanting until Joe—who was bigger than each of them—barreled over to them and shouted, "Hey, he doesn't go over to where you're working and slap the dick out of your mouth, so why don't you let him do his job!"

At that point Adam actually grabbed Joe by the arm and managed to drag him away.

The rest of the students at the rally then began chanting "Cooper! Cooper! Cooper!" until the three dissidents were completely drowned out and finally took their banner and left.

Luke then said, "You know, when progressives get together it's like family. You fight with family, but you always make up for Thanksgiving dinner, and that's what an election's like, right?" The audience laughed and applauded.

After he finished speaking Luke began working the ropeline, shaking hands with students, signing autographs, and smiling for photos as his security detail hovered nearby. Adam began making his way to the private holding area, where Luke would be exiting, to say a quick hello to some of the college's janitorial staff before exiting to his awaiting car. As they walked, Joe said, "That was fucking awesome!"

Adam grabbed Joe by the collar, and though Joe was bigger and stronger than him, Adam practically picked him up off the ground. "What the hell's the matter with you?" he said.

"What's the matter with me? Have you lost your mind, Ad-Man?"

"What were you thinking, yelling at those kids?"

"They were being dicks."

"No, *you* were being a dick. I know it's hard for you to get your head around this, Joe—because it's hard for you to get the head that's *not* in your pants around much of anything—but *this* is not about you. It's about my best friend, who's supposed to be your best friend too. And if you care about him then for once in your life stop acting like some jock asshole stereotype from an eighties teen flick and act like a fucking grown-up."

"What the fuck is the matter with you?" Joe screeched and pulled away. "Who do you think you are?"

Then Adam managed to get Joe in a headlock. "Who do I think I am? Who do I think I am? I *know* that I am a friend of the next president of the United States. Say it with me, 'I am a friend of the next president of the United States.'"

"You're crazy!" Joe yelled.

"Am I?" Adam asked. "Well, then you better hope I don't accidentally snap your neck, because that means I can plead temporary insanity and I'll probably get off. Say it, say 'I am friends with the next president of the United States of America and I will not do or say anything that will hurt him or his campaign.' Say it!"

"Alright! I am friends . . ."

". . . with the next president of the United States. . . ."

"And I will not do or say anything to hurt him . . ."

Joe fell silent and Adam squeezed his neck tighter.

"And I will not do or say anything . . . ," Joe screeched.

"To hurt him or his campaign," Adam said, by way of a reminder.

". . . to hurt him or his campaign."

"Do you mean it?"

"Yes. . . . I can't breathe!"

Adam released Joe.

As Joe stood gasping for air, Adam looked at him and said, "Joe, I'm going to say this only once, and I want you to know that I mean it. If you screw this up for our friend, I will beat the shit out of you."

Joe stood there dumbfounded.

"Now let's go," Adam said. "Luke's waiting for us."

Fifteen minutes later Luke greeted them both with a smile and a hug. "Did you see that crowd?" he exclaimed. "Was that your first rally, Nelson?"

"Yeah," Joe mumbled.

"Did you have fun?"

Adam nudged Joe in the back. "Yeah. It was fun," Joe said. "You're going to make a terrific president. We're all going to do whatever we can to help."

★

After the three of them finished lunch, Adam stepped away to call his wife.

"So are you going to keep me in suspense for forever?"

"What do you mean?" Joe asked.

"Well, what is this I hear about you having a wedding date?"

Joe looked sheepish. "I guess I figured, with my track record, better to just wait to see how things actually turn out before broadcasting the news."

Luke smiled.

"The good news about so many false starts is, you know that this means this one must be pretty special."

"They're all special," Joe said and winked.

Luke rolled his eyes playfully. "When's the wedding?"

"We're planning for next month."

"That's soon?"

"I just don't want to jinx it. You know? It's taken me so long to get here I just kind of want to . . ." He found himself at a loss for words.

"I hear you," Luke added helpfully.

They sat in silence for a bit before Luke asked, "Your dad going to be your best man?"

"I don't think we're going to do all of that. Probably something small. Vegas . . ."

"Smart man. You don't know hell until you've had to spend three hours going over different types of wedding napkins. I spent two of those hours wondering how long it would take me to smother myself to death with one."

Joe laughed.

FIFTEEN YEARS BEFORE
_____

As practically everyone else in the ballroom continued doing the electric slide, Luke crept out of the room. He found Joe standing on the hotel's patio, which had breathtaking views of the entire city.

"Well, looks like I owe Garin twenty bucks."

Joe turned. "For what?"

"When I couldn't find you I was convinced you were off in a closet somewhere with either a bridesmaid or bartender. But Garin said, 'Nah. Not on your wedding day.' He was right."

"Come on. You know how seriously I take being best man, third runner-up."

Since Luke had three brothers, his closest friends had been told that while they wouldn't be official best men, they would be official "best man runners-up."

"Well, I appreciate it. Means a lot to me."

The two stood there staring at the view for a few minutes.

"I can't believe I'm married."

"I can," Joe said.

Luke gave him a puzzled look.

"Your parents are so happy. I can see how you'd want that. Who wouldn't?"

"If Laura and I end up half as happy as they are, I'll be happy."

"You two will be. Anyone watching the way you two looked at each other when you danced could tell you were the real deal." Luke and Laura's first dance had been to Stevie Wonder's "Knocks Me off My Feet."

"It means a lot hearing you say that," Luke replied. "A part of me wondered if you'd demote me as a friend for leaving you hanging out there by yourself."

"Oh I'm not by myself. I've got Sandi, Candi, and Mandi to keep me company," he said with a devilish grin.

"How could I forget?" Luke said, shaking his head at his old friend.

"Seriously, Laura's perfect, Luke. She's beautiful, funny, smart. You were smart to reel her in before someone else got her."

"Thanks, man." Luke was genuinely touched and surprised that Joe sounded so grown up and un-Joe-like for a change.

"I mean, if you're going to be stuck having sex with the same person the rest of your life, might as well look like her."

And then just like that the old Joe returned.

"Hey watch it, you're talking about my wife."

"Sorry," Joe said, though his smile indicated he really wasn't. "Seriously, I wish you both all good stuff."

"Thanks."

They then hugged.

As they embraced they heard a throat being cleared—loudly.

Luke turned to see a perky blonde standing behind them.

"Um. Sorry to interrupt. I just wanted to say I had fun and wanted to make sure you had my number." The woman then passed Joe a napkin. She kissed him on the cheek before walking away.

Joe looked sheepishly at Luke and shrugged like a little boy caught with his hand in the cookie jar. "She's not a bridesmaid," he said, referencing Luke and Garin's bet.

"I know that," Luke said. "She's Laura's boss's daughter."

Joe began to blush.

Luke added, "So I hope you had fun today, because you are going to call her and you are going to see her again or I'm going to have to kill you."

Luke then began to shake his head and said, "What are we going to do with you?"

He then patted his old friend on the back and said, "Come on. The deejay promised me she'd play the chicken dance next. I know how much you love that one."

As they walked away he added, "And Joe, please do me a favor."

"Sure. Name it."

"I really like the deejay and want to be able to hire her for future events, so please don't sleep with her."

"She is cute, isn't she?" Joe said, smiling.

"You are hopeless," Luke said, laughing.

CHAPTER 19

After lunch Joe headed off to stop by the West Coast office of his firm while Adam met up with an old pal from the music industry. He said it was "just to catch up," but Luke knew it was really in hopes of landing a new job. Luke returned to his hotel for a quick change before heading to the Paramount lot to meet up with Marcus so they could travel to the fundraiser together. Mimi traveled with him in case there was any extra money she could squeeze out of his costars or any entertainment executives who might be hanging nearby.

As the widow of a studio executive, Mimi had been on countless lots, so she wasn't impressed. She felt right at home. Within minutes she ran into an old friend, an actor her husband had given his first big break. While Luke tried to play it cool, he did feel a bit like a kid. He saw life-size cartoon characters go by—or two men dressed as them. He then saw an actress who had once co-starred on *Law & Order* walk by. It was his favorite show. Luke tried to be nonchalant, but she could tell he was in awe, so she winked at him.

Just then he saw some large ogre-faced character walking in his direction. Luke moved to let the person by. Then to his surprise and horror "it" came right toward him. Luke blanched before hearing a familiar voice shout, "Hey! There he is!"

It was Marcus.

"What *are* you wearing?" Luke asked, disconcerted.

"Uh—my signature costume. I am working, you know. But thanks for letting me know that you've never watched the show, Governor." He slapped Luke on the arm.

Luke blushed before replying in his best smart-ass voice, "Well, you're not the only one who's busy, Marcus. Given the choice I figured it might be a better investment to use what little free time I have to do little things like checking my voice mail instead of turning on my television."

"Alright. Alright. I got it, Coop. I'm an ass who doesn't call back. Geez, you're worse than a nagging girlfriend. Speaking of, how's Laura?"

Laura never approved of Marcus, considering him a bad influence on Luke, a belief solidified when Laura discovered a small tattoo on her brand-new husband's upper-right butt cheek on their wedding night, courtesy of a raucous night out with Marcus days before their wedding. From that day forward, whenever Laura really needed leverage with Luke she threatened to tell his mother about the tattoo, something that was almost universally frowned on by older Jewish Americans, due to the belief that any form of desecration to the body would prevent a proper burial in a Jewish cemetery.

"Very funny. She's wonderful. Thanks for asking. How's Natalie?" Luke asked.

"Who?" Marcus replied.

"Natalie? Isn't that her name? The model—you know, who's young enough to be your . . ."

"*Niece*? I'm sure that's what you were about to say, right?"

"If that's what you want to tell yourself, sure," Luke said with a mischievous smile.

"Long gone, Coop. Hard to settle down in this business, you know?"

Luke had always assumed that the difference between Joe and Marcus was that while Joe was clearly a commitment-phobe, Marcus really did seem like someone who would hold off on marriage until his career was where he wanted it to be. But there were others, like Garin and Brooke, who assumed that there was a much bigger reason for Marcus's bachelor status. It was only when one of Luke's openly gay campaign staffers asked him directly if Marcus was "seeing anybody" that Luke finally gave any credence to the rumors about Marcus's sexual orientation. Luke didn't care, but he did think it sad that Marcus would feel the need to hide. Marcus was one of the most ambitious people he'd ever met, and if he thought being gay would impact his career, he'd probably go to his grave without publicly acknowledging it.

Marcus's ambition was fueled largely by his father, one of the first black cardiac surgeons to practice at a white hospital. He was elated when his son followed in his footsteps by attending Morehouse but had been greatly disappointed by his son's chosen career. The fact that his father favored his brothers—a dentist and pediatrician—weighed on him heavily.

"How are things going with the job?"

"Honestly, Coop..." Marcus searched for the words. "Look, any actor who's working is a blessed actor. That said, I went to the Yale School of Drama and here I am stuck on this shit show while that twenty-two-year-old rapper who was just released from prison is co-starring in the new Pacino flick. I feel like I might have been better off heading to Rikers after Morehouse instead of grad school."

Just then two scantily clad extras, one blonde and one brunette, walked by the two of them and said in flirtatious unison, "Hiiiii, Marcus..."

"Hi, ladies," Marcus said, turning his head as if wanting to enjoy the view from behind for as long as possible.

"Although the job does have its perks," he said brightly. "Come on, I want to introduce you to a few people in the cast."

★

Luke couldn't believe it when he and Marcus walked into the VIP room of Homecoming, an upscale lounge that had become a favorite after-hours spot for much of so-called Black Hollywood and, increasingly, their non-black friends, acquaintances, and hangers-on. It was like walking into every man's ultimate fantasy. A number of Hollywood's most beautiful black actresses were there. Marcus had dated a few of them, while others were merely longtime friends. Black Hollywood remained a relatively small world. Though it was still tough for most black actors and actresses to land the cover of major magazines or garner paychecks comparable to those of some of their white counterparts (unless your name was Will Smith), there was still a vibrant community of blacks, both onscreen and off, who though not household names to the average white American, were thriving in Hollywood nonetheless. Many of them knew each other, supported each other, and partied together, so when the word spread that Marcus was putting together an event for his friend who was running for president, many of them responded in kind, particularly since a number had been following the up-and-coming governor's career in some of the same magazines and blogs that followed their own professional (and personal) exploits. The event was dubbed "Black Hollywood in Support of 'Cool Hand Luke.'"

Luke was not exactly what you would call hip. Beyond Spike Lee, Denzel Washington, Will Smith, Marcus, and every black cast member of every *Law & Order* franchise, he was not exactly a Black Hollywood aficionado. But while he didn't recognize these people by name, he recognized many faces. Among them, the notoriously press shy Oscar-winning actor Denny Roberts, who wasn't black but whose latest girlfriend was, just like all of his previous girlfriends and wives. He had earned the nickname "Candyman" from a black blogger who joked that Denny had a "sweet tooth," as demonstrated by his love of chocolate.

The room was filled with beautiful brown people. And contrary to stereotype, there was not a single rapper among the Homecoming bunch.

Others in the room included Gaby Washington, the beautiful young actress who had co-starred in a handful of films with Hollywood heavyweights, including Will Smith and Matt Damon, as well as Jonathan Fuchs, one of only a handful of African Americans to be nominated for a best-director Academy Award. The entire cast of the sitcom *Ladies First*, which had been called a black version of *Sex and the City*, was also there.

Luke missed having Laura there, knowing that she would have been fun to navigate the room with because she knew more about who was who than he did.

Afterward, Luke delivered some brief remarks and took questions. More than one of the guests asked him for talking points they could use to convince their parents to switch their support from Beaman. This was the first time Luke could ever remember not actually wanting to leave a fundraiser.

Toward the end of the event he and Garin began chatting with Ramona Jeffries, the actress who had joked she had a "crush on the governor" on an episode of *Live with Regis & Kelly*. She was widely considered one of the most beautiful women in the world, having recently appeared in *People* magazine's "Most Beautiful" issue. In another interview she had mentioned feeling a particular kinship with the governor because being biracial, Jeffries shared a similar experience of being a black child raised by a white parent.

The three of them discussed AIDS funding. She had recently become a celebrity ambassador for the Black AIDS Alliance.

"Well this is something that Luke and I both feel passionately about," Garin said. "Luke has done more than any other governor to increase awareness on this issue in our community."

"Really?" Jeffries replied, clearly impressed.

"Garin, I gotta hire you for the campaign," Luke teased. Garin had a way of being a sort of magnet for beautiful women, and this was yet another example.

"No, seriously, this is such an important issue. In fact I've been trying to get my firm to become more involved on the philanthropic front. I work for an investment firm," Garin said, flashing his thousand-watt grin.

"Really?" Jeffries nodded.

"Yes."

"Do you enjoy that?" she asked him.

"I enjoy making people happy. And when my clients make money, they're happy."

"I guess our jobs are really not so different after all," Jeffries replied. "I feel the same way about moviegoers."

Garin laughed before saying, "Let me give you my card."

"Garin's really great at what he does," Luke chimed in. "You won't find anyone better in looking out for your interests," he said, repaying Garin for his kind words about him.

As Garin fished in his wallet for a business card, they heard a voice say, "I'll second that."

Garin looked stricken.

"Hi, hon. Happy to see me?" Brooke asked.

"Of course!" Garin blurted out. "Surprised, but *so* happy. *So very* happy," he said, his voice three octaves higher than normal.

Luke had to bite his lip to keep from laughing.

"Aren't you going to introduce me to your new friend?"

"Of course," Garin said. "Honey, this is . . . uh . . . uh . . . uh . . ."

"Ramona," the actress replied, helping him out, clearly bemused by it all. She extended her hand.

"I certainly know who you are, Miss Jeffries. It's a pleasure," Brooke replied. "I'm a big fan. So is Garin. Aren't you, honey?"

"I don't go to the movies a lot," Garin stammered.

"Sure you do," Brooke replied. "We just saw your last film with Denzel a few weeks ago. You were fabulous. But I must say you're actually more beautiful in person." She turned to Garin. "Don't you think so, honey?"

"You know what we need?" Garin asked. "Drinks? You need a drink, my love. I'll get you a glass of white wine. Luke, Ramona, can I get you something?"

"I'm good," Ramona said, smiling knowingly.

"Actually, I've got to circulate or I'm going to get in trouble with my fundraising team. Miss Jeffries, I can't thank you enough again for your support, and I will definitely have my staff get in touch regarding your generous offer to campaign at college campuses on my behalf."

"Please call me Ramona. And it's my pleasure."

"Okay. Well thank you, Ramona. Would you mind if I asked you for one more favor?"

"Not at all."

"Would you mind calling my wife? She's a big, big fan of yours and is sad she couldn't make it tonight. Is that lame for me to ask?"

"Happy to do it," Ramona replied sweetly.

Luke pulled out his cell phone and dialed and said, "Hey, gorgeous. I have someone who wants to say hello. It's a surprise. You know the last movie we saw?"

He then passed the phone to Ramona, who opened with, "Hi, Mrs. Cooper, this is Ramona Jeffries. I just want to say two things. One, it's a pleasure to speak with you, and two, if they ever make a movie about you and your husband, I'd be honored to play you as First Lady."

Brooke smiled. Watching the moment take place confirmed what she already knew, that Laura had nothing to worry about with her husband.

Just then Garin returned with a drink for her. He leaned in to kiss her on the lips and she turned her head then whispered, "Are you sure you want to kiss me in front of your new girlfriend?"

Luke heard the exchange and laughed.

★

On the way to the Colby fundraiser Mimi gave Luke a final briefing on some of the donors who would be in the room. She highlighted those who were particularly important targets because she believed that they either were capable of hosting their own event for Luke at a later date or capable of helping the campaign "bundle," as in collect and bundle checks from their rich friends or family members. She also warned him about some of the strong personality types in the room. While Marcus's event, which was successful, was a mid-tier event where the minimum contribution was $500, the Jacobs event was a max event where the minimum ticket to attend was $2,300, due in large part to Brian Colby's attendance. Usually, the higher the ticket price at these things, the bigger the egos involved, and Mimi knew it. Though she had survived so far without having a blowup with Colby's wife Sunny, she knew that there would probably be a few Sunnys in the room that night—only most of them would be wearing a suit and tie. In places like New York and Los Angeles, where celebrity tended to upend the traditional pecking order in the rest of the world where money dictated who was king, those with lots of money tended to act like bigger jerks just to remind everyone that while they may not have an Oscar or an Emmy, they could buy and sell most of the people who did.

When they arrived at the event one thing became crystal clear: Luke was not the star attraction. Brian Colby—all six feet eight inches of him—was. Only instead of being surrounded by a mini-mob scene of scantily clad groupies, Colby was being mobbed by middle-aged rich guys, Mimi's favorite audience (for both professional and personal reasons). Colby's wife Sunny lingered nearby, looking bored in an ultra-revealing dress better suited to the Grammys than a political fundraiser.

When Mimi began trying to work her way through the crowd so that she could grab Brian and escort him to the private office where he and Luke would be formally introduced, it became clear that some of the donors who had written sizable checks to Luke's campaign were there simply to meet Brian. But if there was one thing Mimi was not, it was shy, so she barreled through the mini cluster, ignoring one donor who shouted "Hey, blondie—there's a line!" She hurriedly introduced herself to Brian as Luke's aide and began dragging him in the opposite direction so that he could be escorted to the private office where he and Luke could chat for a bit.

Before Mimi knew what hit her, Sunny Colby was in her face. "Who the hell are you, and where are you going with my husband?"

"Sometimes being an attractive blonde had its downside," Mimi thought to herself.

"Sunny, I presume," Mimi said, extending her hand. "Mimi Van der Wohl. Pleasure to meet you."

Sunny began to turn bright red.

"Oh . . . Ummm . . ."

"I was just going to give Luke and Brian a couple of minutes of privacy to talk. You're welcome to join them, of course."

"Oh . . . okay. Thanks." Sunny then headed into the room, clearly embarrassed.

Mimi asked one of her assistants to locate Buddy Jacobs so that he could also join them.

Luke never ceased to amaze Mimi when it came to his ability to work miracles with his charm. When Mimi first spotted her, Sunny looked so grouchy that she wondered if she had a scowl permanently tattooed on her face. She looked annoyed with the guests, the event, and life in general, but within minutes of meeting Luke she was laughing—and it was not forced laughter, but the kind of laughter that comes only when you feel genuinely relaxed. Brian was smiling too, although he didn't speak as much as his pint-size, uber-assertive wife.

Mimi wasn't surprised to learn that Brian wasn't exactly the brightest bulb in the lamppost, but he seemed nice. Things appeared to be going well. Then the conversation moved to their kids.

Brian asked about Luke's boys and their sports interests. Luke then asked him if he had any sons. Sunny shot both Luke and Brian a dirty look before Brian then changed the subject. Though Mimi immediately got it, Luke was confused as to why the room had turned tense. He wasn't exactly up on celebrity baby mama drama.

But as she so often did, Mimi came to the rescue. "Sunny, I hope you don't mind me asking, but your dress is to die for. Who's it by?"

"Versace," Sunny replied, still annoyed.

Though Mimi's first thought was "I wonder if she can actually spell that?" she said, "And are those the new Louboutins?"

Sunny nodded.

"Well, Brian, you're lucky."

They all looked puzzled before Mimi added dramatically, "Because if your wife didn't look so hot in those shoes, I would have to kill her because I tried to get my hands on a pair after seeing them in *Vogue* and was told they were a special limited edition."

Sunny beamed. "Yeah. I'm one of the only people who has a pair."

"Well, you are wearing the hell out of them, my dear," Mimi replied.

"Thanks," Sunny said cheerily.

"No, thank *you* for participating in our little event."

"Oh, it's our pleasure," Sunny said, then plopped down on Brian's lap and gave him a kiss.

Crisis averted.

Luke asked Brian if he would mind saying hello to a few of his friends. Joe, Garin, Adam, and Brooke filed in.

But Mimi had trouble locating Brock, until one of her aides said the guests seemed to be under control—except for one guy who kept on insisting that he be escorted to the "VIP room." Mimi knew it was Brock. He had once said to her that he was not "impressed by famous people. They put their pants on one leg at a time like the rest of us." But he conveniently mentioned that he was "going to be in L.A. around the time of the fundraiser" and so said he "might stop by" and ordered Mimi to put him on the "VIP list for the event." The event was being hosted in the home of a famous Hollywood director so the entire list was "VIP," but she let Brock continue thinking that he was extra special.

Brian dutifully posed for pictures with Luke's "Dream Team." He then did Luke a special favor by calling Luke's nephew, also named Brian, to chat with him at his bar mitzvah. He actually put him on speakerphone and put the phone to a microphone so the other guests could hear the NBA's MVP say hello.

As the crew then made their way to the main living room where the party was taking place, Joe whispered to Luke, "I have a big surprise for you."

"What is it?" Luke asked.

"Well, if I tell you it won't be a surprise." Joe winked.

Luke displayed his trademark self-deprecating humor when he opened his remarks by saying "I know that most of you are here to hear me speak and not to meet Brian Colby, but I don't want him to feel bad or unloved so with that in mind, I think I'm going to keep my remarks brief so we can allow adequate time to make him feel loved and you all can pretend you're fans who are actually here to see him." People broke into laughter.

Usually at political fundraisers an endless stream of guests waiting to take photos with the candidates is par for the course. This night, however, the photo line was primarily for Colby. Luke took it in stride and floated with Mimi meeting donors. As usual, Mimi worked the room like a general executing a battle plan. There were a handful of starlets in the room (or "starfish," as Mimi called them, because they were "fishing" for the next man to sleep with who could possibly transform them from merely working actresses to superstar), but the $2,300 checks they wrote to be in the same room as Buddy Jacobs was about as much money as she was likely to squeeze out of them. What she needed to line up were more people who were willing to open their homes and fill them with like-minded and like-walleted friends who would also be willing to write checks for the Cooper campaign. Rich nobodies who liked hanging out with somebodies made the best donors. These were Mimi's targets, the suits in the room and their wives. There was one woman, however, who stood out.

One unspoken secret of beautiful people is that they all notice one another, much like two racial minorities in a crowd might smile at each other as if to say, "Nice to see I'm not the only one here." This woman was African American but bore a slight resemblance to Pamela Anderson in her younger years. She looked like she could be an actress, but Mimi didn't recognize her. Although the woman could do with a little less makeup and a lot more bra, she was incredibly attractive, and Mimi wasn't the only one who noticed. She watched as men's heads turned as the brown Barbie-esque figure made her way through the crowd. Within minutes she was standing before them and gave Luke an enthusiastic hug.

"Hey, Monique," Luke said, as the woman leaned over to kiss Luke on both cheeks.

"It's so great to see you!" she exclaimed.

"Lovely to see you too," Luke replied.

"I don't believe we've met," Mimi said, extending her hand.

"Oh hello. Monique. Monique Montgomery."

"Pleasure," Mimi replied. "And how do you two know each other?"

"Monique has been a supporter since way back. She was at one of my very first events last year."

"Yes. I knew him when!" Monique said with a girlish giggle.

Ten seconds into their conversation Mimi could already tell that Monique was precisely the kind of woman that Sunny—and any other wife—should be worried about. Her hug and kiss with Luke were just a tad too familiar and she arched her back in such a way that her breasts were pushed out just a tad too far.

"And what brings you to L.A.? Did you come all this way for our little event?" Mimi asked.

"No. I was here on business, and Brock mentioned the event, so I figured I'd pop by."

"Oh, you know Brock?"

"Doesn't everybody?" she said, giggling.

"And what do you do?" Mimi continued.

"I own a boutique uptown," Monique cheerily said, handing Mimi a card. "You should stop by sometime. We'll take care of you."

"I'm pretty well taken care of," Mimi coolly replied.

Before things turned awkward, Mimi said, "Luke, I want to introduce you to Mr. Morgan before he sneaks out. It was lovely meeting you," she said to Monique, reaching for Luke's arm.

"Monique—thanks as always for the support," Luke said with a bright smile.

"Don't mention it!"

As Mimi walked away with Luke she noticed that Brooke appeared to be watching the two of them. Her bemused expression seemed to indicate that she had been watching the entire exchange with Monique. She then gave Mimi a knowing smile and a nod that seemed to say, "You get it. You get Monique. Nice work." Mimi shot Brooke a little wink, and then grabbed Luke's elbow to continue steering him across the room.

When Colby's wife decided that she had had enough, she displayed her trademark bitchiness, marching right up to Brian in the middle of a picture with a donor, grabbing his hand and announcing, "We're leaving."

Brian just followed behind her like a puppy, even though she was literally half his size.

Mimi made sure Luke was nearby so he could say good-bye to Brian (and his bitchy wife) in person.

Luke thanked him again, and then a fan walked up and asked if Brian would mind returning to the other room for one last photo with his son. Sunny rolled her eyes and sighed very loudly and very rudely, but Brian obliged, following the man into the main living room area. Mimi's cell phone began vibrating and she said, "Sorry—gotta take this," and stepped into the hallway just off the foyer.

That left just Luke and Sunny . . . and it was awkward.

"So . . . ," Luke began. "How old is your little one?"

Asking about kids was almost a surefire way to sustain brief small talk with a married woman, Luke thought.

"She's almost two," Sunny said matter-of-factly, as though disinterested in the subject.

"I've got two myself. . . ."

"Yeah, you said that earlier."

Not sure what to say next, Luke figured he would fall back on his good old, reliable, stock campaign jargon. It had never let him down before.

"That's why I'm running for president . . . you know, I really care about all of our kids and their futures . . ."

Sunny stared at him blankly.

"So it means a lot to have you and your husband's support. I really appreciate it."

"Well, you didn't really have much competition. The other guys running don't have an ass like yours." She then leaned in close and said, "Your wife is very, very lucky."

Out of nowhere, a voice bellowed, "Yes, she is."

It was Brooke. "Too bad the same can't be said for your husband."

Luke felt his brown skin turn bright red.

Sunny looked stunned. A moment later Brian returned. "We're leaving!" Sunny hissed.

"Good," Brooke said under her breath.

Just then Mimi returned. "Sorry about that. What'd I miss?"

Without responding, Sunny turned and dragged Brian out the door.

As they were going out, another woman was coming in.

"Hi, Luke," she said.

Luke stared, speechless.

"I hope you don't mind, but Joe told me to stop by."

With the silence growing increasingly uncomfortable, Mimi extended her hand. "Hello. I'm Luke's finance director, Mimi."

The woman, who Mimi observed was incredibly beautiful, and had an accent Mimi couldn't quite place, extended her hand in kind. "I'm Ranya, an old friend of Luke's." She turned toward Luke. I hope you don't mind, but Joe said it would be okay."

"Not at all," Luke said. He reached out to shake her hand. They shook awkwardly before he finally said, "This is crazy. Come here," and enveloped her in a hug. They hugged tightly before a throat began to clear.

"Hi. I'm Brooke."

"Oh," Ranya said, picking up on the territorial vibe Brooke was throwing out. "You must be Luke's wife. Lovely to meet you," she quickly added, extending her hand.

"No, I'm just an old friend too."

"Oh. Well it's great to meet you."

They all stood there awkwardly for more than a minute before Ranya finally asked, "So can I come inside or . . ."

"Yes! Of course!" Mimi, Luke, and Brooke all said, literally speaking over each other.

As Ranya breezed past them, Mimi said, "Last I saw Joe he was by the bar."

"Thanks," Ranya said, flashing a smile.

"I'll walk with you," Luke said.

Brooke and Mimi locked eyes.

As Luke and Ranya walked ahead of them, Mimi touched Brooke's arm. She leaned in and whispered, "Forgive me for not finding a more ladylike way to say this, but is it just me or did you get the vibe that those two used to fuck?"

"Nope. It's not just you."

"Okay. Just making sure."

"Which is why you will find me by our new-slash-old friend Ranya's side all night."

"And I will be by our friend Luke's side all night."

Brooke added, "As soon as we're alone I'll interrogate Garin to get the full story, and report back."

"Good stuff." She and Mimi high-fived and then made a beeline for the bar, where Luke, Ranya, and Joe were now chatting.

———————————

CHAPTER 20

"Hey, lady!"

Brooke got up and gave Laura a big hug.

"I'm so sorry I'm late!"

"Don't worry about it! Just gave us more time to drink," Brooke said.

Brooke and Tami were already attired in their plush white robes, with a signature *V* on the back, for *Victoria Salon & Spa*. They each had a glass of champagne in hand, one of Victoria's best-known perks.

"Hey, Tami!" Laura said, reaching out to squeeze her hand.

"Hey!"

"How are you?" Laura asked.

"I'm good. How are you?"

"Tired, but I'm hanging in there. Barely. All I know is Election Day can't come soon enough."

"I'll drink to that," Brooke said.

Just then their attendants entered the room.

"Ladies, are you ready to be pampered?"

"I think that is officially my favorite sentence in the English language," Brooke replied.

"I'll drink to that," Tami said.

Laura laughed.

After getting massages and facials, the trio finished up with pedicures.

"I met one of Luke's friends. Someone named Ranya," Brooke said gingerly. She was trying to gauge how much Laura knew about this Ranya woman, if she knew anything at all. "At least I think that was her name."

"Ranya?" Laura said. "Oh, is that the one he used to date?"

"Oh, you know her?" Brooke replied, relieved.

"I never met her. But I've heard about her. Apparently she was a real flake. She was in the arts or something. I think she was a bit nuts, so Luke broke it off with her."

"Oh really?"

"Well I don't remember the details but I do remember thinking at one point that I should send her a thank-you note on my wedding day."

"Why's that?" Brooke asked.

"Because after being with her, Luke seemed so relieved that our relationship was relatively drama free that I think he figured, 'I think I could do this for life.'"

Brooke and Tami laughed, although Brooke wasn't laughing that hard on the inside. From what Garin told her, Luke wasn't really the one who did the dumping. Ranya had been one of his first true loves and had cheated on him, and Luke struggled to get over her before meeting Laura, and after too.

"Luke mentioned that she popped up at some event," Laura continued. "What do you think of this color?"

"I love it," Tami said. "It will look great with your skin tone."

"I agree," Brooke chimed in.

"Thanks, ladies. I'll go with this one," she said to her nail technician.

"Anyway, I wasn't that surprised he ran into her."

"You weren't?"

"No. I've heard from at least ten people who swear they're my long-lost relatives now that he and I are in the news all of the time, so I'm not surprised a crazy ex would come out of the woodwork."

The ladies each took a sip of their champagne.

"What was she like?" Laura asked.

"Oh, nothing special," Brooke lied. She considered Ranya one of the most naturally beautiful women she had seen outside of a magazine cover.

Laura nodded.

"How are things going with the campaign?" Tami asked.

"Oh, they're going," Laura said sarcastically, then smiled.

"Brock says you guys have a lot of momentum right now."

"Well, I never want to get overly confident, but things are actually going pretty well. We're looking good in South Carolina. He's gaining in Florida and catching up in California. But you can just never predict these things, so I just try to focus on treating it like a once-in-a-lifetime experience, like traveling to a foreign country for work. No matter what happens, it's all an amazing experience and I don't want to take a single moment for granted."

"Your schedule must be the hardest part. I have no idea how you do it and manage to look great and raise the boys."

"Honestly, the hardest part is dealing with the staff. I just don't know that I'm ever going to get used to being told what to say by some twenty-two-year-old."

"Seriously, twenty-two?" Brooke asked.

"Well, that may be a slight exaggeration, but not much of one. There are all these twentysomethings running things. I was this close to telling one of them just what she could do with her advice, but Luke keeps saying he has the world's best team, so I'm trying to play nice."

"Well, you just let me know if you need someone to play bad cop. As Garin likes to say, 'Not only am I good at it, but I rather enjoy it.'"

Laura laughed. "Don't be surprised if I take you up on that. Are you going to be able to make our big Women for Cooper event next month? Kerry Washington is cohosting."

"I should be around," Brooke replied.

"What about you, Miss Tami?"

"Oh, I may not be able to make it. Next month is . . ." She paused. "Busy for me."

Brooke and Laura exchanged glances. Tami didn't work outside of the home.

"You traveling somewhere fabulous?" Laura asked.

"No," Tami replied cryptically.

There was a strange silence.

"Everything okay?" Brooke asked.

"Yeah. It's fine."

There was another awkward silence before Tami said, "I just didn't really plan to tell anyone, but I'm having a medical thing."

"Oh, my god," Laura said.

"Are you okay?" Brooke asked.

"No. It's nothing," she insisted.

But they did not appear convinced. Their faces were contorted with worry.

After an uncomfortable pause, Tami finally revealed, "I'm having a tummy tuck, that's all."

While their expressions softened slightly, they were still clearly concerned.

"Well . . . I'm not judging," Brooke said, which clearly meant she was going to. "But why?"

"Well, I just haven't been happy with how I look since I had the twins, and Brock thinks . . ."

"Should have known," Brooke sighed.

"I thought you weren't judging."

"You're not the one I'm judging, Tami," Brooke clarified.

"Brooke, I will be happier when I have the procedure."

"You mean because your overweight husband will finally stop pestering *you* about your weight."

Since she was more of a friend of Brooke's than Tami's, Laura tried to stay out of the fray.

The three women sat in silence for a moment before Brooke finally said, "Look, if this is what you want. . . . You know, if you're happy I'm happy."

She reached for Tami's hand.

"Thanks," Tami said quietly, but moments later tears began to fall. "I just want to make him happy. You know?"

"I know," Brooke said reassuringly.

Laura finally said, "You know what we could use? Some more alcohol."

Minutes later a staff member at Victoria uncorked another bottle of champagne for the trio.

Laura made a toast: "To girlfriends."

"To girlfriends," Tami and Brooke said in unison.

CHAPTER 21

L aura Cooper was not naturally inclined to share herself with
strangers. As the daughter of a successful lawyer and granddaugh-
ter of a successful entrepreneur who owned a string of funeral homes
throughout the South, she was a solid member of the black elite. Yet her
parents were ambivalent about being seen as such. They summered in
Oak Bluffs with other similarly well-heeled families (including, as she
later discovered, relatives of Brooke). But Laura's mother never fully
immersed herself in the world of the Links or other groups that often
defined the lives of the well-to-do wives of black professional men of that
era. Instead, the teacher poured herself into her work with students, setting an example that Laura would follow. But her privileged yet socially
integrated upbringing (including undergraduate studies at Barnard)
instilled in Laura an almost WASP-like sensibility on certain matters,
among them distaste for showiness, bragging, and publicity. Though she
loved fashion, the closest she came to flashing bling was when she wore
the small stud diamonds Luke gifted her for their first anniversary. And
for much of her pre-Luke life she tried to adhere to the golden adage that
a lady of means should appear in the news no more than three times in
her lifetime: upon birth, marriage, and death.

This adage had obviously been turned on its ear, thanks to her husband's political ambitions, and yet no matter how many campaigns
she had participated in, being expected to share a part of yourself with
complete strangers was still not something that came naturally to her.

A week after "Yoga-gate," the older sister of one of Milo's classmates
asked if she could conduct a quick interview with Laura for her high

school newspaper as Laura picked up Milo from school. While Laura really didn't want to, she figured she wouldn't be able to face the girl's mother at school events again if she didn't oblige. The girl promised it would be a brief interview consisting of softball questions, but when she asked Laura "What's your favorite ice cream flavor?" it dawned on Laura that she'd never really given the question much thought. She paused before the girl said, "Well, we can move on to something else. What's your favorite movie?"

"Depends on my mood," Laura replied, "I love *Boomerang* when I need a good laugh. But *Glory* is also one of my favorites. But I also like . . ."

"I can only print one," the girl replied abruptly. After finishing up the other questions she then returned to "What's your favorite ice cream?" Laura paused again trying to think hard about whether or not she actually had a favorite. She had a favorite pie, cake, and cookie, but not an ice cream.

The girl, looking annoyed, finally said, "Honestly, it's a school newspaper. You can say anything."

Laura thought to herself, "What I'd really like to say is, 'What dairy products I choose to consume is really none of your or anyone else's business.'" Instead she said, "I prefer yogurt."

While Luke's local campaigns had required relinquishing some privacy, they were nothing compared to the adjustment demanded by a presidential campaign. People took candid photos of her and the boys as they shopped for groceries. One day in the mall, as she passed a lingerie store, she contemplated buying something sexy to surprise Luke upon his return from one of his campaign trips, but the thought of being recognized while doing so mortified her.

After her remarks about the singer TaMara, the campaign decided to invest in some more-intensive media training for Laura. While she had been taught the basics—like how to stay "on message," which was just a fancy way of saying "don't get distracted by what a reporter wants you to say, just say what you came there to say"—she really hadn't been taught how to dodge verbal bullets and avoid traps of her own making. Every campaign, the media casts characters. There's the hero, the villain, the underdog, and so forth. And there's always one witch, usually one candidate's wife, about whom former staffers have horror stories that they relentlessly feed to the press, ultimately painting the spouse in question as the female version of Mussolini. Though Laura was actually beloved by her staff, she wasn't as beloved by some of the senior staffers. There was always a measure of resentment for the wife who had the candidate's ear, and even sometimes veto power. Among those whose permanent enemies list Laura had made: Johnny Highlands, Luke's former longtime advisor, and his lieutenants, who blamed Laura for Johnny's dismissal. Nate and others were convinced Johnny et al. were now feeding unflattering stories about Laura to the media.

Laura stood a towering six feet, sans heels, but her physical stature belied a somewhat shy demeanor. And yet she didn't hesitate to call one of the campaign's media consultants and demand that he apologize to one of her interns, whom he had made cry during a dressing down. When the consultant hesitated to do so, Laura suggested that this might not be the best campaign for him to continue on. He called and apologized to the intern that afternoon.

He then proceeded to call Laura a number of names behind her back.

Lisa Simmons, a former entertainment reporter turned communications consultant, arrived at the Cooper home late one morning while the boys were at school. Her specialty was prepping high-profile people who were either media shy or downright media reticent, including movie stars who hated discussing their personal lives but were contractually obligated to endure extensive press junkets to promote their films. She also coached "accidental" public figures. These were people who didn't seek fame but became famous anyway—people like the Captain of Flight 101, whose heroism in saving passengers during what was deemed his "miracle" landing made the shy, unassuming grandfather, who was terrified of public speaking, an overnight celebrity. And then there were people who simply had the odd fortune to become famous by association, usually through either marriage or birth. Laura was one such accidental celebrity, since her association with her famous husband made her famous too.

Simmons was bubbly, in a no-nonsense kind of way. The kind of bubbly that Laura could tell was more of a tool for getting what she wanted out of people than anything else.

"So, Laura, it's so lovely to finally meet you, although I feel as though I already know you, having watched you on TV for so long."

"Thanks," Laura replied tentatively. "It's nice to meet you too. Can I offer you some coffee?"

"Never drink the stuff. I'm so naturally jumpy you'd have to bolt me in my chair if I had caffeine."

There was an uncomfortable pause.

"You have a lovely home," Lisa added.

"Thank you."

"And these must be your little ones," she said, picking up a photo.

"Yes."

"They're beautiful."

"Thank you."

"Laura, can I say something?"

"Please."

"I can tell that you'd rather be anywhere but here. That you don't want to be doing *this*. Not this media training. Not this campaign whatnot. But you love your husband so you've made a commitment to him and to yourself to be all in one hundred and ten percent. Right now on TV you come across as half in. I know that's not what you want. So I can help you come across to people the way you want to— like you're one hundred and ten percent committed to this journey, this experience, and most of all to seeing your husband elected president because you believe that's not only what's best for him but what's best for America. I've been doing this a long time. And while I can't cook to save my life, I can't sew, and I can't sing, I'm damn good at this job. So try to trust me, okay?"

"Okay."

For the first half hour they watched clips of Laura's previous interviews so that Lisa could point out where Laura had "missed an opportunity." She never used the words "made a mistake."

And then Lisa trained her in the "three D's." If asked a particularly uncomfortable question she was to employ the three D's in order of importance: deflect, dismiss, defend.

So, for instance, if she was asked "How do you respond to those who say your husband is too young and inexperienced to be president?"

Lisa gave an example of a deflect response: "Well, I talk to voters every single day who tell me they are worried about being able to take care of their families and pay for college and their homes. Those are the issues I have heard voters express concern about, not what year my husband was born."

If the reporter persisted, then Laura was to try to dismiss: "Well, I know that when people are trying to get elected they say lots of things about their opponents. I mean, we all know that's just politics as usual. I really don't pay a lot of attention to it, and honestly I don't think voters pay a lot of attention to it either."

If the reporter pushed, then Laura was to use the defend option—as a last resort, because it's always a fine line between "defending" and being "defensive." The response might go something like: "My husband is smart, compassionate, kind, and cares about people. If we had more leaders with those qualities our country and world would be much better off, so of course I know he would and will make a great president."

She and Lisa practiced using the issue that the campaign knew was most likely to be Luke's, and by default Laura's, Achille's heel: the candidate's religious identity.

Lisa taught her not to get dragged into a back and forth over specifics—ever. Instead, speak broadly, but most of all politely and firmly, to prevent the reporter from pinning Laura down on too many specific details. That would be dangerous territory for a sensitive subject like this. It would sort of be like if a reporter asked a candidate how often he and his spouse argued. The moment you say "twice a month" you've now opened the door to the reporter asking, "When was your last argument and what was it about?" Instead, she was instructed to keep answers to potentially provocative subjects definitive enough to get the question adequately answered yet broad enough to keep the subject in safe territory.

So then they practiced sample questions with Lisa role-playing as the morning reporter from *Wake Up USA*, one of America's leading morning shows.

"So as you know, there are some Americans who have questions about supporting someone with different religious beliefs than them. How do you respond to those Americans?"

"Well first of all, I can completely understand anyone who wants to make sure that whoever leads them has a strong sense of faith, because faith is something that is extremely important to me and to my husband and to our family as well. One of our country's greatest strengths is its diversity. Luke and I have friends who are Baptist, Presbyterian, Jewish, Christian Scientist—you name it—and our extended family reflects this diversity as well, which I think is wonderful. America is a melting pot and so is our family."

In her role as reporter, Lisa then pushed further, following up with, "But what about Americans who specifically want to know if they can support someone whose specific religious practices are so different from their own?"

"With all due respect, I don't think that kind of question gives Americans enough credit. We are such a diverse, open-minded country, filled with tremendous people. If we weren't, my husband and I would not have had the multitude of wonderful opportunities that we have had."

But Lisa pushed again, "I don't mean to be a pest, but you haven't really answered the question, Mrs. Cooper. Let me rephrase. Do you think there are Americans who will not vote for your husband because of his religion, and if so what would you say to them?"

At that Laura went into "defend" mode, but she remembered to do it while employing Lisa's number one rule for defusing conflict: she smiled.

"The American people are smart enough to vote for people on their merits, and I know that ultimately that is what determines who will win the presidency. My husband is smart, kind and qualified, so no, I'm not concerned that his faith will be an obstacle."

Lisa gave her a few more pointers on body language. For instance, she reminded Laura that much of the American people's impression of her would be generated through still photographs, so it was important that she always strive to convey warmth, even if she was standing by Luke in the middle of a snowstorm. They even practiced which direction to lean and tilt her head while listening to her husband or another speaker tell a sad story.

When they finished, Laura felt more confident than she had in months. She gave Lisa a great big hug.

After Lisa finished packing up her belongings, she turned and said, "You know, I don't know that I've ever actually said these words out loud to a client, but I'm going to now. I'd really like to see you as First Lady. Our country would be lucky to have you." She then turned to leave.

★

The campaign began easing Laura into a more aggressive media schedule, beginning with interviews with reporters they deemed relatively safe. Deciding to turn one of the campaign's perceived weaknesses—Laura's trepidation toward the press—into a strength, they announced The Club Reporter Tour, in which Laura would participate in a series of interviews with preselected kid reporters representing local elementary schools in some of the places she was scheduled to campaign. Since one of the most enduring images of American first ladies is that of "America's Mother," the tour represented a perfect opportunity to allow America to begin envisioning her in the role. More important, Laura loved children and actually found being around them a calming distraction from the adult stresses of the campaign.

The Club Reporter Tour was a hit, with adorable images of Laura and the various eight- and nine-year-old reporters interviewing her making the rounds of various newspapers and news sites. When one reporter got so nervous that she couldn't get her question out, and Laura embraced her as she wept and helped the girl eventually get the interview done, the nation let out a collective "Awww."

With The Club Reporter Tour having done wonders for Laura's image, the campaign decided she was ready for her first interview with a major morning show.

Morning shows were known for letting potential first ladies stay in pretty innocuous territory. There would be the usual questions about the Coopers' home life: what kind of husband and father Luke is, and what kind of president he would make. Questions about the mundane, non-presidential aspects of their life: Luke's favorite foods, the family's favorite hobbies, and on the impact the campaign was having on their children. Perhaps questions about Laura's favorite designers but no questions on nuclear disarmament or war treaties, or any similar hard-hitting policy topics. They did know, however, that the Cooper family's unique cultural and religious background might be raised. But Laura was prepared for that.

Unlike her husband, Laura was a practicing Christian. Her mother had been Catholic and her father Protestant. Though raised Catholic, throughout her life she visited a series of churches of various denominations. While she did not attend church every Sunday she did visit a small Episcopalian church in Michigan. It had fewer than 200 members, and while Laura and her family (when they joined her) were clearly the most well known in the congregation, no one ever treated them as such, allowing them to enjoy their privacy and, to some degree anonymity, while there.

The interview with *Wake Up USA* was going well. Laura was coming off as relaxed, funny, charming, and smart. She used an anecdote about asking Luke to pass her a "baking sheet," and him passing her a roll of Saran wrap, to illustrate his inability to find his way around a kitchen—something sure to up his macho cred with men and sure to make Laura relatable to countless women whose own husbands were equally domestically inept.

"What was your first date like?"

"It was pretty funny."

"How so?"

"Well, for our first date he took me skating, and when we got to the rink he said, 'I remembered that you said you liked to skate.' I meant roller skating. He thought I meant ice-skating and I couldn't ice-skate to save my life, but Luke's whole family—coming from Michigan—plays hockey. So he spent much of the evening picking me up off of the ice. But he was such a good sport about it and so sweet. And I knew I'd met a really sweet guy. He worked with me and worked with me and by the end of the date I was able to get around the rink by myself, and now we always take the boys ice-skating as a family."

Then the moment that Laura had practiced and practiced for finally came.

"Your husband has been mentioned as a symbol of unity in our country because of his unique background and family, but as you know there are some Americans who are a bit hesitant about the idea of voting for someone who has different religious beliefs than their own. Are you concerned about that?"

Laura maintained her calm, relaxed smile. "Well, I completely understand that voters want to make sure that whoever leads them has a strong sense of faith, because faith is something that is very important to me and my husband and to our family as well. One of our country's great strengths is its diversity. Our friends and family are Baptist, Presbyterian, Jewish, Christian Scientist—you name it. So I have no concerns, because America is a melting pot and so is our family, and I think that's something Americans really value."

The host then followed up. "Yes, but as you know for some people faith is something that defines who they are, and while they respect religious freedom and other faiths, it's important to them that they feel some sense of a shared belief system with their leaders because oftentimes religious faith can color one's perspective on any number of issues. So if a person of a different religious faith is contemplating not voting for your husband because of that, what would you say to that person?"

Laura went into dismiss mode.

"With all due respect, I don't think that kind of question gives the American people enough credit. You know, I have been traveling around talking to Americans and meeting so many Americans from all over, and they have just furthered my faith in what an open-minded, accepting country we are. And the Americans I talk to talk to me about their hopes and dreams and trying to pay for their children's college education. That's what they care about—electing someone who can help them like my husband can, not about electing someone who is exactly like them in every way."

Campaign workers watching it live at headquarters clapped. They knew Laura had nailed the response and hit it out of the park. That should have been the end of it. But it wasn't.

The host then replied, "I know you once said in an interview, 'Our house is as all-American as apple pie. My husband is Jewish. I am Christian. We are both black but my in-laws are white. Part of my ancestry is Native American and my kids are a little combo of all of that diversity. If America is a melting pot, then just call us American gumbo!' What is it like raising kids in a household filled with such diversity?"

"Our kids have a blast with it all. They know they are unique and special."

"Are they being raised Christian or Jewish?"

Laura's smile began to fade. She felt she had been a pretty good sport enduring this intrusive line of questioning, but now this lady was crossing a line by bringing the details of her children's worship practices into it.

"Well, they are being raised to value their heritage from both sides of their family."

"So that means we could possibly see our very first White House bar mitzvah?"

"That's really none of your business," she said—while maintaining the remnants of a forced smile.

The host was caught off guard. Both women sat there in silence for a moment before the anchor said, "I didn't mean anything by that. I just . . ."

"Sure you didn't," Laura snapped.

At that the host said, "Mrs. Cooper, thank you very much for your time."

"Thank you," Laura said, now not smiling at all.

After the cameras stopped rolling, the host tried to apologize to Laura for "accidentally" offending her. Laura replied curtly, "You should be sorry," before walking off. Of the nearly twelve minutes of footage aired from the interview, the only clip that garnered any real coverage after the fact was the final minute. The exchange had been watched online 100,000 times within twenty-four hours of airing. One blog headline blared "Cool Hand Luke's Mrs. Loses Cool with Reporter." *Late Show* host David Letterman even devoted one of his infamous "Top Ten" lists to the incident with this one titled, "Top Ten Things Not to Ask Mrs. Cooper in an Interview." Though a couple of bloggers defended Laura, questioning whether the line of questioning had been borderline anti-Semitic, overall it was not the coverage the campaign had been hoping for.

The campaign decided they needed help. Instead of bringing in a high-priced consultant for a one-day media training, they decided they needed to bring one of the best campaign communications professionals in the business to work and travel with Laura full time.

Allison Cartwright, a veteran of one previous presidential campaign and two Senate races, joined Laura's team forty-eight hours after the *Wake Up USA* debacle. Cartwright was known for diffusing crisis communications situations quickly, and often quietly, but also for heading off a crisis in the first place. She joined Laura's staff as "Traveling Chief of Staff," which was a fancy way of saying "Laura's campaign-subsidized babysitter." She had a reputation for being a tough but disciplined, and extremely loyal, political operative, and was known for going to the mat for her candidates. But she was also known for expecting the people she was counseling to listen to her, no questions asked. In her first month on board she gave Laura's press operation the equivalent of an extreme home makeover, landing her profiles on a number of blogs and news sites geared to young women, and upcoming profiles in magazines targeting the same demographic, among them *Glamour* and *Marie Claire*. As she had no problem pointing out, Laura was younger and more beautiful than any of the First Lady candidates in recent memory, and Allison wanted the campaign to leverage that more effectively. She also began writing a daily blog on behalf of the First Lady called "Up Close and Personal," which included at least one photo allegedly taken by Laura each day (but usually taken by Allison or her assistant) that was representative of what Laura's life, or her family's life, was like on the campaign trail that day.

She also arranged for more interviews with small publications that candidates never had the time to talk to but that reached specific, targeted constituencies, such as the newsletters that circulated at churches and various senior centers. They were an easy way for Laura to build up goodwill with likely voters without too much effort.

Within weeks Laura's unfavorable rating had gone down again, much like it had after The Club Reporter Tour, and her favorables had gone up, but there had been a couple of hiccups along the way. While the campaign's higher-ups loved Allison, she found getting Laura to like her a challenge. But one of the things Allison had going for her was that she didn't care.

Her relationship with Laura got off to a bumpy start. After Allison landed Laura lunch with the editor of one of the nation's most influential women's magazines, Laura informed her scheduler the day before the lunch that she wouldn't be able to make the trip to New York because her oldest son James was ill. When the scheduler notified Allison that she would be rescheduling the meeting, Allison instructed her not to, saying she wanted to speak with Laura first.

When Laura found out, she sent Allison an e-mail that read,

> **Allison—since you're still relatively new I'm going to give you the benefit of the doubt and assume that there was some sort of miscommunication. My son is ill, as such I instructed Debbie to cancel my obligations for the next 72 hours until he is well. Debbie works for me, not you. Therefore, please do not EVER give her a directive that contradicts one I have given her. Thanks.—L**

After conferring with the campaign's communications director and hearing about the "Chuck E. Cheese Massacre," Allison decided that this particular battle was not one worth fighting, particularly with a boss she was still getting to know. She didn't reply to Laura's e-mail but simply called the magazine editor, explained James's illness, and rescheduled. The editor was not only understanding but actually replied, "It's refreshing to see her putting her kids first despite the campaign craziness," an unexpectedly positive response that caught Allison off guard and that she chose not to share with Laura, lest she make the mistake of believing that she was a bigger expert on these things than Allison.

In the meantime, Laura called one of the few people left on the planet whom she felt she could one hundred percent confide in without being made to feel as though what she just said reflected poorly on the campaign.

"Brooke, do you have a minute?"

"Of course, hon. What's up? You got a Women for Cooper event cookin'?"

There was silence on the line.

"Laura? Are you still there?"

Brooke could then make out the sound of muffled sobs. She waited a few moments before saying, "I absolutely hate it when Garin tells me 'It's not that bad,' without knowing what the hell it is I'm even crying about, so why don't you cry it out and know that I'm here giving you a hug through the phone, and when you're ready to talk it out you let me know. Okay?"

There was silence before she heard Laura's voice say meekly, "I'm nodding. I just realized you wouldn't be able to tell that through the phone." She then laughed lightly.

"Well, Garin has accused me of having eyes in the back of my head, but I haven't quite mastered the art of seeing through objects yet."

Laura laughed ever so slightly again.

"Feel like talking about it?" Brooke asked.

"I just . . . I just . . . I don't know, Brooke . . ."

"What don't you know?"

"I don't know that I can do this. I don't know that I'm strong enough."

"Laura . . . ," Brooke said soothingly.

"I mean it, Brooke. I'm not sleeping. I just worry constantly that I'm going to say or do something to hurt Luke and the campaign. I even worry that what if . . . what if part of me secretly doesn't want him to win, so maybe I'm subconsciously sabotaging the campaign every time I open my mouth and say the wrong thing or wear the wrong thing . . . I feel like if he loses his staff will blame me . . . I could live with that. But I couldn't live with him blaming me."

"Laura, please," Brooke said sternly. "That negro wouldn't have made it to the governor's mansion without you. He knows it and *everybody* who knows him knows it."

Laura stopped sniffling. "What are you talking about?"

"You know I love Luke. But I also know from a very reliable source that the Luke I know and love today is not the Luke that's always been. The reality is, the confidence Luke has today is all because of you. His mother may never say this to you point blank, but one of the reasons she loves you so much is because you gave her son something she never could. You gave him comfort and confidence in his own skin. You made him love who he is in a way she never could, and even going to a black college never could. Don't get me wrong. Luke wouldn't be nothing without you, but he sure as hell wouldn't be the something he is today."

Laura sat there silent and stunned.

"And while we're on the topic," Brooke continued, "that's why his campaign doesn't know exactly what to do with you. They're intimidated by you and what you represent to him and for him."

"You really think so?" Laura asked.

"I know so," Brooke continued. "So you go ahead and get all of your tears out, because sometimes a good cry is good for the soul. It's like cleansing for the spirit. And we all need a good cleansing every now and then. But I can tell you this much, they'd all be crying a lot more tears if you weren't in that man's life."

Laura said quietly, "Thanks, Brooke."

Brooke then replied, "Okay. Now that I've helped you, you've got to repay the favor."

"Of course. Anything," Laura said. "Name it."

"Okay, you're one of my closest girlfriends now, so I can confide in you, right?"

"Absolutely," Laura said, sounding concerned. "I mean, I just had a nervous breakdown in front of you. I owe you."

"I don't know where to start."

"Start from the beginning," Laura said.

"I need some tips for spicing things up in the bedroom." She then blurted out "Garin fell asleep on top of me last night."

There was a long pause before Brooke finally broke it by saying, "Laura. Are you laughing?"

"No," Laura managed to squeak out while biting her lip—the only thing standing between her and a burst of hysterical laughter.

"You're laughing, aren't you?"

"Okay, maybe just a little," Laura said. "I'm sorry. I'm so, so sorry. I'm a terrible friend."

"No, you're not," Brooke said reassuringly, before adding, "it *is* pretty funny. I mean, it would be if it had happened to someone else. Actually, the funny part is not that he fell asleep but that he had to actually start snoring before I even noticed."

At that Laura couldn't hold it in any longer and began laughing loudly—the first laugh she'd had in days.

"Truth be told, I was almost more annoyed by the snoring. When he's congested he sounds like a foghorn."

Brooke then proceeded to make a loud honking noise, her impression of Garin. The ladies then dissolved into giggles.

★

A couple of weeks later, Allison Cartwright, Laura's new aide, decided she had found a battle worth fighting in the war to make Laura Cooper "First Lady ready."

Entertainment Tonight was sending cameras to follow Laura to a couple of events for one of its "A Day on the Trail" profiles of candidate spouses. But when Allison arrived to meet Laura before the cameras arrived, she was not greeted by the Laura whom she, or most Americans, knew. Laura's hair—usually pin-straight—was not straight at all but resembled a slightly less ruly version of Julia Roberts's bushy curls from the *Pretty Woman* era. Laura very rarely wore her hair curly. She didn't have a relaxer like many black women used, but instead usually relied on some combo of pressing comb and flatiron to tame her natural curls. As a white girl from Vermont, Allison didn't know much about pressing combs but she did know she wasn't going to allow her client to go near a TV camera looking like that. At first she tried the subtle approach.

"Ummm . . . your hair is different," she said, trying to sound enthusiastic.

"Yep, I ran out of time and didn't have a chance to flatiron after washing it this morning," Laura replied cheerily.

"Yeah . . . umm . . . maybe we can get someone to come over and take care of it real quick? *Entertainment Tonight* isn't sending a hair person or anything but I can probably try to get one here."

"No, I realize we're already late. I'll just put some product in it so we can head out."

Allison knew this was going to be a tough conversation to have. Having to discuss a candidate's or his family's appearance was tougher than discussing anything else. Allison would almost rather tell a candidate's spouse that he was cheating on her than that she was too fat or too homely or too badly dressed to help her husband get elected to office. She took a deep breath and said, "You know, I really, really like your hair that way. I wish I had big, beautiful curls, but I'm afraid the average voter might not appreciate it as much."

Laura stopped what she was doing. "Oh really? And just why is that?"

"Well . . . ," Allison paused. This conversation would prove just how good—or bad—her communications skills really were, she thought to herself. "Well, I think it might be a bit too . . . too . . . what's the word? . . . ummm . . . ethnic for some voters."

"Oh really?" Laura said, her face shifting. "Too ethnic, huh? Well, you know, Allison, last I checked there were a lot of ethnic voters out there," Laura said, using the bunny-like hand gesture for quotation marks to emphasize her point when she said ethnic.

"Look, Mrs. Cooper, I'm on your side. Really I am, and as I said, I love your hair."

"Great. Then let's roll," Laura said, heading to the door.

Allison realized subtlety wasn't getting the desired result, so she was going to have to play hardball.

"Mrs. Cooper, with all due respect, wouldn't you rather be an asset to your husband's campaign as opposed to a liability? I'm just trying to help you do that. That's my job."

Laura stood there in silence, staring at Allison.

"Mrs. Cooper, I . . ."

Laura cut her off. "And with all due respect to you, Allison, I'm sure with your knowledge and experience you manage to be quite an asset to the campaigns that you find yourself on."

Allison looked confused. Laura's words were conveying what sounded like a compliment, but her face was conveying something else, and it wasn't good.

"Well thank you, Mrs. Cooper. I'd like to think so."

"So I'm going to give you the opportunity to go be an asset on someone else's campaign."

Allison stood there stunned.

"Don't bother finishing out the day." Laura then walked over to the door, opened it, and waited for Allison to walk through it. "Good luck to you," she said.

Immediately after firing Allison, Laura made two phone calls: the second was to the campaign but the first was to Brooke. She got her voice mail and left a message, "Brooke, it's Laura. I need your help. Call me as soon as you get this."

After the *Entertainment Tonight* segment aired, the show's website was inundated with comments about her hair, most of them being some variation of "I LOVE Laura's new do! Did she get a curly perm?" or "I have curly hair and want mine to look like hers. What does she use?"

And the comments were not exclusively from "ethnic" viewers.

Out of the millions of people who saw the segment, Laura received one critical e-mail.

> **Just caught a glimpse of you on 'Entertainment Tonight.' What on Earth was wrong with your hair? It looked like you stuck your finger in a socket. Call me about your next trip to Cali in a few weeks. We should grab lunch while you're here. Xoxo Veronica**

CHAPTER 22

S quirt! In the flesh!" Josh yelled enthusiastically before doing the second most predictable and annoying thing he did whenever he saw Luke, besides calling him Squirt. The former high school champion wrestler enveloped Luke in a big bear hug so tight that he actually lifted Luke off of the ground. "How's my favorite little brother?"

"I thought I was your favorite," David said, entering the room.

"He told me I was," Matt added.

The four Cooper brothers traded hugs.

They were rarely together as a group, so they all looked forward to Thanksgiving, when every member of the Cooper family usually returned to their childhood home.

"Hey Laura!"

"Hey Matt," she said, hugging him before moving on to David and Josh.

"Well, you look great, as usual," Josh said. "We're still trying to figure out what he has on you to get someone like you to marry him. We're guessing you must have felt sorry for him."

As his brothers laughed, Luke replied, "Yeah, and I kept wondering the same thing about Kate. Only I don't have to wonder anymore. She finally told me Mom and Dad paid her off to take you off of their hands."

"Kate, is this true?" Josh shouted.

"Is what true?" Kate shouted from the other room.

"Luke says Mom and Dad paid you to marry me."

"Absolutely!" she replied as his brothers and Laura laughed.

"How are the avocadoes?" Luke whispered, referring to Kate's diet.

"She brought a whole bag for Mom," Josh whispered, then sighed.

"You're kidding."

"I wish!" he said dramatically. "So have you checked yet? Can presidents outlaw avocadoes?"

"Sorry, Josh, but Milo and James want me to outlaw broccoli and brussels sprouts first."

"Oh come on! You've known them, what, less than ten years. You've known us your whole life!" He slapped Luke's back teasingly.

They continued chatting as the men helped set the table while the ladies helped Esther Cooper finish up in the kitchen.

As one of the older grandkids, Brian had control of the remote control.

He had been watching a *Three Stooges* marathon, which caused Luke to remark to his brothers, "I see the great Cooper cultural traditions are being passed down."

But during a commercial he began to flip channels, and stopped on one.

"Well, here's what I know. There are those who talk the talk and there are those who walk the walk. There are candidates who say they care about civil rights and black folks and then there are the candidates who actually show up and stand up for our community and our issues and are here."

"Was that a dig at Governor Cooper, reverend?" another voice on the television replied.

Though all of the adults in the adjoining room had been chatting, they soon fell silent.

"That was a dig at anybody who claims they care about black folks, claim that they want and deserve our votes, then when push comes to shove and we have a forum on the state of civil rights here in America, they can't be bothered to attend."

Another voice then chimed in, "He didn't speak at the conference on civil rights because he was celebrating Rosh Hashanah, one of the most important Jewish holidays. The governor made it clear a long time ago he would be spending the holiday with his family like he always does. And I personally think it would have made him look worse to be out kissing babies if that goes against his faith—or whatever. I mean, I'm Catholic and I wouldn't vote for someone who's out stumping on Christmas, because I think it's tacky. What do you all think?"

Another voice then replied, "Well, in theory you may be right, but I do think while spending time with your family is admirable, missing that civil rights forum, rightly or wrongly, has definitely hurt the governor, who was already struggling to connect with black voters against Beaman, whose family has deep ties to that community."

The anchor's voice then chimed in, "That was a clip from yesterday's episode of *Politics Watch*. The topic? The black vote, which remains up for grabs in this year's primary."

Esther Cooper, who had been in the kitchen, upon entering the room, heard the tail end of the comments and barked, "Turn that crap off."

Everyone remained silent for a few moments before she said, "Luke, why don't you carve the turkey?"

★

After everyone had stuffed themselves, Luke took some time to catch up with his brothers, which he rarely had a chance to do now that the campaign was in high gear.

"So what are you doing with yourself these days, Matt?" Luke asked.

"Playing golf."

"What? I thought you said it wasn't a real sport."

"I never said that."

"You said golf is no different from bowling."

"Exactly."

"And you said bowling's not a real sport," David chimed in.

"I said no such thing."

"You said it's what people do who can't play real sports."

"But I also said it probably requires a lot of skill."

"And zero athleticism," Luke chimed in. "In fact, I think your exact words were, 'It's an activity created to make out-of-shape people have something they can win a trophy at besides eating.'"

"Did I really say that?" Matt looked sheepish.

"Yep," his brothers all said in unison.

"Well, Sharon and her parents have become obsessed with golf in the last few months. And since her father has never exactly been my biggest fan I figured I might as well give it a try. It's actually harder than it looks."

Luke, who played golf and had been teased by Matt for years for doing so, said sarcastically, "No kidding."

David then began typing on his BlackBerry and said, "Hold on, guys, I just got to send this one e-mail."

"Geez, you're worse than me," Luke teased.

"It's my assistant. She's kind of a hardass but she's really good. Really on top of things and makes sure I stay on top of things too."

Josh began giggling then said, "Hey, Dave, you better not let Rebecca hear you talking like that."

"Like what?"

"About Heather's hard ass and her being *on top*."

"Shut up," David said.

"What are you talking about?" Luke asked.

"Didn't you hear? David has a new assistant."

"Really?" Luke asked.

"And apparently Rebecca just loves her," Matt said, needling his brother about his strong-willed wife.

"Luke, you should see her. I can hardly concentrate," David said. "She looks like a Victoria's Secret model. Well, a really short Victoria's Secret model, but you get my point."

"Then why did you hire her? It's not like your concentration's that great to begin with," Luke replied, gently teasing his brother.

"I'm sorry, but have you met our brother before?" Matt replied. Every brother but David laughed. He married Rebecca, a stunningly beautiful former waitress whom their mother was still warming to after almost twenty years because he'd known her for all of six weeks before the wedding.

"Ha. Ha," David said sarcastically.

"Oh, you're never going to believe who's volunteering for the campaign," Luke piped up.

"Who?" Matt asked.

"Ranya."

His brothers stared at him blankly.

"Ranya," Luke repeated. "You remember Ranya, she . . ."

"I remember who she is, Luke," Josh said, then mumbled, "speaking of beautiful distractions . . ." under his breath.

"What?" Luke asked, no longer looking his brother in the eye.

"Who's Ranya?" David asked.

"That crazy broad Luke dated before he met Laura."

"She wasn't crazy," Luke replied.

"Oh, I remember her," David said. "Yeah, she was nuts. But she was *gorgeous.*"

"Well, she didn't sound exactly stable," Josh said.

"What does that mean?" Luke asked.

"What is it Dad always told us about keeping your eye on the ball when you're in the game?" Josh asked.

"What are you talking about?"

"The last thing you need right now is any more distractions."

"You're being ridiculous. Do you know how many old friends from high school and college—hell—kindergarten I've heard from since the campaign started?"

"Yeah, and how many of those did you used to sleep with?"

"More than you know," Luke said, trying to provoke a laugh.

"You wish," Josh replied.

"What'd she do? Write you a piece of fanmail?"

"Stop. She ran into Joe at a party."

"Should have known Joe was involved!" Josh replied.

"What does that mean?" Luke asked.

"I love Joe. You know I do. But there's a reason he's almost fifty and not married. He doesn't exactly have the best judgment."

"Gee-whiz, do you guys approve of any of my friends?"

"All of them except those two," Josh said smiling.

"Well, all I know is you better not let Mom find out," Matt chimed in.

"Why?"

"She *hates* her."

"Please. She probably doesn't even remember her," Luke said.

"Are you kidding? Don't quote me on this, but I'm pretty sure there was talk of a Ranya voodoo doll at one point," Josh added.

"Why on earth would Mom hate her?"

"Because of what she did to you," David piped up.

"But Mom doesn't even know . . ."

Suddenly none of his brothers were looking him in the eyes.

"Unless someone told her," Luke continued. "After I asked them not to . . ."

Josh remained silent.

"Damn. You guys cannot keep a secret!"

"You know how Mom is. It's like waterboarding. She just won't let up until you talk," Josh said.

Just then their mother walked in.

The room fell silent.

"I can't find the cordless phone. Did I leave it in here?"

"No," all of the Cooper boys replied.

"And what are you boys talking about?"

"Nothing," they said in unison again.

Esther Cooper eyed them suspiciously before hearing, "Grandma!!! I need you."

"Be right there, sweetie," she shouted. She turned to leave but stopped to give Luke and Josh the eye for a moment longer. "Waterboarding, huh?" She smiled, then left the room.

The Cooper boys laughed, before Josh whispered to Luke, "Just remember to keep your eye on the ball. Okay, little brother?"

CHAPTER 23

Brooke joined the Cooper campaign as Laura's press secretary a week after the *Entertainment Tonight* blowout with Allison Cartwright. She had no political experience at all, but a ton of experience as a publicist for challenging public personalities in challenging situations. But her most important quality, in Laura's mind, as well as Luke's, was that she had experience putting Laura at ease.

Garin had been hesitant at first when Brooke initially posed the idea. He actually said to Luke, "It's not enough that I've given you the shirt off my back for this campaign, I gotta give you my wife too?" Though Garin laughed when he said it, Luke did initially have reservations about working so closely with a dear friend, but he overcame them after speaking to Laura about how she had felt throughout much of the campaign.

"I feel like I don't have anyone in my corner out there."

"I'm in your corner, babe."

"I know, I know. But all these experts and consultants . . . it's like they talk down to me."

"Who's being disrespectful to you?"

"No, it's not that anyone's blatantly disrespectful. You know I wouldn't put up with that. It's more subtle. It's like this silent condescension . . . like I'm always doing something wrong. I'm a kid they feel like they have to keep from hurting myself, or you . . ."

"I told you that I stand by you one hundred percent for getting rid of that girl who talked about your hair. You know I love your hair however you wear it."

"It's not about that."

"Then what?"

"It's about having someone on *my* team, who's in *my* corner. Someone I can count on to have my back morning, noon, or night. Not someone who's worried about how what I do or say or wear will impact their ability to get hired on another campaign down the road. Brooke has my back and she's great at media. You saw what she did with that Nico chick. She's helped turn her into a star."

"Yeah, and I don't know that we want to tell too many people that we know the person responsible for unleashing Nico onto the world." Luke laughed.

"I'm serious," Laura replied.

Luke sighed before saying, "I want you to be happy. So if this will make you happy . . ." He then leaned in and kissed Laura on the forehead.

Though he didn't show it initially, Garin's reservations about Brooke joining the campaign weighed on him. In addition to concerns about the impact of the schedule on their young daughter, he knew that Brooke's strong personality, while endearing in small doses, could be a lot to take in large ones, and he worried about damaging his relationship with Luke. But she soon proved to be just the addition the Cooper campaign needed.

She was a calming presence for Laura, who trusted her completely. Laura knew that with Brooke on board there would always be at least one person who had her and her husband's best interests—not their own—at heart. She once instructed the campaign to cancel two back-to-back early morning radio interviews because she knew that Laura always battled extreme exhaustion the day before her period. Brooke knew that if Laura was up at 4:30 a.m. for the interviews, she would likely be down and out when that evening's Women for Cooper event rolled around, an event with female elected officials where Laura would need to be her most charming and relaxed self.

Her first coup was landing Laura a guest spot on the talk show of domestic doyenne Martha Ray, who millions of women considered the go-to goddess for tips on maintaining the perfect home. Laura had never seen an episode of the program and was particularly wary of a national interview following the *Wake Up USA* debacle, but Brooke convinced her and the campaign that it would reintroduce Laura to a national daytime audience in a safe setting where she would be assured of not receiving a single question about religion or anything else remotely controversial. And to top it all off, Laura actually liked to cook and loved to bake.

She also secured Laura the covers of the January issues of both *Essence* and *MOMs* magazines. The *MOMs* cover—which was Brooke's idea—featured Laura and her mother-in-law with the headline "Our Future First Ladies?" The cover and accompanying piece celebrated the often-complex relationship between women and their mothers-in-law. Though the piece featured other women as well, the highlight was a Q&A with Laura and Esther Cooper in which Laura talked about the void Esther had filled for her since she lost her own mother years before. Laura also praised Esther for making her husband into the man he had become. For a cover featuring two women who were not A-list celebrities or household names, the *MOMs* issue featuring the Cooper ladies sold surprisingly well, as did the issue of *Essence*, which sold like hotcakes.

Brooke's presence on the campaign trail not only lifted Laura's spirits, it lifted Luke's as well. She was a stabilizing force for both of them, able to fill the roles of both trusted advisor and pseudo-family member on the road. One campaign staffer described her as embodying the toughness of a commando with the diplomacy of a seasoned State Department pro, all wrapped up in a Diane von Furstenberg wrap dress. Luke once joked that Brooke wasn't just a velvet hand in an iron glove. If you crossed her it was more of a velvet fist in an iron boxing glove, making her a natural fit for politics.

Though she had not been looking for a career change, over the last several months she had grown increasingly disillusioned with the world of celebrity PR. It had never been exactly what you'd call fulfilling, but Brooke had always been great at her job and had taken pride in it. Just before receiving Laura's fateful call, though, she encountered the inevitable straw that broke the camel's back.

When a gossip blog e-mailed Brooke for comment on "the controversial Nico tape floating around," Brooke assumed they were referring to her sex tape. She just wasn't sure which one, since her client Nico had a few. But when the blogger in question sent her a link to the video, Brooke soon learned that it was not a sex tape at all. It was something much more scandalous, disgusting, and embarrassing, as far as Brooke was concerned. In it Nico could be seen smoking pot with a friend, who like Nico was white and who was making racist jokes as Nico laughed hysterically. The video ended moments after Nico told a joke using the n-word loud and clear. Brooke left Nico a message to call her. When Nico finally called her back—the following day—and breezily asked, "What do you need?" Brooke calmly replied, "Just to tell you that you need to find yourself a new publicist."

Laura called and asked her to join the campaign the very next day.

The campaign realized just how invaluable Brooke's presence was within weeks, as the campaign weathered one of its first crises.

A report was issued that Brian Colby, the star L. A. Lakers player, had been assaulted at a club where he was celebrating his team's victory over the New York Knicks. Colby was left with a gash above his eye and authorities were left searching for the assailant.

Upon hearing the news, Mimi immediately notified Luke's traveling staff that they should make sure that Luke found time to put in a call to Brian that day, to express his concern. A phone call like this was the type of donor maintenance that could make the difference between Brian Colby hosting one fundraiser for the campaign, or perhaps another down the road.

Mimi had just received the e-mail from Luke's scheduler, letting her know that the call had officially been added to his to-do list for the day, when she noticed there had been an update to the Brian Colby story and scrolled down for more details.

There in black and white was the name of the suspected assailant: Joe Nelson.

Mimi broke a sweat, something she almost never did, and then she talked to herself.

"Okay. There are probably a million Joe Nelsons. It's a common name. Like John Doe. Right . . . Joe Doe. John Doe. John Nelson. Joe Nelson. Relax. Relax."

She closed her eyes and began her meditation breathing.

After a minute she clicked on a link for more info.

"Witnesses say Nelson, who some sources claim is a sports agent, got into a dispute with the NBA great over a woman, reportedly a cheerleader."

At that Mimi did something else she never did. She screamed.

She called Nate. He didn't answer his cell, so an assistant had to hear, "I don't care if he's at a goddamned funeral, you have him call me in the next thirty seconds, or else!"

She also texted in all caps "URGENT."

And sent the same e-mail for good measure.

"In a meeting," Nate texted back. "What's the fire?"

"CALL ME NOW BEFORE THE WHOLE FUCKING HOUSE BURNS DOWN."

Three minutes later her phone rang.

"What's the problem?" Nate asked. Mimi could be a bit of a diva, so Nate assumed Luke had possibly forgotten to thank a donor who felt snubbed and was threatening to cancel an event or something.

"Have you heard about Brian Colby?"

"*That's* what you're calling about?"

"Google the suspect, Nate! Then see if you're still irritated that I interrupted your little meeting."

Mimi sat there silent as he looked on his BlackBerry.

"Okay . . ." Nate replied. "I'm not getting the significance."

"Of course you wouldn't," Mimi snapped.

"Okay, Mimi, do you want to tell me what's going on, or bite my head off?"

"Joe Nelson is one of Luke's oldest friends, Nate!"

There was silence.

"*Now* do you smell the smoke?"

Nate sighed, loudly.

"Okay. Thanks for letting me know."

Mimi didn't reply.

"And for being such a damn good smoke detector," he added.

Mimi didn't say a word. But she smiled.

★

Nate's first call was to the campaign's communications director.

His second call was to Brooke.

Brooke had found herself doing a bit of a delicate dance in her first few weeks on the campaign. She knew that a number of the senior staffers were suspicious of her, wondering if she was a spy planted to report back to the candidate on them and any missteps. While it wasn't unusual for family and friends of the candidate to land campaign jobs, it was unusual for them to land substantive jobs that were more than just ceremonial, jobs where if they screwed up, the campaign could actually suffer. And yet here Brooke was, having never worked on a campaign a day in her life, with a plum position. But so far she had shown herself to be a pro, and while many of them still had their doubts, she was proving herself a little bit more every day.

"Hey, Brooke, Nate here."

"Hi, Nate."

"Listen, first off you've been doing a really solid job, so it's good to have you on board."

"Thanks, Nate. It really means a lot to hear that, especially from you."

"Well it's the truth. Um . . . we have a situation."

"Okay."

"You heard about Brian Colby?"

"I did."

"Okay, here's the thing. It just broke online that the assailant in question is named Joe Nelson."

"What?"

"Yeah. So I'm guessing you consider that pretty significant."

"Well, I don't know. One of Luke's closest friends assaults one of his donors, who happens to be a world famous athlete," she said. "Yeah, I'd say that's pretty significant, Nate. What's our plan?"

"Well, I'm calling you first because I'm sure you have more insight than I do into how Luke's going to react. We have maybe five minutes to hammer this out before Luke hears from someone else or, God forbid, he finds out in the press. What are your thoughts?"

"My first thought is I was right all along about Joe. But I'm guessing that's not the kind of thought you meant. Honestly? Speaking as a member of Luke's campaign staff, I think he needs to distance himself from Joe, plain and simple. Joe's trouble. Always has been. But speaking as Luke's friend, I can tell you that Luke can't really see it and he won't see it, even if you talk to him."

"What do you suggest?" Nate asked.

"The only one he'd probably listen to is my husband, when it comes to this."

"Can you get him to talk to him? Soon?"

"Let me try. I'll call you right back."

"And Brooke, one more thing . . ."

"I know. I won't say anything to anyone, not even Laura, until you tell me we can."

"Thanks."

Brooke had Garin's assistant pull him out of a meeting with his boss.

"Is Allie alright?" were the first words out of his mouth. Brooke didn't have a habit of interrupting his meetings with his boss unless it was a life-or-death emergency.

"She's fine, but Joe's not, and thanks to him soon Luke might not be."

"What do you mean? What's going on?"

"The suspect in the assault on Brian Colby is Joe."

"Bullshit," Garin blurted out. "You're joking."

"Garin, when have you ever known me to pull you out of a meeting with your boss to joke?"

"Shit."

"Now, I need you to listen because we don't have much time. Luke doesn't know yet. Obviously this could have an impact. So we need to make sure that Luke keeps his distance from Joe."

"For how long?"

"As long as it's necessary."

"We haven't even heard Joe's side of the story yet."

"And we don't need to. Look, hon, speaking as your wife, I'm sorry about this, but speaking . . ."

"Oh please, Brooke, you never liked Joe."

Brooke paused. As Garin's wife she wanted to say one thing—something like 'I don't think I like your tone and it better change really quick'—but as a representative of the campaign she had a job to do, so instead she said, "Okay. Fair enough. No, I have never liked him. He's always struck me as immature and irresponsible, and the allegations he's charged with seem to confirm that I was right." She took a breath. "All of that aside, I am sorry. I'm sorry that one or both of your friends may get hurt. I know that that hurts you and I love you and I don't ever like seeing you hurt. But speaking as a press secretary to this campaign, Joe is now officially a liability."

"Luke may be your client but these are my friends we're talking about."

"Honey. I realize that." Brooke softened her tone. "Luke and Laura are my friends too. And because Joe's a friend of yours, I wanted to extend the courtesy of giving you an opportunity to speak with him before we issue a public statement. But most importantly, I wanted to give you an opportunity to speak with Luke. I think it's best if he hears this from you."

"Oh. You think it's best, huh?"

"I do."

"Are you speaking as my wife or as Luke's press person?"

"Both."

Garin sighed. Brooke knew him so well that she could tell by the way he breathed what his mood was. He was upset right now. Garin never cried and rarely raised his voice, but Brooke could tell when he felt like doing both. She usually wore the pants in the family, but when he was really on the verge of an emotional explosion she steered clear.

"Garin?"

"I'm here."

"I don't want to push you, but we don't have much time. Someone's going to have to talk to Luke as soon as possible."

"I'll call him now."

Garin didn't even hang up the phone. He just waited for a new dial tone and then began pushing the numbers. It rang and rang before the voice mail picked up.

"Joe, it's me. Gar. Call me as soon as you can."

★

Nate had notified Luke's aide that he would be receiving an urgent call from his friend Garin and would need to be available to take it as soon as possible.

"Hey! Everything okay with your family? My staff told me it was urgent."

"Yeah. Uh . . . yeah."

"Well, what's going on? You don't sound good."

"It's Joe."

"What's wrong? He all right?" Luke's voice had that extra edge to it that a person gets when he believes he is about to receive bad news from a doctor.

"Not exactly."

"What is it, Garin?"

"You heard about Brian Colby?"

"Yeah. I'm supposed to call him and see how he's doing. It's on my schedule for later today. He got attacked by some crazed fan or something."

"They think it was Joe."

"What?! That's *ridiculous.*"

"No, it's not, I'm afraid."

"This doesn't make any sense."

"I know."

"Is Joe alright? Does he have a lawyer?"

"I haven't been able to get in touch with him just yet, but I wanted you to hear it from me."

"I can't believe this. I can't . . . I mean, Joe is a lot of things but he's not crazy. Only a crazy person would attack one of the biggest sports stars on the planet. The whole thing sounds absurd. I don't believe it."

"I know. I hear you."

"Well, we have to make sure he has a good attorney. We should talk to Brock and . . ."

"No. *We* should not do anything. *You* are running for president right now. The last thing you need are distractions of any kind, and the second-to-last thing you need is to be affiliated with any whiff of scandal. You know I love Joe just as much as you do. He's like a brother, but you, your family, and hundreds of people working for you, including my wife, have worked too hard and sacrificed too much for you to take the chance of pissing it all away by getting dragged into Joe's mess."

"I can't just abandon him. I always said I wouldn't let all of this change me and now you want me to just toss one of my oldest friends overboard?"

"You're not tossing anyone overboard, Luke. You're simply acting like a leader. It would be irresponsible for you to risk the jobs of the hundreds of people working for you to try to help one person who, whether you and I want to admit it or not, is a fuckup. I love Joe, but you and I both know that this whole scenario does not really sound as ridiculous as you and I are trying to convince ourselves it is."

Garin continued, "I will tell him you're worried about him. I'll make sure that message is delivered loud and clear, but if he calls, don't answer. If he e-mails, don't reply."

"For how long?"

"As long as it takes."

CHAPTER 24

New York Post

SCARY MCGUIRE CONNECTED
TO COOPER CAMPAIGN

Joe Nelson, the sports agent accused of assaulting basketball great Brian Colby, is a longtime friend of Michigan governor turned presidential candidate, Luke Cooper. According to numerous sources Nelson is one of the governor's closest friends and confidantes, dating back to their days as students at the exclusive high school for the sons and daughters of Michigan's elite, Langley Prep.

As these exclusive photos reveal, the two men have remained close over the years, this most recent photo taken just weeks ago at a fundraiser hosted for the governor by none other than Brian Colby. The three men are all smiles in the photo, their demeanor a far cry from where their relationships stand today.

According to eyewitness accounts, Nelson approached Colby in Club Amor and confronted him about exchanging flirty text messages with his fiancée, former cheerleader Tiffini Bingham. The two men exchanged words before Nelson hit Colby with a bottle of champagne.

This is not the first time Nelson's temper has gotten him, or the Cooper campaign into trouble. It is alleged that he threatened students at a California College rally where Cooper was speaking after some of the students began heckling the governor over his position on gay rights.

Nelson has previously been arrested for driving under the influence and once was ordered to pay a fine for an incident in which he was accused of threatening another driver who cut him off.

The Cooper campaign released a brief statement on the matter: "Gov. Cooper has made it clear through his words and actions throughout his career that he does not condone violence. He wishes all parties involved in this unfortunate situation a swift and just resolution."

But some political watchers predict the statement may not be enough and that a swift resolution may be wishful thinking and hoping on the governor's part. The young upstart was gaining momentum on frontrunner Abby Beaman, but this episode could turn into a setback.

"People look to leaders to have better judgment than their own. Hanging out with someone who regularly threatens and assaults people does not scream sound judgment," said one Democratic operative who did not wish to be named.

Another added, "Cooper has a lot of pluses going for him. He's good looking, articulate, and bright but the one knock on him has been that he lacks the experience and maturity for the job. Partying with sports agents and ballplayers who are getting into fistfights at clubs doesn't scream mature and really doesn't scream presidential."

★

Despite the fact that the country was facing the possibility of a war, a recession, and countless other serious problems, for weeks the leading news story of the presidential campaign was Luke's connection to the man dubbed "Scary McGuire" thanks to the *New York Post*. The nickname was a play on the name Jerry McGuire, the sports agent immortalized by Tom Cruise in the Hollywood classic of the same name.

Though Nate and the rest of the campaign had initially hoped that the story would be like most scandals and disappear in a few days, this one seemed to be the tabloid equivalent of the never-ending story, with new developments announced every other day. Nate was particularly wary of the possibility of a looming trial that could drag on for months—if not longer—and end up coinciding with the primary or general elections. Nate very rarely allowed worries to get the best of him, but the idea of Luke being called as a witness in a criminal trial was now officially giving him nightmares. On top of it all, though Luke wouldn't say it out loud, the situation with Joe had him down.

It was only one week before the next debate of the campaign and two weeks before the Iowa Caucus. Nate called this time "just before the games," likening it to the window just before the Olympic Games when the sponsors, the media, and the general public really start to narrow their focus on the athletes who matter, and when every sneeze or cough triggers speculation about whether or not someone actually has a shot at a medal or is destined to become another footnote in history—one of those people who sits around telling their grandkids, "I once competed in the Olympics." Though Luke hadn't had any major faux pas on the trail since Joe's arrest, Nate could tell his performance was slightly off, in the way that only someone who was familiar with Luke operating at one hundred ten percent could recognize what eighty percent looked like. Nate could tell that emotionally Luke wasn't in a good place, and it was manifesting on the campaign trail. He wasn't making errors, but this close to the primaries that wasn't enough. He needed to be on his A-game all of the time. As far as Nate was concerned, the next debate was the equivalent of one of those exhibitions where all of the gymnasts do a few tricks for the cameras just before the Games officially begin. No matter how many accolades one has, all it takes is one stumble off the balance beam for the story to move from "X is a frontrunner for an Olympic medal" to "Despite long being perceived as the frontrunner for a medal, the recent fall of X off of the balance beam has insiders second-guessing her hopes for a medal." Nate wanted to make sure that during Tuesday's debate, Luke not only stayed on the balance beam, but nailed his routine. But in recent days Nate could tell that mentally he just wasn't in a place where that was looking likely.

Again, Nate reached out to Brooke for guidance.

"We have a problem. Luke's been . . . well, he's been . . ."

"Miserable?"

"You could say that."

"Yeah, he's been short with me the last couple of times I've spoken with him, and Laura said he hasn't exactly been a barrel of laughs with her either."

"Any ideas?"

"Well, I know Laura said she worries about him getting lonely on the road."

"Occupational hazard, I'm afraid. It's a classic candidate conundrum. They're hardly ever alone for a single moment and yet they're like the most lonely people in the world because there are so few people they feel like they can really chill with."

In what could only be described as a case of Murphy's Law meets the world's worst timing, Adam received a job offer from a record label just days before Colby's assault. He had to start his new job immediately, so Luke found himself without a true friend or family member by his side during one of his most difficult personal moments.

"Actually, I have one idea," Brooke offered.

★

Luke was in a conference room at a small recreation center in South Carolina, in the middle of debate practice with South Carolina Congresswoman Amber Jay, a supporter, playing the role of Senator Beaman.

In the upcoming debate there would be an opportunity for the candidates to ask a question of their fellow candidates, so when Congresswoman Jay turned to Luke and asked, "Governor Cooper, I know that you have been very vocal about how much you value and appreciate religious diversity, and yet when parents in the school district in Minnetonka, Michigan, asked that someone protect their children from being persecuted for simply saying grace each day before beginning lunch, you did nothing. Can you please explain that?"

Luke snapped, "What kind of question is that?"

Replying in character, Jay said, "I think a very fair one to all of the parents out there who, as I do, value their religious faith and don't wish to see our children penalized for practicing it."

"That's way out of line!"

"Is that how you're planning to reply, Luke, because I don't think that's going to play very well on television," the congresswoman said.

"That question was bullshit, John," Luke huffed to his aide, who was playing the role of debate moderator.

"Maybe, Luke, but you can't say that in the debate. Why don't we take a break?" John suggested.

"Sorry to interrupt, but I need to borrow the candidate," another aide said, poking his head in.

"Borrow? What am I, your neighbor's lawnmower? Borrow me for what?"

"I was told to get you for a call with a VIP."

"Who scheduled this call?"

"I'm just following orders, Luke."

"Whose orders?"

He was met with silence.

"Whose orders?" Luke repeated, only this time his voice was testier.

Luke finally exploded, "Well, I guess no one needs to bother telling me anything. I'm just the goddamned candidate. Don't mind me!" He slammed his debate notes down on the podium he was standing behind. They scattered on the floor.

"You tell this so-called VIP that I have a little debate coming up that's probably more important to this campaign right now than they are. Although I realize that every person who gives me a thousand dollars thinks that this campaign revolves around them." Turning back to John portraying the moderator he then said, "Ask the next question."

The tension in the room was palpable.

Luke then barked to John, "Are you deaf? I said ask the next question." His other aide quietly slipped out the door.

"Would you like to grab your notes?" the congresswoman asked.

Luke looked down at the floor. His face began to flush with embarrassment. He took a deep breath. "I'm a little tired today."

"We hadn't noticed," Congresswoman Jay said. Luke cracked a smile. "I'm sorry. I'm just . . ."

Just then the door opened again.

"So I don't count as a VIP, huh? Well excuse me, Mr. President," Garin said.

Luke broke into a wide smile. "What are you doing here?"

"I think the bigger question is why you're claiming you don't have time to hang. I'm guessing you're afraid of what's going to happen on the court now that my leg's better." Garin pulled a basketball from his gym bag. He added, "Please tell me this kid is kidding and I'm not really going to have to sit here and listen to you debate for the next hour. I love you, man. But not that much."

Luke laughed.

"Guys? Is it okay if we end a little early?"

"Fine by me," Congresswoman Jay replied. "Especially since I thought we'd be done about a half hour ago. Your friend's actually a little late." She smiled at Garin.

"You knew about this?" Luke asked her.

She winked at Luke.

Luke walked over to Garin. At first they tried to do one of those über macho half hugs that men do in the presence of others. But then Garin said, "Come here, man" and enveloped Luke in a real hug—the kind of hug you give to family.

Luke's eyes began to well up. "It's so good to see you," he said.

"Okay, rule number one," Garin said as they walked toward the gym. "I'm not Adam or Brock, so no cheating."

"I never cheat!" Luke said.

"Umm. Do we need to revisit the Thanksgiving technical foul?"

"Here we go! That ball was *out*," Luke said, laughing.

"Helen Keller could see that ball was in, Luke. Well, Hellen Keller and your father. Thank you very much."

They laughed.

"What's rule number two?"

"Rule number two? No campaign talk on the court. All of us could use a break."

"All of us?"

As they opened the gym door, Luke then saw whom the "us" referred to.

There stood Brock and Theo, warming up on the court.

"No way!" Luke said.

They stopped what they were doing and headed over to him.

He enveloped them both in a group hug.

"I don't think I've ever been happier to see you guys."

"Let me guess. You need another donation?" Brock deadpanned.

Garin winced, but Luke laughed.

"No, man. We're good. It's just good to see you guys. Really good."

"Okay. Enough talking. Time to play," Garin said.

"Actually, would you all mind if we did a quick prayer?" Theo asked.

After an awkward silence, Luke said, "Not at all."

"Let's all grab hands."

Garin dropped the ball and the four men clasped hands.

"Dear heavenly father," Theo began. "We ask that you bless our dear friend Luke. That you watch over and protect him on this journey. That you give him the wisdom and courage he needs to survive, thrive, and lead successfully, and that if it be your will, that you allow him the strength to triumph."

At that Garin interrupted. "I'd like it noted for the record, God, that he's talking about Luke triumphing on the campaign trail, *not* the basketball court, where I hope to crush my dear old friend."

All of the men burst into laughter. At which point Theo said, "Amen."

For the next forty minutes the four of them played like old times, without a single mention of the campaign. And Garin's prayer was answered. He and Theo beat Brock and Luke by three points.

As they walked off of the court, Luke said, "Well, Garin, it's always great to see you. Now have a safe trip back."

"You're not getting off that easy. I'm hanging around for a few days."

"Lucky me," Luke deadpanned and slapped him on the back.

"So you have some time to improve your game so that I don't embarrass you in our rematch before I go," Garin added.

While Luke and Theo laughed, Brock, never known for his good sportsmanship, appeared to be sulking.

"I think I liked you better when you were limping," Luke chortled.

To which Garin replied, "Yeah, about the only time you actually have a chance is when I can't walk."

Out of nowhere Brock then interjected, "So Garin, how's Joe doing?"

At that the laughter subsided.

"He's hanging in there," Garin replied.

"Well, let me know if he needs any recs for good criminal defense attorneys. I know cases like his can drag on. I heard his agency dropped him so I'm guessing he's not being repped by Paley and Dunn, who I know usually make all of their little athlete problems go away."

Garin wanted to punch him. Instead he said, "That's really thoughtful of you, Brock. And I'll be sure to let him know that you asked after him. But he's fine. In fact, he's more than fine. His father is old golfing buddies with Len Weintraub. You may have heard of him. He's the former attorney general. So his firm is handling Joe's case for him."

"That's terrific," Brock replied, although that's not what his eyes were saying. "In other good news, Luke, my firm's raised another $30,000 this month for the campaign."

"No kidding, Brock. That's great. Really appreciate it," Luke replied.

"Yeah, Brock," Garin seconded. "That's like twice as much as your last fundraiser." Garin winked mischievously in Brock's direction.

Garin and Brock glared at each other.

"Sorry to interrupt, fellas, but I'm starving. Luke, you know where we can grab a bite to eat?" Theo asked.

"Theo, how long have you known me?"

"Too long."

"So what is one thing you know about me?"

"That you always know where to find food."

"There you go."

Luke put his arm around Theo.

After a post-game dinner, Brock had to catch a flight home. He mentioned that Tami was recuperating from "a minor medical procedure," although he wouldn't say what for. He didn't have to. Thanks to Brooke, Garin knew she had had a tummy tuck at Brock's request.

Afterward, Luke, Theo, and Garin played cards in Luke's hotel room until Theo finally called it a night at eleven.

Once Luke and Garin were alone, they finally began to talk about the topic they had spent much of the day trying to avoid with each other—Joe.

"I heard he and Tiffini broke things off," Luke said.

"Yeah. Turns out Joe was actually on to something. She and Colby had had a thing going back off and on a couple of years whenever he was in town. You know cheerleaders and athletes."

Luke knew that Joe always felt insecure about not having the athletic prowess of his father or any of the clients whose million-dollar contracts he negotiated. Nor did he have the power that came with said prowess. So Luke knew that losing his fiancée to an athlete would have been especially devastating for Joe.

"But you know Joe. He will have replaced her with another cheerleader in a month or two." Garin tapped Luke playfully.

Luke didn't crack a smile. "He and I have come a long way."

"You sure have," Garin said, laughing at the memory of the first fight between the friends. Luke hit Joe when he began taunting him with the line "What you talkin' 'bout, Willis?" a reference to the television show *Diff'rent Strokes*, about two black orphans raised by a wealthy white widower. Luke dropped him with a punch that landed them both in the principal's office. Joe actually admitted the fight was his fault and took the punishment that came with his admission, letting Luke off the hook. The moment marked the inauspicious beginning of a lifelong friendship.

"You guys have always had my back. And here he is in trouble and I . . ."

"There's a big difference between having a fight over teasing at sixteen and assaulting someone at forty-six, Luke. You know I love Joe as much as you do, but you didn't get him into this mess, he did."

"I just wish there was something I could do," he said.

"You know what you can do for Joe? You can stop letting this thing with him fuck up what you're trying to do. Out of everything that he's dealing with you know what worries him the most? The idea that he might have ruined his closest friend's life. So if you want to help him, you want to give him something to smile about while his life is in the toilet, go out there, kick some ass, and win this thing."

★

When Garin returned home the campaign staff missed his presence immediately. A number of them commented to Nate about how much more relaxed Luke seemed with Garin around. With the debate around the corner they wanted Luke at his very best, especially since it was the first to be held in South Carolina, the state where Luke was hanging all of his presidential hopes. The campaign had Luke booked to attend a series of events throughout the state in the final hours leading up to it. Luke was pleasant enough, for the most part, but forty-eight hours before the debate, they wanted him more than just pleasant, they wanted him fired up and ready to go. But during an early morning tour of a local factory someone shouted, "Hey, Governor, talked to Scary McGuire lately?" Luke was visibly annoyed but tried to ignore him. But the man continued the heckling before being reprimanded by an aide. Luke was rattled and seemed distracted the remainder of the afternoon.

After a day full of campaign events, he returned to his hotel room at 11 p.m. exhausted.

When his body aide mentioned that he needed to stop by his bedroom to pick up a book, Luke was annoyed.

Minutes later there was a knock at the door.

"About time," he said, before adding "what took you so long?" as he opened the door.

"Well, I'm sorry, but I didn't know you were expecting me," the voice on the other side said. It was Laura.

Luke was speechless.

"Your staff asked me to give you this."

Luke took the briefing book, and promptly tossed it to the floor.

He then pulled Laura close and gave her a big kiss.

"I've missed you," he said.

"How much?"

"This much," and he kissed her again.

A hotel worker then walked by and smiled at them.

"You better invite me inside before you end up with a sex scandal on your hands."

"I don't think it counts as a sex scandal if it's your wife," Luke teased.

"But how does he know I'm your wife?"

"That's true," Luke said. "You're so good looking he probably thinks I have some young, hot girlfriend."

Laura giggled.

He put his arm around her waist and pulled her into the room.

★

PoliticsToday.com

COOPER DOMINATES

Silencing critics who said that he didn't have the maturity to be president, Michigan Governor Luke Cooper dominated last night's debate, the fourth of the primary season. Though confident and affable in interviews, Cooper's performance in previous debates had, even by his own campaign team's admission, been less than stellar. His nerves seemed to get the best of him in the first debate, while in others he struggled to keep up with his opponents, all of whom displayed a greater grasp of foreign affairs.

As political analyst David Gergen put it, "If the Luke Cooper who showed up tonight had showed up in all of the previous debates, he would be the frontrunner."

Though in recent weeks his campaign has been hampered by distractions, including assault charges levied against one of his friends by one of his donors, Cooper performed in tonight's debate as if he didn't have a care in the world.

Perhaps Cooper's campaign planned things this way. With the first primary contest in Iowa one week away, Cooper is now gaining momentum at a time when more voters are paying attention. Cooper chose to sit out both the Iowa and New Hampshire contests to focus his time and resources on the Southern leg of the race—a potentially risky strategy. But if he continues to perform on the campaign trail the way he did this evening it is a strategy that could pay off.

CHAPTER 25

With polls showing him with his first official lead in South Carolina, only a couple of weeks before the state's primary, Luke was
in good spirits. He practically bounded back into his hotel room.

He was surprised to see Nate waiting for him.

"Nate, my man! What's happening?"

Luke was practically singing. Nate had never seen him so happy.

"Not much Luke. You're in a good mood."

"How could I not be in a good mood? We're winning. It's not just the
poll numbers. I *feel* it. So to what do I owe the honor? I don't remember
seeing a meeting on the schedule."

"Yeah, this is sort of a spur of the moment thing. Could you give us a
minute?" he said to Luke's closest traveling aide, who was always lingering close by.

After the aide left the room Luke said, "Uh-oh. Why am I getting the
impression that you don't come bearing good news?"

"Because you have good instincts," Nate replied. "I just got a call from
a source. A reliable source."

"Okay."

"I think you should sit down."

"The fact that you said that makes me think that I should keep standing and pour myself a drink."

"Actually, why don't you pour one for both of us."

Luke stared at Nate, who rarely drank alcohol, then walked over to
the bar in his hotel room, grabbed the bottle of whisky and poured two
glasses.

He passed Nate a glass, before taking a drink from his own. "So what's up?"

"Apparently someone has gathered some of your family members . . . or people claiming to be your family members . . . and they're going to endorse Beaman."

"What are you talking about?" Luke asked. "My whole family is working on the campaign. Hell, I have cousins I haven't seen in twenty years that my mom made go door-knocking for us."

"It's your biological family, Luke."

"What?"

"Someone has organized a few of them to do some sort of press event about how you chose to disassociate yourself from them."

"Chose? I was a kid. It's not like I chose to be adopted by . . . by . . . this is ludicrous. You don't seriously think something like this will actually have any impact."

"There's one more thing. The person organizing the presser is Johnny Highlands."

The thought that the man he once looked to as a second father, who was responsible for Luke's love of politics, was sabotaging his presidential hopes in such a personal and painful way left Luke stricken. He put his glass down.

"I don't believe you. He wouldn't do that."

Nate took a swig of whisky.

"I figured you'd say that. Which is why I needed the drink."

Nate took a deep breath before continuing. "Look, you know I'm not lying about this. You know I have no reason to. I heard it from someone in Burstein's camp. Obviously he has a hand in orchestrating this too. Look, I wish I could give you the time to grieve or cope with this in the way that you need to, but we don't have a lot of time. My understanding is this event is scheduled a couple of days from now. So we need to come up with a plan for how to address it. Because as much as it pains me to admit it, it could make a difference, and not in a good way."

"You can't seriously think that voters are going to fall for this bullshit. I mean, if that's what it takes for someone to be stupid enough to switch their vote, then I don't want their fucking vote anyway." He threw his glass across the room, shattering it.

Nate didn't budge.

"Luke, if you really did surrender every stupid person's vote to our opponents, then you'd be left with, like, five people to vote for you."

Luke didn't laugh.

"I want to talk to him. Johnny and I have had quarrels in the past. We'll get past this just like we have everything else over the years."

"I don't think that's a good idea," Nate replied sternly. "In fact I think it's a very bad idea." He took one last swig of his drink then stood up. "I'll get housekeeping to send someone up to clean up the glass and I'll call you later, once you've had some time to think."

He walked toward the door, then stopped and turned to Luke. "You know what they're going to try to do. Convince just enough black voters that you think you're better than them and that you don't really want to be black, that they can hobble us in South Carolina. Beaman won't beat us here, but she doesn't have to. If we don't win by double digits after pouring everything we have into winning there . . . well . . ." He trailed off before adding, "I'll call you in a few hours."

After Nate left his hotel room, Luke sat on the couch staring into space. The pit of his stomach turned and he was at a loss trying to figure out what to do. Matters concerning his biological family had always affected him more than he let on to his friends and even his family.

★

He was sure he would get the retired Reverend Edwards's voice mail, knowing that he often ignored the telephone if he was working on one of his crossword puzzles, but to his surprise the reverend answered.

"Hello and God bless."

"Hello yourself," Luke replied, trying to feign cheeriness.

"What's wrong?"

Luke chuckled. "I didn't say anything was wrong."

"You don't have to. I always know when something's wrong with one of my kids."

Hearing those words hit Luke like a ton of bricks. "Remember when you told me not to let others lose my way?"

"Uh-huh," the reverend replied.

"I think I may need a compass."

"Talk to me, son."

Luke began to cry, something he never let anyone see him do—not his mother, not his wife.

"You take as long as you need, son, and when you're ready, we'll talk," Reverend Edwards said.

Luke cleared his throat and put on his deepest, most macho voice. "Sorry, Reverend. This is a bit much for me."

"What are you apologizing for? You know why women usually out-live us? Because they don't keep as much nonsense bottled up inside. They release it when they need to, often through tears. Occasionally through throwing something at our heads. Don't ask me how I know."

At that Luke laughed softly.

"You know my Aurelia. She was tougher than a four-star general. I think I saw her cry just once. Wonder if a few more tears would have kept her here by my side just a little while longer."

Luke was silent.

"You there?"

"Yes, sir."

"Well, talk to me."

"It's just . . . I know that I'm blessed . . . to have the wonderful family that I do . . . I know my mom and dad would move heaven and earth for me and my brothers too. But . . . I feel bad saying this but . . . I know I always felt like something was missing. . . . Is that wrong?"

"No, son. Life's a journey. We're all searching for something."

"It's not that I wanted another family . . . I already have one that's wonderful. But I did always feel like a part of me was incomplete . . . and I realize now that I was always searching to find a part of myself, or at least a part of who I am, that I couldn't find at home." Luke sighed before continuing. "My dad taught me a lot of things—how to fish, how to ice-skate. But the one thing he could never teach me is how to get used to being treated differently than my brothers by cops or by sales people in fancy stores." He paused. "You know, my parents always tell the story about how when my dad came home from a business trip and saw my mom holding me for the first time, all he said was 'I thought you said that the next kid in this house would be a little girl.' I know they're so proud of that story—and they should be. It says a lot about who they are. But the one thing I still don't think they realize even now is that even though they don't see me as different—and they really don't—I am different. I am . . . and I think I was always looking to connect with someone who understands what that means for me. Is that crazy?"

"Not at all, son."

"I know that's part of why I became so close with Johnny. It wasn't that I was looking for another father. I already had one—a great one— but I was looking for someone who could teach me not just how to be a man but how to be a black man. I'm rambling . . ."

"No. You're making plenty of sense from where I'm sitting."

"That's why I can't believe Johnny would do this."

"Tell me, what is Johnny doing?"

"My campaign says he's organizing a group of my natural relatives to endorse my opponent."

"Why would he do that?"

"He thinks we betrayed him first by taking him off of the campaign."

"We?"

"Laura thought it was the right thing to do."

"You didn't?"

Luke paused before saying, "I know it was."

"So you either had to hurt him or hurt your campaign. If someone really loves you, they want what's best for you, and if this Johnny fellow is as smart as you always made him out to be then chances are he knows he wasn't the best fit to run your campaign too."

"Then why is he doing this? Why is he trying to hurt me?"

"Because man is not perfect. And when man is hurting, we often behave like animals. You step on a rattlesnake, he'll strike and poison you. Johnny got rattled, son. But one day he'll put the fangs away and come around."

Luke took a deep breath.

"I don't know what to do. My campaign seems to think my family's endorsement might have an impact."

"First off, family is much more than DNA, son. Did Theo ever tell you that you're not the only politician in our family?"

Luke smiled at being referred to as a member of the Edwards family. "No. He never told me."

"My great, great granddaddy was the governor of Mississipi."

Luke furrowed his brow, puzzled.

"That's right. He was the man who once owned my family. That means I got cousins scattered all throughout that state and this one. But they ain't family, son. You get my meaning?"

"Yes, sir."

"So these folks are going to try to hurt the campaign by saying you don't have a real black family. We all know that's not true. You've got plenty of black family, starting with Laura, Theo, me, and all of your Morehouse brothers. Sounds to me like we just got to do a better job letting the rest of the world know. You hear me, son?"

"Yes, sir."

"So let's figure out how we do that."

"Reverend?"

"Yes, son?"

"You know the strange part is that despite what they're doing, a part of me still wants to meet them. To see if we look alike, move alike, sound alike . . . I know that must sound insane."

"You're not crazy to be curious. You'd have to be crazy not to be. We're all curious about what helped make us who we are. We all channel it different ways. Some of us make it a full-time job. How do you think I ended up spending my life in a pulpit?" The reverend laughed.

Luke laughed softly too.

He then confessed to the reverend something he had never told a soul. "You know I thought about trying to find them before but . . . I just worried about . . ."

". . . about hurting your parents."

Luke was quiet before saying, "They never told me not to look for my family. They would never say that, but . . ."

Luke then shared with the reverend all he had ever been told about his biological family and the long-standing tension that developed between them and his adoptive parents that left Luke caught in a lifetime of emotional crossfire. His birth parents had been trying to pursue their own slice of the American Dream, but encountered one obstacle after another. Forced to drop out of college so that they could both work to support their new son, his mother faced even greater hardship when her young husband was killed in a car accident when Luke was just a few months old. She joined a program for young single mothers at the Gorman Center, where she met Esther. The two of them bonded, and when his biological mother was diagnosed with cancer two years later, she asked Esther to raise her son. In Luke's early years Esther tried to maintain relations with his extended family, but money created a gulf. While Luke's mother had never asked Esther for a dime, in the years following her death her siblings asked for an endless series of "loans" during their visits with Luke, loans that were never repaid. When Edmond Cooper finally put his foot down and turned off the financial faucet, one of Luke's aunts threatened to file for custody. While Esther was known for being the muscle in the family, Luke's father was one of those people known for rarely losing his temper—but who became terrifying when he did.

Though Luke never learned the details of exactly what transpired in Edmond and Esther's final verbal exchange with his biological aunt and uncle, his brother would later tell Luke, then a teenager, that Edmond had apparently made them "an offer they couldn't refuse." His brother then said, "Let's just say that Dad made the scene with the horse head in *The Godfather* sound like child's play."

Luke was stunned. *The Godfather* was one of his and his father's favorite movies—they'd watched it together a thousand times—but the idea of his father even implying a physical threat completely threw him. His brother added, "My understanding is that while Mom may have threatened to send someone home in a bodybag for messing with you once, Dad was like 'They won't need a bodybag because they won't find your body if you attempt to take my kid, and if you think I'm joking, just try me.'"

That was the last contact Luke had had with his biological relatives—contact he could now barely remember as an adult.

"So now here we are . . . all these years later . . . I just don't know what to do."

"Well, why don't we start with a prayer?"

"That sounds like a good idea."

He and Reverend Edwards then prayed together.

★

Over the next seventy-two hours Nate convened a focus group of voters to gauge the impact of the looming endorsement by Luke's relatives of his rival.

The results were not encouraging.

Luke later watched video of the responses in his hotel room.

"Well, I lived through segregation," one older African American South Carolina voter began. "And someone who's that age doesn't understand what we all went through before them. And if they're raised by white folks they really don't understand. And if they don't have contact with their blood kin by choice—that gives me even greater pause."

Another chimed in, "You can have all of the book smarts in the world from fancy colleges, but if you don't have the life experience to understand what it's like for those of us who weren't adopted by a rich family that's not black, not that he could help that, but he could help being in touch with his blood relations. And this looks to me like he chose not to, and that's the only reason I could see them wanting to help another candidate."

After watching video after video that sounded the same theme—that Luke wasn't black enough and his relationship with his biological family proved it—Luke finally relented and agreed to do something he had refused to since the campaign began.

He agreed to meet with Reverend Jack Saul. Though he had not preached a single sermon in more than three decades, and his only formal degree consisted of an honorary one bestowed by a college where he occasionally gave speeches, Saul insisted on being introduced as "The Good Reverend Dr. Jack Saul." He got his start as an aide to Dr. King, but was now best known for leading "diversity boycotts," primarily against corporations that had the temerity not to hire him or his sons to lead onsite "diversity seminars," which usually cost six figures.

Nate had tried to convince Luke to meet with Saul early in the campaign—if not to ask for his endorsement then at least to neutralize him and keep him from working against them. Saul had a notorious ego, but Luke had declined, deeming Saul's "diversity training" and boycotts a scam, and Saul himself unethical.

But now that they were in trouble, Nate broached the Saul issue again.

This time Luke relented.

"Set up a meeting."

Twenty-four hours later, Luke found himself sitting in Saul's home in Atlanta.

They engaged in a few minutes of the obligatory chit-chat before Luke cut to the chase.

"Reverend, I'm concerned that I am not connecting as well with older African American voters as I'd like."

"That's an understatement," the reverend, replied taking a sip of his coffee.

"I was wondering if you had any advice."

"Well, that depends."

Luke looked puzzled.

The reverend continued. "Are you asking me as a friend?"

"Of course," Luke replied.

"Because if so I'd find that interesting because I've never considered you a friend, and I know you've never considered me one because if so you would have called me before you found yourself in trouble."

Luke looked startled.

"But then I guess you thought you were too good to be my friend. Isn't that right?"

"Reverend, I don't know who told you that. I . . ." Luke searched for the words. Lying didn't come naturally to him, something his brother once said made politics an unnatural career choice for him.

The reverend put his hand up to silence Luke.

He then continued, "But I'm always happy to make new friends."

A look of relief swept across Luke's face.

"And new friends help each other, don't they, Luke?"

The relief began to dissipate.

"My son would very much like to expand his business ventures into real estate and I'm sure your parents would love to meet him. And as a friend I'm sure you'd be happy to facilitate that introduction."

"I . . ." Luke took a deep breath. "I can certainly introduce your son to one of my brothers, who handles most of our family's operations now. I don't have any say on hiring, but I can certainly handle the introduction."

"Wonderful. And I'm sure as a friend you would be willing to ask your mother to serve on the board of my foundation for the next year. We ask all board members to commit to writing a check for or raising $25,000."

Luke pictured having this conversation with his mother, the conversation where he had to explain to her that he had bartered her time and support of a charity away in exchange for a political endorsement—all without discussing it with her first. He decided that losing in South Carolina would be less painful than having that conversation.

"I'm sorry, Reverend. I should not have come here." Luke stood up and extended his hand.

The reverend didn't take his hand and remained seated.

"I'm sorry too. It will be a shame to see you lose, but perhaps it will teach you a valuable lesson, and you'll learn to show better judgment in how you pick and choose to treat your friends."

★

That evening Luke sat alone in his hotel room pondering the prospects of losing. He then picked up the phone and dialed.

"Hello, Mr. Long. It's Luke. How are you?"

"I'm as well as can be expected considering everyone I'm close to is dying off around me and my arthritis keeps me in constant pain. But I suspect you didn't really call to make idle chitchat. So to what do I owe the honor?"

"Look, Mr. Long, I know we've never been that close. And I'm not entirely sure why. I suspect it's because you think your only daughter could have done better, and that's true. She could have. I can't say I blame you. There's not a day that I don't wake up thinking—knowing—that she could have done better. But I've tried my best to make sure that a day doesn't go by where she regrets that she didn't do better. I love her very much. I've tried to be a good husband, a good father, and a good son-in-law, and I respect you a great deal and I've certainly always tried to show that."

Luke took a breath then continued. "I know you haven't always been particularly thrilled with my choice of career, but I do care a great deal about trying to help people. I know that's something you care about too."

"Luke, I'm in my eighties. It would probably be wise of you to get to the point while I'm still alive and alert enough to listen."

"Yes, sir. I've never asked you for anything except for your daughter's hand in marriage. And at first you said no to that. But I think over the last fifteen years I've proven myself and I'm asking you for something now. And I hope you'll say yes."

"And that is?"

"I know you completed one campaign ad *for* me. But I would like for you to do another *with* me. I'd like for you to tell the world what you know: that I've been a good husband and father and son-in-law. That I'm honest and have integrity and that someone like you, whom I so respect and admire, respects me enough to lead this country."

There was silence.

"Sir?"

"I'm here."

"Would you like some time to think about it?"

"No."

Luke slumped in his chair, dejected.

"I don't need time to think about it," his father-in-law continued. "I'll do whatever you need, son. Frankly, I was just waiting for you to show that you were man enough to ask me yourself instead of having my daughter do your dirty work for you. A leader has to have courage."

★

The day of the press conference Luke did a one-on-one interview with Martin Rolston, one of the few black reporters on a major morning show. Rolston was known for his combative interview style and for wearing ascots, which were part of his signature on-air attire. In the interview, the two men talked about the impact of fatherlessness on the black community, and Luke discussed, in more personal terms than ever before, the impact that never knowing his biological father had had on him. He also discussed how blessed he felt to have so many surrogate fathers in his life. In addition to his adoptive father, he also discussed his father-in-law, who for the first time ever joined Luke on camera to participate in an interview.

In what would become the most replayed clip from the interview, Rolston thanked Griswold Long for his service to the country in World War II, to which he replied, "If you want to thank me proper, then stop saying such knuckleheaded things about my boy."

A bit taken aback, Rolston replied, "I'm sorry, sir? What?"

"You heard me. I read what you said about him not being a strong enough candidate. It was quoted in the paper last week. He's plenty strong. And you're lucky my arthritis is acting up or I'd ask you to step outside, young man."

Luke was so taken aback by his father-in-law's protectiveness that he chuckled, and even Rolston seemed obviously tickled at being threatened by a man in his eighties who occasionally relied on a cane.

Trying to suppress a smile, Rolston awkwardly replied "Yes, sir" before adding, "Well, we can say this much, you certainly have a very loyal team there, Governor."

"Yes, yes I do," Luke beamed.

Luke had to suppress the urge to give Griswold Long a great big hug, but remembering that his father-in-law, forever the military man, wasn't big on public (or private) displays of affection, he instead simply whispered, "Thank you, sir."

When asked throughout the day about the impending endorsement of his opponent by his blood family, Luke said, "Every campaign can tout a roster of diverse supporters and our campaign is very proud of ours."

The day before members of his biological family were scheduled to endorse his rival, Luke was scheduled to unveil a new set of his own headline grabbing endorsements. Reverend Julius Sutton, Reverend P. T. Barclay, and the Reverend Theo Edwards, three heroes of the civil rights movement who had all marched with and been friends and associates of the late Dr. Martin Luther King, Jr. all endorsed Luke. Though officially retired from their respective pulpits, the three were known for being sparing with their endorsements over the years, and both Reverends Barclay and Sutton had initially stated they had no plans to wade into the primary. When asked by a reporter what changed their minds, Reverend Barclay said, "The three of us have known each other a long time and been through a lot together. In a way, we're like family, and when one of us feels strongly about something it's hard for the others not to listen, and let's just say that one of us felt strongly enough about this that we reconsidered."

Reverend Edwards was more succinct. "Luke is like another son to me, and I'm proud to call him that and would be proud to call him Mr. President."

★

24/7News.com

COOPER CAMPAIGN GAINS MOMENTUM
AND NEWFOUND FAMILY

The presidential campaign of Michigan Governor Luke Cooper has had a banner week. Yesterday the campaign not only gained the endorsement of the *South Carolina Herald*, the state's leading paper, but two new family members.

Gov. Cooper, who is adopted, has spoken openly of his unique family story and made it a central narrative of his campaign. Last week, after two of his biological relatives participated in a bizarre press conference in which they announced they were choosing to endorse his opponent, the Cooper campaign was contacted by others claiming to be distant relatives of the candidate. Though the claims of a number of those who got in touch could not be confirmed, two have been verified.

Days ago Gov. Cooper met Lonnie Branson and Jesse Bond for the first time. The two are his second cousins on his biological mother's side. The family resemblance was striking, as Gov. Cooper himself noted upon their first meeting, according to a spokesperson.

Branson and Bond, coincidentally, had both been volunteering for the Cooper campaign headquarters in their home state of North Carolina but said in a brief interview that both plan to travel to South Carolina to help Gov. Cooper in the closing days of his campaign there. As Bond added, "Anything for family."

CHAPTER 26

The seventy-two hours before the South Carolina primary were a whirlwind. While Luke crisscrossed the state in a final bus tour, Laura was her own one-woman political dynamo, visiting dozens of nursing homes, community centers, and churches in the final push. She even personally knocked on some doors and made phone calls to voters from the state headquarters, although unlike the activities of most campaign volunteers, Laura's one-on-one phone chats with voters were usually captured on camera.

She was entering a popular diner to meet patrons when she heard a familiar voice: her own. She looked up to see a television in the diner airing one of the campaign commercials she appeared in. She felt strange seeing it but tried her best to play off it. She recalled how painful the shoot had been, and the International Cookie incident that occurred between the director and her mother-in-law. Despite what a jerk the director had been, Laura had to admit that the ad sounded pretty good and looked even better. Clearly the guy knew what he was doing.

Luke was getting off his campaign bus at one of his final South Carolina stops when he first noticed what appeared to be a sea of supporters dressed in the color maroon. About thirty men in a crowd of nearly 150 were wearing hats and windbreakers that were unmistakably Morehouse colors. They caught Luke's eye, but it wasn't until he noticed that one sign read "MOREHOUSE MEN FOR LUKE" that he knew for sure they were in fact his Morehouse brothers. He made a point to wave and point enthusiastically in their direction.

And they cheered and waved loudly in kind. The moment gave Luke an extra jolt of energy after what had been a long, exhausting few days.

He planned to return to his hotel for the equivalent of a catnap the night before the primary, knowing that even if he had the time he probably wouldn't sleep a wink. The staff booked him and Laura a suite with two rooms at Luke's insistence because he was worried about waking her up when he returned after midnight after his final campaign event.

And yet when he returned to the suite, just before 2 a.m., there she was on the couch.

He tried to creep in as quietly as possible, but he bumped into a floor lamp.

She sat up.

"Honey, I'm sorry," he whispered. "Didn't want to wake you."

"I wanted to see you," she said groggily.

"You should rest. It's going to be a long day tomorrow . . . or today," he said.

"I wanted to see you before," she said.

"Before what?" he asked, making his way over to the couch.

"Before you win," she smiled, her eyes barely open.

He sat down next to her, put his arm around her. She leaned her head on his shoulder. He kissed the top of it.

She wrapped her arm around his tummy. He slipped off his shoes.

"I love you," she whispered.

"I love you more," he replied.

She giggled. "You know, everything's not a competition," she said, before adding, "But for the record, I love *you* more."

He laughed before imitating her voice, "You know everything's not a competition."

He gently kissed her forehead again. As she rested her head on his shoulder, he rested his head on top of hers. They didn't say another word. They just held each other for a few minutes more before drifting off to sleep.

★

Luke had been asked to do a quick thank you/pep talk with his volunteers the morning of the primary. He had barely slept in the last 48 hours and was exhausted. He was irritable and grouchy, and being forced to smile constantly (an official candidate requirement, as Nate reminded him) was making him even grouchier. From his vantage point, if he was going to be up at the crack of dawn he'd rather be talking to voters.

But his scheduler panicked, knowing that standing up volunteers, while possibly small in the big scheme of things of campaign strategy, was exactly the type of move that could be misconstrued. All it would take is one disappointed volunteer telling one reporter looking for an angle, and all of a sudden you had a news story. "Has Cooper Momentum Gone to Candidate's Head?"

His scheduler called the one staffer she knew could make a difference.

"Hello."

"Brooke—I'm sorry. Did I wake you?"

"No. Honestly, I barely slept."

"That makes two of us."

"What's up?" Brooke asked.

"Look, I'm sorry to ask . . . to put you in this kind of position . . . but the thing is Luke was supposed to come by the headquarters to say hi to a bunch of volunteers who have gathered. You know, as sort of one last pep talk to motivate them to go out and work their hearts and souls out for him today."

"Right. I saw it on the schedule."

"Well, he just canceled."

"Why?"

"I think he's tired . . . and from what I gather a little grouchy."

"He's not much of a morning person."

"Yeah, I've learned that the hard way."

They both laughed.

"But we need him to show up. It's important. I know I can't get through to him on this, and frankly I'm afraid to try and I don't know if anyone can, but my guess is you have a better chance than the rest of us."

"Let me see what I can do."

After hanging up, Brooke sent a text message to Laura.

"Hey soon-to-be-1st Lady. Have a sec?"

Laura texted back. "Sure. What's going on?"

"We're scheduled to visit a senior center first thing today but would u mind saying hi to some voluntrs at HQ 1st?"

"Of course not," Laura replied.

"Great. Can u c if Sir Luke would b willing 2 join?"

Sir Luke was the nickname Brooke called Luke to Laura when either of them thought that he was being difficult. It was a play on one of Luke and Laura's all-time favorite songs—"Sir Duke" by Stevie Wonder.

"No prob. We'll be there."

"Thx!"

★

Though Luke had initially resisted going—even sulking in the car on the way there—he eventually said yes. He rarely said no to Laura, particularly when it came to campaign advice since she so rarely offered any.

As they walked into headquarters hand in hand they were greeted with a roar as more than 200 people burst into applause. They were all squished shoulder to shoulder, but no one seemed to mind. Luke broke into a wide grin—one of the first unforced smiles he'd exhibited in days. He and Laura waved to the crowd of supporters, then Laura did something she had not done before in public in all her years as a politician's wife. She began to tear up.

After the applause died down, Luke squeezed her hand. A staff member then appeared with a microphone, handing it to Luke. Laura reached for it and said, "Please don't mind me. These are just tears of joy. I have been so touched by the incredible kindness that you have shown my husband and our family. I always knew that he was a wonderful person and a wonderful leader, and I am so appreciative to every single one of you in this room for making sure the rest of this state—the rest of America—knows it too."

Luke then put his arm around her waist and she leaned her head on his shoulder.

"Won't she make a terrific First Lady?" he asked.

The crowd applauded again. Some even whistled, to which Luke replied, "Watch it. I know she's cute, but she's already taken!"

Luke and the crowd laughed.

He then said, "I know you all have probably heard enough campaign stump speeches to last you a lifetime, so I won't bore you to death with another. I really just want to say thank you for all that you have done. Victory would not be possible without all of you and your hard work. As you know, I'm not just running for myself or just for my family, I'm running for all of you and your families too. . . . So I just want to thank you for all of your hard work. I want to thank your loved ones for putting up with your absences all of the times you were here working late into the night."

After a pause he then said, "You know, I don't know about the other campaigns but we got some good-looking volunteers." Everyone then burst into laughter. "If this were a competition for who has the best looking team, then we'd be all set." The room erupted into laughter and applause. "Seriously," Luke continued, "thank you from the bottom of my heart."

He then waved and he kissed Laura. The two then began circulating and saying hello to people.

Luke was giving a hug to an elderly black volunteer who was in her eighties. She told Luke he was "the son she never had." Luke replied, "Well, then can I call you Mom?" The woman beamed. Luke then shouted, "Someone got a camera? Ma and I are going to get a picture." The campaign's official photographer then scurried over and snapped a pic of the two of them.

He and Laura were surrounded by other volunteers hoping to get a chance to say hi, and then he looked up and saw a familiar face.

"Hey!" Luke said in recognition. Although he couldn't quite remember the name, he knew the man's face looked familiar, and that he knew him through Theo.

He and Luke then did a cross between a high-five and a dap, greeting one another the way they might if they were two old friends meeting for a pickup game.

"Hey, Gov. Nice to see you again. Sam Rollins," the young man, about thirty, said with a bright smile.

"Thanks, man, for coming out," Luke replied.

"My pleasure. Well, you know very few people say no to Reverend Theo."

"Theo sent you?"

"Well, let's just say he asked—in the kind of way that made it clear it was more than a suggestion."

Luke laughed. He had been on the receiving end of a couple of such "requests" from Theo, who was convincing in the way only a man of the cloth could be.

Just then it clicked. Sam's family were members of Mount Sage and Luke had met Sam years ago when he was just a boy, and they had crossed paths a couple more times over the years. Unbeknownst to Luke, after he spoke with the senior Reverend Edwards, he called Theo. As a member of the clergy, Theo, too, could not weigh in officially on endorsing anyone—at least not in his capacity as a minister. But as a friend, there was plenty that he could do to help his brother realize his dream. After speaking with his father, Theo placed a call to Sam, who was not only an active member of Mount Sage, but an active Morehouse alum who was particularly plugged in to the Morehouse under-30 set. He had heard Luke speak at an alumni event, and Theo had also introduced them during the reception that followed his mother's funeral service at Mount Sage a few years before.

Sam had contributed to Luke's gubernatorial and presidential campaigns and had even coordinated a group of Mount Sage parishioners to volunteer at a phone bank for Luke, but when Theo called him after Luke's conversation with his father, he asked him to do more. Their conversation was brief, but during it Theo impressed upon him that he had an opportunity to help make history. Like many people, Sam considered a request from a pastor on par with a personal request from the Office of God.

He said yes without hesitation. Within days Sam had organized an official Morehouse "Men for Coop Group" and had arranged for a couple of hundred of them to be bused in from around the country to ensure Luke's first big primary win.

"So you came all the way down here? Much appreciated."

"And I brought along my brothers," Sam replied.

"You did? Well, thanks! How many brothers do you have?"

"A few thousand. But I could only get a few hundred down to South Carolina—for now," Sam replied, then motioned behind him.

As Luke scanned the room he realized that about seventy-five of the men there were wearing maroon shirts—Morehouse colors, with Morehouse pins next to their Cooper for President pins, just like the ones he had seen at his rally the day before. Sam then said, "Others will be arriving throughout the day."

"Aw, man, thanks," Luke said. He was genuinely touched.

He leaned in and gave Sam a hug. He then said, "Hey, Morehouse men, can we get a photo?" Sam rounded them all up. They gathered around Luke and took what Luke called a "family portrait" with his Morehouse brothers.

Though Luke had been reluctant to do the volunteer visit at first, he found himself having so much fun that he wasn't ready to leave when his staff told him it was time for him and Laura to move on. They had a packed schedule that day. Being surrounded by the love, support, and enthusiasm of his volunteers left him feeling invigorated, proving yet again that his wife knew him best, Luke thought to himself, although he didn't say it. Instead, on their way out of the headquarters, he nuzzled Laura's ear and said, "We're going to win."

★

Nearly thirteen hours later, Luke was staggering back to his hotel. He had spent the whole day running on pure adrenaline but now felt as though he was a car running on empty and headed for a crash. He knew that if he could just get a quick power nap he would be ready for the long night ahead of him—a night he knew he would remember for the rest of his life. He only had a little more than an hour before well-wishers would start to arrive, before his speech in the hotel's ballroom after the final returns came in, and he and Laura both wanted to freshen up and enjoy their last moments of alone time for what would likely be a very long time after today.

But as they stepped into the hotel elevator, Brooke said, "We have to make one quick stop."

"What for?"

"We have to say hello to some people."

"Who?"

"Some VIP volunteers."

"Brooke, I said hello to our volunteers this morning. Let's not push our luck."

His stern tone made it clear that he knew that Brooke had been the one to convince Laura that they needed to go to the headquarters that morning.

"It's one stop, Luke," Laura said in a soothing voice.

"Ten minutes," Luke snapped. "I mean it. I want you to time it."

He then huffed out of the elevator. Brooke was unusually quiet. They walked in silence down the hallway until Brooke stopped and knocked on a door.

The door opened slowly. Luke was still annoyed about it all, so he was looking at the floor thinking about how tired he was when he heard a familiar voice. "So do I have to call you Mr. President yet?"

It was Adam.

"What the hell are you doing here?" Luke said as he laughed and leaned in to give Adam a hug.

"I heard you needed volunteers. I knocked on so many doors today my knuckles almost bled."

He then heard another familiar voice chime in. "I told him if he'd grown up playing a real sport like football instead of tennis, his hands would be tougher." It was Garin. He was wearing a "Cooper for President" T-shirt. He looked exhausted in the way that only someone who has been working around the clock can. Luke soon learned that while he and Laura were speaking to volunteers at headquarters that morning, Garin was already out and about helping the field team put new "Cooper for President" signs up before the polls opened. He'd arrived thirty-six hours before and had been pitching in around the clock, wherever the campaign needed him.

"You know, Garin, if tennis is such a sissy sport," Adam replied, "then why is it that you ended up in a cast the first time you tried to play."

"First of all, it wasn't a cast. It was medical tape. And it wasn't tennis, it was racquetball, smart-ass."

"Oh, excuse me," Adam said as they both laughed. "Back me up here, Coop."

"I'm with Adam on this one, Gar."

"Not surprised, since you play that sissy sport too."

"Who invited Garin?" Luke joked.

"I did," Brooke said smiling as she walked over to Garin, plopped down on his lap, and planted a big kiss on him. They had been apart more than they had been together the last couple of months but it was for a good cause, and for their friend, so they were willing to endure the temporary sacrifice. She kicked off her shoes and rested her head on Garin's shoulder. He squeezed her close.

Upon entering the room Luke saw who the rest of his VIP volunteers were.

Theo was there and sitting next to him was Sam Rollins. "Luke, you remember Sam, don't you? He's been the point man for getting all your Morehouse brothers down here."

"Of course! We caught up this morning. Good to see you again."

"I hope you don't mind me crashing your party here," Sam said.

"Please. You're Morehouse. You're family," Luke warmly replied.

Theo's father was also there. He struggled to stand up, but Luke said, "No, stay right there." He made his way over to where Reverend Edwards was seated then leaned in and gave him a hug. "I can't believe you came all this way."

"Wouldn't miss it," Reverend Edwards replied.

"How are you feeling?" Luke asked.

"Good enough. I've made a vow. I'm going to live to see you elected president if it kills me." Everyone burst into laughter—including the reverend himself.

Tami was also there. Luke gave her a kiss on the cheek. "It's so good to see you."

"It's great to see you too, in person for a change, as opposed to on a television screen."

"Where's Brock?" Luke asked.

"He's been working insane hours on some big case and couldn't get away, but he sent me and he sent this." Tami passed Luke a bottle. The note read, "I wish I could be there to toast you in person. Looking forward to sharing a glass at 1600 Penn Ave. Congrats to my brother. Brock" Brock had a wine cellar that was the envy of many wine connoisseurs. Luke unwrapped the bottle knowing it would not be your run of the mill liquor store purchase, but he was stunned to see it was a bottle of champagne. But not just any champagne. It was a bottle of Louis Roederer Cristal, from 1966. It easily cost the equivalent of some people's mortgage payments. "Wow!" Luke said, holding it up. "Well now I better win this thing or Brock will ask for this back." Everyone within earshot who knew Brock broke into giggles—knowing how apropos the comment really was.

A moment later there was a knock at the door. It was Luke's parents and two of his brothers, Josh and David.

"Heyyyyy!!"

While his brothers each gave him a hug, Luke's mom remained positioned behind a cart that was almost as big as she was.

"What's this?" Luke asked sounding like a little kid.

"It's a surprise."

Luke reached for the lid and she smacked his hand away. Everyone laughed.

"I can't believe she's still smacking me around in my forties," he said teasingly. He winked at his mom.

"Yeah, and being president's not going to change that, so I hope that's not why you're running," Josh said.

"Thanks for the tip, smart-ass," Luke said, hitting his brother in the back of his head.

"Watch your language," Esther scolded.

"Sorry Mom," Luke said, leaning in to give her a kiss.

Josh then stuck his tongue out at Luke.

"And you stop being such a smarty-pants," she said, turning to Josh.

Luke winked. "That's my girl."

Esther pushed the cart farther into the room and said, "I just want to say how proud we are of you and how much we love you."

Practically everyone in the room let out an "awww."

She removed the lid and revealed a cake—but not just any cake: It was her world famous chocolate chip pound cake—Luke's favorite. In red, white, and blue letters, it said "We're proud of you." Sticking out from the cake was a photo of Luke as a toddler.

"The hotel let me take over their kitchen for part of the afternoon so I could make it just the way you like it."

She placed the cake on a coffee table in the center of the room.

Before Luke had a chance to hug her she was being embraced by his friends, many of whom had known her for more than half their lives but had not seen her since his swearing in as governor.

"Hey, hey," Luke said. "Mind if I cut in? She is my mom, after all."

He then leaned in and enveloped her in a big hug.

As his mother sliced the cake, Luke's father gave him a hug. "Hey, son. How are you?"

"Good, Dad. Much better for seeing all of you."

"Wouldn't've missed it. Proud of you."

He then slapped Luke on the back in the reassuring way that only a father can. His brother Josh followed, giving Luke a great big hug followed by his usual big brother ribbing. "I don't know what Mom's been worried about. You look like you've put on a few pounds to me." He then playfully nudged Luke in the gut.

"Oh, that's rich, Josh. You calling *me* fat."

Josh had put on more than a few pounds since his days on the high school wrestling team, pounds he now jokingly referred to as "redistributed muscle."

"It's all muscle. All muscle," Josh said, slapping his gut with a laugh. "Matt wanted to be here but work turned crazy and he missed his flight, so he's going to try to make it later tonight. But he told me to tell you not to worry because you're going to win the rest of these things, so he'll be sure to make it to your next victory lap even if he misses this one."

"Aw. Thanks, bro," Luke said.

"And he asked me to give you this, just in case." Josh then handed Luke a package. Luke unwrapped it and then, reviewing the contents, burst into hysterical laughter, loud enough to capture everyone's attention. Luke announced, "I *love* it," and gave his brother a high-five.

"What is it?" his mom asked.

Luke held the enclosed gift up so that the entire room could see. It was two photos blown up to poster size featuring his brother Matt wearing a T-shirt that on the front read "My brother's running for president," and on the back read ". . . And all I got was this lousy T-shirt!"

The entire room burst into laughter. Matt was known as the comedian in the family.

A moment later Laura's father, Griswold Long, arrived with the boys and with Brooke and Garin's daughter Allie, who was sound asleep in his arms. The boys were all thrilled to see a room filled with their grandparents, godparents, and assorted aunts and uncles—all of the people they knew could be counted on to spoil them the most.

Laura's father carefully laid Allie on a couch so she could continue her nap while Milo made a beeline for "Uncle Garin," who immediately began tossing him around like a beanbag before Brooke said, "Be careful. Laura said he had a bag of Cheetos earlier. You don't want him to get sick and make a mess."

"Relax, Auntie Brooke," Garin said with a smile.

Milo then parroted him, "Yeah, relax, Auntie Brooke."

"Excuse me?" Brooke said in a stern tone.

Milo then whispered to Garin, "Uh-oh . . . are we about to get a time out?"

To which Garin whispered back, "Don't worry about it, little man. I'm not afraid of her." He then quickly added, "But why don't we go ahead and grab a slice of cake . . . over there." He then led Milo across the room—away from the wife, the one that he was *not* afraid of.

The friends and family continued to catch up over cake, along with the ice cream, coffee, and pizza that had been delivered to the room. But the food wasn't the only surprise that arrived later.

Upon hearing another knock, they all assumed it was room service yet again.

When Brooke opened the door she couldn't believe her eyes.

Standing before her was Laura's cousin Veronica—only she didn't look like herself. Instead of being clad in her usual designer pumps, with designer duds to match, she was clad in something Brooke didn't even know she owned: jeans and sneakers.

"Well, are you going to invite me in or not?" Veronica snapped.

But she still sounded like the same old Veronica, Brooke thought to herself.

"Of course," Brooke said.

Veronica didn't bother saying hello but sauntered in, wearing a "Cooper for President" T-shirt and matching campaign hat.

"Hey, cuz!" Laura said enthusiastically.

"Hey yourself."

They exchanged air kisses.

"Thanks for coming to help."

"Veronica, I didn't know you would be volunteering," Luke said.

"Well, truth be told, I didn't know I would be either until a few nights ago. I asked the campaign what more I could do to help. I thought they'd ask me to throw another party, but they said you needed people knocking on doors, so here I am."

Luke was stunned.

"Well, thanks. That means a lot."

"Anything for family," Veronica said in a very un-Veronica-sounding way.

She then turned to Laura and added, "Please tell me you're letting someone fix your makeup before you go in front of the TV cameras."

And once again she sounded like her old self.

They all spent the next half hour catching up before Theo's father, Reverend Edwards, began stomping his cane on the floor to let everyone know he wanted to speak.

Luke was the first to notice. "You need something, Rev?" he asked.

"I was wondering," Reverend Edwards began, "if we might have a moment of prayer? Would anyone mind?"

"Not at all," Luke replied. "Excuse me, guys." He continued without much response, "Guys?"

"Hey! Hey! Hey!" Brooke said in a booming voice. "The reverend has graciously offered to lead us in a word of prayer."

Luke's mother said, "That's a lovely idea" and walked over to Reverend Edwards and reached for his hand.

Everyone followed suit, clasping hands until they stood in a unified ring around the room.

"Actually," the reverend continued, "I was hoping that you might be so kind as to lead us, Mrs. Cooper."

"Oh, I don't know about that. I'm not a very good public speaker, not like my son."

"You're not in public, Mom. We're all family here," Luke said.

"I tell you what," the reverend said. "Why don't I start us off and then I'll squeeze your hand and then you finish up. We'll work as a team."

"Go, Mrs. Cooper!" Garin cheered. Others joined until the room was a mix of cheers and applause.

"Well . . . okay," she said.

They all bowed their heads in prayer.

★

Three hours later after the Associated Press declared Luke Cooper the winner of the South Carolina primary with a solid 12-point victory, he and Laura prepared to take the stage in the hotel's ballroom. It would be their first time greeting the world as more than just a presidential candidate and his wife, but as a possible president and First Lady.

After a couple of final notes from aides, the two glided out onto the stage hand in hand.

Luke then slipped his arm around Laura's waist as they waved to supporters. Laura then turned toward him and affectionately straightened his tie. She leaned into him. He kissed her on the head just before he made his way to the podium to begin his speech. Before he let her go, she leaned in and whispered, "Someone's getting lucky tonight."

She then winked mischievously at him before turning to walk away. Luke watched her walk—all of her—and for a moment forgot about everyone else in the room.

★

New York Post

LUCKY MAN:

Cooper Wins Primary and Prime Offer from his Wife

Gov. Luke Cooper may have just experienced his luckiest day yet. On the night that his campaign celebrated his first victory of the presidential primary, his wife invited him to a private celebration featuring just the two of them. That's the speculation among those who heard comments Michigan's First Lady meant to share with just her husband, but inadvertently shared with the world. Though the audio is low, Laura Cooper can be clearly heard saying the words, "Someone's getting lucky tonight," just as she leaves her husband's side before he begins his victory speech to supporters in the ballroom of the South Carolina Hyatt.

According to sources, in addition to the microphone at the podium, unbeknownst to the possible future First Lady, the stage had two small, alternate microphones positioned near the podium as backups. One of those microphones picked up her no longer private remarks.

When asked for comment the campaign initially refused, before Mrs. Cooper's press secretary, Brooke Andrews, issued the following coy statement: "Mrs. Cooper has made no secret of the fact that she loves her husband very much and considers him an incredibly smart and capable governor and candidate for president. But now it looks like the secret is out that she also considers him cute and irresistible."

CHAPTER 27

There were two weeks to go before the next round of primaries, in the states of California, Michigan, and Pennsylvania. Since Beaman represented Pennsylvania, and Luke Michigan, those states were essentially a guaranteed win for both candidates, which meant California would be the most watched primary of that day. Beaman had long been heavily favored to win in that state, though, owing to her family ties there, which included an endorsement from the governor, who had once interned for her father years before.

But Luke's convincing win in South Carolina had done exactly what Nate had predicted it would months before—turned the campaign from a three-man race to a one-man, one-woman race, specifically a race between Abigail Beaman and Luke Cooper. Luke's newfound standing as a viable threat to Beaman's planned coronation for the primary had put the equivalent of a political bull's-eye on his back. And less than 36 hours after his South Carolina win, the first dart was thrown. An organization called Americans for Religious Freedom, which described itself as devoted to protecting the legal rights of Christians in the workplace and educational institutions, began airing ads claiming that Luke, as governor, had not done enough to protect the rights of Christians. They cited the case that Congresswoman Jay asked Luke about during debate prep, involving parents in a Michigan school district who sued because they believed their children were being bullied for saying grace and the school district was not doing anything to stop it. As governor there was really little Luke could do—a fact that any legal scholar or political strategist trying to score points would know, but many voters likely would

not. Still, his office had issued a statement at the time denouncing bullying of a student in any form as "reprehensible." The ad was the political
equivalent of a warning shot. The more Luke won—the closer he got to
the nomination—the worse they would get, Nate warned him.

Luke's response: "Bring it on."

Mimi knew that donors were more fickle about determining which
candidates and causes they were willing to support than a toddler with
a new toy, so she made sure the campaign struck while the iron was
hot. Her team had so many fundraisers scheduled she could hardly
keep up. Most of the "new" donors were really pre-existing donors
of some of the candidates who had dropped out of the race. It was
tradition in campaigns that when one candidate dropped out, other
candidates began circling their donors like buzzards. Some might have
assumed that the morning after his big South Carolina win Luke would
be taking it easy, sleeping in, and savoring his victory just for a bit.
Instead, Mimi had him working the phones, making his standard
pitch. "You're right. Senator Jamison is a terrific guy and he ran a great
race, and I certainly hope for his counsel and support now that he's
no longer in the race. I'm also hoping that I can count on you for your
support as well."

★

After their big South Carolina win, Laura and the boys were to return to
Michigan for a couple of days of downtime, or "mom time," in Laura's
words. Brooke was also given a couple of days off to spend with her
daughter Allie, whom she had seen sporadically since joining the campaign. Brooke was glad to be traveling back from South Carolina with
Garin, savoring the increasingly rare moments alone with her family.
Though Tami was originally booked on a later flight they encouraged
her to join them. Primary night had been so chaotic after the returns
started coming in that they hadn't had that much time to catch up, so
Tami changed her reservation and joined Brooke and Garin on their
flight to New York.

Before Brooke and Tami said their goodbyes at the airport they
made a spa date. Time for things like bikini waxes had become an exotic
luxury on the campaign trail, so they decided to meet for a Girls' Day
Out the following day. Tami booked their appointment at J. Sisters, the

salon where everyone from Vanessa Williams to Naomi Campbell went for their world famous bikini waxes.

She was looking forward to a day of pampering with her friend.

★

It wasn't like Tami to be late for a spa appointment, and after waiting fifteen minutes for her to arrive Brooke was becoming antsy. She tried reaching Tami on her cell phone and landline, but got no answer. Concerned that they would lose their appointments, Brooke proceeded inside for her wax. After her wax was finished, she dressed and stepped out of the private room, almost running into another woman. "Oh, excuse me," Brooke said.

She was about to pass by her before realizing that it was Tami. "Oh my gosh! I almost passed right by you!" Brooke said with a laugh.

She barely recognized her. Tami was wearing big sunglasses and had her hair hidden underneath a baseball cap, and her outfit looked . . . well, not like Tami. She was wearing a pair of sweatpants with a stain on them, UGG boots, and a down coat—something, Tami once joked, that "should be fashionably permissible only on ski slopes or in rural Canada."

"Are you okay? I was getting worried about you," Brooke said.

"Sorry I was late," Tami mumbled.

"It's okay. I'm sure they'll squeeze you in."

The woman who performed Brooke's wax said, "Mrs. Simpson, I'm ready for you."

"Okay . . . ," Tami said.

"I'll wait right out here for you and then we can go down and get our pedis together."

"Okay," Tami said without looking up.

"You sure you're okay?"

"Fine," she said quietly.

Tami silently followed the woman into the same room in which she performed Brooke's wax.

A few minutes later Brooke could hear the aesthetician say in a loud, alarmed voice "Is this your first time?" followed by "Miss . . . miss . . . are you okay? Miss, what's wrong?"

Brooke then heard weeping, which grew louder and louder. She then shouted through the curtain, "Tami? It's me. Are you okay?"

The aesthetician then poked her head out. "I think your friend is not well."

Because the room was barely big enough for two people, let alone three, Brooke asked the aesthetician if they could trade places briefly.

"Tami—I'm coming in."

There was Tami, still dressed in her down coat on top but wearing nothing on the bottom except for the little disposable panties they provide for those too modest to strip totally naked for their wax. Her sunglasses were off and it was clear why she had worn them. She looked terrible. She had no makeup on. Her lips were dry and cracked. She was hysterical.

"What is it? Tam—talk to me."

"I . . . I . . ."

It then came pouring out. After arriving five hours early from South Carolina she returned to find Brock at home in the middle of the afternoon, taking a bubble bath with Monique Montgomery.

Tami picked up the nearest thing that mattered to him that she could get her hands on—his degree from Columbia Law. It was lying on their dresser in a cracked picture frame that Tami had promised him she'd have replaced that week.

She threw it and the frame broke, leaving Monique screaming at the shattered glass and Brock's degree floating in the tub.

"Shit, Tami! You got it all wet!" he screamed.

Tami fled their home in tears. She walked aimlessly around the city before finally returning that evening when she knew he would be out at a meeting. At least that's where he'd told her he'd be the week before. Who knew if that was another one of his lies. She grabbed a bag and started packing. Then it dawned on her. Where would she take the boys? She could go to a hotel, but what kind of parent would move their children into one—just to spite their father. And she couldn't abandon them. Instead she put her overnight bag away and grabbed Brock's. She threw in a few pairs of underwear, some socks, grabbed his toiletry bag, placed two suits in a garment bag, then placed it all in a pile by the front door. She then told the boys they were having a slumber party and would be sleeping in Mommy and Daddy's room that night. Once the boys were tucked comfortably in the bed she used to share with her husband, she locked the door to their master suite.

After waking up the following morning she saw that his pile of belongings by the front door were gone, to where she didn't know. After getting the twins off to preschool she dragged herself to J. Sisters.

"Oh, Tami . . . I'm so sorry."

★

When Brooke told Garin he was immediately filled with compassion for Tami. He genuinely liked her. "That's terrible. She's so nice." He then said, "Stay out of it, Brooke."

"Garin, he told her if she ever left him she'd get nothing. That's not right. You see the way he treats her," Brooke replied.

To which Garin responded, "Yes, Brock's an asshole, but she had to know that when she married him."

"She's our friend."

"Correction. She's *your* friend. Brock's Luke's friend. And Luke's *your* boss. Not to mention my best friend. I'm begging you: *stay out of it.*"

"Correction. Laura's my boss. And besides, Luke would never approve of this. He's not that kind of guy. He has integrity."

"Yes, he does. Luke also has enough on his plate at the moment without adding marital counselor to his responsibilities and so do you. Leave it alone, Brooke. Leave it alone."

Brooke left the conversation there . . . with Garin. She knew that despite his protests she was going to ignore him and tell Laura, which would be the same as telling Luke.

Tami had asked Brooke to keep things quiet until she knew for sure what she wanted to do. When they finally spoke, Brock insisted that the "incident" with Monique "meant nothing" to him. When Tami asked him if that had been the first time, he refused to respond. Instead he offered to buy her the Mercedes convertible she'd had her eye on. When that didn't elicit the expected reaction, he then added, "I've also taken the liberty of increasing your clothing allowance. I thought you would appreciate that."

"Are you going to apologize?" she asked.

"What do you think the Mercedes is?"

"That's not the same thing!"

"Does that mean you don't want the car?"

Tami finally shouted, "I want your respect, Brock."

Brock stared at her blankly and walked out.

Later that day Tami e-mailed Brooke and asked her if she had any recommendations for a good divorce attorney. Though Brooke was sad to see anyone divorce, she was secretly elated that Tami had finally told that overbearing egomaniac where to go.

★

Brooke and Laura were traveling to a campaign event in California when Brooke received the e-mail from Tami.

"What is it?" Laura asked, hearing Brooke say, "*wow.*"

"It's Tami."

"Is she alright?"

"She's terrific now that she's leaving Brock."

"What?" Laura said, before adding, "Well frankly, I'm surprised it took her so long."

Brooke smiled then nodded.

Laura decided it would be a mistake to distract Luke with news of the impending divorce, so they decided they would wait until Brock spoke with Luke directly, which they surmised would not be for quite some time. Since Tami was leaving him and not the other way around, Brock would likely try to keep the news as quiet as possible for as long as possible.

They made their way to the Women for Cooper event, where Laura wowed the enthusiastic crowd.

★

After a day of glad-handing voters, Luke was exhausted. He returned to his hotel after midnight. He was sad to have missed Laura, who despite being in the same state that day had had a jam-packed schedule herself elsewhere. The campaign was much like a military operation at this point and they had to spread out.

Luke's body aide handed him his briefing book, asked him if he needed anything else, then bid the candidate good night.

Luke loosened his tie and reached for the hotel phone to call Laura.

Luke then heard a ringing. He looked around to see if it was his cell. It wasn't.

But he could swear there was a phone ringing somewhere.

Laura then answered.

Her voice sounded so crisp and clear. Like she was right there with him.

"What are you wearing?" he asked flirtatiously, like he often did when he was traveling and couldn't see her.

"Why don't you come in the bathroom and find out?" she replied.

"What are you talking about?"

Luke made his way into the bathroom of his suite and there was his beautiful wife covered in bubbles and surrounded by candles in the huge tub.

"What are you doing here? I thought you wanted to get back to tuck the boys in."

"Well, I decided to stay here and tuck you in instead," she giggled mischievously. "Going to join me?"

"Try and stop me," he said grinning from ear to ear.

CHAPTER 28

The Cooper campaign was now within striking distance of Beaman in some key states, including California, the next significant primary. The more Beaman's campaign, and its surrogates, attacked Luke, labeling him "inexperienced" and "not up for the job," and challenged his ability to connect with "a majority of Americans on religious values," the more confident Nate became that Luke really was going to win, not just the California primary, but the nomination.

Their internal polls now had them three points behind Beaman in California, which was the equivalent of a statistical tie. If they actually won there—something that Nate hadn't even considered a possibility in the early planning stages of the campaign—that would be the ultimate game changer. Luke would officially trade places with Beaman as they headed to Florida and then on to other primary states with sizable black populations, where Luke would be competitive. Even more significant, Luke was gaining ground on Beaman with women, due in part to the "Someone's getting lucky tonight" moment that took place the night of the South Carolina primary. Rumors swirled that Beaman and her husband had a less than warm and fuzzy relationship, but were more like political business partners.

"Can you believe it?" Luke had actually never heard Nate so excited.

Luke laughed. "Yeah, I can, actually. If you'll recall, a certain advisor of mine predicted we were going to win, remember?"

"Yeah, but I didn't think we'd be so close so soon. It's like it snuck up on us."

"Well, we're not there yet. As you keep reminding me. It's not official until the last man—or woman—standing makes that last concession call. Remember?"

"You know I never count a victory before it's in the bag, but let me say I'm a lot happier with where we are today than I expected to be."

With three days to go before California voters went to the polls, Luke asked, "Any final words of wisdom for me, Mr. Senior Advisor?"

"Yeah. Don't fuck up over the next seventy-two hours."

Luke laughed. "Gee, thanks. So that's the kind of genius I'm paying all that dough for each month."

"I think that's pretty sound advice, all things considered." They both laughed.

Luke had hung up with Nate for only a few moments before his cell rang.

"Hello."

"It's me."

"Hey Brooke!" Luke said.

"We need to talk."

"What's up?"

"Now Luke, I'm going to say this off the bat. You know I love you like family and I love Laura too. But you should know this. I have a firm rule. I won't work with people who lie to me, and any client that does, I will sever my business relationship with them immediately."

"Brooke, what are you talking about?"

"I'm going to ask you something and I want you to think very carefully before you answer."

"What is it?"

"Are you having an affair?"

"*What?!* What are you talking about?"

"Well, the good news is you sound convincingly shocked that I asked you the question, which is a good sign. The bad news is you didn't actually answer the question, which is a bad sign."

"Brooke, what on earth are you talking about!?"

"I'm talking about Ranya, Luke."

"Ranya? I don't understand."

"And yet you still haven't answered the question."

"Where is this coming from?"

"And yet again you didn't answer the question . . ."

"You know I dated her—like twenty years ago! It's not a secret. You know that, Laura knows that . . . everybody knows that . . ."

"But you haven't been with her recently?"

"Hell no! And why the hell are you asking me this?"

"Well, I'm sorry, and relieved. Very relieved. I heard from a friend who knows people at one of the celeb blogs overseas. There are items floating around about the two of you. Apparently there is something worse than a woman scorned, and that's a woman broke and scorned."

"Ranya's scorned over a relationship that ended almost two decades ago? I find that hard to believe."

"Not Ranya. Tiffini. Joe's Tiffini. She's been talking to the press. Apparently Brian Colby ended things with her for good after Sunny threatened to leave him and take half. So Tiffini just sold a tell-all interview to one of the UK tabloids."

"Okay, so what does this have to do with me?"

"Apparently she's not just dishing on Colby but on her relationship with Joe."

"Why would a UK tabloid care about a tell-all from someone who dated a sports agent in the U.S.?"

"They're not interested in what she has to say because she dated a sports agent. They're interested in what she has to say because she dated someone who knows the secrets of someone who may become the next president of the United States. You're sure there's nothing you want to tell me? I haven't said a word to anyone about this yet. Not Nate and certainly not Laura. But obviously I'm going to have to."

"Brooke, I'm not lying to you."

"Well, I guess it's unlikely they'd give her a nice payday or a cover if she didn't have a really good story, so it's not beyond the realm of possibility that she would embellish her story to add a couple of zeroes to her check." Finally she said, "I'm going to call Nate now. You should act surprised when he gets in touch with you. I really shouldn't have gone over his and your communications director's head with this, but I really care about you guys and hearing this freaked me out so much I couldn't see straight."

"I understand," Luke said quietly.

★

California Confidential

COOPER'S CAMPAIGN CUTIE?

Mysterious Muslim Beauty Could Rock Presidential Race

Her name is Ranya Shafiq. While Governor Luke Cooper's spokesperson describes her as nothing more than a "campaign volunteer" who has "made a few calls on behalf of the campaign," another source says she did much more than that for the governor and may just end up being the woman who ends his marriage and presidential hopes.

Tiffini Bingham is the woman at the heart of a love triangle between L.A. Laker Brian Colby and sports agent Joe Nelson, accused of assaulting the basketball great in a dispute over the affections of Bingham, a former Rockette. The revelation caused Colby and his wife Sunny to temporarily split before reconciling several weeks ago.

Bingham recently gave a tell-all interview to UK tabloid *The Sun*, in which she alleges that during her relationship with Colby and Nelson, both men shared secrets with her about their high-profile colleagues, clients and friends. In Nelson's case, this includes Gov. Luke Cooper, whom he has known since high school.

Thanks to his recent win in South Carolina, the Michigan governor has emerged as a serious contender for this year's Democratic nomination, but his relationship with Nelson has already proved embarrassing for his campaign. Brian Colby had just hosted a fundraiser for the governor when Nelson allegedly attacked Colby in a nightclub in a dispute over Bingham. A number of political observers speculated that the incident could handicap Cooper with voters and prove to be a distraction during a crucial point of the campaign. Ultimately Cooper defied the skeptics, pulling off an impressive double-digit win in the presidential election's first Southern primary. But weathering two scandals in one election cycle is a tall order for even the most seasoned political veterans and may prove a particularly tall order for the young governor, who only recently emerged on the national stage. And according to Bingham this second scandal is a doozy.

Bingham claims that the governor has been carrying on a relationship with Shafiq, a former flame from his law school days, and that Joe Nelson, his friend, served as the go-between, allowing Shafiq to attend campaign events without arousing suspicion. Not only do the allegations threaten to shatter Cooper's image as a devoted family man, but they also have caused some to question his fitness for the presidency. According to sources, Ms. Shafiq is a distant relative of Omar Mohamed, a leader of the terrorist organization Hu Sia. One political watcher, who requested anonymity, citing his relationship with senior staffers on the governor's campaign, said, "Let's say he didn't sleep with her. Even if that's true, bringing someone with ties to a terrorist organization in to even lick a stamp for your campaign is not exactly the kind of judgment that screams presidential, I don't care how good of a 'friend' she is."

The Cooper campaign has come out swinging, denouncing the allegations as "pure fiction" and adding that they "will sue any party who knowingly slanders the reputation of the governor or his family." They then took direct aim at Ms. Bingham by adding, "In this country we have a name for someone who will do, say and sell anything for money to the highest bidder. We will refrain from calling Ms. Bingham that name but we will call her another that certainly fits: liar."

★

"I love him like a brother but I would never lie to you," Garin said to Brooke.

"Honestly?"

"Honestly. I mean, depending on the situation I might not volunteer every detail unless you specifically asked, but I would never ever lie to you and he would never ask me to. How's Laura doing?" Garin asked.

"Actually she seems to be holding up better than I am. It's like she never doubted him for a minute so she completely skipped that whole phase and went straight into 'how-dare-they-try-to-screw-with-my-husband mode.' She's had us working overtime to increase the number of events she's doing each day so she can campaign even more."

"Well, believe it or not, unconditional trust in a marriage can be a comforting thing, from what I hear," Garin said sarcastically.

"Okay, I already know I can be a bit of a hard-ass. I don't need you to remind me."

Brooke was not only infamous for making sure that no third party interfered in the marriages of her friends but her own. Garin's longtime personal trainer who also worked for many of his Wall Street friends, was a part-time fitness model who had been profiled in a number magazines. After meeting her at their engagement party, Brooke found a not-so-subtle way of telling Garin he had to hire a new trainer. As a birthday gift, she gave him a prepaid gift certificate for a year's worth of sessions with Alex Guillaume, a former professional football player turned personal trainer to the stars who was also one of Brooke's early clients.

"Have you heard from Joe yet?"

"I already told you he's in rehab, Brooke."

"Well, he could really help clear all of this up. In fact, he's the only one who really can."

"I know. I know. And I'm sure he would want to help if he knew, but I told you that communication is severely restricted while he's there, especially the first week or two. And with this being part of his plea deal for the Colby thing, he can't take any chances in not following the rules, or he'll end up in prison."

"And that's a bad thing?"

"You know what I think? We shouldn't talk about this anymore," Garin said abruptly.

"I'm sorry. That was a stupid thing to say about your friend."

"Yes, it was." Garin sighed. "How bad's the damage?"

"Well, in the short term? We had a shot at winning California. That's not going to happen now. In the long term? Can't say just yet."

★

Campaign Daily

AMID SCANDAL AND CALIFORNIA LOSS, COOPER CAMPAIGN LOOKS AHEAD

On the strength of his commanding South Carolina victory and a number of recent prominent endorsements, Gov. Luke Cooper seemed poised to become the Cinderella story of this year's presidential election. At the start of the campaign the fact that Sen. Abigail Beaman would become the Democratic nominee was a given, but in recent weeks speculation reached fever pitch that the charismatic Cooper may change that as he began gaining on Beaman in some key states.

But the fairy tale appears to have been short-lived.

The Cooper campaign has been rocked by allegations that the governor carried on an extramarital affair with a former flame with ties to a terrorist organization. While the governor and his campaign have vehemently denied the allegations, they have clearly taken a toll. He had begun to make significant strides in California, with some predicting he could pull out a surprise win, but it was not to be.

Female voters who were credited with being crucial to the governor's sizable South Carolina victory appear to have returned to Sen. Beaman's fold, at least for the moment.

Polls had shown them giving Gov. Cooper a bounce in a number of upcoming primary states, most notably Florida and Ohio. A recent focus group showed why the governor appeared to be gaining ground with women, who were originally considered part of Abigail Beaman's core base of voters.

Pollster Lunden Franks called it the "Lucky Effect." When Gov. Cooper's wife Laura was famously caught on a microphone sharing a private moment with the governor following his triumph in South Carolina, pollsters say it conveyed a genuine warmth and affection between the couple. This served as a distinct contrast to the Beaman marriage, which has been notoriously bumpy over the years, including rumors of infidelity that caused the couple to separate briefly ten years ago.

Now with the infidelity allegations against Gov. Cooper, some voters are deciding that there isn't much difference between the two couples in terms of their marriages and personal lives, so instead of voting on likability they might as well vote on experience, and that is now giving an edge back to Sen. Beaman.

★

"Well, if we're the *Titanic*, let's just say that not only have we hit the iceberg but we're running low on lifeboats," Nate said to Luke.

"What do we do?" Luke asked with nervousness in his voice.

"Luke, you know I hate to ask, but . . ."

"No, there is absolutely no truth to this at all, and I told you I didn't know about her uncle. If I had I never would have let her volunteer. I'm guilty of stupidity, not infidelity."

"Well then, I think the voters need to hear that."

"I've said it once, but you know I'll say it as many times as it takes. Just tell me when."

"Not from you. From her. We need Ranya's help on this."

"I thought you said we need to keep as much distance as possible from her."

"We do. But we've got to get her on the record with this thing but not look like we called her and begged her to save our asses. How do you suggest we reach out to her?"

"Want me to call her?"

"Out of the question! What are our other options?"

"Well, I'm tempted to joke that maybe Joe should get in touch with her, but I guess considering the state of things that's not that funny."

"No, it's not," Nate replied.

"Garin knows her, but they haven't spoken in years."

"Well now is as good a time as any."

"Well, whatever you do, don't let Brooke get ahold of her contact info. Because if she gets in touch with Ranya, no telling what she might say."

At that Nate let out a laugh, his first in days.

CHAPTER 29

Ranya had been attending a meditation retreat, but responded when Garin left her an urgent voice mail. She didn't hesitate to do an interview after speaking with Nate. Though the campaign initially thought to arrange the interview with a liberal talk show host or bloggers that they knew would be sympathetic, they ultimately decided that if they wanted to have a chance at winning back female voters, a morning show would be better, despite the potential risks involved in appearing on one. So they went with *Wake Up USA*.

The interview was taped ten days before the Florida and Ohio primaries in an undisclosed location.

"First off, I'd like to thank you for joining me during what has clearly been a very difficult time for you," the host said.

"You're welcome," Ranya replied in accented English. She wore an oversized purple silk blouse and black leggings over her petite frame. Ballet flats and a gold bangle bracelet finished off the look, giving her the appearance of a wealthy heiress dressing the part of an artist.

"What made you decide to finally talk to the media?"

"Well, I was tired of seeing how many lies were being told about me and my friends."

"What lies are you talking about?"

"I don't even know where to start, there are so many ridiculous stories."

"Well, the one that's at the forefront of everyone's mind. Tiffini Bingham claims that you had an affair with Governor Cooper. Is that true?"

"I had a relationship with Luke when we were kids."

"When he was in college?"

"I was in college and he was in law school."

"And how long did that relationship last?"

"A couple of years. Maybe three or more, but very off and on."

"Why was that? Did your religious differences play a part?"

"There were many things that played a part."

"What finally caused things to end?"

"We were practically kids, and I know I was very immature about certain things."

"How did you become involved in his campaign?"

"I ran into his friend at a party last year . . ."

"Joe Nelson?"

"Yes, and he invited me to a fundraiser and I attended and I saw Luke and told him I would like to help."

"And had you been in touch with the governor over the years?"

"No, that was the first time I had seen him since we were kids."

"Do you have any idea why Tiffini Bingham would tell this story?"

"No. I don't know the woman. But from what I hear she was compensated for the story. And that's the only thing I can presume, is that she was motivated by something like money, because I can't think of another compelling reason to try to destroy the lives of strangers."

"So let's talk about your involvement with the campaign. What exactly was your job for the Cooper presidential campaign?"

"It wasn't a job. I volunteered to help where I could. I gave them the names of some people in the film industry I thought they may want to contact for fundraising, and made a few calls to some of them."

"About how much time did you spend working on the campaign?"

"Well again, I wasn't a worker. I was a volunteer. And I may have helped a total of eight hours, if that."

"As you know there have been questions raised about your background, specifically about your possible connection to Omar Mohamed. Is there a connection?"

"He is my grandfather's much younger half brother. I've never met him, not a single time in my life."

"Omar Mohamed is believed to be connected to an organization of Islamic extremists. What are your thoughts on their alleged crimes?"

"Well, I am a pacifist, so I don't condone or support any violence, and

I am actually an agnostic so I wouldn't have ties to any Islamic group of any kind, or any religious group. In fact that was one of the things that Luke and I disagreed over when we dated. He's very spiritual and very much believes in God."

"And you don't?"

"Well, I'm open-minded. I'm just not entirely sure what's out there."

"Have you met the governor's wife?"

"No. I haven't had the opportunity, but I've seen her and she's very beautiful and elegant."

"Do you ever wonder about what might have been? You know, think about the fact that that could have been you in line to become the next First Lady of the United States?"

Ranya laughed, then said, "No. Because first of all I don't know that the U.S. would be ready for a First Lady like me. As your questions make clear, there's a lot about me that I think doesn't necessarily convey First Lady to a lot of people. Second, I actually value my privacy and can't imagine what it would be like to be under a microscope like this all of the time. But I say God bless to those who are willing to go through the hassle in an effort to serve their country."

"God bless?"

"It's a figure of speech," she said cheerily then laughed.

After the interview Nate and the other advisors cheered. It had gone even better than they expected. Ranya came off as honest and sincere, and she praised both Luke and, more important, Laura, something a true "other woman" would be unlikely to do on camera.

Nate called Luke. "I think we may have just plugged the hole from the iceberg," he said, returning to his *Titanic* metaphor.

Laura and Brooke had been watching too from a hotel in a town in Ohio where Laura was scheduled to visit a senior citizens' home later that morning.

Brooke was so happy and relieved she practically danced a jig when the interview finished, but Laura didn't seem equally elated. She seemed more tense after the interview aired, not less.

"Wasn't that great, Laura?"

"Uh-huh," Laura said non-commitally. "I have a headache, Brooke. I don't know that I can make it to the senior center."

Brooke was puzzled. Laura had seemed fine only minutes earlier.

"Laura," she said gently, "you know I'm on your side, and of course I don't want to push you when you're not well, but today's really important. The press is really going to be on high alert for any reaction from you on the whole Ranya thing and they will seize upon any and every little sign of deviation from your normal routine and try to extrapolate from that. I'm worried that if you cancel your first public appearance right after her interview they may think something's up."

"What the press extrapolates is not my problem." Laura enunciated the word "extrapolates" in a condescending tone that had a sharpness to it Brooke had never heard before. "I'm not going to the appearance," Laura continued. "Now are you going to call my scheduler, or shall I?"

"I'll take care of it," Brooke mumbled before walking out the door.

Once Brooke was gone, Laura picked up her phone. It rang several times before voice mail picked up and she said, "It's me. We need to talk. Call me when you get this."

★

Eight hours later Laura was standing in Luke's hotel room, waiting for him.

When he walked in the door his face lit up.

"Hey, babe. What a nice surprise."

Laura's face was expressionless.

Luke leaned in to kiss her on the mouth. She turned her head, causing him to peck her cheek by default.

"We need to talk."

"Yeah, I got your message. Is everything alright, hon?"

"I caught the interview with Ranya," Laura said icily.

A look of concern on Luke's face turned into one of bewilderment.

"It was good, right? You heard what she said about you?" He forced a smile.

"I did," Laura said calmly. "I also heard what she said about you. And about your relationship."

"What do you mean?" Luke asked, although his facial expression indicated that he knew exactly what she meant.

"I'm only going to ask you this once. When was the last time you were with her, Luke?"

Luke was quiet for what felt like an eternity before clearing his throat. "I don't remember the exact date."

"Well, I don't need an exact date. How about ballpark?"

"It was so long ago. . . . I mean, who can remember something like that?"

"Apparently she can. She said you were together for three years. You told me you were together for one, which means one of you is either wrong or lying, or really bad at telling time. Because if you were with her for three years, that means you were with her when you were also with me."

Luke's usually decent poker face faded completely.

"Did you sleep with her while we were together?" Laura asked.

"Never when we were married," he said emphatically.

"What about before we were married when we were together?"

Luke took a deep breath.

"Well, I guess that answers that," she said. "How long? When did it stop? When we were dating? When we were engaged? When?"

"I told her I couldn't . . . I couldn't see her after we . . . you and I were going to get married."

"I'm not one of your voters, so don't try to talk in circles around me. I asked you a direct question and I want a direct answer. Were you with her when you were with me?"

"I . . . I . . . don't remember the last time I was with her . . . It wasn't that memorable . . . I mean, after I met you my whole world changed . . ."

Laura responded by picking up her BlackBerry and throwing it at his head.

He ducked, but felt the breeze as it zoomed close to his eye.

"Don't make me ask you again. And don't make me throw your laptop next!"

"I slept with her after you and I were together."

"What does that mean 'together'? Together as in we'd had one date? Or together as in right before the wedding?"

He couldn't look her in the eye.

"Luke, did you sleep with another woman right before you married me? That better not be what you're telling me."

"The last time was right after we got engaged. I just . . ."

"Just wanted to be sure you weren't making a mistake?"

"No. No . . . I just . . . I don't know . . . things ended so abruptly with her . . . It was like I needed to know there was nothing left . . . and there wasn't."

"Clearly there was something. I mean, you didn't almost sleep with her. You did sleep with her."

"And then I left her, Laura. I left her for you."

"Is that supposed to make me feel better?"

"I don't know! I don't know . . . I mean the truth is . . . bullshit aside . . . I . . . I . . ."

"You what?"

"I wanted to hurt her. I wanted to hurt her the way she hurt me. That's not the kind of thing I'm proud to admit. It doesn't exactly make me sound like a very good person or even a decent person, but it's the truth. I wanted to wound her and sleeping with her right before marrying someone else I figured would do that."

"So you married me to get back at someone else?"

"Would you *stop* and just listen for a minute? I didn't mean to sleep with her. We met for coffee to catch up, mainly. Yes—so I could rub in her face that I had met someone else—someone terrific and I was moving on with my life with you. I planned to drop the bomb about the engagement and we started drinking, then one thing led to another . . . afterwards we were lying in bed and she told me that she loved me and had always loved me. And I told her I was in love too . . . with someone else . . . with you, and I told her I was going to marry you. And she said, hearing me say that I loved you didn't hurt her. But the way that I said it did. Because she said she could tell that I meant it. And that was the last time I saw her."

"Until the campaign."

"She was a volunteer. That was *it*."

Laura sighed and closed her eyes for a moment then began rubbing her temples.

They sat in silence for several minutes.

Luke finally reached for her hand. She pulled it away.

"I need a little time to process," she said.

He nodded then said, "I do love you and I've never been unfaithful."

She glared at him.

"Never have I broken our vows, Laura. *Never*. You believe me, don't you? I need you to believe me. If you don't believe in me, nothing else matters."

★

In the days that followed Laura canceled all of her campaign appearances. While the campaign blamed her absence on the need to be back home temporarily to provide some "sense of normalcy for the boys," rumors swirled among campaign staffers that the couple had had a blowout and that she would not be returning to the campaign trail anytime soon.

In her absence Esther Cooper, who had been limiting her campaign appearances to a few times a month, took over much of Laura's schedule, but also added several more stops in Florida, which had a sizable Jewish population. Esther would spend days campaigning from sunup to sundown there, often wearing a button that said "MADAM PRESIDENT" in large letters, with the words "of Jewish Moms for Cooper" underneath, a gift from her son Matt, the funnyman in the family.

As they were preparing to leave for one of the largest Florida rallies to date, she had a moment alone with Luke.

"What happened?" she asked in a stern tone.

"What do you mean?"

"Why is Laura home and not out here helping you?"

"I made a mistake, Mom," he said.

"Obviously. She told me that part. What she won't tell me is what exactly you did to hurt her so. Please tell me you did not have an affair with that woman. That Reina woman."

"Ranya. Her name is Ranya."

"I don't care what her name is. I did not raise my boys to be cheaters. Is that what you did?"

"Not exactly."

"Not exactly? What does that mean?"

"It means I made a mistake but . . ."

"But what?"

"Ma—with all due respect this is really between Laura and me."

At that point Esther Cooper said, "You have something on your face."

Luke began wiping at the spot she pointed to before Esther finally said, "Come here."

He leaned down so that she could reach his face. She licked her thumb the way she always did before preparing to clean it as she had so many times before. She then reached up, only instead of grabbing his chin, she grabbed for his ear and squeezed as hard as she could. Luke squealed. "Ow!!!"

"You tell me what you did!"

"I cheated on Laura, but not when we were married, when we were dating," he said.

"Is that all?"

". . . and also when we were engaged."

Esther let go of his ear.

Luke rubbed it and said, "Damn, Mom. I think I'm going to need to ice it."

"Good. You're lucky you're too big for me . . ."

". . . to put over your knee. I know. I know."

Luke smiled and for the first time since the start of the conversation she smiled back.

"Laura actually threw her phone at my head."

"Did it hit you?"

He shook his head no.

"Lucky for you. The last time I threw something at your father—well, let's just say my aim's a little better than hers. Even the happiest couples have their moments. And we certainly had ours."

"I never knew that."

"Well, that wasn't for you boys to know."

"But you got through it?"

"Well, it's been almost sixty years and I'm still with him. What do you think?"

She laughed.

"I really messed up, Mom." He sat down on the couch.

She sat next to him.

"Yes, you did. We all make mistakes and you haven't done anything unforgivable or unfixable."

"How do I fix it, Mom? She won't even talk to me."

"You know I love you and there's nothing I wish I could do more than take your pain away when you're hurting. But if you're planning to be the leader of the free world and solve the world's problems, then you're going to have to be able to solve your own."

★

"You knew this all along and you never told me!" Brooke thundered at Garin. "I thought you said you would never lie to me for him."

"And I also told you I wouldn't volunteer any information you didn't specifically ask for. You asked me if he cheated on Laura while they were married and he didn't."

"Do you think you're being cute?"

"Always," Garin said in his best smooth operator voice, trying to lighten the mood.

"I'm not amused."

"Are you ever?"

"What's that supposed to mean?"

"It means this is really none of your business, Brooke, what goes on in someone else's marriage."

"He made it my business the day he hired me to give up weekends with my daughter to slave day and night trying to get his ass elected president."

"Okay. Well, did you care when that football player you were working for got another woman knocked up while he was married? I don't remember you dropping him as a client or ranting about how upset you were. In fact, I think you helped make it go away in the press, and if I remember correctly you used the bonus that he gave you to surprise me with a Caribbean vacation for our anniversary that year."

"That is not the same thing and you know it!" she screamed.

"Why is it not the same thing? Why, Brooke?"

"Because it's not!"

"Why?"

For one rare moment Brooke was speechless.

Garin plowed on. "The only reason you're pissed is because Luke turned out to be human just like every one of us. He's not Mr. Perfect like you've made him out to be all these years. The only perfect man was

Jesus Christ . . . and I guess your father, of course," Garin said, landing a dig at the father Brooke worshipped but could never please.

"I can't believe you said that, Garin," she said through tears.

"Listen," he said gently. "I shouldn't have said that. But sometimes you're just so hard on people, Brooke. We're all going to disappoint you at some point. Even those of us who love you. And you have to try to forgive us and love us anyway. Luke's a good man and a good friend and a good boss and a good candidate. Tell me if you think I'm wrong."

She didn't say a word—a rarity for Brooke in an argument.

"So why don't you do for Luke and Laura what you would for any of your clients that you value. Try to help them find their way out of this mess. That's what they need from you as a publicist and as a friend. Not judgment, but help."

He could hear her sniffling before saying, "You're right."

★

By the following morning Brooke was in the living room of the Cooper home in Michigan.

"I know what happened."

"I'm sure you do. How long ago did Garin tell you?"

"I just found out the other day."

"Really, Brooke? You expect me to believe that?"

"Laura, it's the truth. You know I wouldn't have withheld something like that from you, which is probably why Garin never told me. As angry as I was at him for holding out on me, I now know it was the right thing for him to do because, as he suspected, I never would have been able to keep something like that from a friend, and you're one of my best friends."

Laura's expression softened. "I just feel so stupid. How could I not have known? And I wonder how many other people knew. How many of them were laughing behind my back?"

"No one."

Laura gave her a "you must be kidding" look.

"According to Garin, Luke was so embarrassed he didn't even tell his brothers. He knew he'd made a mistake by . . . doing whatever it was he did with what's her face, and he was terrified that if you found out you'd call off the wedding. So he made the choice not to tell a soul besides Garin, and he swore him to secrecy. Garin said all Luke kept saying was 'I can't let this ruin the best thing that ever happened to me.' He was talking about you."

"Did the campaign send you here, Brooke?"

"No. I'm not here as your publicist. I'm here as your friend. And as Luke's friend. You know you belong together and you're going to be together long after this campaign ends."

"And?"

"And so you don't want to do anything that you may regret after."

"What is that supposed to mean?"

"It means that if Luke had cheated on you while you were married, that might be unforgivable. But he didn't. But if you abandon him during the most important moment of his life, that might be unforgivable, and even if he says it isn't it will always be there between you."

"Brooke, I'm really surprised to hear you defending him."

"I'm not defending him. Lord knows I probably would have thrown something a lot more lethal than my BlackBerry. Like my shoe."

Laura laughed.

"But sometimes the people we love aren't perfect. Just like we're not perfect. It's a lesson I'm still learning to accept. But unconditional love requires it."

Just then Laura and Luke's son James came in. "Mom, can I have some juice?"

"Sure, hon." Laura touched his head lovingly then turned to Brooke. "He's home with a cold." She then left the room to grab a glass of juice.

While she was gone James said to Brooke, "Mom's been sad."

"I know, honey," Brooke replied.

Laura returned with the glass of juice moments later. "You should be up in bed," she said to James as she passed him the glass.

He gave her a tight hug with his free arm. "Love you, Mom."

"I love you too, sweetie."

She smiled. After he was up the staircase she turned to Brooke and said, "I need some time to think."

"Okay. But you know we don't have a lot of time."

"I know."

Days later Laura called Brooke. "Okay. I'm ready."

Laura rejoined the campaign trail, although she pointedly kept a separate campaign schedule from her husband.

★

AddictedToPolitics.com

_____

BEAMAN TAKES AIM AT COOPER,
AS GOV. REGAINS HIS FOOTING

If there were such a thing as political last rites, many started administering them to the campaign of Gov. Luke Cooper this month, after his campaign was shaken by a series of embarrassing rumors and missteps. But just weeks after the presidential campaign of the Michigan governor seemed to be on life support, he appears to have made one of the most impressive comebacks in recent memory.

Although he was trailing Sen. Abigail Beaman and Rep. Jay Billings only two short weeks ago, a new Quinnipiac poll shows the governor trailing Senator Beaman by just one percentage point in Florida, a statistical dead heat. The numbers appear to be consistent with the Beaman campaign's own internal polling, as the senator has noticeably increased the attacks on the governor, unleashing a barrage of negative ads in the primary's final days.

Though the Cooper campaign has been hesitant to attack, insisting that they plan to run a "positive" campaign, they have fired back with what some are calling the campaign's "not so secret weapon." The campaign recently released a new ad starring the candidate's mother, Esther Cooper, titled "Whispers." In it she confronts the recent fliers that began appearing in largely Jewish communities challenging the governor's religious identity. The governor, who is African-American, was adopted and raised in the Jewish faith by the Cooper family.

In the thirty-second spot Esther Cooper looks into the camera and says, "Part of being a parent means eventually having to let your children leave the nest, spread their wings and fly on their own. That means letting them fight their own battles. But when someone attacks the faith of my family they are no longer just

messing with my kids, they are messing with me. The attacks on
my son and his religious faith are simply not true. How do I know?
Because I raised him." The ad then ends with a photo of the Cooper
family, including Luke, his mother, father, and three brothers.

It remains to be seen just how much of an impact the ads are
having, but political watchers say it is one of the most effective of
the primary season.

★

Two days before the Florida primary Brooke received a hysterical call
from Tami. One of Brooke's friends had given her a referral for a powerhouse divorce attorney. According to Tami, who was barely audible
through her sobs, after Brock received his first correspondence from her
legal counsel he went ballistic and she returned home to find that the
locks to their apartment had been changed. The housekeeper allowed
her in to collect some belongings, but upon trying to check into a hotel
Tami discovered that her credit cards had been canceled. Tami's attorney
told her Brock was just trying to "bully" her by playing "hardball." It was
merely an "intimidation tactic." "Well, it's working!" Tami screamed at
him from her cell phone. (She was later informed by her carrier that her
cell phone service would be disconnected at the end of the month.)

"I don't know what I'm going to do, Brooke," she wailed.

"Well, I do. I'm going to call Garin. How much do you think you need
to get you through the month?"

"Brooke, I couldn't . . ."

"This is not up for discussion. I'm calling Garin this instant."

With the Florida primary rapidly approaching, every interview,
every speech, and every single interaction with voters counted, and
Brooke didn't want to distract Laura with this latest unfortunate piece
of news from their friend. She decided to wait until their day wrapped
up to tell her.

After Laura finished her last event—a meet and greet at a bingo night
at a local Florida church—she broke the news.

"That jackass. Is she alright? What can we do to help?"

"Garin checked her into a hotel and is paying ahead a week at a time,
but Laura, you know how Brock is. He's so stubborn and competitive.

You know he hates to lose. I didn't want to scare Tami, but part of me is wondering if maybe she really should consider . . ."

"She can't go back to him," Laura said anticipating the rest of Brooke's thought.

"I'll speak with Luke. Hopefully he can talk some sense into him before this thing gets any uglier. They have their two kids to think about."

"Laura," Brooke began. "Garin told me to stay out of this. He specifically told me not to drag you and Luke into it because of the campaign and all. You both already have plenty on your plate."

"Nothing comes before family, including a campaign. Tami and Brock are like family. Don't worry, Brooke. This will work itself out. I'll speak with Luke. But do you think it can wait until after the primary's over? I really don't want to distract him."

"Of course," Brooke replied.

"Boy. The two of us really are lucky."

"Lucky?"

"That we're not married to him," Laura replied.

"Isn't that the truth."

In the weeks since the Ranya "affair" things had remained chilly between Luke and Laura, but hearing about Brock's treatment of Tami reminded Laura of just how lucky she really was.

A little more than forty-eight hours later, in the early morning hours after the Florida primary, the Associated Press called the race. Though extremely close, Congressman Jay Billings was declared the surprise winner by one point, while Luke came in second and Abigail Beaman came in one point behind him. According to political watchers the sniping between the Beaman and Cooper camps allowed Billings, the dark horse, to mount a surprise come-from-behind victory.

Laura's schedulers had informed Luke's several days before that she would not be by his side as he gave his speech that night.

As he strode out of the door of his hotel room to head down to thank his supporters, he grabbed his mother's hand. She would be his First Lady for the evening. She squeezed his hand tight and told Luke she was proud of him. As they waited for the elevator that would take them downstairs, another elevator opened and out stepped Laura.

Luke's face lit up. "You're here!"

"I'm here," she replied.

"I thought . . . I thought . . ." Self-conscious about the staffers and his mother milling about nearby, he simply said, "I thought you wouldn't make it."

"Well, I was in the neighborhood." She then stroked his face.

"Glad you were."

"I'm glad I was too."

"I love you."

"I love you too."

They then kissed.

After a few moments, they both heard a throat being cleared.

It was an aide.

"Sorry, but we have a couple of hundred people waiting."

As he made his way to the hotel ballroom to give one of the more difficult speeches of his career, Luke found himself standing between the two women he loved more than anything: his mother on his left and his wife on his right.

★

Brooke was usually a drill sergeant when it came to being on time for interviews, but she couldn't help but laugh when Laura overslept for a radio interview the morning after the Florida primary and confessed that she was "exhausted" because Luke kept her up all night "fooling around." "I didn't get an ounce of sleep," Laura said.

"Well, I certainly can't tell the press that, Laura. Maybe we should say you have the flu instead?" At that Laura laughed.

CHAPTER 30

Though Luke was disappointed by the Florida loss, the fact that he came so close after such a tough month left him, and just as important, Nate, cautiously optimistic.

"We had a rough couple of weeks," Nate said. "If we hadn't, we would have won this thing. No questions asked. But we've got to look forward." They didn't have a single moment to spare looking back. Super Tuesday was right around the corner. The remaining candidates would compete in eight states on a single day, and Nate knew that their campaign, battered by the previous round of bad press and a fresh loss, was in rough shape, particularly financially speaking.

During the weeks that the Ranya scandal had dominated the news, the campaign's fundraising operation essentially ground to a halt and, despite the near win in Florida, had never fully recovered. Now the campaign was heading into Super Tuesday with a severe financial handicap. The Beaman campaign had outraised them 3 to 1 in the preceding month and now some tough choices had to be made, namely whether or not to abandon some states altogether in an effort to have a shot at winning others.

Furthermore, at the height of the Ranya controversy a number of donors postponed their fundraisers, while one—Phyllis Fletcher, a prominent Christian feminist activist whose endorsement had been a major coup for the Cooper campaign—canceled hers altogether.

One Cooper donor decided to go forward with her fundraiser . . . for another candidate.

Diamond Moon, the lawyer turned unemployed talk show host who famously didn't bother to show up for the fundraiser she was to headline for Luke, popped up on the host committee for an upcoming Beaman fundraiser. When Page Six got wind of this tidbit, they gleefully ran an item that was a play on the title of the talk show Diamond was infamously fired from.

★

"LOVE HIM AND LEAVE HIM?"

Diamond Moon has apparently had a change of heart. The lawyer turned yakker, who was famously fired from her gabfest *Love Him or Leave Him*, was the star attraction at a fundraiser for Gov. Luke Cooper last year (which she famously missed, citing "illness," as reported in this column). However, this week she is listed as a member of the host committee for a "Women for Beaman" fundraiser taking place at the nightspot The Duchess. When reached for comment, a spokesperson for the diva replied, "Diamond is thrilled to support a qualified candidate for president who not only respects women but has made protecting the rights of women a cornerstone of her career." When asked if that means she's had second thoughts about whether or not Gov. Cooper respects women, her flack replied, "No comment."

★

The move was the epitome of kicking someone when they're down. Luke's cousin Jessica, who had to deal with Diamond's outrageous behavior when helping with the earlier fundraiser, was furious. She knew that Diamond had orchestrated this on purpose as a way of getting back at Luke and his campaign for the unflattering item Page Six had run about her and her husband following their event. Jessica was so livid she decided to take the next few weeks off from her job to devote herself to helping Luke's campaign.

The campaign's fundraising operation had gone from a sprint to a crawl virtually overnight, and at this rate would soon cease altogether. Mimi knew what was happening. Political fundraising was a bloodsport, and she knew that the other campaigns, like sharks, likely smelled blood in the water and had already begun trying to poach her donors. Mimi called a member of the campaign's finance committee who told her point blank that he had been approached by Senator Burstein about "switching teams." The senator had made a hard sell, arguing that "despite spending most of his resources in Florida, Governor Cooper had lost there and it was only a matter of weeks before his campaign would be broke" and those donors who were on board sooner rather than later would be "remembered and rewarded down the road."

Against Nate's wishes, Mimi insisted that Luke begin calling major donors to reassure them. Nate worried it would make Luke look weak. But Mimi was more worried about the campaign going bankrupt—and taking her professional reputation along with it. There was only one major event still pending. It was being hosted by Marjorie and Sol Leventhal, or as Luke called them, Mr. and Mrs. Leventhal, his best friend Adam's parents.

Though Mr. Leventhal was a lifelong Republican, he called Luke his "other son" and said this time he would make an exception and support, as well as raise money for, a Democrat. When the Ranya story broke Adam e-mailed asking if he and Laura were okay. "Let me know if you need anything." Luke thanked him and apologized saying, "I'll completely understand if your mom and dad want to postpone the event."

When Adam didn't reply Luke assumed he had his answer: Adam's parents, wanted out of the event and Luke's oldest friend was trying to think of the right way to tell him so.

Instead, Luke received an e-mail from Mr. Leventhal. The subject line read: "What the hell's the matter with you?"

> **Dear Luke:**
> Of course we're not canceling the event. If I stopped supporting every candidate who did something stupid I'd just give up and find a nice, warm communist country to move to.
> (Maybe Cuba? I hear the beaches there are great . . .)
> This is non-negotiable. See you at the event.
> Hang in there son.
> Yours truly . . .
> SL

It was classic Mr. Leventhal: caustic, witty, and a bit of tough love thrown in for good measure. Since their teen years Adam had complained that his father showed Luke more patience and affection than he showed his own son. This was the first moment Luke realized that Adam was right. Mr. Leventhal would have disinherited Adam if a rumor like this had become public and embarrassed their family. But here he was going forth with an event for Luke because he cared about him. Luke was touched.

After Luke's round of calls Mimi then scheduled an emergency call with the campaign's national finance team and asked Nate to be on the line for moral support. On the call she stressed that it was time to "put up or shut up." They needed to raise money—and fast—or the campaign would go under. "If there are any money sources you have been holding out on—friends and family members you've been hesitant to ask, neighbors who owe you a favor—this is the time to ask. I am not saying this for dramatic effect, as Nate will attest. This is it. Luke's last stand. It is up to you. If we can't kickstart our fundraising, and soon, Luke might as well drop out because in a few weeks he will become virtually invisible. He won't be able to run a single advertisement on any station anywhere."

"I'd just like to add to that, if I may, Mimi."

"Go right ahead, Nate."

"It's not just that the ads will stop—although that will happen. The electricity will go out. Vendors won't get paid so they will stop making the campaign signs that you see our volunteers holding. We won't be able to pay our staff. Our phone service and BlackBerries will be turned off, which means that calls like this won't be possible." What Nate didn't add was that he and two other consultants on the campaign were forgoing their paychecks for the next month in an effort to leave the campaign with more cash, a move that was usually the first real sign of a sinking political ship, which is why he wanted to keep the information from becoming public as long as possible and therefore did not disclose it on the call.

Nate continued, "I very rarely panic, but in about a week or two I won't be left with any other choice. So you guys are the campaign equivalent of the Navy SEALs. You turn to your finance team for rescue when all other operations fail, and right now they're failing."

At that point one donor chimed in. "Hey, guys, Steve Abrams here. Look, I'll be honest. You know I've been trying. As many of you on this call know I raised a lot of money for Luke's gubernatorial campaign and told him I'd do everything I could to get him from the governor's mansion to the White House, but right now let's just say the water pressure on the faucets is running pretty low . . . I mean, I have business colleagues who had been leaning towards holding events, but ever since this Ranya thing they just kind of think Beaman is unstoppable."

"But we almost stopped her in Florida."

"Almost, but you didn't. I'm sorry. I like Luke. I really do, but I don't know what else to really say . . ."

"Say you'll keep trying," Mimi said.

"Don't worry, we'll keep trying, Mimi. This is Garin speaking."

"Thanks, Garin."

"I'll make a few calls today and report back to you," he added.

"Sounds good," Mimi replied.

"Can everyone send me an update by close of this week?"

There was an audible silence.

"Hello?" Mimi said to a series of unenthusiastic murmurs.

One of the reasons Garin had worked so hard all of his life was so he would never, ever have to go to anyone with his hand out, the way so many people in his neighborhood had when he was growing up. But that afternoon, after the finance committee call, there he sat, calling friends, acquaintances, and colleagues, some of whom he couldn't stand, to beg for money.

"Only for Luke," he thought to himself.

One of his first calls was to one of his least favorite people on the planet, Luke's Morehouse friend Marcus Templeton. Marcus had agreed to host another fundraiser for Luke when he was riding high following his South Carolina victory, but since the Ranya drama he had done what he always did whenever Luke, or any other friend, was no longer of any use to him—he disappeared.

"Hey Marcus," Garin said.

"Sorry, who is this?"

"Garin Andrews."

"Who?"

"Garin Andrews."

Silence.

"Luke's friend. We were in his wedding party together."

"Oh right. Look, you kinda caught me in the middle of something. Can I call you back soon?"

Garin knew Marcus well enough to know that "soon" meant never, so he said, "This will only take a minute. I realize how busy you must be so I wanted to let you know that a staffer from Luke's campaign would be happy to take over the planning of the next fundraiser you agreed to do for Luke."

"Garin, this really isn't a good time for me."

Since playing nice didn't seem to be getting him anywhere, Garin switched gears.

"Well, Marcus, any time I'm forced to have a conversation with you isn't really a good time for me either, but I endure it because Luke has always vouched for what a great guy you are even when I told him otherwise."

"I'm sorry, is that your definition of persuasion? Because if so, you're lousy at it."

"Well, how about you overlook my shitty persuasive skills if I overlook what a shitty friend you are?"

"What's your problem, man?"

"My problem, Marcus? My problem is that when you didn't want to ask your folks for cash so you could keep pursuing this acting thing, you called Luke and he gave you the lifeline you needed to hang in there. Then when you finally got your big break he almost never heard from you. Then when all those tabloids were sniffing around about your personal life, out of the blue you called your old 'friend' the governor to vouch for what a macho dog you had allegedly been in college, even though we all know that's not true. Don't we, Marcus?"

"I don't know what you're talking about," Marcus said quietly, yet defiantly, in a tone that made clear that he did and that he was uncomfortable. He then added, "I'll have my assistant get the campaign another check this afternoon and I'll see if I can get a couple more friends to send something in."

"Thanks, Marcus."

★

The response on the call did not leave Mimi feeling particularly confident. In the last several months she had enjoyed the benefits of working for an A-list candidate. Though fundraising could rarely be described as "easy," they were raising at a brisk enough pace that she actually had the luxury of being able to turn down events. If someone offered to host a fundraiser—so that they could meet Luke and introduce him to their friends—but could not make a commitment to raise a minimum of $50,000, then they were "encouraged" to reconsider hosting an event, and instead "advised" to collect their friends' contributions and send them into the campaign with a note. If the amount received was $20,000 or more, then the candidate would call them personally to thank them. It wasn't quite the same as having him in their home, but it allowed the donors a few bragging rights and usually spurred them to raise more so that they could up the ante by getting Luke into their home to further show off to their friends. But the tables had turned overnight. Mimi found herself doing something she hadn't done much of in months: calling a low-dollar donor.

When Sheryl and Jason Matthews hosted a successful Young Professionals for Cooper event in Harlem months before, Mimi had been so impressed that she thought perhaps it might be a good idea to replicate them nationwide, but when things became so busy with their high-dollar donors YPL simply slipped off her radar. Now it was back on in a big way. Mimi knew how it would look if she simply called Sheryl after all of these months, especially considering the recent scandal. It would look desperate. Then she remembered Luke's cousin. "What was her name again? Jenna? Jane? Jessica? Something with a J," Mimi thought to herself. She had helped with the Harlem event and had offered to help in the future if Mimi needed it. She could reach out to them and it would probably seem more like an overture from a concerned relative instead of a mercenary act from a desperate fundraiser. After the call with the finance committee she placed a call to Jessica.

★

Though they had had a wonderful night together following his Florida loss, Luke knew Laura well enough to know that things were still not 100 percent okay between them. So when she greeted him in his hotel room at the end of a full day of campaigning in New York with the words "We need to talk," he assumed it was about their marriage, not someone else's.

"Okay," he said quietly. He began to remove his tie. Laura then said, "There's something I haven't told you."

"Okay," he said taking a deep breath. He made his way over to the mini bar, opened it, and poured himself a drink.

"I'm all ears," he said.

"Brock and Tami are getting a divorce."

Luke was so relieved that that was all. His kids weren't sick. His wife wasn't leaving him. No one he loved was terminally ill and Laura wasn't pregnant.

"That's terrible," he finally said. "When . . . what happened?"

"Tami caught him with someone else. Monique Montgomery, that model."

A look of recognition fell over his face. Laura had to stop herself from accidentally saying out loud, "And apparently not just when he and Tami were engaged."

Instead she said simply, "She's leaving him."

"How long have you known?"

"A few days. We didn't want to distract you."

"And you didn't think it would be distracting now?'

"Didn't have a choice. Brock threw Tami out of their home and cut her off. She's destitute."

"What?" Luke said stunned.

"Brooke and Garin had to give her money."

Luke was momentarily speechless before finally sputtering, "What about the kids?"

"They're living in the house with him and a nanny he hired. He told her if she attempted to take them out of the home he would have her arrested for kidnapping."

"This is insane. There has to be a mistake." Luke leaned against the mini bar.

Laura got up from the bed and walked over to him.

"I'm afraid not, hon," she said softly. She then leaned in and rested her head on his shoulder and wrapped her arms around his waist.

They stood there for a while, until the silence was disrupted by the vibration of his cell phone.

"You're the only one who can talk some sense into him," Laura said.

Laura could feel his head nodding in agreement.

"What time is it?"

Laura unwrapped her arms, looked at the hotel clock, and said, "Just before midnight."

"I'll call him tomorrow."

This time it was Laura's turn to nod. They didn't fool around that night but they slept in an embrace.

★

The morning after his conversation with Laura, Luke made a point to ask his schedulers to carve out at least 20 minutes of time for a personal call later that afternoon. He did not tell them with whom or about what, and his scheduler could tell by his tone not to ask.

Luke had given thousands of speeches in front of audiences large and small in his years as a candidate—so many that he almost never became nervous beforehand anymore, yet the thought of broaching this subject with one of his closest friends left him filled with butterflies. He couldn't eat at all beforehand, instead floating from one event to the next on nothing more than coffee. He had e-mailed Brock that morning to make sure he would be available so they wouldn't miss each other. Finally, at 2 p.m., he called.

"How are you, man?" Luke began.

"I'm good. Drowning in work, as usual, but wouldn't have it any other way."

A staple of any conversation with Brock was being reminded first and foremost that he was extremely busy and in fact probably busier than you, no matter how busy you are—even if you were running for president.

"How's the campaign?"

It dawned on Luke that he had received only one e-mail from Brock in the last couple of weeks. He had thought it somewhat strange that after the Ranya story broke he hadn't called to check in to see how his friend was doing. But now after learning about Brock's own marital woes it made a bit more sense, although with Brock it could be hard to tell. He didn't exactly do emotional intimacy. The last contact the two men— best friends—had had was the morning after Luke lost the Pennsylvania primary, which had been largely expected because it was Beaman turf. Brock sent Luke an e-mail that simply read: "The only decent thing to come out of Pennsylvania is the Steelers (and they've been questionable at best the last few years) so don't worry about it." That was about as close as Brock came to sentimentality.

"We're plugging along," Luke replied in response to Brock's question about the campaign. "Plugging along, but I'm not going to lie. The last couple of weeks have been a rough stretch, brother. The last week or so I've been asking myself how the hell my friends could let me get myself into this mess. If you really liked me, weren't you supposed to say something like, 'Luke—instead of running for president, why don't you try something a little bit easier and more realistic—like becoming an astronaut.'"

Brock let out a laugh.

Luke chuckled for a moment too, then added, "No seriously, I'm sure you've heard the stories and rumors. It's been tough on Laura. She tries to act so strong, but I know it's been hard on her."

Brock didn't say a word.

"Brock, is everything okay?"

"Yeah . . ." he said. "Just a bit swamped here," he added. "Not to rush you off the phone, Luke, but did you just call to catch up?"

Luke took a deep breath.

"I was just wondering . . . I just wanted to check in on the kids."

"They're great," Brock said.

"Brock . . . I know about Tami."

"What are you talking about?"

"I know about the divorce."

"I see you've been talking to big-mouthed Brooke. Yes, we are taking some time apart at the moment, but I have no doubt that it will be temporary. Once Tami gets this nonsense out of her system she will come to her senses and come back home."

"Brock, I'm not trying to overstep my boundaries here . . ."

"Then don't."

"Brock, you know I love you guys like family, which is why I'm just trying to look out for you both."

"I appreciate your concern. But this is not your family, Luke. It's mine."

"I understand that and I respect that. I love you like a brother, Brock, but I think we can both agree that throwing the mother of your children out into the streets is probably not what's best for your kids."

"Into the streets? Is that what she told you?" he asked. "After twenty years of friendship you accuse me of that?"

"Brock . . ."

"You know I didn't call and ask if you fucked that Ranya chick while you were married to Laura. I gave you the benefit of the doubt because that's what friends are supposed to do."

Luke was caught off guard by his tone. "Brock, I . . ."

"While we're on the subject, maybe you should spend more time focusing on your own marriage instead of worrying about someone else's."

Luke was stunned that Brock would speak to him that way, but he was equally stunned as the realization began to sink in that everything Laura had told him about what Brock had done was true. One of the strategies that made Brock such a successful attorney was his ability to deflect blame when necessary. Luke was well aware of that. He never once directly answered the question about whether or not he had forced Tami out of their home. When he referenced Ranya shortly thereafter, Luke knew he was grasping for straws. Brock and Luke knew each other better than just about anyone else knew them, other than their families. In Brock's case he knew the likelihood of Luke cheating on Laura was about as likely as him running off and joining the circus. Luke, on the other hand, knew that Brock was always striving to have the best of everything—best house, best car, and best-looking wife. Therefore it was not beyond the realm of possibility that he would cheat on Tami if she was no longer measuring up to his increasingly impossible-to-live-up-to standards.

Determined not to take the bait, Luke ignored the Ranya remark and instead said as calmly as possible, "Brock, you know how much I care about all of you. That's the only reason I'm calling."

"After all of these years—after everything I've done for you—I cannot believe you would take that bitch's side."

"Brock, I'm not taking anyone's side . . . except the kids. I gotta look out for my namesake, right?" he said, referring to his godson little Luke, in an effort to lighten the mood somewhat.

It didn't work.

"I find that hard to believe. I should have known you were involved."

"What are you talking about? Involved?"

"I knew Tami's ass wasn't smart enough to pull this off on her own."

"Pull what off? Brock, I just called because last night Laura told me what's going on."

"Yeah, and it's just a coincidence that Tami goes out and hires Roddy as her divorce attorney? Yeah, I'll bet you and that wife of yours had nothing to do with that . . ."

Now it all made sense. Why Brock was so angry and irrational sounding. He had hated Roddy since their law school days, and if he resented Roddy so much that he wouldn't attend a political fundraiser he was hosting, then Roddy representing Tami in a divorce would have him on the verge of going postal.

"Roddy's her attorney?"

"Yeah, like you're really surprised," Brock said.

"Brock, I . . . I had no idea. I swear to you, Laura just told me about your separation last night . . . I don't think she even knows."

"Oh please, I've seen the way she and Brooke talk to Tami . . . like she's some field slave and they show up every now and then bringing news of freedom from the North. Trying to convince her that I wasn't a good husband when I'm slaving away to give her every goddamn thing she ever wanted . . . but no . . . the two of them were always running their mouths, always hovering around her like the witches from *Macbeth* . . . so don't tell me that one of them didn't give her the idea to hire him as the ultimate *fuck you* to me. I know they did, because Lord knows Tami's not smart enough to come up with something like that on her own. Well, she wanted to teach me a lesson. Mission accomplished. Now I'm teaching her one. And once she's learned it, she's welcome to come home."

Luke was now too sad to be stunned. He had asked for privacy for this call but there was a knock at the door, meaning it must be something urgent. His aide poked his head in. Luke gave him the signal for one more minute, then said, "Brock, I only have two more things to say and then I'll let you go. First, please don't let this thing get any more out of hand than it already is. Regardless of what's happened between you two in the past, it's never too late to start doing what's best for your kids and for you. Anger is not a good place to start from. You and Tami are wonderful people. Please just remember to act like it for the sake of your kids. Just be fair, Brock. That's all I'm asking. Just be fair."

"Luke—" Brock began.

"I wasn't finished," Luke interjected. "The second thing I wanted to say is that what you say about your own wife is one thing, but don't you ever speak of my wife like that again."

Luke could hear Brock breathing deeply. Finally he said, "I should have known that you would let running for president go to your head. You think you're so fucking smart. So special. Well, let's see if you feel that way when you lose."

Then the phone went dead.

When Laura asked Luke how the conversation had gone he simply replied, "Not well." He then added, "You should check in with Brooke and find out how much Tami needs to last her the next few months. We can afford to help. And can you also call Josh and ask him to put her in touch with Hank Elliot? He's a friend of my dad's and I'm sure he can cut her a deal on an apartment in one of his buildings."

Laura had never been prouder of her husband.

CHAPTER 31

In the days following his falling out with Brock, Luke was stoic, but Laura could sense a sadness about him.

Though Brooke had been one of the slowest in his inner circle to thaw following the Ranya allegations, the day after his conversation with Brock she walked over to Luke and gave him a hug, just a squeeze and a quick peck on the cheek, then turned around and went right back to work. At Brooke's urging, Garin took a leave of absence from work to join Luke on the trail. He had no official title, although Luke jokingly called him "Friend in Chief," and unlike a lot of friends of candidates (or "Focs") he actually didn't drive Luke's staff crazy. He was the ideal. He stayed out of their way, didn't throw his weight around, and pitched in when and where they needed it, holding signs up during photo ops and campaign visibilities, and generally kept Luke in good spirits. They also squeezed in a game of basketball when they could.

It took a lot of effort to keep Luke smiling when Garin didn't feel like smiling himself. The more they campaigned, the more Garin began to sense that his best friend was losing this race.

Garin never said a word about his thoughts to anyone—especially Brooke, who was literally killing herself everyday to help their friend fulfill his dream. Garin had always known that Brooke was a workaholic, but he had never seen her like this. Luke's campaign was clearly more than just a job for her. It had become a mission. He was proud of her and didn't want to ruin it all by saying something negative.

Garin had been surprised to realize that on the campaign trail he really didn't get to see Brooke all that much more than he did when they were in different states. She and Laura kept a different schedule, in different states, from the one he and Luke followed. When they did see each other they were usually exhausted. Garin was used to working a lot of hours in finance, but bankers and traders weren't expected to do fifteen hours of work with a smile. From about 6 a.m. to 11 p.m. each day, Luke and Laura and even Brooke had these Stepford wife-like expressions plastered on their faces. "Any person you speak to may be a voter, and you don't get a second chance to make a first impression on them, especially during a thirty-second conversation, which is what most of our interactions with them are," Brooke told him. On those nights when Garin and Brooke could be together, he would usually just hold her hand and stroke her hair until she drifted off to sleep.

★

Garin was mortified. There he was, standing with other volunteers holding up signs behind Luke as he gave a televised speech on a college campus, when his cell phone began to ring. It almost seemed like the ringing got louder the longer it continued, and while Luke was trying to ignore it Garin could feel hundreds of eyes on him. He tried reaching for the phone in his pocket to shut it off while juggling the sign. Finally the sign went flying from his hands. He just turned and disappeared through the curtains of the stage they were standing on to answer the phone. He heard Luke announce to the crowd, "Guess he's an undecided voter," to loud laughter. Garin was so befuddled he didn't notice the incoming number.

"Gar?" he heard on the other end.

"Yeah. Who's this?"

"It's Joe."

"Joe?"

"Yeah . . . Catch you at a bad time?"

"No. I can talk." Since I'm already off of the stage now, he thought to himself.

"Oh good. Your office said you're on leave. Everything okay?"

"Yeah . . . yeah, I'm just . . . I'm just . . . doing some traveling," Garin said, catching himself.

"Are you helping with the campaign?"

"Sort of. Traveling with Luke . . ."

"That's great."

"How are you?" Garin asked.

"Good. Really good, actually. Sorry I've been out of touch. I've been away at a place called Serenity. It's a rehabilitation center."

"How'd you like it?" was all he could think of to say. Congrats didn't seem appropriate. "I mean . . . how are you?"

"Garin. It's okay. You can relax."

And just like that Garin did. "You sound good."

"I feel good," Joe replied. "For the first time in a long time I feel really good. So I'm sorry I missed all your calls. Is everything okay? What'd I miss?"

"Nothing much. Just that Tiffini told the world that Luke and Ranya were having an affair. He lost California and Florida and his campaign's been limping along ever since. Oh, and Brock and Tami are getting a divorce."

"What? Are you kidding?"

"About Brock and Tami getting a divorce?"

"You know what I mean. You're telling me Luke lost Florida because of some bullshit rumor Tiffini was peddling?"

"Well, I'm learning that politics isn't really that black and white, but the Ranya stuff certainly didn't help things . . . I mean, I guess we'll never know what might have been in Florida, at least."

They thought separately in silence about how much had hit the fan since they last spoke.

"Is there anything I can do? I mean, I guess it's a little late, but I wish there was something I could do to make this all up to him . . . I don't think Hallmark makes a card to apologize for ruining someone's chance at the presidency."

Garin laughed before finally saying, "Just pray."

"You know that's never really been my thing, Gar. But considering the mess I've helped cause, I guess I can make an exception for Luke."

"I'm sure he'd appreciate that." He then added, "Actually, Joe, there is something you might be able to help with."

★

Garin called Mimi with the news that he had secured $40,000 in commitments for the campaign. She couldn't believe it.

"Did you do something illegal that I should know about?" she asked with a mischievous laugh. "I mean, I'm not going to end up finding compromising photos of you and some older female donors on the Internet, am I? Although we're so desperate at this point that it's not like I'd really care."

"Not quite," Garin replied.

"Well, where's all this money coming from all of a sudden? I mean, if there's a money tree out there somewhere, I'd sure like to know so we can shake the hell out of it."

Garin laughed but didn't volunteer any additional information.

"Seriously, some industry looking for a helping hand on the regulation side in Michigan?"

"Since when do you care where the money comes from? As long as it keeps coming." Garin loved keeping Mimi in suspense.

"I'm a nosy old broad. So sue me."

"It's from the sports world."

"More professional-athlete dollars, huh? Well please, just make sure your buddy doesn't go assaulting these donors." The moment the words left her mouth Mimi added, "Forgive me, Garin. That was not a nice thing to say, especially after all you've done."

"No, it wasn't, especially after all Joe's done. The donors are all friends of his father. He played football with some of them and is golf buddies with some of the others. He even got Anthony Paduano, the golf legend, to agree to lend his name to a fundraising letter we can e-mail around."

"Well, there's not much left to say except that I'm really glad I wore my Manolos today, because if I'm going to insert my foot this far in my mouth I at least want to be wearing nice shoes."

Garin didn't laugh, but he did smile.

"Seriously, my apologies, Garin. And please thank Joe. He's really helping to save our asses right now."

★

It was four days before Super Tuesday. Luke had just walked into his hotel room after a long day of campaigning.

"Shit, Crosby, you scared me," Luke said upon seeing Nate sitting on the couch.

"We need to talk and I figured it was better to do so in person."

"Sure," Luke said.

His body aide milled about before Nate asked, "Can you give us a minute?"

The aide replied, "Sure. Let me just finish putting together these briefing notes . . ."

Nate then barked "Take a hike," in a tone that was very un-Nate-like.

The aide scurried out the door.

"What's up, Nate?"

"We have a decision to make. Probably the toughest call of the campaign."

Luke took a deep breath. This was it. They were out of money and he was going to have to decide whether or not to bow out gracefully or to drive what was left of his campaign off a cliff like Thelma and Louise.

"Okay," he said.

"I have come into possession of some photos. Embarrassing photos."

Though his mouth said, "Of who?" Luke's head said, "Please don't let them be of Laura or someone else I care about."

"Of Abigail Beaman," Nate replied.

The look of relief that swept across Luke's face was so palpable that Nate actually said, "What? Did you take some naked pictures I don't know about?"

Luke relaxed and let out a laugh. "What's so embarrassing about the photos?"

"Well, she's not in them alone and she's not in them with her husband, if you get my meaning."

Luke was surprised. Having grown up in one of America's foremost political families, Abigail Beaman was, if nothing else, a savvy politician, and the idea that she would make such a rookie mistake was shocking.

"How on earth did that happen?"

"The guy's an asshole. Like the guy who sold out Princess Diana. Held on to the pics, just in case."

"When are they from?"

"A few years ago. Apparently she ended things so she could run for president."

"How did you get ahold of them?"

"That's not something you as the candidate need to know. Here's the thing, Luke. I'm sure you've figured out by now that we're losing. The way things are looking it's only a matter of when, not if, but *when* we run out of money and have to throw in the towel. At this point we need a game changer and this . . . well you can say it's a lot of things but it could potentially be a game changer."

"Nate, I don't want to win like this."

"I guess the question becomes, do you want to win at all?"

"I gotta be honest. I'm surprised you . . ."

". . . would stoop to this? Well, I haven't. Not yet. I'm not the one who gets to make the decision or tell you what to do. But I have a responsibility to give you the option. How would you feel after the fact if we lost and you found out these existed and I knew but never told you?"

Luke thought about it for a moment.

"In any case, we obviously don't have a lot of time to make a decision on this. Clock is ticking. I'll need an answer by tomorrow at the latest." As he headed for the door Nate turned back. "And one more thing. Obviously this is supersensitive, so we need to be extremely discreet in terms of who we share this with."

★

"Hey Luke? Everything okay?" Brooke asked, since Luke was calling unusually late.

"Yeah. Yeah."

"Can I help you with something?"

"I need your advice. But I need you to keep this in confidence. From . . . everyone."

"I understand."

"If someone gave you incriminating information on one of the other candidates, what would you do with it?"

"Depends on how incriminating. Are we talking a sex tape?"

"Not exactly."

"Not exactly!?" she exclaimed. "What does that mean?"

"Someone has pictures of one of the other candidates. Embarrassing pictures, but . . . I don't know."

"What don't you know, Luke?"

"I mean who wants to win like that?"

"Winners, that's who."

"So you think we should use it?"

"No. I think you should use and abuse it. Hell, plaster it on your campaign signs if you can."

"Don't you think it could potentially backfire? I mean won't some voters be turned off by that kind of tactic?"

"Of course, but they'll be balanced out by the number of voters who are turned off by the behavior depicted in the photo and end up voting for you as a result. Honestly, Luke, I don't know why you're even having to debate this in your head. If the shoe—or picture, shall I say—were on the other foot, they would have already distributed a copy of the photo to every registered voter in every upcoming primary state in the nation."

"Yeah, but I've been making the case to voters that I'm not like the other guys running, remember?"

"And you can prove that once you are elected. But you have to get elected first and this may be our . . ." She then caught herself. "I mean your only hope."

The words hit Luke like an arrow. He then said quietly, "Thanks for the advice."

"Anytime."

★

After sleeping on the dilemma, Luke awoke to find an e-mail from Nate. "We need to make a decision. Just write back yes or no to let me know what you want to do. It's up to you."

Luke took a sip of his coffee then clicked reply on the e-mail but before he began to type his phone rang.

"Hello."

"Hey, hon, it's me."

"Hey you. It's great to hear your voice."

"It's great to hear yours too. Aren't you going to ask me what I'm wearing?"

"What are you wearing?" he obliged teasingly.

"That old, ugly bathrobe you hate." She let out a laugh.

"Sexy!" he said. "How are you?"

"I'm good. So tired I can't even remember what state I'm in today but I'm good."

"You are officially the hardest working person on this campaign and I'm so lucky to have you."

"Awww. Thanks, sweetie."

They giggled.

"So I called to tell you something really funny."

"I'm all ears."

"I just got off of the phone with Veronica. She was just in St. Barts on vacation . . ."

"Gee, your cousin has such a rough life . . ."

". . . and she said she cut her vacation from three weeks to two to come back and help us."

"Well, isn't that nice?" Luke said sarcastically.

"Be nice!" Laura scolded, though she was clearly trying to stifle a laugh herself. "She means well and she's trying to help."

"I'm sorry," Luke said in mock seriousness. "So what's so funny about it?"

"Well, she said that she heard from one of her vacation pals that it's common knowledge that Senator Beaman had an affair with some guy who used to work for her family or something."

Luke almost spit out the coffee he had just taken a quick sip of.

"Did you hear me?" Laura asked.

"Yeah, I did."

"Well, Veronica is so crazy she said, 'I have the secret to Luke's victory! He should use this to expose her for the fraud that she is!' She really sounded serious. Isn't that funny? She was like, 'I have a friend who's friendly with Barbara Walters so we won't have any trouble getting the word out.' Now of course the idea of Veronica judging anyone else's private life is the funniest part of all." Veronica had been promiscuous in her younger years during her search for Mr. Right, specifically Mr. Rich Right. "The other funny part is that she actually thought you'd be interested in using something like that. Can you imagine?"

Noticing the silence, she added, "Hon, are you there?"

"I'm here."

"Well, can you imagine that?"

"No. I can't," he said.

"Anyway, I knew you'd think it was hysterical."

"Yeah. It's funny. Your cousin is a trip." He then added the non sequitur, "I miss you a lot."

"Well, I miss you too."

"No, I *really* miss you, babe."

"Uh-oh. Someone's feeling frisky."

"That's not what I mean," Luke replied in a surprisingly serious tone. "You know what I really won't miss when this thing is over? Not getting to spend enough time with you and the boys. You're my world."

Laura was so touched she was almost speechless.

She finally said, "I love you so much and I can't wait to see you . . . all of you."

They chatted for a few more minutes.

After hanging up the phone Luke picked up his BlackBerry, opened Nate's e-mail, and typed the word "No."

★

The Hill Chronicle

_____

SUPER TUESDAY LOSSES SIGNAL UNCERTAIN FUTURE FOR COOPER CAMPAIGN

After suffering losses in seven out of the eight Super Tuesday primary races, Gov. Luke Cooper's presidential campaign appears to be on life support.

While his spokesperson refused to say whether or not the governor will end his candidacy in the coming days, he did acknowledge that they have no immediate plans for him to campaign in the remaining primary states.

CHAPTER 32

Luke Cooper was sound asleep in his own bed for the first time in a long time when he was awakened by what sounded like a loud thud.

He sat up startled to discover that his son Milo had done a somersault onto the bed.

"Hi, Daddy!"

"Hey, little man. You okay?"

"We made you breakfast."

"You did?" Luke gave him a squeeze and saw James holding a breakfast tray while Laura stood nearby.

"Mommy helped," James added.

"Aww, this is for me?" Luke yawned before asking, "What time is it?"

"Almost noon," Laura said.

"You're kidding? I never sleep that late."

"Your body needed it after a year of hardly any sleep."

Milo then said, "I'm glad you're home, Daddy."

"I'm glad I'm home too, son." He kissed him on the forehead.

★

After breakfast he and his boys watched another hour of cartoons as Luke thought about one of his last conversations with Sen. Beaman, on the night he called to concede the California primary to her.

"Senator Beaman, Luke Cooper here."

"Hi, Governor."

"I just want to congratulate you on your hard-fought win."

"Thank you. Thanks a lot, Governor. You ran a hell of a race, and frankly I had no idea how things were going to turn out until the very end. I know I'm not supposed to say this but you had me wishing I had your staff for a few days there."

Luke laughed. "Well, I wish you well going forward," Beaman added.

"Thank you. Same to you and your family."

"Governor?"

"Yes?"

"I know it may be a little late in coming but I want you to hear it directly from me. I had absolutely nothing to do with that nonsense being peddled about your family."

Luke was silent but Beaman continued. "I've always believed that families should be entirely off limits and I tried very hard to relay that to my team. I made it clear that anyone that was caught distributing anything unpleasant or unfounded about you or your marriage would no longer be welcome on my staff—or in any capacity in my campaign."

"I did receive your note a few weeks ago and I appreciated it. I hope you received my reply."

"I did. But I still wanted to say it out loud."

"Well, thank you. That means a lot."

"I try to remember that at the end of the day none of this really matters if the people we love aren't okay in the long run. It's funny, but I ran into Jack in the capitol after he dropped out of the race and I asked him how he's doing. He told me he was great because he'd had dinner with his kids every night for the last week. I really envied him in that moment."

"I hear you," Luke said.

It was the longest one-on-one conversation the two of them had ever had, and the first where they didn't talk like two adversaries worried about being quoted by a reporter later. Concession calls are known for two things: their brevity and lack of sincerity. Rarely does the person who has spent months telling strangers how unqualified and unworthy you are to hold the office genuinely "wish you well." Most likely, they wish that you would get hit by a bus.

But this concession call felt different. Abigail Beaman surprised him.

★

Nate warned Luke that he was likely to start hearing from Beaman and Billings more regularly in the days since he left the race.

"They both want your endorsement. Just think, this will be the best couple of months for you of the entire campaign. After nearly a year of trashing you, both of them are going to start kissing your ass nonstop to get your support."

Luke tried to take comfort in the idea, but he was too overwhelmed with worry about so much else.

Johnny, Luke's long-time advisor before Nate, once described the end of a campaign as "like falling off of a cliff." Adding that, "the only difference between winning or losing is that winning is like having a parachute to soften your fall. Losing feels like this terrifying death spiral, and only time will tell how badly the landing will hurt or whether or not you'll survive."

After enjoying a charmed political life of endless victory, Luke now knew how it felt to fall without a parachute.

Though Nate was partially right that Luke now had some leverage thanks to both candidates' desire for his endorsement, the same wasn't true for those around Luke. He was sad that he lost, but he was much more concerned about how his loss affected others. There were hundreds of campaign staffers throughout the nation who were unemployed or soon would be. Some of them had received offers from the other campaigns and had turned them down to work for him, and now he had lost. He was now trying to find as many parachutes as he could for them.

"Anyone I endorse must hire some of our team. It's got to be part of the package."

"Well, I can't guarantee anything but we can certainly bring it up in the conversations," Nate replied. "Although Luke," he added, "you know I'm not going to tell you what to do . . . who to endorse. My feelings on Burstein aside, this has got to be your decision and yours alone."

"Why do I sense a but coming?"

"But . . . we can't pretend those photos don't exist. We also can't pretend we're the only ones that know about them."

"Well, how do we know we're not?"

"Luke, my mom has a saying: You want something to stay a secret, don't tell anybody; once you do, it's not a secret anymore. Not only does the guy in the pic know, it's well known Beaman's hubby knows, if not about the photos then certainly about the guy she's in them with. My point is once three people know something, it's no longer a secret and it's only a matter of time before others find out. If not during the primary then definitely after."

"So you think having an affair should preclude someone from being elected president?"

"No. I'm not saying that it should. But I'm saying that it can. Especially when there are photos and . . ."

"Especially when the candidate is a woman."

"I didn't say that. Again, I can't tell you what to do. I just want you to weigh all of the facts and make a decision you're comfortable with."

★

Laura made a candlelit dinner and put the music of Anita Baker on in the background. The boys were staying with Luke's parents, so they had the house to themselves for a date night.

"How's your steak?"

"Good," Luke replied.

"I got a new haircut. Do you like it?"

"It's great," Luke said without glancing up to see that she had not changed her hair a bit.

"I also bought a $10,000 handbag today and found out I was pregnant."

"That's nice," Luke said without looking at her.

"Okay," Laura said dropping her fork on the plate. "What is going on?"

"What?"

"Luke Cooper, look at me. What is going on? With *you*?" She lingered on the word "you" for effect. "You've been like a zombie all evening."

"I'm sorry. I'm sorry, hon." He reached across the table and squeezed her hand.

"Is something wrong? What is it?"

"I'm sorry. I'm sorry. It's work."

"No kidding."

"I want to ask you something."

"Sure."

"If you knew something about someone, something embarrassing, and it was someone that you worked with, and let's say you knew you and that person would be competing for the same promotion, would you give the person a heads up that you know or that someone knows? Or would you let your boss find out?"

"Depends on whether it's just embarrassing or is it something that could actually impact their ability to do the job? If someone's in to creative stuff in bed, they might not want the other teachers or parents at the elementary school to know, but that has nothing to do with their ability to teach. On the other hand, if they used to be a stripper, while I personally may not judge, plenty of parents would, so maybe the principal has a right to hear it from someone."

Luke nodded then took a sip of his wine.

"Why? What's going on? Did you find out something about someone at the State House?"

"No."

"You know something about Beaman or Billings? Something bad?"

Luke saw a twinkle in her eye.

He shrugged noncommittally.

"Well, what is it?"

"I don't want to say."

"Honey. You know I won't say a word to anyone."

But he knew that, much like his mother, Laura had actually been angrier about some of the allegations and dirty tricks directed at their family on the campaign trail than Luke had.

"There are pictures of one of them with someone they had a relationship with."

"And let me guess. This someone is not the someone they are married to."

Luke nodded.

"Sort of changes the equation."

"What do you mean?"

"Well, answering to a few parents or a principal at a school is one thing. Answering to voters is something else. I wish I could say it's a personal matter for their family but you and I both know that's not entirely true. How long have you known?"

"A while."

A look of realization fell over Laura's face.

"Oh my gosh. Veronica was right. The Beaman rumor. She was right, wasn't she? You could have used this to beat her."

Luke didn't say anything.

Laura's eyes began to well.

"You think I should have?"

Laura rose from her seat, knelt down beside Luke, leaned in and gave him a big kiss.

"I'm so proud of you," she said, and enveloped him in a hug.

★

In the weeks after Luke withdrew from the presidential race Garin made a point to call "to check in and see how you're doing." But after more than two weeks of Garin's super-attentive friend routine, Luke finally said, "You know I love you, man, and it's always great to hear from you, but are you calling so much because you and Laura are worried that I'm depressed or because *you're* depressed?"

Garin let out a loud laugh.

Two months later Luke and Laura would come to New York—not for fundraising or campaigning, for a change, but just for a getaway. No kids. No staff. Just the two of them.

The day they arrived Brooke and Laura had a girls' date scheduled at a spa with Tami while Luke and Garin were on their own before the couples reconnected that evening to take in a Broadway show.

★

Brooke and Laura met each other at the spa with a big hug. They had gone from being attached at the hip every day on the campaign to corresponding by phone and e-mail without seeing each other in recent weeks.

"How are you, Tami?" Laura asked.

"I'm good. I feel good," she said. She certainly looked it, having lost at least 15 pounds. Ditching Brock was like having a weight lifted both spiritually and literally.

"Please, she's better than good. Tell her," Brooke said.

"Brooke, you know I don't like to gloat at anyone's misfortune."

"Then let me," Brooke said giddily. "Rumor has it Monique Montgomery left Brock for a rapper."

"And not just any rapper," Tami added. "He used to be one of Brock's clients."

"You're kidding!" Laura said.

"No," Brooke and Tami said in unison.

"Excuse me, could we get a bottle of champagne? A great big bottle and three glasses so we can toast. We're celebrating," Laura said to a member of the spa staff.

★

"Brooke never told you about the photos?" Luke asked as he and Garin finished their lunch. "I have to admit I'm surprised, pleasantly so."

Garin was quiet.

"She did tell you, didn't she?" Luke said in a moment of realization.

"Well, in her defense, she held out for a while. I didn't know until things were over."

"Was she pissed? I know Brooke. She hates to lose. I guess I can't say I blame her. I mean I pretty much took my career, along with hers and a bunch of other people's, down with me."

"First of all, she doesn't look at it that way. If it weren't for you she'd still be stuck representing a bunch of entitled C-list celebrity assholes that she hates, and complaining to me about them every day. Instead she found what she believes she was meant to be doing all along, only she never knew it. She already has these local politicians here knocking on her door looking to hire her to consult for them."

"Really?"

"Yeah. Besides, she seemed kind of . . . relieved."

"Relieved?"

"To see that you really are who she always thought you were. Releasing those photos would have been very Brooke. I'm not saying that makes her a bad person." He smiled. "You know I love her, but she knows it would not have been you."

He added, "And as far as how things ended, she and I didn't talk about this much but she missed Allie and Allie really missed her. She's practically spent more time with her this week than she had in all the time she worked on the campaign. Everything happens for a reason. I'm not saying I'm glad you lost, but I am happy to have my wife and the mother of my child back, and she seems pretty happy to be back."

Luke let out a sigh of relief, then said, "Well then, maybe I shouldn't tell you this."

"Tell me what?"

"The other thing that's factoring into this whole endorsement scenario. If Billings wins he wants me to consider being his VP."

"Get out of here! When did you find out?"

"Nate called right before we left."

"Well, so . . . what does that mean?"

"It means I have some thinking to do."

"About what?"

"About whether I want to start this all over again. I mean, I put my family through this once already. It's like we're finally getting back to normal."

"Normal? Luke, no one goes into politics because they want a normal life. Besides, vice president is like a way better job anyway. I mean, think about it, you get a lot of the perks of president—big, free house, reservations at any restaurant around the world, your own plane, and—none of the pressure. You're a heartbeat away from the big chair. It's like being second in line to the throne. The older brother gets the crown, but the baby brother always has the most fun and the hottest wife."

Luke laughed.

"Besides, Luke, in all seriousness you told me you ran because you wanted to be able to help more people. You wanted to make a difference. You wanted black boys who don't have you for a dad to be able to look at you and see that they have a shot at being whatever they want to be. Now be honest. Can you reach more of them sitting at the governor's desk in Michigan or being on the world stage as vice president?"

"Yeah, but what does it say to those boys if we lose? I mean, if they see me lose twice, how does that help them believe in anything?"

"Well, I don't know. How does seeing Michael Jordan lose or Kobe Bryant lose affect them? It shows them that even the greats lose sometimes, but it's not about losing, it's about how they come back after. What they learn from the loss means something . . . you know, whether or not they give up or come back stronger."

"You're not going to make this easy for me, are you?"

"Make it easy for you to give up, and feel sorry for yourself? Nope. Especially after all of the dough I invested in you. If I don't get to call you Mr. President, I'll be willing to settle for calling you Mr. Vice President."

Luke smiled but was quiet.

Garin pushed. "What does Laura think?"

"She didn't say. I think she's waiting to hear how I'm leaning first. Doesn't want to sway me one way or the other."

"Bullshit. She may not have said it yet but she wants you to do it."

"What makes you say that?"

"You guys went through hell the last year, and to have nothing to show for it in the end . . ."

"Gee, thanks, Gar."

"You know what I mean."

"I'm just saying that I'm sure she thinks that it would be nice to have something to show for all that you guys went through. And the vice presidency is not a bad consolation prize. "Besides. I was just messing with you before. I love my wife but can't wait for her to get back to work full-time again. She's been on my ass nonstop since she got home." He then imitated Brooke's voice, "'You never clean. You're not doing Allie's hair right. What time will you be home? Don't be late!' and on and on and on. It never ends." Luke laughed.

★

National Herald-Journal

SLOW AND STEADY WINS THE RACE?

*On the Heels of Beaman Sex Scandal Rep. Billings Poised to
Secure Democratic Nomination*

In one of the most remarkable turn of events in recent political memory, Congressman Jay Billings all but secured the Democratic nomination with his sweep of the Southern primary states yesterday.

Less than a month ago Sen. Abigail Beaman was considered a lock for the nomination, until a sex scandal crippled her campaign. Having ousted the other strongest opponent in the race, Michigan Governor Luke Cooper, on Super

Tuesday, Beaman's victory had long been considered a question of when, not if. But Billings, buoyed by Cooper's withdrawal and support from a number of his supporters who were looking for an alternative to Beaman, vowed to hang in there until the Southern primary, arguing that it would give his campaign just the boost he needed. Some are now wondering if Billings had a crystal ball and could see into the future, considering the developments of recent weeks.

After her Super Tuesday triumph a website published photos of Sen. Beaman in an embrace with a man other than her husband, and subsequent photos showed them kissing. After refusing to comment on the photos for several days, the Beaman campaign finally confirmed their authenticity, releasing a statement that read in part:

"Sen. Beaman has previously acknowledged that her marriage has not always been perfect but that she loves her family very much."

Though her campaign tried to steer the focus back on to the issues, the ensuing media frenzy consumed her campaign. She then made a decision that appears to have proven costly. She began avoiding the media altogether in the days preceding the next round of primaries in Western states and the South. According to polls, these voters place a greater emphasis on issues such as "character" and "values," and they abandoned Beaman for Billings in the closing days of the primary.

CHAPTER 33

The meeting was top secret. The only ones who knew Luke was visiting Jay Billings's twenty-acre ranch were the congressman's three senior advisors, along with Laura, Nate, and Luke's chief of staff at the governor's office.

Luke joined the congressman and his wife for a cup of coffee in their living room before he and the congressman headed outside. They sat on a porch overlooking a lake.

"I taught my boys how to fish right over there," Billings said. "Do your boys fish?"

"They're learning. Still a bit small, but they love the water."

"What about hunting?"

"Not so much."

The congressman let out a hearty laugh. Gun control had been one of the issues that set them apart.

"It's funny that we both come from a family of so many boys."

Luke smiled. "Yeah. It kind of is. How many brothers do you have again?"

"Four, and then my wife and I have three boys."

"I have three brothers and Laura and I have our two boys."

"And I have three grandsons so far. But one of my sons has another on the way. My wife begged them not to tell her what the doctor says about the sex of the baby so she won't be disappointed. I told her not to worry, and that I'm sure this boy will be healthy too."

The congressman winked.

Luke laughed.

"It's not the only thing we have in common, you know, Luke. I think people would actually be surprised at how much we have in common."

Luke looked quizzically.

"I'm serious. Both of us were elected at relatively young ages. Both of us take our religious faith seriously. Both of us are extremely close to our families. Happily married. I ran for president when I was younger and lost. But in many ways that was the beginning of my career, not the end. I think this could represent a new beginning for you too. You know you're not the only one I've met with, but I've told my team I think you're the right person for the job. The right person to be my number two on the ticket. What do you think?"

"I think it sounds like a wonderful opportunity and I'm honored to be considered."

"Well, if you're here I'm assuming that means you're more than honored. I'm assuming that means you're ready and willing to answer the call of service to your country."

Luke paused and thought for a moment.

"With all due respect, do you mind my asking why me?"

"Well, I could tell you that I admire the campaign that you ran, that I admire your handling and grasp of the issues. And that's all true. But the reality, Luke, is you're likable. People respond to you in a way that they don't to a lot of politicians. I don't have that. I have foreign policy chops. I have the ability to talk in detail about arcane federal policy. But I don't have the ability to grab a crowd the way you do. And I'd be lying if I didn't mention that I find the idea of helping our country make history by breaking barriers a very appealing concept. Even if you and I accomplished nothing else, just by winning we would have helped make our country a little better than it was the day before we won, just by virtue of you being the first to make it to the vice presidency."

Luke thought about that for a moment then asked, "Do I have to give you my answer right now?"

The congressman smiled. "It would help. But no. Take your time. Not too much time, but you can take some."

★

That evening Luke picked up the phone and dialed.

"Nate, it's me. I know what I want to do."

ACKNOWLEDGMENTS

Without question, completing this book was one of the most rewarding, yet challenging, undertakings of my professional career. So while I am incredibly proud to have made it to the finish line, I know it would not have been possible without my round-the-clock cheering section.

First off, I'd like to thank my fabulous agent and dear friend Michele Rubin for being my champion, sounding board, occasional therapist, and for telling me I could do it over and over again on the days I had my doubts. This book would not have been possible without her and the entire team at Writers House, including Brianne Johnson and Michael Mejias.

Next I'd like to thank my editor Malaika Adero for believing in this project, and in me, from day one, and for turning this blogger into a real-life fiction writer through a combination of tough love, patience, and humor—always executed with impeccable style. I'd also like to thank publisher Judith Curr for her leadership and boundless enthusiasm for this project. To the rest of the Atria team, Todd Hunter, and Adiya Mobley: THANK YOU.

There are not enough words in the English language for me to express my gratitude to Ken Sunshine and his tireless staff at Sunshine Sachs, who served as the publicists for my first book *Party Crashing*. I've often said that by now I'm used to being the least famous person in every room I enter in New York, and that was certainly the case when I joined the client roster there. Yet Ken, and the rest of the team (led by the world's best publicist and my dear friend, Jessica Berger), consistently made me feel like a superstar, and saw possibilities in my career that I had never even imagined. They also introduced me to one of my other earliest cheerleaders (to whom I also owe a tremendous debt of gratitude), Arianna Huffington, who championed my work long before I had given her, or anyone else, a really good reason to and continues to be one of my biggest champions today.

Many thanks to Darrell Williams, my publisher at TheLoop21.com, and the entire team there, for their incredible support and for their tireless commitment to accurately telling the stories of people of color that so often go overlooked in mainstream media.

I must also thank Jesse Rodriguez, Steve Friedman, and the entire team at *The Dylan Ratigan Show* for making me feel like a member of the Ratigan Show family. And I must extend an extra special thank you to Dylan Ratigan for so generously providing a regular platform for so many diverse voices on air, including my own.

I don't think it's too much of an exaggeration to say that this book may not have been completed without the generosity of Anthony Paduano and Ruth Porat, who provided me with the most lovely writers retreat an author could hope for, in the form of their home. It is so beautiful there that I'm tempted to write another book just so I have an excuse to go back. A million thanks to you both.

At various times Jose Antonio Vargas, the Mann family (Linda, Howard, Josh, Matt, Katie, and Chloe), and Sara Roccisano and her family also graciously opened their homes to me when I needed a change of scenery to kick-start the writing. I remain incredibly appreciative.

A heartfelt shout out to Crystal Smith, Jenisha Watts, and Eileen deParrie, for taking the oath of friendship to another level by reading various drafts of the book. Thanks for finishing all of them and finding something honest yet nice to say, even when that wasn't always easy to do.

And to David Katz: Thanks for your friendship and for reminding me not to let things "rent space in my head," and for starting it all by connecting me with Dan Lazar, who introduced me to the wonderful Ms. Rubin, my agent.

I cannot thank Kim Leiken, and her predecessor Marketa Friedland, enough for helping me maintain my sanity by being such wonderful assistants.

To my other cheerleaders: Kate Betts, Jenna Bond-Louden, Diogo and Ali Bustani, Gwen Cooper and Laurence Lerman, Tyler Doran,

Gloria Feldt, James Fou, Susan Fales-Hill, Amanda Loureiro, Ron Oppenheim, Babette Perry (and her whole crew at IMG), Juliette Powell, Elon Rutberg, Dr. Tod Sinett, Len Weintraub, Amber Winsor, Zulma Zayas—THANK YOU. THANK YOU. THANK YOU.

I'd also like to thank every person who has taken the time to send me an encouraging note about my work via e-mail, Facebook, or twitter (and even those of you who have sent me not-so-encouraging notes :) You have all made me grow as a writer and I appreciate you taking the time to do so.

Lastly, I'd like to thank my grandmother Katherine Hill Venable, for reminding me to always eat my vegetables.